AFTER DARK

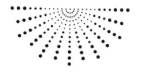

WILKIE COLLINS

ALICIA EDITIONS

CONTENTS

THE ANGLER'S STORY OF THE LADY OF GLENWITH GRANGE.

THE NUN'S STORY OF GABRIEL'S MARRIAGE

THE PROFESSOR'S STORY OF THE YELLOW MASK.

PREFACE TO "AFTER DARK."

I have taken some pains to string together the various stories contained in this Volume on a single thread of interest, which, so far as I know, has at least the merit of not having been used before.

The pages entitled "Leah's Diary" are, however, intended to fulfill another purpose besides that of serving as the frame-work for my collection of tales. In this part of the book, and subsequently in the Prologues to the stories, it has been my object to give the reader one more glimpse at that artist-life which circumstances have afforded me peculiar opportunities of studying, and which I have already tried to represent, under another aspect, in my fiction, "Hide-and-Seek." This time I wish to ask some sympathy for the joys and sorrows of a poor traveling portrait-painter — presented from his wife's point of view in "Leah's Diary," and supposed to be briefly and simply narrated by himself in the Prologues to the stories. I have purposely kept these two portions of the book within certain limits; only giving, in the one case, as much as the wife might naturally write in her diary at intervals of household leisure; and, in the other, as much as a modest and sensible man would be likely to say about himself and about the characters he met with in his wanderings. If I have been so fortunate as to make my idea intelligible by this brief and simple mode of treatment, and if I have, at the same time, achieved the necessary object of gathering several separate stories together as neatly-fitting parts of one complete whole, I shall have succeeded in a design which I have for some time past been very anxious creditably to fulfill.

Of the tales themselves, taken individually, I have only to say, by way of necessary explanation, that "The Lady of Glenwith Grange" is now offered to the reader for the first time; and that the other stories have appeared in the columns of *Household Words* . My best thanks are due to Mr. Charles Dickens for his kindness in allowing me to set them in their present frame-work.

I must also gratefully acknowledge an obligation of another kind to the accomplished artist, Mr. W. S. Herrick, to whom I am indebted for the curious and interesting facts on which the tales of "The Terribly Strange Bed" and "The Yellow Mask" are founded.

Although the statement may appear somewhat superfluous to those who know me, it may not be out of place to add, in conclusion, that these stories are entirely of my own imagining, constructing, and writing. The fact that the events of some of my tales occur on foreign ground, and are acted out by foreign personages, appears to have suggested in some quarters the inference that the stories themselves might be of foreign origin. Let me, once for all, assure any readers who may honor me with their attention, that in this, and in all other cases, they may depend on the genuineness of my literary offspring. The little children of my brain may be weakly enough, and may be sadly in want of a helping hand to aid them in their first attempts at walking on the stage of this great world; but, at any rate, they are not borrowed children. The members of my own literary family are indeed increasing so fast as to render the very idea of borrowing quite out of the question, and to suggest serious apprehension that I may not have done adding to the large book-population, on my own sole responsibility, even yet.

LEAVES FROM LEAH'S DIARY.

26th February, 1827.— The doctor has just called for the third time to examine my husband's eyes. Thank God, there is no fear at present of my poor William losing his sight, provided he can be prevailed on to attend rigidly to the medical instructions for preserving it. These instructions, which forbid him to exercise his profession for the next six months at least, are, in our case, very hard to follow. They will but too probably sentence us to poverty, perhaps to actual want; but they must be borne resignedly, and even thankfully, seeing that my husband's forced cessation from work will save him from the dreadful affliction of loss of sight. I think I can answer for my own cheerfulness and endurance, now that we know the worst. Can I answer for our children also? Surely I can, when there are only two of them. It is a sad confession to make, but now, for the first time since my marriage, I feel thankful that we have no more.

17th.— A dread came over me last night, after I had comforted William as well as I could about the future, and had heard him fall off to sleep, that the doctor had not told us the worst. Medical men do sometimes deceive their patients, from what has always seemed to me to be misdirected kindness of heart. The mere suspicion that I had been trifled with on the subject of my husband's illness, caused me such uneasiness, that I made an excuse to get out, and went in secret to the doctor. Fortunately, I found him at home, and in three words I confessed to him the object of my visit.

He smiled, and said I might make myself easy; he had told us the worst.

"And that worst," I said, to make certain, "is, that for the next six months my husband must allow his eyes to have the most perfect repose?"

"Exactly," the doctor answered. "Mind, I don't say that he may not dispense with his green shade, indoors, for an hour or two at a time, as the inflammation gets subdued. But I do most positively repeat that he must not *employ* his eyes. He must not touch a brush or pencil; he must not think of taking another likeness, on any consideration whatever, for the next six months. His persisting in finishing those two portraits, at the time when his eyes first began to fail, was the real cause of all the bad symptoms that we have had to combat ever since. I warned him (if you remember, Mrs. Kerby?) when he first came to practice in our neighborhood."

"I know you did, sir," I replied. "But what was a poor traveling portrait-painter like my husband, who lives by taking likenesses first in one place and then in another, to do? Our bread depended on his using his eyes, at the very time when you warned him to let them have a rest."

"Have you no other resources? No money but the money Mr. Kerby can get by portrait-painting?" asked the doctor.

"None," I answered, with a sinking at my heart as I thought of his bill for medical attendance.

"Will you pardon me?" he said, coloring and looking a little uneasy, "or, rather, will you ascribe it to the friendly interest I feel in you, if I ask whether Mr. Kerby realizes a comfortable income by the practice of his profession? Don't," he went on anxiously, before I could reply —"pray don't think I make this inquiry from a motive of impertinent curiosity!"

I felt quite satisfied that he could have no improper motive for asking the question, and so answered it at once plainly and truly.

"My husband makes but a small income," I said. "Famous London portrait-painters get great prices from their sitters; but poor unknown artists, who only travel about the country, are obliged to work hard and be contented with very small gains. After we have paid all that we owe here, I am afraid we shall have little enough left to retire on, when we take refuge in some cheaper place."

"In that case," said the good doctor (I am so glad and proud to remember that I always liked him from the first!), "in that case, don't make yourself anxious about my bill when you are thinking of clearing off your debts here. I can afford to wait till Mr. Kerby's eyes are well again, and I shall then ask him for a likeness of my little daughter. By that arrangement we are sure to be both quits, and both perfectly satisfied."

He considerately shook hands and bade me farewell before I could say half the grateful words to him that were on my lips. Never, never shall I forget that he relieved me of my two heaviest anxieties at the most anxious time of my life. The merciful, warm-hearted man! I could almost have knelt down and kissed his doorstep, as I crossed it on my way home.

18th.— If I had not resolved, after what happened yesterday, to look only at the cheerful side of things for the future, the events of today would have robbed me of all my courage, at the very outset of our troubles. First, there was the casting up of our bills, and the discovery, when the amount of them was balanced against all the money we have saved up, that we shall only have between three and four pounds left in the cash-box, after we have got out of debt. Then there was the sad necessity of writing letters in my husband's name to the rich people who were ready to employ him, telling them of the affliction that had overtaken him, and of the impossibility of his executing their orders for portraits for the next six months to come. And, lastly, there was the heart-breaking business for me to go through of giving our landlord warning, just as we had got comfortably settled in our new abode. If William could only have gone on with his work, we might have stopped in this town, and in these clean, comfortable lodgings for at least three or four months. We have never had the use of a nice empty garret before, for the children to play in; and I never met with any landlady so pleasant to deal with in the kitchen as the landlady here. And now we must leave all this comfort and happiness, and go — I hardly know where. William, in his bitterness, says to the workhouse; but that shall never be, if I have to go out to service to prevent it. The darkness is coming on, and we must save in candles, or I could write much more. Ah, me! what a day this has been. I have had but one pleasant moment since it began; and that was in the morning, when I set my little Emily to work on a bead purse for the kind doctor's daughter. My child, young as she is, is wonderfully neat-handed at stringing beads; and even a poor little empty purse as a token of our gratitude, is better than nothing at all.

19th.— A visit from our best friend — our only friend here — the doctor. After he had examined William's eyes, and had reported that they were getting on as well as can be hoped at present, he asked where we thought of going to live? I said in the cheapest place we could find, and added that I was about to make inquiries in the by-streets of the town that very day. "Put off those inquiries," he said, "till you hear from me again. I am going now to see a patient at a farmhouse five miles off. (You needn't look at the children, Mrs. Kerby, it's nothing infectious — only a clumsy lad, who has broken his collar-bone by a fall from a horse.) They receive lodgers occasionally at the farm-house, and I know no reason why they should not be willing to receive you. If you want to be well housed and well fed at a cheap rate, and if you like the society of honest, hearty people, the farm of Appletreewick is the very place for you. Don't thank me till you know whether I can get you these new lodgings or not. And in the meantime settle all your business affairs here, so as to be able to move at a moment's notice." With those words the kind-hearted

6 | WILKIE COLLINS

gentleman nodded and went out. Pray heaven he may succeed at the farm-house! We may be sure of the children's health, at least, if we live in the country. Talking of the children, I must not omit to record that Emily has nearly done one end of the bead purse already.

20th.— A note from the doctor, who is too busy to call. Such good news! They will give us two bedrooms, and board us with the family at Apple-treewick for seventeen shillings a week. By my calculations, we shall have three pounds sixteen shillings left, after paying what we owe here. That will be enough, at the outset, for four weeks' living at the farmhouse, with eight shillings to spare besides. By embroidery-work I can easily make nine shillings more to put to that, and there is a fifth week provided for. Surely, in five weeks' time — considering the number of things I can turn my hand to — we may hit on some plan for getting a little money. This is what I am always telling my husband, and what, by dint of constantly repeating it, I am getting to believe myself. William, as is but natural, poor fellow, does not take so lighthearted view of the future as I do. He says that the prospect of sitting idle and being kept by his wife for months to come, is something more wretched and hopeless than words can describe. I try to raise his spirits by reminding him of his years of honest hard work for me and the children, and of the doctor's assurance that his eyes will get the better, in good time, of their present helpless state. But he still sighs and murmurs — being one of the most independent and high spirited of men — about living a burden on his wife. I can only answer, what in my heart of hearts I feel, that I took him for Better and for Worse; that I have had many years of the Better, and that, even in our present trouble, the Worse shows no signs of coming yet!

The bead purse is getting on fast. Red and blue, in a pretty striped pattern.

21st.— A busy day. We go to Appletreewick tomorrow. Paying bills and packing up. All poor William's new canvases and painting-things huddled together into a packing-case. He looked so sad, sitting silent with his green shade on, while his old familiar working materials were disappearing around him, as if he and they were never to come together again, that the tears would start into my eyes, though I am sure I am not one of the crying sort. Luckily, the green shade kept him from seeing me: and I took good care, though the effort nearly choked me, that he should not hear I was crying, at any rate.

The bead purse is done. How are we to get the steel rings and tassels for it? I am not justified now in spending sixpence unnecessarily, even for the best of purposes.

22d.———

23d. *The Farm of Appletreewick.* — Too tired, after our move yesterday, to write a word in my diary about our journey to this delightful place. But now that we are beginning to get settled, I can manage to make up for past omissions.

My first occupation on the morning of the move had, oddly enough, nothing to do with our departure for the farmhouse. The moment breakfast was over I began the day by making Emily as smart and nice-looking as I could, to go to the doctor's with the purse. She had her best silk frock on, showing the mending a little in some places, I am afraid, and her straw hat trimmed with my bonnet ribbon. Her father's neck-scarf, turned and joined so that nobody could see it, made a nice mantilla for her; and away she went to the doctor's, with her little, determined step, and the purse in her hand (such a pretty hand that it is hardly to be regretted I had no gloves for her). They were delighted with the purse — which I ought to mention was finished with some white beads; we found them in rummaging among our boxes, and they made beautiful rings and tassels, contrasting charmingly with the blue and red of the rest of the purse. The doctor and his little girl were, as I have said, delighted with the present; and they gave Emily, in return, a workbox for herself, and a box of sugar-plums for her baby sister. The child came back all flushed with the pleasure of the visit, and quite helped to keep up her father's spirits with talking to him about it. So much for the highly interesting history of the bead purse.

Toward the afternoon the light cart from the farmhouse came to fetch us and our things to Appletreewick. It was quite a warm spring day, and I had another pang to bear as I saw poor William helped into the cart, looking so sickly and sad, with his miserable green shade, in the cheerful sunlight. "God only knows, Leah, how this will succeed with us," he said, as we started; then sighed, and fell silent again.

Just outside the town the doctor met us. "Good luck go with you!" he cried, swinging his stick in his usual hasty way; "I shall come and see you as soon as you are all settled at the farmhouse." "Good-by, sir," says Emily, struggling up with all her might among the bundles in the bottom of the cart; "good-by, and thank you again for the work-box and the sugar-plums." That was my child all over! she never wants telling. The doctor kissed his hand, and gave another flourish with his stick. So we parted.

How I should have enjoyed the drive if William could only have looked, as I did, at the young firs on the heath bending beneath the steady breeze; at the shadows flying over the smooth fields; at the high white clouds moving on and on, in their grand airy procession over the gladsome blue sky! It was a hilly road, and I begged the lad who drove us not to press the horse; so we were nearly an hour, at our slow rate of going, before we drew up at the gate of Appletreewick.

24th February to 2d March.— We have now been here long enough to know something of the place and the people. First, as to the place: Where the farmhouse now is, there was once a famous priory. The tower is still standing, and the great room where the monks ate and drank — used at present as a granary. The house itself seems to have been tacked on to the ruins anyhow. No two rooms in it are on the same level. The children do nothing but tumble about the passages, because there always happens to be a step up or down, just at the darkest part of every one of them. As for staircases, there seems to me to be one for each bedroom. I do nothing but lose my way — and the farmer says, drolling, that he must have sign-posts put up for me in every corner of the house from top to bottom. On the ground-floor, besides the usual domestic offices, we have the best parlor — a dark, airless, expensively furnished solitude, never invaded by anybody; the kitchen, and a kind of hall, with a fireplace as big as the drawing-room at our town lodgings. Here we live and take our meals; here the children can racket about to their hearts' content; here the dogs come lumbering in, whenever they can get loose; here wages are paid, visitors are received, bacon is cured, cheese is tasted, pipes are smoked, and naps are taken every evening by the male members of the family. Never was such a comfortable, friendly dwelling-place devised as this hall; I feel already as if half my life had been passed in it.

Out-of-doors, looking beyond the flower-garden, lawn, back yards, pigeon-houses, and kitchen-gardens, we are surrounded by a network of smooth grazing-fields, each shut off from the other by its neat hedgerow and its sturdy gate. Beyond the fields the hills seem to flow away gently from us into the far blue distance, till they are lost in the bright softness of the sky. At one point, which we can see from our bedroom windows, they dip suddenly into the plain, and show, over the rich marshy flat, a strip of distant sea — a strip sometimes blue, sometimes gray; sometimes, when the sun sets, a streak of fire; sometimes, on showery days, a flash of silver light.

The inhabitants of the farmhouse have one great and rare merit — they are people whom you can make friends with at once. Between not knowing them at all, and knowing them well enough to shake hands at first sight, there is no ceremonious interval or formal gradation whatever. They received us, on our arrival, exactly as if we were old friends returned from some long traveling expedition. Before we had been ten minutes in the hall, William had the easiest chair and the snuggest corner; the children were eating bread-and-jam on the window-seat; and I was talking to the farmer's wife, with the cat on my lap, of the time when Emily had the measles.

The family numbers seven, exclusive of the indoor servants, of course. First came the farmer and his wife — he is a tall, sturdy, loud-voiced, active old man — she the easiest, plumpest and gayest woman of sixty I ever met with. They have three sons and two daughters. The two eldest of the young men are employed on the farm; the third is a sailor, and is making holiday-time of it just now at Appletreewick. The daughters are pictures of health and freshness. I have but one complaint to make against them — they are beginning to spoil the children already.

In this tranquil place, and among these genial, natural people, how happily my time might be passed, were it not for the saddening sight of William's affliction, and the wearing uncertainty of how we are to provide for future necessities! It is a hard thing for my husband and me, after having had the day made pleasant by kind words and friendly offices, to feel this one anxious thought always forcing itself on us at night: Shall we have the means of stopping in our new home in a month's time?

3d.— A rainy day; the children difficult to manage; William miserably despondent. Perhaps he influenced me, or perhaps I felt my little troubles with the children more than usual: but, however it was, I have not been so heavy-hearted since the day when my husband first put on the green shade. A listless, hopeless sensation would steal over me; but why write about it? Better to try and forget it. There is always tomorrow to look to when today is at the worst.

4th.— To-morrow has proved worthy of the faith I put in it. Sunshine again out-of-doors; and as clear and true a reflection of it in my own heart as I can hope to have just at this time. Oh! that month, that one poor month of respite! What are we to do at the end of the month?

5th.— I made my short entry for yesterday in the afternoon just before tea-time, little thinking of events destined to happen with the evening that would be really worth chronicling, for the sake of the excellent results to which they are sure to lead. My tendency is to be too sanguine about everything, I know; but I am, nevertheless, firmly persuaded that I can see a new way out of our present difficulties — a way of getting money enough to keep us all in comfort at the farmhouse until William's eyes are well again.

The new project which is to relieve us from all uncertainties for the next six months actually originated with *me!* It has raised me many inches higher in my own estimation already. If the doctor only agrees with my view of the case when he comes tomorrow, William will allow himself to be persuaded, I know; and then let them say what they please, I will answer for the rest.

This is how the new idea first found its way into my head:

We had just done tea. William, in much better spirits than usual, was talking with the young sailor, who is jocosely called here by the very ugly name of "Foul-weather Dick." The farmer and his two eldest sons were composing themselves on the oaken settles for their usual nap. The dame was knitting, the two girls were beginning to clear the tea-table, and I was darning the children's socks. To all appearance, this was not a very propitious state of things for the creation of new ideas, and yet my idea grew out of it, for all that. Talking with my husband on various subjects connected with life in ships, the young sailor began giving us a description of his hammock; telling us how it was slung; how it was impossible to get into it any other way than "stern foremost" (whatever that may mean); how the rolling of the ship made it rock like a cradle; and how, on rough nights, it sometimes swayed to and fro at such a rate as to bump bodily against the ship's side and wake him up with the sensation of having just received a punch on the head from a remarkably hard fist. Hearing all this, I ventured to suggest that it must be an immense relief to him to sleep on shore in a good, motionless, solid four-post bed. But, to my surprise, he scoffed at the idea; said he never slept comfortably out of his hammock; declared that he quite missed his occasional punch on the head from the ship's side; and ended by giving a most comical account of all the uncomfortable sensations he felt when he slept in a four-post bed. The odd nature of one of the young sailor's objections to sleeping on shore reminded my husband (as indeed it did me too) of the terrible story of a bed in a French gambling-house, which he once heard from a gentleman whose likeness he took.

"You're laughing at me," says honest Foul-weather Dick, seeing William turn toward me and smile.—"No, indeed," says my husband; "that last objection of yours to the four-post beds on shore seems by no means ridiculous to *me,* at any rate. I once knew a gentleman, Dick, who practically realized your objection."

"Excuse me, sir," says Dick, after a pause, and with an appearance of great bewilderment and curiosity; "but could you put 'practically realized' into plain English, so that a poor man like me might have a chance of understanding you?"—"Certainly!" says my husband, laughing. "I mean that I once knew a gentleman who actually saw and felt what you say in jest you are afraid of seeing and feeling whenever you sleep in a four-post bed. Do you understand that?" Foul-weather Dick understood it perfectly, and begged with great eagerness to hear what the gentleman's adventure really was. The dame, who had been listening to our talk, backed her son's petition; the two girls sat down expectant at the half-cleared tea-table; even the farmer and his drowsy sons roused themselves lazily on the settle — my husband saw that he stood fairly committed to the relation of the story, so he told it without more ado.

I have often heard him relate that strange adventure (William is the best teller of a story I ever met with) to friends of all ranks in many different parts of England, and I never yet knew it fail of producing an effect. The farmhouse audience were, I may almost say, petrified by it. I never before saw people look so long in the same direction, and sit so long in the same attitude, as they did. Even the servants stole away from their work in the kitchen, and, unrebuked by master or mistress, stood quite spell-bound in the doorway to listen. Observing all this in silence, while my husband was going on with his narrative, the thought suddenly flashed across me, "Why should William not get a wider audience for that story, as well as for others which he has heard from time to time from his sitters, and which he has hitherto only repeated in private among a few friends? People tell stories in books and get money for them. What if we told our stories in a book? and what if the book sold? Why freedom, surely, from the one great anxiety that is now preying on us! Money enough to stop at the farmhouse till William's eyes are fit for work again!" I almost jumped up from my chair as my thought went on shaping itself in this manner. When great men make wonderful discoveries, do they feel sensations like mine, I wonder? Was Sir Isaac Newton within an ace of skipping into the air when he first found out the law of gravitation? Did Friar Bacon long to dance when he lit the match and heard the first charge of gunpowder in the world go off with a bang?

I had to put a strong constraint on myself, or I should have communicated all that was passing in my mind to William before our friends at the farm-house. But I knew it was best to wait until we were alone, and I did wait. What a relief it was when we all got up at last to say good-night!

The moment we were in our own room, I could not stop to take so much as a pin out of my dress before I began. "My dear," said I, "I never heard you tell that gambling-house adventure so well before. What an effect it had upon our friends! what an effect, indeed, it always has wherever you tell it!"

So far he did not seem to take much notice. He just nodded, and began to pour out some of the lotion in which he always bathes his poor eyes the last thing at night.

"And as for that, William," I went on, "all your stories seem to interest people. What a number you have picked up, first and last, from different sitters, in the fifteen years of your practice as a portrait-painter! Have you any idea how many stories you really do know?"

No: he could not undertake to say how many just then. He gave this answer in a very indifferent tone, dabbing away all the time at his eyes with the sponge and lotion. He did it so awkwardly and roughly, as it seemed to me, that I took the sponge from him and applied the lotion tenderly myself.

"Do you think," said I, "if you turned over one of your stories carefully in your mind beforehand — say the one you told to-night, for example — that you could repeat it all to me so perfectly and deliberately that I should be able to take it down in writing from your lips?"

Yes: of course he could. But why ask that question?

"Because I should like to have all the stories that you have been in the habit of relating to our friends set down fairly in writing, by way of preserving them from ever being forgotten."

Would I bathe his left eye now, because that felt the hottest to-night? I began to forbode that his growing indifference to what I was saying would soon end in his fairly going to sleep before I had developed my new idea, unless I took some means forthwith of stimulating his curiosity, or, in other words, of waking him into a proper state of astonishment and attention. "William," said I, without another syllable of preface, "I have got a new plan for finding all the money we want for our expenses here."

He jerked his head up directly, and looked at me. What plan?

"This: The state of your eyes prevents you for the present from following your profession as an artist, does it not? Very well. What are you to do with your idle time, my dear? Turn author! And how are you to get the money we want? By publishing a book!"

"Good gracious, Leah! are you out of your senses?" he exclaimed.

I put my arm round his neck and sat down on his knee (the course I always take when I want to persuade him to anything with as few words as possible).

"Now, William, listen patiently to me," I said. "An artist lies under this great disadvantage in case of accidents — his talents are of no service to him unless he can use his eyes and fingers. An author, on the other hand, can turn his talents to account just as well by means of other people's eyes and fingers as by means of his own. In your present situation, therefore, you have nothing for it, as I said before, but to turn author. Wait! and hear me out. The book I want you to make is a book of all your stories. You shall repeat them, and I will write them down from your dictation. Our manuscript shall be printed; we will sell the book to the public, and so support ourselves honorably in adversity, by doing the best we can to interest and amuse others."

While I was saying all this — I suppose in a very excitable manner — my husband looked, as our young sailor-friend would phrase it, quite *taken aback.* "You were always quick at contriving, Leah," he said; "but how in the world came you to think of this plan?"

"I thought of it while you were telling them the gambling-house adventure downstairs," I answered.

"It is an ingenious idea, and a bold idea," he went on, thoughtfully. "But it is one thing to tell a story to a circle of friends, and another thing to put it into a printed form for an audience of strangers. Consider, my dear, that we are neither of us used to what is called writing for the press."

"Very true," said I, "but nobody is used to it when they first begin, and yet plenty of people have tried the hazardous literary experiment successfully. Besides, in our case, we have the materials ready to our hands; surely we can succeed in shaping them presentably if we aim at nothing but the simple truth."

"Who is to do the eloquent descriptions and the striking reflections, and all that part of it?" said William, perplexedly shaking his head.

"Nobody!" I replied. "The eloquent descriptions and the striking reflections are just the parts of a story-book that people never read. Whatever we do, let us not, if we can possibly help it, write so much as a single sentence that can be conveniently skipped. Come! come!" I continued, seeing him begin to shake his head again; "no more objections, William, I am too certain of the success of my plan to endure them. If you still doubt, let us refer the new project to a competent arbitrator. The doctor is coming to see you tomorrow. I will tell him all that I have told you; and if you will promise on your side, I will engage on mine to be guided entirely by his opinion."

William smiled, and readily gave the promise. This was all I wanted to send me to bed in the best spirits. For, of course, I should never have thought of mentioning the doctor as an arbitrator, if I had not known beforehand that he was sure to be on my side.

6th.— The arbitrator has shown that he deserved my confidence in him. He ranked himself entirely on my side before I had half done explaining to him what my new project really was. As to my husband's doubts and difficulties, the dear good man would not so much as hear them mentioned. "No objections," he cried, gayly; "set to work, Mr. Kerby, and make your fortune. I always said your wife was worth her weight in gold — and here she is now, all ready to get into the bookseller's scales and prove it. Set to work! set to work!"

"With all my heart," said William, beginning at last to catch the infection of our enthusiasm. "But when my part of the work and my wife's has been completed, what are we to do with the produce of our labor?"

"Leave that to me," answered the doctor. "Finish your book and send it to my house; I will show it at once to the editor of our country newspaper. He has plenty of literary friends in London, and he will be just the man to help you. By-the-by," added the doctor, addressing me, "you think of everything, Mrs. Kerby; pray have you thought of a name yet for the new book?"

At that question it was my turn to be "taken aback." The idea of naming the book had never once entered my head.

"A good title is of vast importance," said the doctor, knitting his brows thoughtfully. "We must all think about that. What shall it be? eh, Mrs. Kerby, what shall it be?"

"Perhaps something may strike us after we have fairly set to work," my husband suggested. "Talking of work," he continued, turning to me, "how are you to find time, Leah, with your nursery occupations, for writing down all the stories as I tell them?"

"I have been thinking of that this morning," said I, "and have come to the conclusion that I shall have but little leisure to write from your dictation in the day-time. What with dressing and washing the children, teaching them, giving them their meals, taking them out to walk, and keeping them amused at home — to say nothing of sitting sociably at work with the dame and her two girls in the afternoon — I am afraid I shall have few opportunities of doing my part of the book between breakfast and tea-time. But when the children are in bed, and the farmer and his family are reading or dozing, I should have at least three unoccupied hours to spare. So, if you don't mind putting off our working-time till after dark —"

"There's the title!" shouted the doctor, jumping out of his chair as if he had been shot.

"Where?" cried I, looking all round me in the surprise of the moment, as if I had expected to see the title magically inscribed for us on the walls of the room.

"In your last words, to be sure!" rejoined the doctor. "You said just now that you would not have leisure to write from Mr. Kerby's dictation till *after dark*. What can we do better than name the book after the time when the book is written? Call it boldly, *After dark*. Stop! before anybody says a word for or against it, let us see how the name looks on paper."

I opened my writing-desk in a great flutter. The doctor selected the largest sheet of paper and the broadest-nibbed pen he could find, and wrote in majestic round-text letters, with alternate thin and thick strokes beautiful to see, the two cabalistic words

AFTER DARK.

We all three laid our heads together over the paper, and in breathless silence studied the effect of the round-text: William raising his green shade in the excitement of the moment, and actually disobeying the doctor's orders about not using his eyes, in the doctor's own presence! After a good long stare, we looked round solemnly in each other's faces and nodded. There was no doubt whatever on the subject after seeing the round-text. In one happy moment the doctor had hit on the right name.

"I have written the title-page," said our good friend, taking up his hat to go. "And now I leave it to you two to write the book."

Since then I have mended four pens and bought a quire of letter-paper at the village shop. William is to ponder well over his stories in the daytime, so as to be quite ready for me "after dark." We are to commence our new occupation this evening. My heart beats fast and my eyes moisten when I think of it. How many of our dearest interests depend upon the one little beginning that we are to make to-night!

THE TRAVELER'S STORY OF A TERRIBLY STRANGE BED.

PROLOGUE TO THE FIRST STORY.

*B*efore I begin, by the aid of my wife's patient attention and ready pen, to relate any of the stories which I have heard at various times from persons whose likenesses I have been employed to take, it will not be amiss if I try to secure the reader's interest in the following pages, by briefly explaining how I became possessed of the narrative matter which they contain.

Of myself I have nothing to say, but that I have followed the profession of a traveling portrait-painter for the last fifteen years. The pursuit of my calling has not only led me all through England, but has taken me twice to Scotland, and once to Ireland. In moving from district to district, I am never guided beforehand by any settled plan. Sometimes the letters of recommendation which I get from persons who are satisfied with the work I have done for them determine the direction in which I travel. Sometimes I hear of a new neighbor-hood in which there is no resident artist of ability, and remove thither on spec-ulation. Sometimes my friends among the picture-dealers say a good word on my behalf to their rich customers, and so pave the way for me in the large towns. Sometimes my prosperous and famous brother-artists, hearing of small commissions which it is not worth their while to accept, mention my name, and procure me introductions to pleasant country houses. Thus I get on, now in one way and now in another, not winning a reputation or making a fortune, but happier, perhaps, on the whole, than many men who have got both the one and the other. So, at least, I try to think now, though I started in my youth with as high an ambition as the best of them. Thank God, it is not my business here to speak of past times and their disappointments. A twinge of the old hopeless heartache comes over me sometimes still, when I think of my student days.

One peculiarity of my present way of life is, that it brings me into contact with all sorts of characters. I almost feel, by this time, as if I had painted every civilized variety of the human race. Upon the whole, my experience of the world, rough as it has been, has not taught me to think unkindly of my fellow-creatures. I have certainly received such treatment at the hands of some of my sitters as I could not describe without saddening and shocking any kind-hearted reader; but, taking one year and one place with another, I have cause to remember with gratitude and respect — sometimes even with friendship and affection — a very large proportion of the numerous persons who have employed me.

Some of the results of my experience are curious in a moral point of view. For example, I have found women almost uniformly less delicate in asking me about my terms, and less generous in remunerating me for my services, than men. On the other hand, men, within my knowledge, are decidedly vainer of their personal attractions, and more vexatiously anxious to have them done full justice to on canvas, than women. Taking both sexes together, I have found young people, for the most part, more gentle, more reasonable, and more considerate than old. And, summing up, in a general way, my experience of different ranks (which extends, let me premise, all the way down from peers to publicans), I have met with most of my formal and ungracious receptions among rich people of uncertain social standing: the highest classes and the lowest among my employers almost always contrive — in widely different ways, of course, to make me feel at home as soon as I enter their houses.

The one great obstacle that I have to contend against in the practice of my profession is not, as some persons may imagine, the difficulty of making my sitters keep their heads still while I paint them, but the difficulty of getting them to preserve the natural look and the every-day peculiarities of dress and manner. People will assume an expression, will brush up their hair, will correct any little characteristic carelessness in their apparel — will, in short, when they want to have their likenesses taken, look as if they were sitting for their pictures. If I paint them, under these artificial circumstances, I fail of course to present them in their habitual aspect; and my portrait, as a necessary consequence, disappoints everybody, the sitter always included. When we wish to judge of a man's character by his handwriting, we want his customary scrawl dashed off with his common workaday pen, not his best small-text, traced laboriously with the finest procurable crow-quill point. So it is with portrait-painting, which is, after all, nothing but a right reading of the externals of character recognizably presented to the view of others.

Experience, after repeated trials, has proved to me that the only way of getting sitters who persist in assuming a set look to resume their habitual expression, is to lead them into talking about some subject in which they are greatly interested. If I can only beguile them into speaking earnestly, no matter on what topic, I am sure of recovering their natural expression; sure of seeing all the little precious everyday peculiarities of the man or woman peep out, one after another, quite unawares. The long, maundering stories about nothing, the wearisome recitals of petty grievances, the local anecdotes unrelieved by the faintest suspicion of anything like general interest, which I have been condemned to hear, as a consequence of thawing the ice off the features of formal sitters by the method just described, would fill hundreds of volumes, and promote the repose of thousands of readers. On the other hand, if I have suffered under the tediousness of the many, I have not been without my compensating gains from the wisdom and experience of the few. To some of my sitters I have been indebted for information which has enlarged my mind — to some for advice which has lightened my heart — to some for narratives of strange adventure which riveted my attention at the time, which have served to interest and amuse my fireside circle for many years past, and which are now, I would fain hope, destined to make kind friends for me among a wider audience than any that I have yet addressed.

Singularly enough, almost all the best stories that I have heard from my sitters have been told by accident. I only remember two cases in which a story was volunteered to me, and, although I have often tried the experiment, I cannot call to mind even a single instance in which leading questions (as the lawyers call them) on my part, addressed to a sitter, ever produced any result worth recording. Over and over again, I have been disastrously successful in encouraging dull people to weary me. But the clever people who have something interesting to say, seem, so far as I have observed them, to acknowledge no other stimulant than chance. For every story which I propose including in the present collection, excepting one, I have been indebted, in the first instance, to the capricious influence of the same chance. Something my sitter has seen about me, something I have remarked in my sitter, or in the room in which I take the likeness, or in the neighborhood through which I pass on my way to work, has suggested the necessary association, or has started the right train of recollections, and then the story appeared to begin of its own accord. Occasionally the most casual notice, on my part, of some very unpromising object has smoothed the way for the relation of a long and interesting narrative. I first heard one of the most dramatic of the stories that will be presented in this book, merely through being carelessly inquisitive to know the history of a stuffed poodle-dog.

It is thus not without reason that I lay some stress on the desirableness of prefacing each one of the following narratives by a brief account of the curious manner in which I became possessed of it. As to my capacity for repeating these stories correctly, I can answer for it that my memory may be trusted. I may claim it as a merit, because it is after all a mechanical one, that I forget nothing, and that I can call long-passed conversations and events as readily to my recollection as if they had happened but a few weeks ago. Of two things at least I feel tolerably certain beforehand, in meditating over the contents of this book: First, that I can repeat correctly all that I have heard; and, secondly, that I have never missed anything worth hearing when my sitters were addressing me on an interesting subject. Although I cannot take the lead in talking while I am engaged in painting, I can listen while others speak, and work all the better for it.

So much in the way of general preface to the pages for which I am about to ask the reader's attention. Let me now advance to particulars, and describe how I came to hear the first story in the present collection. I begin with it because it is the story that I have oftenest "rehearsed," to borrow a phrase from the stage. Wherever I go, I am sooner or later sure to tell it. Only last night, I was persuaded into repeating it once more by the inhabitants of the farmhouse in which I am now staying.

Not many years ago, on returning from a short holiday visit to a friend settled in Paris, I found professional letters awaiting me at my agent's in London, which required my immediate presence in Liverpool. Without stopping to unpack, I proceeded by the first conveyance to my new destination; and, calling at the picture-dealer's shop, where portrait-painting engagements were received for me, found to my great satisfaction that I had remunerative employment in prospect, in and about Liverpool, for at least two months to come. I was putting up my letters in high spirits, and was just leaving the picture-dealer's shop to look out for comfortable lodgings, when I was met at the door by the landlord of one of the largest hotels in Liverpool — an old acquaintance whom I had known as manager of a tavern in London in my student days.

"Mr. Kerby!" he exclaimed, in great astonishment. "What an unexpected meeting! the last man in the world whom I expected to see, and yet the very man whose services I want to make use of!"

"What, more work for me?" said I; "are all the people in Liverpool going to have their portraits painted?"

"I only know of one," replied the landlord, "a gentleman staying at my hotel, who wants a chalk drawing done for him. I was on my way here to inquire of any artist whom our picture-dealing friend could recommend. How glad I am that I met you before I had committed myself to employing a stranger!"

"Is this likeness wanted at once?" I asked, thinking of the number of engagements that I had already got in my pocket.

"Immediately — today — this very hour, if possible," said the landlord. "Mr. Faulkner, the gentleman I am speaking of, was to have sailed yesterday for the Brazils from this place; but the wind shifted last night to the wrong quarter, and he came ashore again this morning. He may of course be detained here for some time; but he may also be called on board ship at half an hour's notice, if the wind shifts back again in the right direction. This uncertainty makes it a matter of importance that the likeness should be begun immediately. Undertake it if you possibly can, for Mr. Faulkner's a liberal gentleman, who is sure to give you your own terms."

I reflected for a minute or two. The portrait was only wanted in chalk, and would not take long; besides, I might finish it in the evening, if my other engagements pressed hard upon me in the daytime. Why not leave my luggage at the picture-dealer's, put off looking for lodgings till night, and secure the new commission boldly by going back at once with the landlord to the hotel? I decided on following this course almost as soon as the idea occurred to me — put my chalks in my pocket, and a sheet of drawing paper in the first of my portfolios that came to hand — and so presented myself before Mr. Faulkner, ready to take his likeness, literally at five minutes' notice.

I found him a very pleasant, intelligent man, young and handsome. He had been a great traveler; had visited all the wonders of the East; and was now about to explore the wilds of the vast South American Continent. Thus much he told me good-humoredly and unconstrainedly while I was preparing my drawing materials.

As soon as I had put him in the right light and position, and had seated myself opposite to him, he changed the subject of conversation, and asked me, a little confusedly as I thought, if it was not a customary practice among portrait-painters to gloss over the faults in their sitters' faces, and to make as much as possible of any good points which their features might possess.

"Certainly," I answered. "You have described the whole art and mystery of successful portrait-painting in a few words."

"May I beg, then," said he, "that you will depart from the usual practice in my case, and draw me with all my defects, exactly as I am? The fact is," he went on, after a moment's pause, "the likeness you are now preparing to take is intended for my mother. My roving disposition makes me a great anxiety to her, and she parted from me this last time very sadly and unwillingly. I don't know how the idea came into my head, but it struck me this morning that I could not better employ the time, while I was delayed here on shore, than by getting my likeness done to send to her as a keepsake. She has no portrait of me since I was a child, and she is sure to value a drawing of me more than anything else I could send to her. I only trouble you with this explanation to prove that I am really sincere in my wish to be drawn unflatteringly, exactly as I am."

Secretly respecting and admiring him for what he had just said, I promised that his directions should be implicitly followed, and began to work immediately. Before I had pursued my occupation for ten minutes, the conversation began to flag, and the usual obstacle to my success with a sitter gradually set itself up between us. Quite unconsciously, of course, Mr. Faulkner stiffened his neck, shut his month, and contracted his eyebrows — evidently under the impression that he was facilitating the process of taking his portrait by making his face as like a lifeless mask as possible. All traces of his natural animated expression were fast disappearing, and he was beginning to change into a heavy and rather melancholy-looking man.

This complete alteration was of no great consequence so long as I was only engaged in drawing the outline of his face and the general form of his features. I accordingly worked on doggedly for more than an hour — then left off to point my chalks again, and to give my sitter a few minutes' rest. Thus far the likeness had not suffered through Mr. Faulkner's unfortunate notion of the right way of sitting for his portrait; but the time of difficulty, as I well knew, was to come. It was impossible for me to think of putting any expression into the drawing unless I could contrive some means, when he resumed his chair, of making him look like himself again. "I will talk to him about foreign parts," thought I, "and try if I can't make him forget that he is sitting for his picture in that way."

While I was pointing my chalks Mr. Faulkner was walking up and down the room. He chanced to see the portfolio I had brought with me leaning against the wall, and asked if there were any sketches in it. I told him there were a few which I had made during my recent stay in Paris; "In Paris?" he repeated, with a look of interest; "may I see them?"

I gave him the permission he asked as a matter of course. Sitting down, he took the portfolio on his knee, and began to look through it. He turned over the first five sketches rapidly enough; but when he came to the sixth, I saw his face flush directly, and observed that he took the drawing out of the portfolio, carried it to the window, and remained silently absorbed in the contemplation of it for full five minutes. After that, he turned round to me, and asked very anxiously if I had any objection to part with that sketch.

It was the least interesting drawing of the collection — merely a view in one of the streets running by the backs of the houses in the Palais Royal. Some four or five of these houses were comprised in the view, which was of no particular use to me in any way; and which was too valueless, as a work of art, for me to think of selling it. I begged his acceptance of it at once. He thanked me quite warmly; and then, seeing that I looked a little surprised at the odd selection he had made from my sketches, laughingly asked me if I could guess why he had been so anxious to become possessed of the view which I had given him?

"Probably," I answered, "there is some remarkable historical association connected with that street at the back of the Palais Royal, of which I am ignorant."

"No," said Mr. Faulkner; "at least none that *I* know of. The only association connected with the place in *my* mind is a purely personal association. Look at this house in your drawing — the house with the water-pipe running down it from top to bottom. I once passed a night there — a night I shall never forget to the day of my death. I have had some awkward traveling adventures in my time; but *that* adventure —! Well, never mind, suppose we begin the sitting. I make but a bad return for your kindness in giving me the sketch by thus wasting your time in mere talk."

"Come! come!" thought I, as he went back to the sitter's chair, "I shall see your natural expression on your face if I can only get you to talk about that adventure." It was easy enough to lead him in the right direction. At the first hint from me, he returned to the subject of the house in the back street. Without, I hope, showing any undue curiosity, I contrived to let him see that I felt a deep interest in everything he now said. After two or three preliminary hesitations, he at last, to my great joy, fairly started on the narrative of his adventure. In the interest of his subject he soon completely forgot that he was sitting for his portrait — the very expression that I wanted came over his face — and my drawing proceeded toward completion, in the right direction, and to the best purpose. At every fresh touch I felt more and more certain that I was now getting the better of my grand difficulty; and I enjoyed the additional gratification of having my work lightened by the recital of a true story, which possessed, in my estimation, all the excitement of the most exciting romance.

This, as I recollect it, is how Mr. Faulkner told me his adventure:

THE TRAVELER'S STORY OF A
TERRIBLY STRANGE BED.

*S*hortly after my education at college was finished, I happened to be staying at Paris with an English friend. We were both young men then, and lived, I am afraid, rather a wild life, in the delightful city of our sojourn. One night we were idling about the neighborhood of the Palais Royal, doubtful to what amusement we should next betake ourselves. My friend proposed a visit to Frascati's; but his suggestion was not to my taste. I knew Frascati's, as the French saying is, by heart; had lost and won plenty of five-franc pieces there, merely for amusement's sake, until it was amusement no longer, and was thoroughly tired, in fact, of all the ghastly respectabilities of such a social anomaly as a respectable gambling-house. "For Heaven's sake," said I to my friend, "let us go somewhere where we can see a little genuine, blackguard, poverty-stricken gaming with no false gingerbread glitter thrown over it all. Let us get away from fashionable Frascati's, to a house where they don't mind letting in a man with a ragged coat, or a man with no coat, ragged or otherwise." "Very well," said my friend, "we needn't go out of the Palais Royal to find the sort of company you want. Here's the place just before us; as blackguard a place, by all report, as you could possibly wish to see." In another minute we arrived at the door, and entered the house, the back of which you have drawn in your sketch.

When we got upstairs, and had left our hats and sticks with the door-keeper, we were admitted into the chief gambling-room. We did not find many people assembled there. But, few as the men were who looked up at us on our entrance, they were all types — lamentably true types — of their respective classes.

We had come to see blackguards; but these men were something worse. There is a comic side, more or less appreciable, in all blackguardism — here there was nothing but tragedy — mute, weird tragedy. The quiet in the room was horrible. The thin, haggard, long-haired young man, whose sunken eyes fiercely watched the turning up of the cards, never spoke; the flabby, fat-faced, pimply player, who pricked his piece of pasteboard perseveringly, to register how often black won, and how often red — never spoke; the dirty, wrinkled old man, with the vulture eyes and the darned great-coat, who had lost his last *sou,* and still looked on desperately, after he could play no longer — never spoke. Even the voice of the croupier sounded as if it were strangely dulled and thickened in the atmosphere of the room. I had entered the place to laugh, but the spectacle before me was something to weep over. I soon found it necessary to take refuge in excitement from the depression of spirits which was fast stealing on me. Unfortunately I sought the nearest excitement, by going to the table and beginning to play. Still more unfortunately, as the event will show, I won — won prodigiously; won incredibly; won at such a rate that the regular players at the table crowded round me; and staring at my stakes with hungry, superstitious eyes, whispered to one another that the English stranger was going to break the bank.

The game was *Rouge et Noir* . I had played at it in every city in Europe, without, however, the care or the wish to study the Theory of Chances — that philosopher's stone of all gamblers! And a gambler, in the strict sense of the word, I had never been. I was heart-whole from the corroding passion for play. My gaming was a mere idle amusement. I never resorted to it by necessity, because I never knew what it was to want money. I never practiced it so incessantly as to lose more than I could afford, or to gain more than I could coolly pocket without being thrown off my balance by my good luck. In short, I had hitherto frequented gambling-tables — just as I frequented ball-rooms and opera-houses — because they amused me, and because I had nothing better to do with my leisure hours.

But on this occasion it was very different — now, for the first time in my life, I felt what the passion for play really was. My success first bewildered, and then, in the most literal meaning of the word, intoxicated me. Incredible as it may appear, it is nevertheless true, that I only lost when I attempted to estimate chances, and played according to previous calculation. If I left everything to luck, and staked without any care or consideration, I was sure to win — to win in the face of every recognized probability in favor of the bank. At first some of the men present ventured their money safely enough on my color; but I speedily increased my stakes to sums which they dared not risk. One after another they left off playing, and breathlessly looked on at my game.

Still, time after time, I staked higher and higher, and still won. The excitement in the room rose to fever pitch. The silence was interrupted by a deep-muttered chorus of oaths and exclamations in different languages, every time the gold was shoveled across to my side of the table — even the imperturbable croupier dashed his rake on the floor in a (French) fury of astonishment at my success. But one man present preserved his self-possession, and that man was my friend. He came to my side, and whispering in English, begged me to leave the place, satisfied with what I had already gained. I must do him the justice to say that he repeated his warnings and entreaties several times, and only left me and went away after I had rejected his advice (I was to all intents and purposes gambling drunk) in terms which rendered it impossible for him to address me again that night.

Shortly after he had gone, a hoarse voice behind me cried: "Permit me, my dear sir — permit me to restore to their proper place two napoleons which you have dropped. Wonderful luck, sir! I pledge you my word of honor, as an old soldier, in the course of my long experience in this sort of thing, I never saw such luck as yours — never! Go on, sir — *Sacre mille bombes!* Go on boldly, and break the bank!"

I turned round and saw, nodding and smiling at me with inveterate civility, a tall man, dressed in a frogged and braided surtout.

If I had been in my senses, I should have considered him, personally, as being rather a suspicious specimen of an old soldier. He had goggling, blood-shot eyes, mangy mustaches, and a broken nose. His voice betrayed a barrack-room intonation of the worst order, and he had the dirtiest pair of hands I ever saw — even in France. These little personal peculiarities exercised, however, no repelling influence on me. In the mad excitement, the reckless triumph of that moment, I was ready to "fraternize" with anybody who encouraged me in my game. I accepted the old soldier's offered pinch of snuff; clapped him on the back, and swore he was the honestest fellow in the world — the most glorious relic of the Grand Army that I had ever met with. "Go on!" cried my military friend, snapping his fingers in ecstasy —"Go on, and win! Break the bank — *Mille tonnerres!* my gallant English comrade, break the bank!"

And I *did* go on — went on at such a rate, that in another quarter of an hour the croupier called out, "Gentlemen, the bank has discontinued for to-night." All the notes, and all the gold in that "bank," now lay in a heap under my hands; the whole floating capital of the gambling-house was waiting to pour into my pockets!

"Tie up the money in your pocket-handkerchief, my worthy sir," said the old soldier, as I wildly plunged my hands into my heap of gold. "Tie it up, as we used to tie up a bit of dinner in the Grand Army; your winnings are too heavy for any breeches-pockets that ever were sewed. There! that's it — shovel them in, notes and all! *Credie!* what luck! Stop! another napoleon on the floor! *Ah! sacre petit polisson de Napoleon!* have I found thee at last?

Now then, sir — two tight double knots each way with your honorable permission, and the money's safe. Feel it! feel it, fortunate sir! hard and round as a cannon-ball — *Ah, bah!* if they had only fired such cannon-balls at us at Austerlitz — *nom d'une pipe!* if they only had! And now, as an ancient grenadier, as an ex-brave of the French army, what remains for me to do? I ask what? Simply this: to entreat my valued English friend to drink a bottle of Champagne with me, and toast the goddess Fortune in foaming goblets before we part!"

Excellent ex-brave! Convivial ancient grenadier! Champagne by all means! An English cheer for an old soldier! Hurrah! hurrah! Another English cheer for the goddess Fortune! Hurrah! hurrah! hurrah!

"Bravo! the Englishman; the amiable, gracious Englishman, in whose veins circulates the vivacious blood of France! Another glass? *Ah, bah!* — the bottle is empty! Never mind! *Vive le vin!* I, the old soldier, order another bottle, and half a pound of bonbons with it!"

"No, no, ex-brave; never — ancient grenadier! *Your* bottle last time; *my* bottle this. Behold it! Toast away! The French Army! the great Napoleon! the present company! the croupier! the honest croupier's wife and daughters — if he has any! the Ladies generally! everybody in the world!"

By the time the second bottle of Champagne was emptied, I felt as if I had been drinking liquid fire — my brain seemed all aflame. No excess in wine had ever had this effect on me before in my life. Was it the result of a stimulant acting upon my system when I was in a highly excited state? Was my stomach in a particularly disordered condition? Or was the Champagne amazingly strong?

"Ex-brave of the French Army!" cried I, in a mad state of exhilaration, "*I* am on fire! how are *you?* You have set me on fire! Do you hear, my hero of Austerlitz? Let us have a third bottle of Champagne to put the flame out!"

The old soldier wagged his head, rolled his goggle-eyes, until I expected to see them slip out of their sockets; placed his dirty forefinger by the side of his broken nose; solemnly ejaculated "Coffee!" and immediately ran off into an inner room.

The word pronounced by the eccentric veteran seemed to have a magical effect on the rest of the company present. With one accord they all rose to depart. Probably they had expected to profit by my intoxication; but finding that my new friend was benevolently bent on preventing me from getting dead drunk, had now abandoned all hope of thriving pleasantly on my winnings. Whatever their motive might be, at any rate they went away in a body. When the old soldier returned, and sat down again opposite to me at the table, we had the room to ourselves. I could see the croupier, in a sort of vestibule which opened out of it, eating his supper in solitude. The silence was now deeper than ever.

A sudden change, too, had come over the "ex-brave." He assumed a portentously solemn look; and when he spoke to me again, his speech was ornamented by no oaths, enforced by no finger-snapping, enlivened by no apostrophes or exclamations.

"Listen, my dear sir," said he, in mysteriously confidential tones —"listen to an old soldier's advice. I have been to the mistress of the house (a very charming woman, with a genius for cookery!) to impress on her the necessity of making us some particularly strong and good coffee. You must drink this coffee in order to get rid of your little amiable exaltation of spirits before you think of going home — you *must,* my good and gracious friend! With all that money to take home to-night, it is a sacred duty to yourself to have your wits about you. You are known to be a winner to an enormous extent by several gentlemen present to-night, who, in a certain point of view, are very worthy and excellent fellows; but they are mortal men, my dear sir, and they have their amiable weaknesses. Need I say more? Ah, no, no! you understand me! Now, this is what you must do — send for a cabriolet when you feel quite well again — draw up all the windows when you get into it — and tell the driver to take you home only through the large and well-lighted thoroughfares. Do this; and you and your money will be safe. Do this; and tomorrow you will thank an old soldier for giving you a word of honest advice."

Just as the ex-brave ended his oration in very lachrymose tones, the coffee came in, ready poured out in two cups. My attentive friend handed me one of the cups with a bow. I was parched with thirst, and drank it off at a draught. Almost instantly afterwards, I was seized with a fit of giddiness, and felt more completely intoxicated than ever. The room whirled round and round furiously; the old soldier seemed to be regularly bobbing up and down before me like the piston of a steam-engine. I was half deafened by a violent singing in my ears; a feeling of utter bewilderment, helplessness, idiocy, overcame me. I rose from my chair, holding on by the table to keep my balance; and stammered out that I felt dreadfully unwell — so unwell that I did not know how I was to get home.

"My dear friend," answered the old soldier — and even his voice seemed to be bobbing up and down as he spoke —"my dear friend, it would be madness to go home in *your* state; you would be sure to lose your money; you might be robbed and murdered with the greatest ease. *I* am going to sleep here; do *you* sleep here, too — they make up capital beds in this house — take one; sleep off the effects of the wine, and go home safely with your winnings tomorrow — tomorrow, in broad daylight."

I had but two ideas left: one, that I must never let go hold of my handkerchief full of money; the other, that I must lie down somewhere immediately, and fall off into a comfortable sleep. So I agreed to the proposal about the bed, and took the offered arm of the old soldier, carrying my money with my disengaged hand. Preceded by the croupier, we passed along some passages and up a flight of stairs into the bedroom which I was to occupy. The ex-brave shook me warmly by the hand, proposed that we should breakfast together, and then, followed by the croupier, left me for the night.

I ran to the wash-hand stand; drank some of the water in my jug; poured the rest out, and plunged my face into it; then sat down in a chair and tried to compose myself. I soon felt better. The change for my lungs, from the fetid atmosphere of the gambling-room to the cool air of the apartment I now occupied, the almost equally refreshing change for my eyes, from the glaring gaslights of the "salon" to the dim, quiet flicker of one bedroom-candle, aided wonderfully the restorative effects of cold water. The giddiness left me, and I began to feel a little like a reasonable being again. My first thought was of the risk of sleeping all night in a gambling-house; my second, of the still greater risk of trying to get out after the house was closed, and of going home alone at night through the streets of Paris with a large sum of money about me. I had slept in worse places than this on my travels; so I determined to lock, bolt, and barricade my door, and take my chance till the next morning.

Accordingly, I secured myself against all intrusion; looked under the bed, and into the cupboard; tried the fastening of the window; and then, satisfied that I had taken every proper precaution, pulled off my upper clothing, put my light, which was a dim one, on the hearth among a feathery litter of wood-ashes, and got into bed, with the handkerchief full of money under my pillow.

I soon felt not only that I could not go to sleep, but that I could not even close my eyes. I was wide awake, and in a high fever. Every nerve in my body trembled — every one of my senses seemed to be preternaturally sharpened. I tossed and rolled, and tried every kind of position, and perseveringly sought out the cold corners of the bed, and all to no purpose. Now I thrust my arms over the clothes; now I poked them under the clothes; now I violently shot my legs straight out down to the bottom of the bed; now I convulsively coiled them up as near my chin as they would go; now I shook out my crumpled pillow, changed it to the cool side, patted it flat, and lay down quietly on my back; now I fiercely doubled it in two, set it up on end, thrust it against the board of the bed, and tried a sitting posture. Every effort was in vain; I groaned with vexation as I felt that I was in for a sleepless night.

What could I do? I had no book to read. And yet, unless I found out some method of diverting my mind, I felt certain that I was in the condition to imagine all sorts of horrors; to rack my brain with forebodings of every possible and impossible danger; in short, to pass the night in suffering all conceivable varieties of nervous terror.

I raised myself on my elbow, and looked about the room — which was brightened by a lovely moonlight pouring straight through the window — to see if it contained any pictures or ornaments that I could at all clearly distinguish. While my eyes wandered from wall to wall, a remembrance of Le Maistre's delightful little book, "Voyage autour de ma Chambre," occurred to me. I resolved to imitate the French author, and find occupation and amusement enough to relieve the tedium of my wakefulness, by making a mental inventory of every article of furniture I could see, and by following up to their sources the multitude of associations which even a chair, a table, or a wash-hand stand may be made to call forth.

In the nervous unsettled state of my mind at that moment, I found it much easier to make my inventory than to make my reflections, and thereupon soon gave up all hope of thinking in Le Maistre's fanciful track — or, indeed, of thinking at all. I looked about the room at the different articles of furniture, and did nothing more.

There was, first, the bed I was lying in; a four-post bed, of all things in the world to meet with in Paris — yes, a thorough clumsy British four-poster, with the regular top lined with chintz — the regular fringed valance all round — the regular stifling, unwholesome curtains, which I remembered having mechanically drawn back against the posts without particularly noticing the bed when I first got into the room. Then there was the marble-topped wash-hand stand, from which the water I had spilled, in my hurry to pour it out, was still dripping, slowly and more slowly, on to the brick floor. Then two small chairs, with my coat, waistcoat, and trousers flung on them. Then a large elbow-chair covered with dirty-white dimity, with my cravat and shirt collar thrown over the back. Then a chest of drawers with two of the brass handles off, and a tawdry, broken china inkstand placed on it by way of ornament for the top. Then the dressing-table, adorned by a very small looking-glass, and a very large pincushion. Then the window — an unusually large window. Then a dark old picture, which the feeble candle dimly showed me. It was a picture of a fellow in a high Spanish hat, crowned with a plume of towering feathers. A swarthy, sinister ruffian, looking upward, shading his eyes with his hand, and looking intently upward — it might be at some tall gallows at which he was going to be hanged. At any rate, he had the appearance of thoroughly deserving it.

This picture put a kind of constraint upon me to look upward too — at the top of the bed. It was a gloomy and not an interesting object, and I looked back at the picture. I counted the feathers in the man's hat — they stood out in relief — three white, two green. I observed the crown of his hat, which was of conical shape, according to the fashion supposed to have been favored by Guido Fawkes. I wondered what he was looking up at. It couldn't be at the stars; such a desperado was neither astrologer nor astronomer. It must be at the high gallows, and he was going to be hanged presently. Would the executioner come into possession of his conical crowned hat and plume of feathers? I counted the feathers again — three white, two green.

While I still lingered over this very improving and intellectual employment, my thoughts insensibly began to wander. The moonlight shining into the room reminded me of a certain moonlight night in England — the night after a picnic party in a Welsh valley. Every incident of the drive homeward, through lovely scenery, which the moonlight made lovelier than ever, came back to my remembrance, though I had never given the picnic a thought for years; though, if I had *tried* to recollect it, I could certainly have recalled little or nothing of that scene long past. Of all the wonderful faculties that help to tell us we are immortal, which speaks the sublime truth more eloquently than memory? Here was I, in a strange house of the most suspicious character, in a situation of uncertainty, and even of peril, which might seem to make the cool exercise of my recollection almost out of the question; nevertheless, remembering, quite involuntarily, places, people, conversations, minute circumstances of every kind, which I had thought forgotten forever; which I could not possibly have recalled at will, even under the most favorable auspices. And what cause had produced in a moment the whole of this strange, complicated, mysterious effect? Nothing but some rays of moonlight shining in at my bedroom window.

I was still thinking of the picnic — of our merriment on the drive home — of the sentimental young lady who *would* quote "Childe Harold" because it was moonlight. I was absorbed by these past scenes and past amusements, when, in an instant, the thread on which my memories hung snapped asunder; my attention immediately came back to present things more vividly than ever, and I found myself, I neither knew why nor wherefore, looking hard at the picture again.

Looking for what?

Good God! the man had pulled his hat down on his brows! No! the hat itself was gone! Where was the conical crown? Where the feathers — three white, two green? Not there! In place of the hat and feathers, what dusky object was it that now hid his forehead, his eyes, his shading hand?

Was the bed moving?

I turned on my back and looked up. Was I mad? drunk? dreaming? giddy again? or was the top of the bed really moving down — sinking slowly, regularly, silently, horribly, right down throughout the whole of its length and breadth — right down upon me, as I lay underneath?

My blood seemed to stand still. A deadly paralysing coldness stole all over me as I turned my head round on the pillow and determined to test whether the bed-top was really moving or not, by keeping my eye on the man in the picture.

The next look in that direction was enough. The dull, black, frowzy outline of the valance above me was within an inch of being parallel with his waist. I still looked breathlessly. And steadily and slowly — very slowly — I saw the figure, and the line of frame below the figure, vanish, as the valance moved down before it.

I am, constitutionally, anything but timid. I have been on more than one occasion in peril of my life, and have not lost my self-possession for an instant; but when the conviction first settled on my mind that the bed-top was really moving, was steadily and continuously sinking down upon me, I looked up shuddering, helpless, panic-stricken, beneath the hideous machinery for murder, which was advancing closer and closer to suffocate me where I lay.

I looked up, motionless, speechless, breathless. The candle, fully spent, went out; but the moonlight still brightened the room. Down and down, without pausing and without sounding, came the bed-top, and still my panic-terror seemed to bind me faster and faster to the mattress on which I lay — down and down it sank, till the dusty odor from the lining of the canopy came stealing into my nostrils.

At that final moment the instinct of self-preservation startled me out of my trance, and I moved at last. There was just room for me to roll myself sidewise off the bed. As I dropped noiselessly to the floor, the edge of the murderous canopy touched me on the shoulder.

Without stopping to draw my breath, without wiping the cold sweat from my face, I rose instantly on my knees to watch the bed-top. I was literally spellbound by it. If I had heard footsteps behind me, I could not have turned round; if a means of escape had been miraculously provided for me, I could not have moved to take advantage of it. The whole life in me was, at that moment, concentrated in my eyes.

It descended — the whole canopy, with the fringe round it, came down — down — close down; so close that there was not room now to squeeze my finger between the bed-top and the bed. I felt at the sides, and discovered that what had appeared to me from beneath to be the ordinary light canopy of a four-post bed was in reality a thick, broad mattress, the substance of which was concealed by the valance and its fringe. I looked up and saw the four posts rising hideously bare. In the middle of the bed-top was a huge wooden screw that had evidently worked it down through a hole in the ceiling, just as ordinary presses are worked down on the substance selected for compression. The frightful apparatus moved without making the faintest noise. There had been no creaking as it came down; there was now not the faintest sound from the room above. Amid a dead and awful silence I beheld before me — in the nineteenth century, and in the civilized capital of France — such a machine for secret murder by suffocation as might have existed in the worst days of the Inquisition, in the lonely inns among the Hartz Mountains, in the mysterious tribunals of Westphalia! Still, as I looked on it, I could not move, I could hardly breathe, but I began to recover the power of thinking, and in a moment I discovered the murderous conspiracy framed against me in all its horror.

My cup of coffee had been drugged, and drugged too strongly. I had been saved from being smothered by having taken an overdose of some narcotic. How I had chafed and fretted at the fever fit which had preserved my life by keeping me awake! How recklessly I had confided myself to the two wretches who had led me into this room, determined, for the sake of my winnings, to kill me in my sleep by the surest and most horrible contrivance for secretly accomplishing my destruction! How many men, winners like me, had slept, as I had proposed to sleep, in that bed, and had never been seen or heard of more! I shuddered at the bare idea of it.

But, ere long, all thought was again suspended by the sight of the murderous canopy moving once more. After it had remained on the bed — as nearly as I could guess — about ten minutes, it began to move up again. The villains who worked it from above evidently believed that their purpose was now accomplished. Slowly and silently, as it had descended, that horrible bed-top rose towards its former place. When it reached the upper extremities of the four posts, it reached the ceiling, too. Neither hole nor screw could be seen; the bed became in appearance an ordinary bed again — the canopy an ordinary canopy — even to the most suspicious eyes.

Now, for the first time, I was able to move — to rise from my knees — to dress myself in my upper clothing — and to consider of how I should escape. If I betrayed by the smallest noise that the attempt to suffocate me had failed, I was certain to be murdered. Had I made any noise already? I listened intently, looking towards the door.

No! no footsteps in the passage outside — no sound of a tread, light or heavy, in the room above — absolute silence everywhere. Besides locking and bolting my door, I had moved an old wooden chest against it, which I had found under the bed. To remove this chest (my blood ran cold as I thought of what its contents *might* be!) without making some disturbance was impossible; and, moreover, to think of escaping through the house, now barred up for the night, was sheer insanity. Only one chance was left me — the window. I stole to it on tiptoe.

My bedroom was on the first floor, above an *entresol,* and looked into a back street, which you have sketched in your view. I raised my hand to open the window, knowing that on that action hung, by the merest hair-breadth, my chance of safety. They keep vigilant watch in a House of Murder. If any part of the frame cracked, if the hinge creaked, I was a lost man! It must have occupied me at least five minutes, reckoning by time — five *hours,* reckoning by suspense — to open that window. I succeeded in doing it silently — in doing it with all the dexterity of a house-breaker — and then looked down into the street. To leap the distance beneath me would be almost certain destruction! Next, I looked round at the sides of the house. Down the left side ran a thick water-pipe which you have drawn — it passed close by the outer edge of the window. The moment I saw the pipe I knew I was saved. My breath came and went freely for the first time since I had seen the canopy of the bed moving down upon me!

To some men the means of escape which I had discovered might have seemed difficult and dangerous enough — to *me* the prospect of slipping down the pipe into the street did not suggest even a thought of peril. I had always been accustomed, by the practice of gymnastics, to keep up my school-boy powers as a daring and expert climber; and knew that my head, hands, and feet would serve me faithfully in any hazards of ascent or descent. I had already got one leg over the window-sill, when I remembered the handkerchief filled with money under my pillow. I could well have afforded to leave it behind me, but I was revengefully determined that the miscreants of the gambling-house should miss their plunder as well as their victim. So I went back to the bed and tied the heavy handkerchief at my back by my cravat.

Just as I had made it tight and fixed it in a comfortable place, I thought I heard a sound of breathing outside the door. The chill feeling of horror ran through me again as I listened. No! dead silence still in the passage — I had only heard the night air blowing softly into the room. The next moment I was on the window-sill — and the next I had a firm grip on the water-pipe with my hands and knees.

I slid down into the street easily and quietly, as I thought I should, and immediately set off at the top of my speed to a branch "Prefecture" of Police, which I knew was situated in the immediate neighborhood. A "Sub-prefect," and several picked men among his subordinates, happened to be up, maturing, I believe, some scheme for discovering the perpetrator of a mysterious murder which all Paris was talking of just then. When I began my story, in a breath-less hurry and in very bad French, I could see that the Sub-prefect suspected me of being a drunken Englishman who had robbed somebody; but he soon altered his opinion as I went on, and before I had anything like concluded, he shoved all the papers before him into a drawer, put on his hat, supplied me with another (for I was bareheaded), ordered a file of soldiers, desired his expert followers to get ready all sorts of tools for breaking open doors and ripping up brick flooring, and took my arm, in the most friendly and familiar manner possible, to lead me with him out of the house. I will venture to say that when the Sub-prefect was a little boy, and was taken for the first time to the play, he was not half as much pleased as he was now at the job in prospect for him at the gambling-house!

Away we went through the streets, the Sub-prefect cross-examining and congratulating me in the same breath as we marched at the head of our formidable *posse comitatus*. Sentinels were placed at the back and front of the house the moment we got to it; a tremendous battery of knocks was directed against the door; a light appeared at a window; I was told to conceal myself behind the police — then came more knocks and a cry of "Open in the name of the law!" At that terrible summons bolts and locks gave way before an invisible hand, and the moment after the Sub-prefect was in the passage, confronting a waiter half-dressed and ghastly pale. This was the short dialogue which immediately took place:

"We want to see the Englishman who is sleeping in this house?"

"He went away hours ago."

"He did no such thing. His friend went away; *he* remained. Show us to his bedroom!"

"I swear to you, Monsieur le Sous-prefect, he is not here! he —"

"I swear to you, Monsieur le Garcon, he is. He slept here — he didn't find your bed comfortable — he came to us to complain of it — here he is among my men — and here am I ready to look for a flea or two in his bedstead. Renaudin! (calling to one of the subordinates, and pointing to the waiter) collar that man and tie his hands behind him. Now, then, gentlemen, let us walk upstairs!"

Every man and woman in the house was secured — the "Old Soldier" the first. Then I identified the bed in which I had slept, and then we went into the room above.

No object that was at all extraordinary appeared in any part of it. The Sub-prefect looked round the place, commanded everybody to be silent, stamped twice on the floor, called for a candle, looked attentively at the spot he had stamped on, and ordered the flooring there to be carefully taken up. This was done in no time. Lights were produced, and we saw a deep raftered cavity between the floor of this room and the ceiling of the room beneath. Through this cavity there ran perpendicularly a sort of case of iron thickly greased; and inside the case appeared the screw, which communi-cated with the bed-top below. Extra lengths of screw, freshly oiled; levers covered with felt; all the complete upper works of a heavy press — constructed with infernal ingenuity so as to join the fixtures below, and when taken to pieces again, to go into the smallest possible compass — were next discovered and pulled out on the floor. After some little difficulty the Sub-prefect succeeded in putting the machinery together, and, leaving his men to work it, descended with me to the bedroom. The smothering canopy was then lowered, but not so noiselessly as I had seen it lowered. When I mentioned this to the Sub-prefect, his answer, simple as it was, had a terrible significance. "My men," said he, "are working down the bed-top for the first time — the men whose money you won were in better practice."

We left the house in the sole possession of two police agents — every one of the inmates being removed to prison on the spot. The Sub-prefect, after taking down my "proces verbal" in his office, returned with me to my hotel to get my passport. "Do you think," I asked, as I gave it to him, "that any men have really been smothered in that bed, as they tried to smother *me?* "

"I have seen dozens of drowned men laid out at the Morgue," answered the Sub-prefect, "in whose pocket-books were found letters stating that they had committed suicide in the Seine, because they had lost everything at the gaming table. Do I know how many of those men entered the same gambling-house that *you* entered? won as *you* won? took that bed as *you* took it? slept in it? were smothered in it? and were privately thrown into the river, with a letter of explanation written by the murderers and placed in their pocket-books? No man can say how many or how few have suffered the fate from which you have escaped. The people of the gambling-house kept their bedstead machinery a secret from *us* — even from the police! The dead kept the rest of the secret for them. Good-night, or rather good-morning, Monsieur Faulkner! Be at my office again at nine o'clock — in the meantime, *au revoir!* "

The rest of my story is soon told. I was examined and re-examined; the gambling-house was strictly searched all through from top to bottom; the prisoners were separately interrogated; and two of the less guilty among them made a confession. I discovered that the Old Soldier was the master of the gambling-house — *justice* discovered that he had been drummed out of the army as a vagabond years ago; that he had been guilty of all sorts of villainies since; that he was in possession of stolen property, which the owners identified; and that he, the croupier, another accomplice, and the woman who had made my cup of coffee, were all in the secret of the bedstead. There appeared some reason to doubt whether the inferior persons attached to the house knew anything of the suffocating machinery; and they received the benefit of that doubt, by being treated simply as thieves and vagabonds. As for the Old Soldier and his two head myrmidons, they went to the galleys; the woman who had drugged my coffee was imprisoned for I forget how many years; the regular attendants at the gambling-house were considered "suspicious" and placed under "surveillance"; and I became, for one whole week (which is a long time) the head "lion" in Parisian society. My adventure was dramatized by three illustrious play-makers, but never saw theatrical daylight; for the censorship forbade the introduction on the stage of a correct copy of the gambling-house bedstead.

One good result was produced by my adventure, which any censorship must have approved: it cured me of ever again trying "Rouge et Noir" as an amusement. The sight of a green cloth, with packs of cards and heaps of money on it, will henceforth be forever associated in my mind with the sight of a bed canopy descending to suffocate me in the silence and darkness of the night.

Just as Mr. Faulkner pronounced these words he started in his chair, and resumed his stiff, dignified position in a great hurry. "Bless my soul!" cried he, with a comic look of astonishment and vexation, "while I have been telling you what is the real secret of my interest in the sketch you have so kindly given to me, I have altogether forgotten that I came here to sit for my portrait. For the last hour or more I must have been the worst model you ever had to draw from!"

"On the contrary, you have been the best," said I. "I have been trying to catch your likeness; and, while telling your story, you have unconsciously shown me the natural expression I wanted to insure my success."

NOTE BY MRS. KERBY.

I cannot let this story end without mentioning what the chance saying was which caused it to be told at the farmhouse the other night. Our friend the young sailor, among his other quaint objections to sleeping on shore, declared that he particularly hated four-post beds, because he never slept in one without doubting whether the top might not come down in the night and suffocate him. I thought this chance reference to the distinguishing feature of William's narrative curious enough, and my husband agreed with me. But he says it is scarcely worth while to mention such a trifle in anything so important as a book. I cannot venture, after this, to do more than slip these lines in modestly at the end of the story. If the printer should notice my few last words, perhaps he may not mind the trouble of putting them into some out-of-the-way corner.

L. K.

THE LAWYER'S STORY OF A STOLEN LETTER.

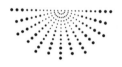

PROLOGUE TO THE SECOND STORY.

*T*he beginning of an excellent connection which I succeeded in establishing in and around that respectable watering-place, Tidbury-on-the-Marsh, was an order for a life-size oil portrait of a great local celebrity — one Mr. Boxsious, a solicitor, who was understood to do the most thriving business of any lawyer in the town.

The portrait was intended as a testimonial "expressive (to use the language of the circular forwarded to me at the time) of the eminent services of Mr. Boxsious in promoting and securing the prosperity of the town." It had been subscribed for by the "Municipal Authorities and Resident Inhabitants" of Tidbury-on-the-Marsh; and it was to be presented, when done, to Mrs. Boxsious, "as a slight but sincere token"— and so forth. A timely recommendation from one of my kindest friends and patrons placed the commission for painting the likeness in my lucky hands; and I was instructed to attend on a certain day at Mr. Boxsious's private residence, with all my materials ready for taking a first sitting.

On arriving at the house, I was shown into a very prettily furnished morning-room. The bow-window looked out on a large inclosed meadow, which represented the principal square in Tidbury. On the opposite side of the meadow I could see the new hotel (with a wing lately added), and close by, the old hotel obstinately unchanged since it had first been built. Then, further down the street, the doctor's house, with a colored lamp and a small door-plate, and the banker's office, with a plain lamp and a big door-plate — then some dreary private lodging-houses — then, at right angles to these, a street of shops; the cheese-monger's very small, the chemist's very smart, the pastrycook's very dowdy, and the green-grocer's very dark, I was still looking out at the view thus presented, when I was suddenly apostrophized by a glib, disputatious voice behind me.

"Now, then, Mr. Artist," cried the voice, "do you call that getting ready for work? Where are your paints and brushes, and all the rest of it? My name's Boxsious, and I'm here to sit for my picture."

I turned round, and confronted a little man with his legs astraddle, and his hands in his pockets. He had light-gray eyes, red all round the lids, bristling pepper-colored hair, an unnaturally rosy complexion, and an eager, impudent, clever look. I made two discoveries in one glance at him: First, that he was a wretched subject for a portrait; secondly, that, whatever he might do or say, it would not be of the least use for me to stand on my dignity with him.

"I shall be ready directly, sir," said I.

"Ready directly?" repeated my new sitter. "What do you mean, Mr. Artist, by ready directly? I'm ready now. What was your contract with the Town Council, who have subscribed for this picture? To paint the portrait. And what was my contract? To sit for it. Here am I ready to sit, and there are you not ready to paint me. According to all the rules of law and logic, you are committing a breach of contract already. Stop! let's have a look at your paints. Are they the best quality? If not, I warn you, sir, there's a second breach of contract! Brushes, too? Why, they're old brushes, by the Lord Harry! The Town Council pays you well, Mr. Artist; why don't you work for them with new brushes? What? you work best with old? I contend, sir, that you can't. Does my housemaid clean best with an old broom? Do my clerks write best with old pens? Don't color up, and don't look as if you were going to quarrel with me! You can't quarrel with me. If you were fifty times as irritable a man as you look, you couldn't quarrel with me. I'm not young, and I'm not touchy — I'm Boxsious, the lawyer; the only man in the world who can't be insulted, try it how you like!"

He chuckled as he said this, and walked away to the window. It was quite useless to take anything he said seriously, so I finished preparing my palette for the morning's work with the utmost serenity of look and manner that I could possibly assume.

"There!" he went on, looking out of the window; "do you see that fat man slouching along the Parade, with a snuffy nose? That's my favorite enemy, Dunball. He tried to quarrel with me ten years ago, and he has done nothing but bring out the hidden benevolence of my character ever since. Look at him! look how he frowns as he turns this way. And now look at me! I can smile and nod to him. I make a point of always smiling and nodding to him — it keeps my hand in for other enemies. Good-morning! (I've cast him twice in heavy damages) good-morning, Mr. Dunball. He bears malice, you see; he won't speak; he's short in the neck, passionate, and four times as fat as he

THE LAWYER'S STORY OF A STOLEN LETTER.

ought to be; he has fought against my amiability for ten mortal years; when he can't fight any longer, he'll die suddenly, and I shall be the innocent cause of it."

Mr. Boxsious uttered this fatal prophecy with extraordinary complacency, nodding and smiling out of the window all the time at the unfortunate man who had rashly tried to provoke him. When his favorite enemy was out of sight, he turned away, and indulged himself in a brisk turn or two up and down the room. Meanwhile I lifted my canvas on the easel, and was on the point of asking him to sit down, when he assailed me again.

"Now, Mr. Artist," he cried, quickening his walk impatiently, "in the interests of the Town Council, your employers, allow me to ask you for the last time when you are going to begin?"

"And allow me, Mr. Boxsious, in the interest of the Town Council also," said I, "to ask you if your notion of the proper way of sitting for your portrait is to walk about the room!"

"Aha! well put — devilish well put!" returned Mr. Boxsious; "that's the only sensible thing you have said since you entered my house; I begin to like you already." With these words he nodded at me approvingly, and jumped into the high chair that I had placed for him with the alacrity of a young man.

"I say, Mr. Artist," he went on, when I had put him into the right position (he insisted on the front view of his face being taken, because the Town Council would get the most for their money in that way), "you don't have many such good jobs as this, do you?"

"Not many," I said. "I should not be a poor man if commissions for life-size portraits often fell in my way."

"You poor!" exclaimed Mr. Boxsious, contemptuously. "I dispute that point with you at the outset. Why, you've got a good cloth coat, a clean shirt, and a smooth-shaved chin. You've got the sleek look of a man who has slept between sheets and had his breakfast. You can't humbug me about poverty, for I know what it is. Poverty means looking like a scarecrow, feeling like a scarecrow, and getting treated like a scarecrow. That was *my* luck, let me tell you, when I first thought of trying the law. Poverty, indeed! Do you shake in your shoes, Mr. Artist, when you think what you were at twenty? I do, I can promise you."

He began to shift about so irritably in his chair, that, in the interests of my work, I was obliged to make an effort to calm him.

"It must be a pleasant occupation for you in your present prosperity," said I, "to look back sometimes at the gradual processes by which you passed from poverty to competence, and from that to the wealth you now enjoy."

"Gradual, did you say?" cried Mr. Boxsious; "it wasn't gradual at all. I was sharp — damned sharp, and I jumped at my first start in business slap into five hundred pounds in one day."

"That was an extraordinary step in advance," I rejoined. "I suppose you contrived to make some profitable investment —"

"Not a bit of it! I hadn't a spare sixpence to invest with. I won the money by my brains, my hands, and my pluck; and, what's more, I'm proud of having done it. That was rather a curious case, Mr. Artist. Some men might be shy of mentioning it; I never was shy in my life and I mention it right and left everywhere — the whole case, just as it happened, except the names. Catch me ever committing myself to mentioning names! Mum's the word, sir, with yours to command, Thomas Boxsious."

"As you mention 'the case' everywhere," said I, "perhaps you would not be offended with me if I told you I should like to hear it?"

"Man alive! haven't I told you already that I can't be offended? And didn't I say a moment ago that I was proud of the case? I'll tell you, Mr. Artist — but stop! I've got the interests of the Town Council to look after in this business. Can you paint as well when I'm talking as when I'm not? Don't sneer, sir; you're not wanted to sneer — you're wanted to give an answer — yes or no?"

"Yes, then," I replied, in his own sharp way. "I can always paint the better when I am hearing an interesting story."

"What do you mean by talking about a story? I'm not going to tell you a story; I'm going to make a statement. A statement is a matter of fact, therefore the exact opposite of a story, which is a matter of fiction. What I am now going to tell you really happened to me."

I was glad to see that he settled himself quietly in his chair before he began. His odd manners and language made such an impression on me at the time, that I think I can repeat his "statement" now, almost word for word as he addressed it to me.

THE LAWYER'S STORY OF A STOLEN LETTER.

I served my time — never mind in whose office — and I started in business for myself in one of our English country towns, I decline stating which. I hadn't a farthing of capital, and my friends in the neighborhood were poor and useless enough, with one exception. That exception was Mr. Frank Gatliffe, son of Mr. Gatliffe, member for the county, the richest man and the proudest for many a mile round about our parts. Stop a bit, Mr. Artist, you needn't perk up and look knowing. You won't trace any particulars by the name of Gatliffe. I'm not bound to commit myself or anybody else by mentioning names. I have given you the first that came into my head.

Well, Mr. Frank was a stanch friend of mine, and ready to recommend me whenever he got the chance. I had contrived to get him a little timely help — for a consideration, of course — in borrowing money at a fair rate of interest; in fact, I had saved him from the Jews. The money was borrowed while Mr. Frank was at college. He came back from college, and stopped at home a little while, and then there got spread about all our neighborhood a report that he had fallen in love, as the saying is, with his young sister's governess, and that his mind was made up to marry her. What! you're at it again, Mr. Artist! You want to know her name, don't you? What do you think of Smith?

Speaking as a lawyer, I consider report, in a general way, to be a fool and a liar. But in this case report turned out to be something very different. Mr. Frank told me he was really in love, and said upon his honor (an absurd expression which young chaps of his age are always using) he was determined to marry Smith, the governess — the sweet, darling girl, as *he* called her; but I'm not sentimental, and I call her Smith, the governess. Well, Mr. Frank's father, being as proud as Lucifer, said "No," as to marrying the governess, when Mr. Frank wanted him to say "Yes." He was a man of business, was old Gatliffe, and he took the proper business course. He sent the governess away with a first-rate character and a spanking present, and then he, looked about him to get something for Mr. Frank to do. While he was looking about, Mr. Frank bolted to London after the governess, who had nobody alive belonging to her to go to but an aunt — her father's sister. The aunt refuses to let Mr. Frank in without the squire's permission. Mr. Frank writes to his father, and says he will marry the girl as soon as he is of age, or shoot himself. Up to town comes the squire and his wife and his daughter, and a lot of sentimentality, not in the slightest degree material to the present statement, takes places among them; and the upshot of it is that old Gatliffe is forced into withdrawing the word No, and substituting the word Yes.

I don't believe he would ever have done it, though, but for one lucky peculiarity in the case. The governess's father was a man of good family — pretty nigh as good as Gatliffe's own. He had been in the army; had sold out; set up as a wine-merchant — failed — died; ditto his wife, as to the dying part of it. No relation, in fact, left for the squire to make inquiries about but the father's sister — who had behaved, as old Gatliffe said, like a thorough-bred gentlewoman in shutting the door against Mr. Frank in the first instance. So, to cut the matter short, things were at last made up pleasant enough. The time was fixed for the wedding, and an announcement about it — Marriage in High Life and all that — put into the county paper. There was a regular biography, besides, of the governess's father, so as to stop people from talking — a great flourish about his pedigree, and a long account of his services in the army; but not a word, mind ye, of his having turned wine-merchant afterward. Oh, no — not a word about that!

I knew it, though, for Mr. Frank told me. He hadn't a bit of pride about him. He introduced me to his future wife one day when I met him out walking, and asked me if I did not think he was a lucky fellow. I don't mind admitting that I did, and that I told him so. Ah! but she was one of my sort, was that governess. Stood, to the best of my recollection, five foot four. Good lissom figure, that looked as if it had never been boxed up in a pair of stays. Eyes that made me feel as if I was under a pretty stiff cross-examination the moment she looked at me. Fine red, kiss-and-come-again sort of lips. Cheeks and complexion — No, Mr. Artist, you wouldn't identify her by her cheeks and complexion, if I drew you a picture of them this very moment. She has had a family of children since the time I'm talking of; and her cheeks are a trifle fatter, and her complexion is a shade or two redder now, than when I first met her out walking with Mr. Frank.

The marriage was to take place on a Wednesday. I decline mentioning the year or the month. I had started as an attorney on my own account —

say six weeks, more or less, and was sitting alone in my office on the Monday morning before the wedding-day, trying to see my way clear before me and not succeeding particularly well, when Mr. Frank suddenly bursts in, as white as any ghost that ever was painted, and says he's got the most dreadful case for me to advise on, and not an hour to lose in acting on my advice.

"Is this in the way of business, Mr. Frank?" says I, stopping him just as he was beginning to get sentimental. "Yes or no, Mr. Frank?" rapping my new office paper-knife on the table, to pull him up short all the sooner.

"My dear fellow"— he was always familiar with me —"it's in the way of business, certainly; but friendship —"

I was obliged to pull him up short again, and regularly examine him as if he had been in the witness-box, or he would have kept me talking to no purpose half the day.

"Now, Mr. Frank," says I, "I can't have any sentimentality mixed up with business matters. You please to stop talking, and let me ask questions. Answer in the fewest words you can use. Nod when nodding will do instead of words."

I fixed him with my eye for about three seconds, as he sat groaning and wriggling in his chair. When I'd done fixing him, I gave another rap with my paper-knife on the table to startle him up a bit. Then I went on.

"From what you have been stating up to the present time," says I, "I gather that you are in a scrape which is likely to interfere seriously with your marriage on Wednesday?"

(He nodded, and I cut in again before he could say a word):

"The scrape affects your young lady, and goes back to the period of a transaction in which her late father was engaged, doesn't it?"

(He nods, and I cut in once more):

"There is a party, who turned up after seeing the announcement of your marriage in the paper, who is cognizant of what he oughtn't to know, and who is prepared to use his knowledge of the same to the prejudice of the young lady and of your marriage, unless he receives a sum of money to quiet him? Very well. Now, first of all, Mr. Frank, state what you have been told by the young lady herself about the transaction of her late father. How did you first come to have any knowledge of it?"

"She was talking to me about her father one day so tenderly and prettily, that she quite excited my interest about him," begins Mr. Frank; "and I asked her, among other things, what had occasioned his death. She said she believed it was distress of mind in the first instance; and added that this distress was connected with a shocking secret, which she and her mother had kept from everybody, but which she could not keep from me, because she was deter-mined to begin her married life by having no secrets from her husband." Here

Mr. Frank began to get sentimental again, and I pulled him up short once more with the paper-knife.

"She told me," Mr. Frank went on, "that the great mistake of her father's life was his selling out of the army and taking to the wine trade. He had no talent for business; things went wrong with him from the first. His clerk, it was strongly suspected, cheated him —"

"Stop a bit," says I. "What was that suspected clerk's name?"

"Davager," says he.

"Davager," says I, making a note of it. "Go on, Mr. Frank."

"His affairs got more and more entangled," says Mr. Frank; "he was pressed for money in all directions; bankruptcy, and consequent dishonor (as he considered it) stared him in the face. His mind was so affected by his troubles that both his wife and daughter, toward the last, considered him to be hardly responsible for his own acts. In this state of desperation and misery, he —" Here Mr. Frank began to hesitate.

We have two ways in the law of drawing evidence off nice and clear from an unwilling client or witness. We give him a fright, or we treat him to a joke. I treated Mr. Frank to a joke.

"Ah!" says I, "I know what he did. He had a signature to write; and, by the most natural mistake in the world, he wrote another gentleman's name instead of his own — eh?"

"It was to a bill," says Mr. Frank, looking very crestfallen, instead of taking the joke. "His principal creditor wouldn't wait till he could raise the money, or the greater part of it. But he was resolved, if he sold off everything, to get the amount and repay —"

"Of course," says I, "drop that. The forgery was discovered. When?"

"Before even the first attempt was made to negotiate the bill. He had done the whole thing in the most absurdly and innocently wrong way. The person whose name he had used was a stanch friend of his, and a relation of his wife's — a good man as well as a rich one. He had influence with the chief creditor, and he used it nobly. He had a real affection for the unfortunate man's wife, and he proved it generously."

"Come to the point," says I. "What did he do? In a business way, what did he do?"

"He put the false bill into the fire, drew a bill of his own to replace it, and then — only then — told my dear girl and her mother all that had happened. Can you imagine anything nobler?" asks Mr. Frank.

"Speaking in my professional capacity, I can't imagine anything greener," says I. "Where was the father? Off, I suppose?"

"Ill in bed," says Mr. Frank, coloring. "But he mustered strength enough to write a contrite and grateful letter the same day, promising to prove himself worthy of the noble moderation and forgiveness extended to him, by selling off everything he possessed to repay his money debt. He did sell off everything, down to some old family pictures that were heirlooms; down to the little plate he had; down to the very tables and chairs that furnished his drawing-room. Every farthing of the debt was paid; and he was left to begin the world again, with the kindest promises of help from the generous man who had forgiven him. It was too late. His crime of one rash moment — atoned for though it had been — preyed upon his mind. He became possessed with the idea that he had lowered himself forever in the estimation of his wife and daughter, and —"

"He died," I cut in. "Yes, yes, we know that. Let's go back for a minute to the contrite and grateful letter that he wrote. My experience in the law, Mr. Frank, has convinced me that if everybody burned everybody else's letters, half the courts of justice in this country might shut up shop. Do you happen to know whether the letter we are now speaking of contained anything like an avowal or confession of the forgery?"

"Of course it did," says he. "Could the writer express his contrition properly without making some such confession?"

"Quite easy, if he had been a lawyer," says I. "But never mind that; I'm going to make a guess — a desperate guess, mind. Should I be altogether in error if I thought that this letter had been stolen; and that the fingers of Mr. Davager, of suspicious commercial celebrity, might possibly be the fingers which took it?"

"That is exactly what I wanted to make you understand," cried Mr. Frank.

"How did he communicate the interesting fact of the theft to you?"

"He has not ventured into my presence. The scoundrel actually had the audacity —"

"Aha!" says I. "The young lady herself! Sharp practitioner, Mr. Davager."

"Early this morning, when she was walking alone in the shrubbery," Mr. Frank goes on, "he had the assurance to approach her, and to say that he had been watching his opportunity of getting a private interview for days past. He then showed her — actually showed her — her unfortunate father's letter; put into her hands another letter directed to me; bowed, and walked off; leaving her half dead with astonishment and terror. If I had only happened to be there at the time!" says Mr. Frank, shaking his fist murderously in the air, by way of a finish.

"It's the greatest luck in the world that you were not," says I. "Have you got that other letter?"

He handed it to me. It was so remarkably humorous and short, that I remember every word of it at this distance of time. It began in this way:

"To Francis Gatliffe, Esq., Jun.

"SIR— I have an extremely curious autograph letter to sell. The price is a five-hundred-pound note. The young lady to whom you are to be married on

Wednesday will inform you of the nature of the letter, and the genuineness of the autograph. If you refuse to deal, I shall send a copy to the local paper, and shall wait on your highly-respected father with the original curiosity, on the afternoon of Tuesday next. Having come down here on family business, I have put up at the family hotel — being to be heard of at the Gatliffe Arms. Your very obedient servant, ALFRED DAVAGER."

"A clever fellow that," says I, putting the letter into my private drawer.

"Clever!" cries Mr. Frank, "he ought to be horsewhipped within an inch of his life. I would have done it myself; but she made me promise, before she told me a word of the matter, to come straight to you."

"That was one of the wisest promises you ever made," says I. "We can't afford to bully this fellow, whatever else we may do with him. Do you think I am saying anything libelous against your excellent father's character when I assert that if he saw the letter he would certainly insist on your marriage being put off, at the very least?"

"Feeling as my father does about my marriage, he would insist on its being dropped altogether, if he saw this letter," says Mr. Frank, with a groan. "But even that is not the worst of it. The generous, noble girl herself says that if the letter appears in the paper, with all the unanswerable comments this scoundrel would be sure to add to it, she would rather die than hold me to my engagement, even if my father would let me keep it."

As he said this his eyes began to water. He was a weak young fellow, and ridiculously fond of her. I brought him back to business with another rap of the paper-knife.

"Hold up, Mr. Frank," says I. "I have a question or two more. Did you think of asking the young lady whether, to the best of her knowledge, this infernal letter was the only written evidence of the forgery now in existence?"

"Yes, I did think directly of asking her that," says he; "and she told me she was quite certain that there was no written evidence of the forgery except that one letter."

"Will you give Mr. Davager his price for it?" says I.

"Yes," says Mr. Frank, quite peevish with me for asking him such a question. He was an easy young chap in money matters, and talked of hundreds as most men talk of sixpences.

"Mr. Frank," says I, "you came here to get my help and advice in this extremely ticklish business, and you are ready, as I know without asking, to remunerate me for all and any of my services at the usual professional rate. Now, I've made up my mind to act boldly — desperately, if you like — on the hit or miss, win all or lose all principle — in dealing with this matter. Here is my proposal. I'm going to try if I can't do Mr. Davager out of his letter. If I don't succeed before tomorrow afternoon, you hand him the money, and I charge you nothing for professional services. If I do succeed, I hand you the letter instead of Mr. Davager, and you give me the money instead of giving it to him. It's a precious risk for me, but I'm ready to run it. You must pay your five hundred any way. What do you say to my plan? Is it Yes, Mr. Frank, or No?"

"Hang your questions!" cries Mr. Frank, jumping up; "you know it's Yes ten thousand times over. Only you earn the money and —"

"And you will be too glad to give it to me. Very good. Now go home. Comfort the young lady — don't let Mr. Davager so much as set eyes on you — keep quiet — leave everything to me — and feel as certain as you please that all the letters in the world can't stop your being married on Wednesday." With these words I hustled him off out of the office, for I wanted to be left alone to make my mind up about what I should do.

The first thing, of course, was to have a look at the enemy. I wrote to Mr. Davager, telling him that I was privately appointed to arrange the little business matter between himself and "another party" (no names!) on friendly terms; and begging him to call on me at his earliest convenience. At the very beginning of the case, Mr. Davager bothered me. His answer was, that it would not be convenient to him to call till between six and seven in the evening. In this way, you see, he contrived to make me lose several precious hours, at a time when minutes almost were of importance. I had nothing for it but to be patient, and to give certain instructions, before Mr. Davager came, to my boy Tom.

There never was such a sharp boy of fourteen before, and there never will be again, as my boy Tom. A spy to look after Mr. Davager was, of course, the first requisite in a case of this kind; and Tom was the smallest, quickest, quietest, sharpest, stealthiest little snake of a chap that ever dogged a gentleman's steps and kept cleverly out of range of a gentleman's eyes. I settled it with the boy that he was not to show at all when Mr. Davager came; and that he was to wait to hear me ring the bell when Mr. Davager left. If I rang twice, he was to show the gentleman out. If I rang once, he was to keep out of the way, and follow the gentleman whereever he went till he got back to the inn. Those were the only preparations I could make to begin with; being obliged to wait, and let myself be guided by what turned up.

About a quarter to seven my gentleman came.

In the profession of the law we get somehow quite remarkably mixed up with ugly people, blackguard people, and dirty people. But far away the ugliest and dirtiest blackguard I ever saw in my life was Mr. Alfred Davager. He had greasy white hair and a mottled face. He was low in the forehead, fat in the stomach, hoarse in the voice, and weak in the legs. Both his eyes were bloodshot, and one was fixed in his head. He smelled of spirits, and carried a toothpick in his mouth. "How are you? I've just done dinner," says he; and he lights a cigar, sits down with his legs crossed, and winks at me.

I tried at first to take the measure of him in a wheedling, confidential way; but it was no good. I asked him, in a facetious, smiling manner, how he had got hold of the letter. He only told me in answer that he had been in the confidential employment of the writer of it, and that he had always been famous since infancy for a sharp eye to his own interests. I paid him some compliments; but he was not to be flattered. I tried to make him lose his temper; but he kept it in spite of me. It ended in his driving me to my last resource — I made an attempt to frighten him.

"Before we say a word about the money," I began, "let me put a case, Mr. Davager. The pull you have on Mr. Francis Gatliffe is, that you can hinder his marriage on Wednesday. Now, suppose I have got a magistrate's warrant to apprehend you in my pocket? Suppose I have a constable to execute it in the next room? Suppose I bring you up tomorrow — the day before the marriage — charge you only generally with an attempt to extort money, and apply for a day's remand to complete the case? Suppose, as a suspicious stranger, you can't get bail in this town? Suppose —"

"Stop a bit," says Mr. Davager. "Suppose I should not be the greenest fool that ever stood in shoes? Suppose I should not carry the letter about me? Suppose I should have given a certain envelope to a certain friend of mine in a certain place in this town? Suppose the letter should be inside that envelope, directed to old Gatliffe, side by side with a copy of the letter directed to the editor of the local paper? Suppose my friend should be instructed to open the envelope, and take the letters to their right address, if I don't appear to claim them from him this evening? In short, my dear sir, suppose you were born yesterday, and suppose I wasn't?" says Mr. Davager, and winks at me again.

He didn't take me by surprise, for I never expected that he had the letter about him. I made a pretense of being very much taken aback, and of being quite ready to give in. We settled our business about delivering the letter, and handing over the money, in no time. I was to draw out a document, which he was to sign. He knew the document was stuff and nonsense, just as well as I did, and told me I was only proposing it to swell my client's bill. Sharp as he was, he was wrong there. The document was not to be drawn out to gain money from Mr. Frank, but to gain time from Mr. Davager. It served me as an excuse to put off the payment of the five hundred pounds till three o'clock on the Tuesday afternoon. The Tuesday morning Mr. Davager said he should devote to his amusement, and asked me what sights were to be seen in the neighborhood of the town. When I had told him, he pitched his toothpick into my grate, yawned, and went out.

I rang the bell once — waited till he had passed the window — and then looked after Tom. There was my jewel of a boy on the opposite side of the street, just setting his top going in the most playful manner possible. Mr.

Davager walked away up the street toward the market-place. Tom whipped his top up the street toward the market-place, too.

In a quarter of an hour he came back, with all his evidence collected in a beautifully clear and compact state. Mr. Davager had walked to a public-house just outside the town, in a lane leading to the highroad. On a bench outside the public-house there sat a man smoking. He said "All right?" and gave a letter to Mr. Davager, who answered "All right!" and walked back to the inn. In the hall he ordered hot rum-and-water, cigars, slippers, and a fire to be lit in his room. After that he went upstairs, and Tom came away.

I now saw my road clear before me — not very far on, but still clear. I had housed the letter, in all probability for that night, at the Gatliffe Arms. After tipping Tom, I gave him directions to play about the door of the inn, and refresh himself when he was tired at the tart-shop opposite, eating as much as he pleased, on the understanding that he crammed all the time with his eye on the window. If Mr. Davager went out, or Mr. Davager's friend called on him, Tom was to let me know. He was also to take a little note from me to the head chambermaid — an old friend of mine — asking her to step over to my office, on a private matter of business, as soon as her work was done for that night. After settling these little matters, having half an hour to spare, I turned to and did myself a bloater at the office fire, and had a drop of gin-and-water hot, and felt comparatively happy.

When the head chambermaid came, it turned out, as good luck would have it, that Mr. Davager had drawn her attention rather too closely to his ugliness, by offering her a testimony of his regard in the shape of a kiss. I no sooner mentioned him than she flew into a passion; and when I added, by way of clinching the matter, that I was retained to defend the interests of a very beautiful and deserving young lady (name not referred to, of course) against the most cruel underhand treachery on the part of Mr. Davager, the head chambermaid was ready to go any lengths that she could safely to serve my cause. In a few words I discovered that Boots was to call Mr. Davager at eight the next morning, and was to take his clothes downstairs to brush as usual. If Mr. D ——— had not emptied his own pockets overnight, we arranged that Boots was to forget to empty them for him, and was to bring the clothes downstairs just as he found them. If Mr. D———'s pockets were emptied, then, of course, it would be necessary to transfer the searching process to Mr. D ———'s room. Under any circumstances, I was certain of the head chambermaid; and under any circumstances, also, the head chambermaid was certain of Boots.

I waited till Tom came home, looking very puffy and bilious about the face; but as to his intellects, if anything, rather sharper than ever. His report was uncommonly short and pleasant. The inn was shutting up; Mr. Davager was going to bed in rather a drunken condition; Mr. Davager's friend had never appeared. I sent Tom (properly instructed about keeping our man in view all the next morning) to his shake-down behind the office-desk, where I heard him hiccoughing half the night, as even the best boys will, when over-excited and too full of tarts.

At half-past seven next morning, I slipped quietly into Boots's pantry.

Down came the clothes. No pockets in trousers. Waistcoat-pockets empty. Coat-pockets with something in them. First, handkerchief; secondly, bunch of keys; thirdly, cigar-case; fourthly, pocketbook. Of course I wasn't such a fool as to expect to find the letter there, but I opened the pocketbook with a certain curiosity, notwithstanding.

Nothing in the two pockets of the book but some old advertisements cut out of newspapers, a lock of hair tied round with a dirty bit of ribbon, a circular letter about a loan society, and some copies of verses not likely to suit any company that was not of an extremely free-and-easy description. On the leaves of the pocketbook, people's addresses scrawled in pencil, and bets jotted down in red ink. On one leaf, by itself, this queer inscription:

"MEM. 5 ALONG. 4 ACROSS."

I understood everything but those words and figures, so of course I copied them out into my own book.

Then I waited in the pantry till Boots had brushed the clothes, and had taken them upstairs. His report when he came down was, that Mr. D——— had asked if it was a fine morning. Being told that it was, he had ordered breakfast at nine, and a saddle-horse to be at the door at ten, to take him to Grimwith Abbey — one of the sights in our neighborhood which I had told him of the evening before.

"I'll be here, coming in by the back way, at half-past ten," says I to the head chambermaid.

"What for?" says she.

"To take the responsibility of making Mr. Davager's bed off your hands for this morning only," says I.

"Any more orders?" says she.

"One more," says I. "I want to hire Sam for the morning. Put it down in the order-book that he's to be brought round to my office at ten."

In case you should think Sam was a man, I'd better perhaps tell you he was a pony. I'd made up my mind that it would be beneficial to Tom's health, after the tarts, if he took a constitutional airing on a nice hard saddle in the direction of Grimwith Abbey.

"Anything else?" says the head chambermaid.

"Only one more favor," says I. "Would my boy Tom be very much in the way if he came, from now till ten, to help with the boots and shoes, and stood at his work close by this window which looks out on the staircase?"

"Not a bit," says the head chambermaid.

"Thank you," says I; and stepped back to my office directly.

When I had sent Tom off to help with the boots and shoes, I reviewed the whole case exactly as it stood at that time.

There were three things Mr. Davager might do with the letter. He might give it to his friend again before ten — in which case Tom would most likely see the said friend on the stairs. He might take it to his friend, or to some other friend, after ten — in which case Tom was ready to follow him on Sam the pony. And, lastly, he might leave it hidden somewhere in his room at the inn — in which case I was all ready for him with a search-warrant of my own granting, under favor always of my friend the head chambermaid. So far I had my business arrangements all gathered up nice and compact in my own hands. Only two things bothered me; the terrible shortness of the time at my disposal, in case I failed in my first experiments, for getting hold of the letter, and that queer inscription which I had copied out of the pocketbook:

"MEM. 5 ALONG. 4 ACROSS."

It was the measurement most likely of something, and he was afraid of forgetting it; therefore it was something important. Query — something about himself? Say "5" (inches) "along"— he doesn't wear a wig. Say "5" (feet) "along"— it can't be coat, waistcoat, trousers, or underclothing. Say "5" (yards) "along"— it can't be anything about himself, unless he wears round his body the rope that he's sure to be hanged with one of these days. Then it is *not* something about himself. What do I know of that is important to him besides? I know of nothing but the Letter. Can the memorandum be connected with that? Say, yes. What do "5 along" and "4 across" mean, then? The measurement of something he carries about with him? or the measurement of something in his room? I could get pretty satisfactorily to myself as far as that; but I could get no further.

Tom came back to the office, and reported him mounted for his ride. His friend had never appeared. I sent the boy off, with his proper instructions, on Sam's back — wrote an encouraging letter to Mr. Frank to keep him quiet — then slipped into the inn by the back way a little before half-past ten. The head chambermaid gave me a signal when the landing was clear. I got into his room without a soul but her seeing me, and locked the door immediately.

The case was, to a certain extent, simplified now. Either Mr. Davager had ridden out with the letter about him, or he had left it in some safe hiding-place in his room. I suspected it to be in his room, for a reason that will a little astonish you — his trunk, his dressing-case, and all the drawers and cupboards, were left open. I knew my customer, and I thought this extraordinary carelessness on his part rather suspicious.

Mr. Davager had taken one of the best bedrooms at the Gatliffe Arms. Floor carpeted all over, walls beautifully papered, four-poster, and general furniture first-rate. I searched, to begin with, on the usual plan, examining everything in every possible way, and taking more than an hour about it. No discovery. Then I pulled out a carpenter's rule which I had brought with me. Was there anything in the room which — either in inches, feet, or yards — answered to "5 along" and "4 across"? Nothing. I put the rule back in my pocket — measurement was no good, evidently. Was there anything in the room that would count up to 5 one way and 4 another, seeing that nothing would measure up to it? I had got obstinately persuaded by this time that the letter must be in the room — principally because of the trouble I had had in looking after it. And persuading myself of that, I took it into my head next, just as obstinately, that "5 along" and "4 across" must be the right clew to find the letter by — principally because I hadn't left myself, after all my searching and thinking, even so much as the ghost of another guide to go by. "Five along"— where could I count five along the room, in any part of it?

Not on the paper. The pattern there was pillars of trellis-work and flowers, inclosing a plain green ground — only four pillars along the wall and only two across. The furniture? There were not five chairs or five separate pieces of any furniture in the room altogether. The fringes that hung from the cornice of the bed? Plenty of them, at any rate! Up I jumped on the counterpane, with my pen-knife in my hand. Every way that "5 along" and "4 across" could be reckoned on those unlucky fringes I reckoned on them — probed with my penknife — scratched with my nails — crunched with my fingers. No use; not a sign of a letter; and the time was getting on — oh, Lord! how the time did get on in Mr. Davager's room that morning.

I jumped down from the bed, so desperate at my ill luck that I hardly cared whether anybody heard me or not. Quite a little cloud of dust rose at my feet as they thumped on the carpet.

"Hullo!" thought I, "my friend the head chambermaid takes it easy here. Nice state for a carpet to be in, in one of the best bedrooms at the Gatliffe Arms." Carpet! I had been jumping up on the bed, and staring up at the walls, but I had never so much as given a glance down at the carpet. Think of me pretending to be a lawyer, and not knowing how to look low enough!

The carpet! It had been a stout article in its time, had evidently began in a drawing-room; then descended to a coffee-room; then gone upstairs altogether to a bedroom. The ground was brown, and the pattern was bunches of leaves and roses speckled over the ground at regular distances. I reckoned up the bunches. Ten along the room — eight across it. When I had stepped out five one way and four the other, and was down on my knees on the center bunch, as true as I sit on this chair I could hear my own heart beating so loud that it quite frightened me.

I looked narrowly all over the bunch, and I felt all over it with the ends of my fingers, and nothing came of that. Then I scraped it over slowly and gently with my nails. My second finger-nail stuck a little at one place. I parted the pile of the carpet over that place, and saw a thin slit which had been hidden by the pile being smoothed over it — a slit about half an inch long, with a little end of brown thread, exactly the color of the carpet ground, sticking out about a quarter of an inch from the middle of it. Just as I laid hold of the thread gently, I heard a footstep outside the door.

It was only the head chambermaid. "Haven't you done yet?" she whispers.

"Give me two minutes," says I, "and don't let anybody come near the door — whatever you do, don't let anybody startle me again by coming near the door."

I took a little pull at the thread, and heard something rustle. I took a longer pull, and out came a piece of paper, rolled up tight like those candle-lighters that the ladies make. I unrolled it — and, by George! there was the letter!

The original letter! I knew it by the color of the ink. The letter that was worth five hundred pounds to me! It was all that I could do to keep myself at first from throwing my hat into the air, and hurrahing like mad. I had to take a chair and sit quiet in it for a minute or two, before I could cool myself down to my proper business level. I knew that I was safely down again when I found myself pondering how to let Mr. Davager know that he had been done by the innocent country attorney, after all.

It was not long before a nice little irritating plan occurred to me. I tore a blank leaf out of my pocketbook, wrote on it with my pencil, "Change for a five-hundred-pound note," folded up the paper, tied the thread to it, poked it back into the hiding-place, smoothed over the pile of the carpet, and then bolted off to Mr. Frank. He in his turn bolted off to show the letter to the young lady, who first certified to its genuineness, then dropped it into the fire, and then took the initiative for the first time since her marriage engagement, by flinging her arms round his neck, kissing him with all her might, and going into hysterics in his arms. So at least Mr. Frank told me, but that's not evidence. It is evidence, however, that I saw them married with my own eyes on the Wednesday; and that while they went off in a carriage-and-four to spend the honeymoon, I went off on my own legs to open a credit at the Town and County Bank with a five-hundred-pound note in my pocket.

As to Mr. Davager, I can tell you nothing more about him, except what is derived from hearsay evidence, which is always unsatisfactory evidence, even in a lawyer's mouth.

My inestimable boy, Tom, although twice kicked off by Sam the pony, never lost hold of the bridle, and kept his man in sight from first to last. He had nothing particular to report except that on the way out to the Abbey Mr. Davager had stopped at the public-house, had spoken a word or two to his friend of the night before, and had handed him what looked like a bit of paper. This was no doubt a clew to the thread that held the letter, to be used in case of accidents. In every other respect Mr. D. had ridden out and ridden in like an ordinary sightseer. Tom reported him to me as having dismounted at the hotel about two. At half-past I locked my office door, nailed a card under the knocker with "not at home till tomorrow" written on it, and retired to a friend's house a mile or so out of the town for the rest of the day.

Mr. Davager, I have been since given to understand, left the Gatliffe Arms that same night with his best clothes on his back, and with all the valuable contents of his dressing-case in his pockets. I am not in a condition to state whether he ever went through the form of asking for his bill or not; but I can positively testify that he never paid it, and that the effects left in his bedroom did not pay it either. When I add to these fragments of evidence that he and I have never met (luckily for me, you will say) since I jockeyed him out of his banknote, I have about fulfilled my implied contract as maker of a statement with you, sir, as hearer of a statement. Observe the expression, will you? I said it was a Statement before I began; and I say it's a Statement now I've done. I defy you to prove it's a Story! How are you getting on with my portrait? I like you very well, Mr. Artist; but if you have been taking advantage of my talking to shirk your work, as sure as you're alive I'll split upon you to the Town Council!

I attended a great many times at my queer sitter's house before his likeness was completed. To the last he was dissatisfied with the progress I made. Fortunately for me, the Town Council approved of the portrait when it was done. Mr. Boxsious, however, objected to them as being much too easy to please. He did not dispute the fidelity of the likeness, but he asserted that I had not covered the canvas with half paint enough for my money. To this day (for he is still alive), he describes me to all inquiring friends as "The Painter-Man who jockeyed the Town Council."

THE FRENCH GOVERNESS'S STORY OF SISTER ROSE.

PROLOGUE TO THE THIRD STORY.

It was a sad day for me when Mr. Lanfray, of Rockleigh Place, discovering that his youngest daughter's health required a warm climate, removed from his English establishment to the South of France. Roving from place to place, as I am obliged to do, though I make many acquaintances, I keep but few friends. The nature of my calling is, I am quite aware, mainly answerable for this. People cannot be blamed for forgetting a man who, on leaving their houses, never can tell them for certain when he is likely to be in their neighborhood again.

Mr. Lanfray was one of the few exceptional persons who always remembered me. I have proofs of his friendly interest in my welfare in the shape of letters which I treasure with grateful care. The last of these is an invitation to his house in the South of France. There is little chance at present of my being able to profit by his kindness; but I like to read his invitation from time to time, for it makes me fancy, in my happier moments, that I may one day really be able to accept it.

My introduction to this gentleman, in my capacity of portrait-painter, did not promise much for me in a professional point of view. I was invited to Rockleigh — or to "The Place," as it was more frequently called among the people of the county — to take a likeness in water-colors, on a small scale, of the French governess who lived with Mr. Lanfray's daughters. My first idea on hearing of this was, that the governess was about to leave her situation, and that her pupils wished to have a memorial of her in the shape of a portrait. Subsequent inquiry, however, informed me that I was in error. It was the eldest of Mr. Lanfray's daughters, who was on the point of leaving the house to accompany her husband to India; and it was for her that the portrait had been ordered as a home remembrance of her best and dearest friend. Besides these particulars, I discovered that the governess, though still called "mademoiselle," was an old lady; that Mr. Lanfray had been introduced to her many years since in France, after the death of his wife; that she was absolute mistress in the house; and that her three pupils had always looked up to her as a second mother, from the time when their father first placed them under her charge.

These scraps of information made me rather anxious to see Mademoiselle Clairfait, the governess.

On the day appointed for my attendance at the comfortable country house of Rockleigh, I was detained on the road, and did not arrive at my destination until late in the evening. The welcome accorded to me by Mr. Lanfray gave an earnest of the unvarying kindness that I was to experience at his hands in after-life. I was received at once on equal terms, as if I had been a friend of the family, and was presented the same evening to my host's daughters. They were not merely three elegant and attractive young women, but — what means much more than that — three admirable subjects for pictures, the bride particularly. Her young husband did not strike me much at first sight; he seemed rather shy and silent. After I had been introduced to him, I looked round for Mademoiselle Clairfait, but she was not present; and I was soon afterward informed by Mr. Lanfray that she always spent the latter part of the evening in her own room.

At the breakfast-table the next morning, I again looked for my sitter, and once more in vain. "Mamma, as we call her," said one of the ladies, "is dressing expressly for her picture, Mr. Kerby. I hope you are not above painting silk, lace, and jewelry. The dear old lady, who is perfection in everything else, is perfection also in dress, and is bent on being painted in all her splendor."

This explanation prepared me for something extraordinary; but I found that my anticipations had fallen far below the reality when Mademoiselle Clairfait at last made her appearance, and announced that she was ready to sit for her portrait.

Never before or since have I seen such perfect dressing and such active old age in combination. "Mademoiselle" was short and thin; her face was perfectly white all over, the skin being puckered up in an infinite variety of the smallest possible wrinkles. Her bright black eyes were perfect marvels of youthfulness and vivacity. They sparkled, and beamed, and ogled, and moved about over everybody and everything at such a rate, that the plain gray hair above them looked unnaturally venerable, and the wrinkles below an artful piece of masquerade to represent old age. As for her dress, I remember few harder pieces of work than the painting of it. She wore a silver-gray silk gown that seemed always flashing out into some new light whenever she moved. It was as stiff as a board, and rustled like the wind. Her head, neck, and bosom were enveloped in clouds of the airiest-looking lace I ever saw, disposed about each part of her with the most exquisite grace and propriety, and glistening at all sorts of unexpected places with little fairy-like toys in gold and precious stones. On her right wrist she wore three small bracelets, with the hair of her three pupils worked into them; and on her left, one large bracelet with a miniature let in over the clasp. She had a dark crimson and gold scarf thrown coquettishly over her shoulders, and held a lovely little feather-fan in her hand. When she first presented herself before me in this costume, with a brisk courtesy and a bright smile, filling the room with perfume, and gracefully flirting the feather-fan, I lost all confidence in my powers as a portrait-painter immediately. The brightest colors in my box looked dowdy and dim, and I myself felt like an unwashed, unbrushed, unpresentable sloven.

"Tell me, my angels," said mademoiselle, apostrophizing her pupils in the prettiest foreign English, "am I the cream of all creams this morning? Do I carry my sixty years resplendently? Will the savages in India, when my own love exhibits my picture among them, say, 'Ah! smart! smart! this was a great dandy?' And the gentleman, the skillful artist, whom it is even more an honor than a happiness to meet, does he approve of me for a model? Does he find me pretty and paintable from top to toe?" Here she dropped me another brisk courtesy, placed herself in a languishing position in the sitter's chair, and asked us all if she looked like a shepherdess in Dresden china.

The young ladies burst out laughing, and mademoiselle, as gay as any of them and a great deal shriller, joined in the merriment. Never before had I contended with any sitter half as restless as that wonderful old lady. No sooner had I begun than she jumped out of the chair, and exclaiming, "*Grand Dieu!* I have forgotten to embrace my angels this morning," ran up to her pupils, raised herself on tiptoe before them in quick succession, put the two first fingers of each hand under their ears, kissed them lightly on both cheeks, and was back again in the chair before an English governess could have said, "Good-morning, my dears, I hope you all slept well last night."

I began again. Up jumped mademoiselle for the second time, and tripped across the room to a cheval-glass. "No!" I heard her say to herself, "I have not discomposed my head in kissing my angels. I may come back and pose for my picture."

Back she came. I worked from her for five minutes at the most. "Stop!" cries mademoiselle, jumping up for the third time; "I must see how this skillful artist is getting on. *Grand Dieu!* why he has done nothing!"

For the fourth time I began, and for the fourth time the old lady started out of her chair. "Now I must repose myself," said mademoiselle, walking lightly from end to end of the room, and humming a French air, by way of taking a rest.

I was at my wit's end, and the young ladies saw it. They all surrounded my unmanageable sitter, and appealed to her compassion for me. "Certainly!" said mademoiselle, expressing astonishment by flinging up both her hands with all the fingers spread out in the air. "But why apostrophize me thus? I am here, I am ready, I am at the service of this skillful artist. Why apostrophize me?"

A fortunate chance question of mine steadied her for some time. I inquired if I was expected to draw the whole of my sitter's figure as well as her face. Mademoiselle replied by a comic scream of indignation. If I was the brave and gifted man for whom she took me, I ought to be ready to perish rather than leave out an inch of her anywhere. Dress was her passion, and it would be an outrage on her sentiments if I did not do full justice to everything she had on — to her robe, to her lace, to her scarf, to her fan, to her rings, her jewels, and, above all, to her bracelets. I groaned in spirit at the task before me, but made my best bow of acquiescence. Mademoiselle was not to be satisfied by a mere bow; she desired the pleasure of specially directing my attention, if I would be so amiable as to get up and approach her, to one of her bracelets in particular — the bracelet with the miniature, on her left wrist. It had been the gift of the dearest friend she ever had, and the miniature represented that friend's beloved and beautiful face. Could I make a tiny, tiny copy of that likeness in my drawing! Would I only be so obliging as to approach for one little moment, and see if such a thing were possible?

I obeyed unwillingly enough, expecting, from mademoiselle's expression, to see a commonplace portrait of some unfortunate admirer whom she had treated with unmerited severity in the days of her youth. To my astonishment, I found that the miniature, which was very beautifully painted, represented a woman's face — a young woman with kind, sad eyes, pale, delicate cheeks, light hair, and such a pure, tender, lovely expressions that I thought of Raphael's Madonnas the moment I looked at her portrait.

The old lady observed the impression which the miniature produced on me, and nodded her head in silence. "What a beautiful, innocent, pure face!" I said.

Mademoiselle Clairfait gently brushed a particle of dust from the miniature with her handkerchief, and kissed it. "I have three angels still left," she said, looking at her pupils. "They console me for the fourth, who has gone to heaven."

She patted the face on the miniature gently with her little, withered, white fingers, as if it had been a living thing. "Sister Rose!" she sighed to herself; then, looking up again at me, said, "I should like it put into my portrait, sir, because I have always worn it since I was a young woman, for 'Sister Rose's' sake."

The sudden change in her manner, from the extreme of flighty gayety to the extreme of quiet sadness, would have looked theatrical in a woman of any other nation. It seemed, however, perfectly natural and appropriate in her. I went back to my drawing, rather perplexed. Who was "Sister Rose"? Not one of the Lanfray family, apparently. The composure of the young ladies when the name was mentioned showed plainly enough that the original of the miniature had been no relation of theirs.

I tried to stifle my curiosity on the subject of Sister Rose, by giving myself entirely to my work. For a full half-hour, Mademoiselle Clairfait sat quietly before me, with her hands crossed on her lap, and her eyes fixed on the bracelet. This happy alteration enabled me to do something toward completing the outline of her face and figure. I might even, under fortunate circumstances, have vanquished the preliminary difficulties of my task at one effort; but the fates were against me that day. While I was still working rapidly and to my satisfaction, a servant knocked at the door to announce luncheon, and mademoiselle lightly roused herself from her serious reflection and her quiet position in a moment.

"Ah me!" she said, turning the miniature round on her wrist till it was out of sight. "What animals we are, after all! The spiritual part of us is at the mercy of the stomach. My heart is absorbed by tender thoughts, yet I am not the less ready for luncheon! Come, my children and fellow-mortals. *Allons cultiver notre jardin!*"

With this quotation from "Candide," plaintively delivered, the old lady led the way out of the room, and was followed by her younger pupils. The eldest sister remained behind for a moment, and reminded me that the lunch was ready.

"I am afraid you have found the dear old soul rather an unruly sitter," she said, noticing the look of dissatisfaction with which I was regarding my drawing. "But she will improve as you go on. She has done better already for the last half-hour, has she not?"

"Much better," I answered. "My admiration of the miniature on the bracelet seemed — I suppose, by calling up some old associations — to have a strangely soothing effect on Mademoiselle Clairfait."

"Ah yes! only remind her of the original of that portrait, and you change her directly, whatever she may have been saying or doing the moment before. Sometimes she talks of *Sister Rose,* and of all that she went through in the time of the French Revolution, by the hour together. It is wonderfully interesting — at least we all think so."

"I presume that the lady described as 'Sister Rose' was a relation of Mademoiselle Clairfait's?"

"No, only a very dear friend. Mademoiselle Clairfait is the daughter of a silk-mercer, once established at Chalons-sur-Marne. Her father happened to give an asylum in his office to a lonely old man, to whom 'Sister Rose' and her brother had been greatly indebted in the revolutionary time; and out of a train of circumstances connected with that, the first acquaintance between mademoiselle and the friend whose portrait she wears, arose. After the time of her father's bankruptcy, and for many years before we were placed under her charge, our good old governess lived entirely with 'Sister Rose' and her brother. She must then have heard all the interesting things that she has since often repeated to my sisters and myself."

"Might I suggest," said I, after an instant's consideration, "that the best way to give me a fair chance of studying Mademoiselle Clairfait's face at the next sitting, would be to lead her thoughts again to that quieting subject of the miniature, and to the events which the portrait recalls? It is really the only plan, after what I have observed this morning, that I can think of for enabling me to do myself and my sitter justice."

"I am delighted to hear you say so," replied the lady; "for the execution of your plan, by me or by my sisters, will be the easiest thing in the world. A word from us at any time will set mademoiselle thinking, and talking too, of the friend of her youthful days. Depend on our assistance so far. And now let me show you the way to the luncheon-table."

Two good results followed the ready rendering of the help I had asked from my host's daughters. I succeeded with my portrait of Mademoiselle Clairfait, and I heard the story which occupies the following pages.

In the case of the preceding narratives, I have repeated what was related to me, as nearly as possible in the very words of my sitters. In the case of this third story, it is impossible for me to proceed upon the same plan. The circumstances of "Sister Rose's" eventful history were narrated to me at different times, and in the most fragmentary and discursive manner. Mademoiselle Clairfait characteristically mixed up with the direct interest of her story, not only references to places and people which had no recognizable connection with it, but outbursts of passionate political declamation, on the extreme liberal side — to say nothing of little tender apostrophes to her beloved friend, which sounded very prettily as she spoke them, but which would lose their effect altogether by being transferred to paper. Under these circumstances, I have thought it best to tell the story in my own way — rigidly adhering to the events of it exactly as they were related; and never interfering on my own responsibility except to keep order in the march of the incidents, and to present them, to the best of my ability, variously as well as interestingly to the reader.

PART FIRST. CHAPTER I.

"*W*ell, Monsieur Guillaume, what is the news this evening?"

"None that I know of, Monsieur Justin, except that Mademoiselle Rose is to be married tomorrow."

"Much obliged, my respectable old friend, for so interesting and unexpected a reply to my question. Considering that I am the valet of Monsieur Danville, who plays the distinguished part of bridegroom in the little wedding comedy to which you refer, I think I may assure you, without offense, that your news is, so far as I am concerned, of the stalest possible kind. Take a pinch of snuff, Monsieur Guillaume, and excuse me if I inform you that my question referred to public news, and not to the private affairs of the two families whose household interests we have the pleasure of promoting."

"I don't understand what you mean by such a phrase as promoting household interests, Monsieur Justin. I am the servant of Monsieur Louis Trudaine, who lives here with his sister, Mademoiselle Rose. You are the servant of Monsieur Danville, whose excellent mother has made up the match for him with my young lady. As servants, both of us, the pleasantest news we can have any concern with is news that is connected with the happiness of our masters. I have nothing to do with public affairs; and, being one of the old school, I make it my main object in life to mind my own business. If our homely domestic politics have no interests for you, allow me to express my regret, and to wish you a very good-evening."

"Pardon me, my dear sir, I have not the slightest respect for the old school, or the least sympathy with people who only mind their own business. However, I accept your expressions of regret; I reciprocate your 'Good-evening'; and I trust to find you improved in temper, dress, manners, and appearance the next time I have the honor of meeting you. Adieu, Monsieur Guillaume, and! *Vive la bagatelle!"*

These scraps of dialogue were interchanged on a lovely summer evening in the year seventeen hundred and eighty-nine, before the back door of a small house which stood on the banks of the Seine, about three miles westward of the city of Rouen. The one speaker was lean, old, crabbed and slovenly; the other was plump, young, oily-mannered and dressed in the most gorgeous livery costume of the period. The last days of genuine dandyism were then rapidly approaching all over the civilized world; and Monsieur Justin was, in his own way, dressed to perfection, as a living illustration of the expiring glories of his epoch.

After the old servant had left him, he occupied himself for a few minutes in contemplating, superciliously enough, the back view of the little house before which he stood. Judging by the windows, it did not contain more than six or eight rooms in all. Instead of stables and outhouses, there was a conservatory attached to the building on one side, and a low, long room, built of wood, gayly painted, on the other. One of the windows of this room was left uncurtained and through it could be seen, on a sort of dresser inside, bottles filled with strangely-colored liquids oddly-shaped utensils of brass and copper, one end of a large furnace, and other objects, which plainly proclaimed that the apartment was used as a chemical laboratory.

"Think of our bride's brother amusing himself in such a place as that with cooking drugs in saucepans," muttered Monsieur Justin, peeping into the room. "I am the least particular man in the universe, but I must say I wish we were not going to be connected by marriage with an amateur apothecary. Pah! I can smell the place through the window."

With these words Monsieur Justin turned his back on the laboratory in disgust, and sauntered toward the cliffs overhanging the river.

Leaving the garden attached to the house, he ascended some gently rising ground by a winding path. Arrived at the summit, the whole view of the Seine, with its lovely green islands, its banks fringed with trees, its gliding boats, and little scattered water-side cottages, opened before him. Westward, where the level country appeared beyond the further bank of the river, the landscape was all aglow with the crimson of the setting sun. Eastward, the long shadows and mellow intervening lights, the red glory that quivered on the rippling water, the steady ruby fire glowing on cottage windows that reflected the level sunlight, led the eye onward and onward, along the windings of the Seine, until it rested upon the spires, towers, and broadly-massed houses of Rouen, with the wooded hills rising beyond them for background. Lovely to look on at any time, the view was almost supernaturally beautiful now under the gorgeous evening light that glowed up in it. All its attractions, however, were lost on the valet; he stood yawning with his hands in his pockets, looking neither to the right nor to the left, but staring straight before him at a little hollow, beyond which the ground sloped away smoothly to the brink of the cliff. A bench was placed here, and three persons — an old lady, a gentleman, and a young girl — were seated on it, watching the sunset, and by consequence turning their backs on Monsieur Justin. Near them stood two gentlemen, also looking toward the river and the distant view. These five figures attracted the valet's attention, to the exclusion of every other object around him.

"There they are still," he said to himself, discontentedly. "Madame Danville in the same place on the seat; my master, the bridegroom, dutifully next to her; Mademoiselle Rose, the bride, bashfully next to him; Monsieur Trudaine, the amateur apothecary brother, affectionately next to her; and Monsieur Lomaque, our queer land-steward, officially in waiting on the whole party. There they all are indeed, incomprehensibly wasting their time still in looking at nothing! Yes," continued Monsieur Justin, lifting his eyes wearily, and staring hard, first up the river at Rouen, then down the river at the setting sun; "yes, plague take them! looking at nothing, absolutely and positively at nothing, all this while."

Here Monsieur Justin yawned again, and, returning to the garden, sat himself down in an arbor and resignedly went to sleep.

If the valet had ventured near the five persons whom he had been apostrophizing from a distance, and if he had been possessed of some little refinement of observation, he could hardly have failed to remark that the bride and bridegroom of the morrow, and their companions on either side, were all, in a greater or less degree, under the influence of some secret restraint, which affected their conversation, their gestures, and even the expression of their faces. Madame Danville — a handsome, richly-dressed old lady, with very bright eyes, and a quick, suspicious manner — looked composedly and happily enough, as long as her attention was fixed on her son. But when she turned from him toward the bride, a hardly perceptible uneasiness passed over her face — an uneasiness which only deepened to positive distrust and dissatisfaction whenever she looked toward Mademoiselle Trudaine's brother. In the same way, her son, who was all smiles and happiness while he was speaking with his future wife, altered visibly in manner and look exactly as his mother altered, whenever the presence of Monsieur Trudaine specially impressed itself on his attention. Then, again, Lomaque, the land-steward — quiet, sharp, skinny Lomaque, with the submissive manner, and the red-rimmed eyes — never looked up at his master's future brother-inlaw without looking away again rather uneasily, and thoughtfully drilling holes in the grass with his long sharp-pointed cane. Even the bride herself — the pretty, innocent girl, with her childish shyness of manner — seemed to be affected like the others. Doubt, if not distress, overshadowed her face from time to time, and the hand which her lover held trembled a little, and grew restless, when she accidentally caught her brother's eye.

Strangely enough there was nothing to repel, but, on the contrary, everything to attract in the look and manner of the person whose mere presence seemed to exercise such a curiously constraining influence over the wedding-party. Louis Trudaine was a remarkably handsome man. His expression was singularly kind and gentle; his manner irresistibly winning in its frank, manly firmness and composure. His words, when he occasionally spoke, seemed as unlikely to give offense as his looks; for he only opened his lips in courteous reply to questions directly addressed to him. Judging by a latent mournfulness in the tones of his voice, and by the sorrowful tenderness which clouded his kind, earnest eyes whenever they rested on his sister, his thoughts were certainly not of the happy or the hopeful kind. But he gave them no direct expression; he intruded his secret sadness, whatever it might be, on no one of his companions. Nevertheless, modest and self-restrained as he was, there was evidently some reproving or saddening influence in his presence which affected the spirits of every one near him, and darkened the eve of the wedding to bride and bridegroom alike.

As the sun slowly sank in the heavens, the conversation flagged more and more. After a long silence, the bridegroom was the first to start a new subject.

"Rose, love," he said, "that magnificent sunset is a good omen for our marriage; it promises another lovely day tomorrow."

The bride laughed and blushed.

"Do you really believe in omens, Charles?" she said.

"My dear," interposed the old lady, before her son could answer, "if Charles does believe in omens, it is nothing to laugh at. You will soon know better, when you are his wife, than to confound him, even in the slightest things, with the common herd of people. All his convictions are well founded — so well, that if I thought he really did believe in omens, I should most assuredly make up my mind to believe in them too."

"I beg your pardon, madame," Rose began, tremulously, "I only meant —"

"My dear child, have you so little knowledge of the world as to suppose that I could be offended —"

"Let Rose speak," said the young man.

He turned round petulantly, almost with the air of a spoiled child, to his mother, as he said those words. She had been looking fondly and proudly on him the moment before. Now her eyes wandered disconcertedly from his face; she hesitated an instant with a sudden confusion which seemed quite foreign to her character, then whispered in his ear,

"Am I to blame, Charles, for trying to make her worthy of you?"

Her son took no notice of the question. He only reiterated sharply, "Let Rose speak."

"I really had nothing to say," faltered the young girl, growing more and more confused.

"Oh, but you had!"

There was such an ungracious sharpness in his voice, such an outburst of petulance in his manner as he spoke, that his mother gave him a warning touch on the arm, and whispered "Hush!"

Monsieur Lomaque, the land-steward, and Monsieur Trudaine, the brother, both glanced searchingly at the bride, as the words passed the bridegroom's lips. She seemed to be frightened and astonished, rather than irritated or hurt. A curious smile puckered up Lomaque's lean face, as he looked demurely down on the ground, and began drilling a fresh hole in the turf with the sharp point of his cane. Trudaine turned aside quickly, and, sighing, walked away a few paces; then came back, and seemed about to speak, but Danville interrupted him.

"Pardon me, Rose," he said; "I am so jealous of even the appearance of any want of attention toward you, that I was nearly allowing myself to be irritated about nothing."

He kissed her hand very gracefully and tenderly as he made his excuse; but there was a latent expression in his eye which was at variance with the apparent spirit of his action. It was noticed by nobody but observant and submissive Monsieur Lomaque, who smiled to himself again, and drilled harder than ever at his hole in the grass.

"I think Monsieur Trudaine was about to speak," said Madame Danville. "Perhaps he will have no objection to let us hear what he was going to say."

"None, madame," replied Trudaine, politely. "I was about to take upon myself the blame of Rose's want of respect for believers in omens, by confessing that I have always encouraged her to laugh at superstitions of every kind."

"You a ridiculer of superstitions?" said Danville, turning quickly on him. "You, who have built a laboratory; you, who are an amateur professor of the occult arts of chemistry — a seeker after the Elixir of Life. On my word of honor, you astonish me!"

There was an ironical politeness in his voice, look, and manner as he said this, which his mother and his land-steward, Monsieur Lomaque, evidently knew how to interpret. The first touched his arm again and whispered, "Be careful!" the second suddenly grew serious, and left off drilling his hole in the grass. Rose neither heard the warning of Madame Danville, nor noticed the alteration in Lomaque. She was looking round at her brother, and was waiting with a bright, affectionate smile to hear his answer. He nodded, as if to reassure her, before he spoke again to Danville.

"You have rather romantic ideas about experiments in chemistry," he said, quietly. "Mine have so little connection with what you call the occult arts that all the world might see them, if all the world thought it worth while. The only Elixirs of Life that I know of are a quiet heart and a contented mind. Both those I found, years and years ago, when Rose and I first came to live together in the house yonder."

He spoke with a quiet sadness in his voice, which meant far more to his sister than the simple words he uttered. Her eyes filled with tears; she turned for a moment from her lover, and took her brother's hand. "Don't talk, Louis, as if you thought you were going to lose your sister, because —" Her lips began to tremble, and she stopped suddenly.

"More jealous than ever of your taking her away from him!" whispered Madame Danville in her son's ear. "Hush! don't, for God's sake, take any notice of it," she added, hurriedly, as he rose from the seat and faced Trudaine with undisguised irritation and impatience in his manner. Before he could speak, the old servant Guillaume made his appearance, and announced that coffee was ready. Madame Danville again said "Hush!" and quickly took one of his arms, while he offered the other to Rose. "Charles," said the young girl, amazedly, "how flushed your face is, and how your arm trembles!"

He controlled himself in a moment, smiled, and said to her: "Can't you guess why, Rose? I am thinking of tomorrow." While he was speaking, he passed close by the land-steward, on his way back to the house with the ladies. The smile returned to Monsieur Lomaque's lean face, and a curious light twinkled in his red-rimmed eyes as he began a fresh hole in the grass.

"Won't you go indoors, and take some coffee?" asked Trudaine, touching the land-steward on the arm.

Monsieur Lomaque started a little and left his cane sticking in the ground. "A thousand thanks, monsieur," he said; "may I be allowed to follow you?"

"I confess the beauty of the evening makes me a little unwilling to leave this place just yet."

"Ah! the beauties of Nature — I feel them with you, Monsieur Trudaine; I feel them here." Saying this, Lomaque laid one hand on his heart, and with the other pulled his stick out of the grass. He had looked as little at the landscape or the setting sun as Monsieur Justin himself.

They sat down, side by side, on the empty bench; and then there followed an awkward pause. Submissive Lomaque was too discreet to forget his place, and venture on starting a new topic. Trudaine was preoccupied, and disinclined to talk. It was necessary, however, in common politeness, to say something. Hardly attending himself to his own words, he began with a commonplace phrase: "I regret, Monsieur Lomaque, that we have not had more opportunities of bettering our acquaintance."

"I feel deeply indebted," rejoined the land-steward, "to the admirable

Madame Danville for having chosen me as her escort hither from her son's estate near Lyons, and having thereby procured for me the honor of this introduction." Both Monsieur Lomaque's red-rimmed eyes were seized with a sudden fit of winking, as he made this polite speech. His enemies were accustomed to say that, whenever he was particularly insincere, or particularly deceitful, he always took refuge in the weakness of his eyes, and so evaded the trying ordeal of being obliged to look steadily at the person whom he was speaking with.

"I was pleased to hear you mention my late father's name, at dinner, in terms of high respect," continued Trudaine, resolutely keeping up the conversation. "Did you know him?"

"I am indirectly indebted to your excellent father," answered the landsteward, "for the very situation which I now hold. At a time when the good word of a man of substance and reputation was needed to save me from poverty and ruin, your father spoke that word. Since then I have, in my own very small way, succeeded in life, until I have risen to the honor of superintending the estate of Monsieur Danville."

"Excuse me, but your way of speaking of your present situation rather surprises me. Your father, I believe, was a merchant, just as Danville's father was a merchant; the only difference between them was that one failed and the other realized a large fortune. Why should you speak of yourself as honored by holding your present place?"

"Have you never heard?" exclaimed Lomaque, with an appearance of great astonishment, "or can you have heard, and forgotten, that Madame Danville is descended from one of the noble houses of France? Has she never told you, as she has often told me, that she condescended when she married her late husband; and that her great object in life is to get the title of her family (years since extinct in the male line) settled on her son?"

"Yes," replied Trudaine; "I remember to have heard something of this, and to have paid no great attention to it at the time, having little sympathy with such aspirations as you describe. You have lived many years in Danville's service, Monsieur Lomaque; have you"— he hesitated for a moment, then continued, looking the land-steward full in the face —"have you found him a good and kind master?"

Lomaque's thin lips seemed to close instinctively at the question, as if he were never going to speak again. He bowed — Trudaine waited — he only bowed again. Trudaine waited a third time. Lomaque looked at his host with perfect steadiness for an instant, then his eyes began to get weak again. "You seem to have some special interest," he quietly remarked, "if I may say so without offense, in asking me that question."

"I deal frankly, at all hazards, with every one," returned Trudaine; "and stranger as you are, I will deal frankly with you. I acknowledge that I have an interest in asking that question — the dearest, the tenderest of all interests." At those last words, his voice trembled for a moment, but he went on firmly; "from the beginning of my sister's engagement with Danville, I made it my duty not to conceal my own feelings; my conscience and my affection for Rose counseled me to be candid to the last, even though my candor should distress or offend others. When we first made the acquaintance of Madame Danville, and when I first discovered that her son's attentions to Rose were not unfavorably received, I felt astonished, and, though it cost me a hard effort, I did not conceal that astonishment from my sister —"

Lomaque, who had hitherto been all attention, started here, and threw up his hands in amazement. "Astonished, did I hear you say? Astonished, Monsieur Trudaine, that the attentions of a young gentleman, possessed of all the graces and accomplishments of a highly-bred Frenchman, should be favorably received by a young lady! Astonished that such a dancer, such a singer, such a talker, such a notoriously fascinating ladies' man as Monsieur Danville, should, by dint of respectful assiduity, succeed in making some impression on the heart of Mademoiselle Rose! Oh, Monsieur Trudaine, venerated Monsieur Trudaine, this is almost too much to credit!"

Lomaque's eyes grew weaker than ever, and winked incessantly as he uttered this apostrophe. At the end, he threw up his hands again, and blinked inquiringly all round him, in mute appeal to universal nature.

"When, in the course of time, matters were further advanced," continued Trudaine, without paying any attention to the interruption; "when the offer of marriage was made, and when I knew that Rose had in her own heart accepted it, I objected, and I did not conceal my objections —"

"Heavens!" interposed Lomaque again, clasping his hands this time with a look of bewilderment; "what objections, what possible objections to a man young and well-bred, with an immense fortune and an uncompromised character? I have heard of these objections; I know they have made bad blood; and I ask myself again and again, what can they be?"

"God knows I have often tried to dismiss them from my mind as fanciful and absurd," said Trudaine, "and I have always failed. It is impossible, in your presence, that I can describe in detail what my own impressions have been, from the first, of the master whom you serve. Let it be enough if I confide to you that I cannot, even now, persuade myself of the sincerity of his attachment to my sister, and that I feel — in spite of myself, in spite of my earnest desire to put the most implicit confidence in Rose's choice — a distrust of his character and temper, which now, on the eve of the marriage, amounts to positive terror. Long secret suffering, doubt, and suspense, wring this confession from me, Monsieur Lomaque, almost unawares, in defiance of caution, in defiance of all the conventionalities of society. You have lived for years under the same roof with this man; you have seen him in his most unguarded and private moments. I tempt you to betray no confidence — I only ask you if you can make me happy by telling me that I have been doing your master grievous injustice by my opinion of him? I ask you to take my hand, and tell me if you can, in all honor, that my sister is not risking the happiness of her whole life by giving herself in marriage to Danville tomorrow!"

He held out his hand while he spoke. By some strange chance, Lomaque happened just at that moment to be looking away toward those beauties of Nature which he admired so greatly. "Really, Monsieur Trudaine, really such an appeal from you, at such a time, amazes me." Having got so far, he stopped and said no more.

"When we first sat down together here, I had no thought of making this appeal, no idea of talking to you as I have talked," pursued the other. "My words have escaped me, as I told you, almost unawares; you must make allowances for them and for me. I cannot expect others, Monsieur Lomaque, to appreciate and understand my feelings for Rose. We two have lived alone in the world together; father, mother, kindred, they all died years since, and left us. I am so much older than my sister that I have learned to feel toward her more as a father than as a brother. All my life, all my dearest hopes, all my highest expectations, have centered in her. I was past the period of my boyhood when my mother put my little child sister's hand in mine, and said to me on her death-bed: 'Louis, be all to her that I have been, for she has no one left to look to but you.' Since then the loves and ambitions of other men have not been my loves or my ambitions. Sister Rose — as we all used to call her in those past days, as I love to call her still — Sister Rose has been the one aim, the one happiness, the one precious trust, the one treasured reward, of all my life. I have lived in this poor house, in this dull retirement, as in a paradise, because Sister Rose — my innocent, happy, bright-faced Eve — has lived here with me. Even if the husband of her choice had been the husband of mine, the necessity of parting with her would have been the hardest, the bitterest of trials. As it is, thinking what I think, dreading what I dread, judge what my feelings must be on the eve of her marriage; and know why, and with what object, I made the appeal which surprised you a moment since, but which cannot surprise you now. Speak if you will — I can say no more." He sighed bitterly; his head dropped on his breast, and the hand which he had extended to Lomaque trembled as he withdrew it and let it fall at his side.

The land-steward was not a man accustomed to hesitate, but he hesitated now. He was not usually at a loss for phrases in which to express himself, but he stammered at the very outset of his reply. "Suppose I answered," he began, slowly; "suppose I told you that you wronged him, would my testimony really be strong enough to shake opinions, or rather presumptions, which have been taking firmer and firmer hold of you for months and months past? Suppose, on the other hand, that my master had his little" (Lomaque hesitated before he pronounced the next word)—"his little — infirmities, let me say; but only hypothetically, mind that — infirmities; and suppose I had observed them, and was willing to confide them to you, what purpose would such a confidence answer now, at the eleventh hour, with Mademoiselle Rose's heart engaged, with the marriage fixed for tomorrow? No! no! trust me —"

Trudaine looked up suddenly. "I thank you for reminding me, Monsieur Lomaque, that it is too late now to make inquiries, and by consequence too late also to trust in others. My sister has chosen; and on the subject of that choice my lips shall be henceforth sealed. The events of the future are with God; whatever they may be, I hope I am strong enough to bear my part in them with the patience and the courage of a man! I apologize, Monsieur Lomaque, for having thoughtlessly embarrassed you by questions which I had no right to ask. Let us return to the house — I will show you the way."

Lomaque's lips opened, then closed again; he bowed uneasily, and his sallow complexion whitened for a moment.

Trudaine led the way in silence back to the house; the land-steward following slowly at a distance of several paces, and talking in whispers to himself. "His father was the saving of me," muttered Lomaque; "that is truth, and there is no getting over it; his father was the saving of me; and yet here am I— no! it's too late!— too late to speak — too late to act — too late to do anything!"

Close to the house they were met by the old servant.

"My young lady has just sent me to call you in to coffee, monsieur," said Guillaume. "She has kept a cup hot for you, and another cup for Monsieur Lomaque."

The land-steward started — this time with genuine astonishment. "For me!" he exclaimed. "Mademoiselle Rose has troubled herself to keep a cup of coffee hot for me?" The old servant stared; Trudaine stopped and looked back.

"What is there so very surprising," he asked, "in such an ordinary act of politeness on my sister's part?"

"Excuse me, Monsieur Trudaine," answered Lomaque; "you have not passed such an existence as mine — you are not a friendless old man — you have a settled position in the world, and are used to be treated with consideration. I am not. This is the first occasion in my life on which I find myself an object for the attention of a young lady, and it takes me by surprise. I repeat my excuses; pray let us go in."

Trudaine made no reply to this curious explanation. He wondered at it a little, however, and he wondered still more when, on entering the drawing-room, he saw Lomaque walk straight up to his sister, and — apparently not noticing that Danville was sitting at the harpsichord and singing at the time — address her confusedly and earnestly with a set speech of thanks for his hot cup of coffee. Rose looked perplexed, and half inclined to laugh, as she listened to him. Madame Danville, who sat by her side, frowned, and tapped the land-steward contemptuously on the arm with her fan.

"Be so good as to keep silent until my son has done singing," she said. Lomaque made a low bow, and retiring to a table in a corner, took up a newspaper lying on it. If Madame Danville had seen the expression that came over his face when he turned away from her, proud as she was, her aristocratic composure might possibly have been a little ruffled.

Danville had finished his song, had quitted the harpsichord, and was talking in whispers to his bride; Madame Danville was adding a word to the conversation every now and then; Trudaine was seated apart at the far end of the room, thoughtfully reading a letter which he had taken from his pocket, when an exclamation from Lomaque, who was still engaged with the newspaper, caused all the other occupants of the apartment to suspend their employments and look up.

"What is it?" asked Danville, impatiently.

"Shall I be interrupting if I explain?" inquired Lomaque, getting very weak in the eyes again, as he deferentially addressed himself to Madame Danville.

"You have already interrupted us," said the old lady, sharply; "so you may now just as well explain."

"It is a passage from the *Scientific Intelligence* which has given me great delight, and which will be joyful news for every one here." Saying this, Lomaque looked significantly at Trudaine, and then read from the newspaper these lines:

"ACADEMY OF SCIENCES, PARIS.— The vacant sub-professorship of chemistry has been offered, we are rejoiced to hear, to a gentleman whose modesty has hitherto prevented his scientific merits from becoming sufficiently prominent in the world. To the members of the academy he has been long since known as the originator of some of the most remarkable improvements in chemistry which have been made of late years — improvements, the credit of which he has, with rare, and we were almost about to add, culpable moderation, allowed others to profit by with impunity. No man in any profession is more thoroughly entitled to have a position of trust and distinction conferred on him by the State than the gentleman to whom we refer — M. Louis Trudaine."

Before Lomaque could look up from the paper to observe the impression which his news produced, Rose had gained her brother's side and was kissing him in a flutter of delight.

"Dear Louis," she cried, clapping her hands, "let me be the first to congratulate you! How proud and glad I am! You accept the professorship, of course?"

Trudaine, who had hastily and confusedly put his letter back in his pocket the moment Lomaque began to read, seemed at a loss for an answer. He patted his sister's hand rather absently, and said:

"I have not made up my mind; don't ask me why, Rose — at least not now, not just now." An expression of perplexity and distress came over his face, as he gently motioned her to resume her chair.

"Pray, is a sub-professor of chemistry supposed to hold the rank of a gentleman?" asked Madame Danville, without the slightest appearance of any special interest in Lomaque's news.

"Of course not," replied her son, with a sarcastic laugh; "he is expected to work and make himself useful. What gentleman does that?"

"Charles!" exclaimed the old lady, reddening with anger.

"Bah!" cried Danville, turning his back on her, "enough of chemistry. Lomaque, now you have begun reading the newspaper, try if you can't find something interesting to read about. What are the last accounts from Paris? Any more symptoms of a general revolt?"

Lomaque turned to another part of the paper. "Bad, very bad prospects for the restoration of tranquillity," he said. "Necker, the people's Minister, is dismissed. Placards against popular gatherings are posted all over Paris. The Swiss Guards have been ordered to the Champs Elysees, with four pieces of artillery. No more is yet known, but the worst is dreaded. The breach between the aristocracy and the people is widening fatally almost hour by hour."

Here he stopped and laid down the newspaper. Trudaine took it from him, and shook his head forebodingly as he looked over the paragraph which had just been read.

"Bah!" cried Madame Danville. "The People, indeed! Let those four pieces of artillery be properly loaded, let the Swiss Guards do their duty, and we shall hear no more of the People!"

"I advise you not to be sure of that," said her son, carelessly; "there are rather too many people in Paris for the Swiss Guards to shoot conveniently. Don't hold your head too aristocratically high, mother, till we are quite certain which way the wind really does blow. Who knows if I may not have to bow just as low one of these days to King Mob as ever you courtesied in your youth to King Louis the Fifteenth?"

He laughed complacently as he ended, and opened his snuff-box. His mother rose from her chair, her face crimson with indignation.

"I won't hear you talk so — it shocks, it horrifies me!" she exclaimed, with vehement gesticulation. "No, no! I decline to hear another word. I decline to sit by patiently while my son, whom I love, jests at the most sacred principles, and sneers at the memory of an anointed king. This is my reward, is it, for having yielded and having come here, against all the laws of etiquette, the night before the marriage? I comply no longer; I resume my own will and my own way. I order you, my son, to accompany me back to Rouen.

We are the bridegroom's party, and we have no business overnight at the house of the bride. You meet no more till you meet at the church. Justin, my coach! Lomaque, pick up my hood. Monsieur Trudaine, thanks for your hospitality; I shall hope to return it with interest the first time you are in our neighborhood. Mademoiselle, put on your best looks tomorrow, along with your wedding finery; remember that my son's bride must do honor to my son's taste. Justin! my coach — drone, vagabond, idiot, where is my coach?"

"My mother looks handsome when she is in a passion, does she not, Rose?" said Danville, quietly putting up his snuff-box as the old lady sailed out of the room. "Why, you seem quite frightened, love," he added, taking her hand with his easy, graceful air; "frightened, let me assure you, without the least cause. My mother has but that one prejudice, and that one weak point, Rose. You will find her a very dove for gentleness, as long as you do not wound her pride of caste. Come, come, on this night, of all others, you must not send me away with such a face as that."

He bent down and whispered to her a bridegroom's compliment, which brought the blood back to her cheek in an instant.

"Ah, how she loves him — how dearly she loves him!" thought her brother, watching her from his solitary corner of the room, and seeing the smile that brightened her blushing face when Danville kissed her hand at parting.

Lomaque, who had remained imperturbably cool during the outbreak of the old lady's anger — Lomaque, whose observant eyes had watched sarcastically the effect of the scene between mother and son on Trudaine and his sister, was the last to take leave. After he had bowed to Rose with a certain gentleness in his manner, which contrasted strangely with his wrinkled, haggard face, he held out his hand to her brother "I did not take your hand when we sat together on the bench," he said; "may I take it now?"

Trudaine met his advance courteously, but in silence. "You may alter your opinion of me one of these days." Adding those words in a whisper, Monsieur Lomaque bowed once more to the bride and went out.

For a few minutes after the door had closed the brother and sister kept silence. "Our last night together at home!" That was the thought which now filled the heart of each. Rose was the first to speak. Hesitating a little as she approached her brother, she said to him, anxiously:

"I am sorry for what happened with Madame Danville, Louis. Does it make you think the worse of Charles?"

"I can make allowance for Madame Danville's anger," returned Trudaine, evasively, "because she spoke from honest conviction."

"Honest?" echoed Rose, sadly, "honest?— ah, Louis! I know you are thinking disparagingly of Charles's convictions, when you speak so of his mother's."

Trudaine smiled and shook his head; but she took no notice of the gesture of denial — only stood looking earnestly and wistfully into his face. Her eyes began to fill; she suddenly threw her arms round his neck, and whispered to him: "Oh, Louis, Louis! how I wish I could teach you to see Charles with my eyes!"

He felt her tears on his cheek as she spoke, and tried to reassure her.

"You shall teach me, Rose — you shall, indeed. Come, come, we must keep up our spirits, or how are you to look your best tomorrow?"

He unclasped her arms, and led her gently to a chair. At the same moment there was a knock at the door, and Rose's maid appeared, anxious to consult her mistress on some of the preparations for the wedding ceremony. No interruption could have been more welcome just at that time. It obliged Rose to think of present trifles, and it gave her brother an excuse for retiring to his study.

He sat down by his desk, doubting and heavy-hearted, and placed the letter from the Academy of Sciences open before him.

Passing over all the complimentary expressions which it contained, his eye rested only on these lines at the end: "During the first three years of your professorship, you will be required to reside in or near Paris nine months out of the year, for the purpose of delivering lectures and superintending experiments from time to time in the laboratories." The letter in which these lines occurred offered him such a position as in his modest self-distrust he had never dreamed of before; the lines themselves contained the promise of such vast facilities for carrying on his favorite experiments as he could never hope to command in his own little study, with his own limited means; and yet, there he now sat doubting whether he should accept or reject the tempting honors and advantages that were offered to him — doubting for his sister's sake!

"Nine months of the year in Paris," he said to himself, sadly; "and Rose is to pass her married life at Lyons. Oh, if I could clear my heart of its dread on her account — if I could free my mind of its forebodings for her future — how gladly I would answer this letter by accepting the trust it offers me!"

He paused for a few minutes, and reflected. The thoughts that were in him marked their ominous course in the growing paleness of his cheek, in the dimness that stole over his eyes. "If this cleaving distrust from which I cannot free myself should be in very truth the mute prophecy of evil to come — to come, I know not when — if it be so (which God forbid!), how soon she may want a friend, a protector near at hand, a ready refuge in the time of her trouble! Where shall she then find protection or refuge? With that passionate woman? With her husband's kindred and friends?"

He shuddered as the thought crossed his mind, and opening a blank sheet of paper, dipped his pen in the ink. "Be all to her, Louis, that I have been," he murmured to himself, repeating his mother's last words, and beginning the letter while he uttered them. It was soon completed. It expressed in the most respectful terms his gratitude for the offer made to him, and his inability to accept it, in consequence of domestic circumstances which it was needless to explain. The letter was directed, sealed; it only remained for him to place it in the post-bag, lying near at hand. At this last decisive act he hesitated. He had told Lomaque, and he had firmly believed himself, that he had conquered all ambitions for his sister's sake. He knew now, for the first time, that he had only lulled them to rest — he knew that the letter from Paris had aroused them. His answer was written, his hand was on the post-bag, and at that moment the whole struggle had to be risked over again — risked when he was most unfit for it! He was not a man under any ordinary circumstances to procrastinate, but he procrastinated now.

"Night brings counsel; I will wait till tomorrow," he said to himself, and put the letter of refusal in his pocket, and hastily quitted the laboratory.

PART FIRST. CHAPTER II.

*I*nexorably the important morrow came: irretrievably, for good or for evil, the momentous marriage-vow was pronounced. Charles Danville and Rose Trudaine were now man and wife. The prophecy of the magnificent sunset overnight had not proved false. It was a cloudless day on the marriage morning. The nuptial ceremonies had proceeded smoothly throughout, and had even satisfied Madame Danville. She returned with the wedding-party to Trudaine's house, all smiles and serenity. To the bride she was graciousness itself. "Good girl," said the old lady, following Rose into a corner, and patting her approvingly on the cheek with her fan; "good girl, you have looked well this morning — you have done credit to my son's taste. Indeed, you have pleased me, child! Now go upstairs, and get on your traveling-dress, and count on my maternal affection as long as you make Charles happy."

It had been arranged that the bride and bridegroom should pass their honeymoon in Brittany, and then return to Danville's estate near Lyons. The parting was hurried over, as all such partings should be. The carriage had driven off; Trudaine, after lingering long to look after it, had returned hastily to the house; the very dust of the whirling wheels had all dispersed; there was absolutely nothing to see; and yet there stood Monsieur Lomaque at the outer gate; idly, as if he was an independent man — calmly, as if no such responsibilities as the calling of Madame Danville's coach, and the escorting of Madame Danville back to Lyons, could possibly rest on his shoulders.

Idly and calmly, slowly rubbing his hands one over the other, slowly nodding his head in the direction by which the bride and bridegroom had departed, stood the eccentric land-steward at the outer gate. On a sudden the sound of footsteps approaching from the house seemed to arouse him. Once more he looked out into the road, as if he expected still to see the carriage of the newly-married couple. "Poor girl! ah, poor girl!" said Monsieur Lomaque softly to himself, turning round to ascertain who was coming from the house.

It was only the postman with a letter in his hand, and the post-bag crumpled up under his arm.

"Any fresh news from Paris, friend?" asked Lomaque.

"Very bad, monsieur," answered the postman. "Camille Desmoulins has appealed to the people in the Palais Royal; there are fears of a riot."

"Only a riot!" repeated Lomaque, sarcastically. "Oh, what a brave Government not to be afraid of anything worse! Any letters?" he added, hastily dropping the subject.

"None *to* the house," said the postman, "only one *from* it, given me by Monsieur Trudaine. Hardly worth while," he added, twirling the letter in his hand, "to put it into the bag, is it?"

Lomaque looked over his shoulder as he spoke, and saw that the letter was directed to the President of the Academy of Sciences, Paris.

"I wonder whether he accepts the place or refuses it?" thought the land-steward, nodding to the postman, and continuing on his way back to the house.

At the door he met Trudaine, who said to him, rather hastily, "You are going back to Lyons with Madame Danville, I suppose?"

"This very day," answered Lomaque.

"If you should hear of a convenient bachelor lodging, at Lyons, or near it," continued the other, dropping his voice and speaking more rapidly than before, "you would be doing me a favor if you would let me know about it."

Lomaque assented; but before he could add a question which was on the tip of his tongue, Trudaine had vanished in the interior of the house.

"A bachelor lodging!" repeated the land-steward, standing alone on the doorstep. "At or near Lyons! Aha! Monsieur Trudaine, I put your bachelor lodging and your talk to me last night together, and I make out a sum total which is, I think, pretty near the mark. You have refused that Paris appointment, my friend; and I fancy I can guess why."

He paused thoughtfully, and shook his head with ominous frowns and bitings of his lips.

"All clear enough in that sky," he continued, after a while, looking up at the lustrous midday heaven. "All clear enough there; but I think I see a little cloud rising in a certain household firmament already — a little cloud which hides much, and which I for one shall watch carefully."

PART SECOND. CHAPTER I.

Five years have elapsed since Monsieur Lomaque stood thoughtfully at the gate of Trudaine's house, looking after the carriage of the bride and bridegroom, and seriously reflecting on the events of the future. Great changes have passed over that domestic firmament in which he prophetically discerned the little warning cloud. Greater changes have passed over the firmament of France.

What was revolt five years ago is Revolution now — revolution which has ingulfed thrones, and principalities, and powers; which has set up crownless, inhereditary kings and counselors of its own, and has bloodily torn them down again by dozens; which has raged and raged on unrestrainedly in fierce earnest, until but one king can still govern and control it for a little while. That king is named Terror, and seventeen hundred and ninety-four is the year of his reign.

Monsieur Lomaque, land-steward no longer, sits alone in an official-looking room in one of the official buildings of Paris. It is another July evening, as fine as that evening when he and Trudaine sat talking together on the bench overlooking the Seine. The window of the room is wide open, and a faint, pleasant breeze is beginning to flow through it. But Lomaque breathes uneasily, as if still oppressed by the sultry midday heat; and there are signs of perplexity and trouble in his face as he looks down absently now and then into the street.

The times he lives in are enough of themselves to sadden any man's face. In the Reign of Terror no living being in all the city of Paris can rise in the morning and be certain of escaping the spy, the denunciation, the arrest, or the guillotine, before night. Such times are trying enough to oppress any man's spirits; but Lomaque is not thinking of them or caring for them now. Out of a mass of papers which lie before him on his old writing-table, he has just taken up and read one, which has carried his thoughts back to the past, and to the changes which have taken place since he stood alone on the doorstep of Trudaine's house, pondering on what might happen.

More rapidly even than he had foreboded those changes had occurred. In less time even than he had anticipated, the sad emergency for which Rose's brother had prepared, as for a barely possible calamity, overtook Trudaine, and called for all the patience, the courage, the self-sacrifice which he had to give for his sister's sake. By slow gradations downward, from bad to worse, her husband's character manifested itself less and less disguisedly almost day by day. Occasional slights, ending in habitual neglect; careless estrangement, turning to cool enmity; small insults, which ripened evilly to great injuries — these were the pitiless signs which showed her that she had risked all and lost all while still a young woman — these were the unmerited afflictions which found her helpless, and would have left her helpless, but for the ever-present comfort and support of her brother's self-denying love. From the first, Trudaine had devoted himself to meet such trials as now assailed him; and like a man he met them, in defiance alike of persecution from the mother and of insult from the son.

The hard task was only lightened when, as time advanced, public trouble began to mingle itself with private grief. Then absorbing political necessities came as a relief to domestic misery. Then it grew to be the one purpose and pursuit of Danville's life cunningly to shape his course so that he might move safely onward with the advancing revolutionary tide — he cared not whither, as long as he kept his possessions safe and his life out of danger. His mother, inflexibly true to her Old-World convictions through all peril, might entreat and upbraid, might talk of honor, and courage, and sincerity — he heeded her not, or heeded only to laugh. As he had taken the false way with his wife, so he was now bent on taking it with the world.

The years passed on; destroying changes swept hurricane-like over the old governing system of France; and still Danville shifted successfully with the shifting times. The first days of the Terror approached; in public and in private — in high places and in low — each man now suspected his brother. Crafty as Danville was, even he fell under suspicion at last, at headquarters in Paris, principally on his mother's account. This was his first political failure; and, in a moment of thoughtless rage and disappointment, he wreaked the irritation caused by it on Lomaque. Suspected himself, he in turn suspected the land-steward. His mother fomented the suspicion — Lomaque was dismissed.

In the old times the victim would have been ruined, in the new times he was simply rendered eligible for a political vocation in life. Lomaque was poor, quick-witted, secret, not scrupulous. He was a good patriot; he had good patriot friends, plenty of ambition, a subtle, cat-like courage, nothing to dread — and he went to Paris. There were plenty of small chances there for men of his caliber. He waited for one of them. It came; he made the most of it; attracted favorably the notice of the terrible Fouquier-Tinville; and won his way to a place in the office of the Secret Police.

Meanwhile, Danville's anger cooled down; he recovered the use of that cunning sense which had hitherto served him well, and sent to recall the discarded servant. It was too late. Lomaque was already in a position to set him at defiance — nay, to put his neck, perhaps, under the blade of the guillo-tine. Worse than this, anonymous letters reached him, warning him to lose no time in proving his patriotism by some indisputable sacrifice, and in silencing his mother, whose imprudent sincerity was likely ere long to cost her her life. Danville knew her well enough to know that there was but one way of saving her, and thereby saving himself. She had always refused to emigrate; but he now insisted that she should seize the first opportunity he could procure for her of quitting France until calmer times arrived.

Probably she would have risked her own life ten times over rather than have obeyed him; but she had not the courage to risk her son's too; and she yielded for his sake. Partly by secret influence, partly by unblushing fraud, Danville procured for her such papers and permits as would enable her to leave France by way of Marseilles. Even then she refused to depart, until she knew what her son's plans were for the future. He showed her a letter which he was about to dispatch to Robespierre himself, vindicating his suspected patriotism, and indignantly demanding to be allowed to prove it by filling some office, no matter how small, under the redoubtable triumvirate which then governed, or more properly terrified, France. The sight of this document reassured Madame Danville. She bade her son farewell, and departed at last, with one trusty servant, for Marseilles.

Danville's intention, in sending his letter to Paris, had been simply to save himself by patriotic bluster. He was thunderstruck at receiving a reply, taking him at his word, and summoning him to the capital to accept employment there under the then existing Government. There was no choice but to obey. So to Paris he journeyed, taking his wife with him into the very jaws of danger. He was then at open enmity with Trudaine; and the more anxious and alarmed he could make the brother feel on the sister's account, the better he was pleased. True to his trust and his love, through all dangers as through all persecutions, Trudaine followed them; and the street of their sojourn at Paris, in the perilous days of the Terror, was the street of his sojourn too.

Danville had been astonished at the acceptance of his proffered services; he was still more amazed when he found that the post selected for him was one of the superintendent's places in that very office of Secret Police in which

Lomaque was employed as agent. Robespierre and his colleagues had taken the measure of their man — he had money enough, and local importance enough to be worth studying. They knew where he was to be distrusted, and how he might be made useful. The affairs of the Secret Police were the sort of affairs which an unscrupulously cunning man was fitted to help on; and the faithful exercise of that cunning in the service of the State was insured by the presence of Lomaque in the office. The discarded servant was just the right sort of spy to watch the suspected master. Thus it happened that, in the office of the Secret Police at Paris, and under the Reign of Terror, Lomaque's old master was, nominally, his master still — the superintendent to whom he was ceremonially accountable, in public — the suspected man, whose slightest words and deeds he was officially set to watch, in private.

Ever sadder and darker grew the face of Lomaque as he now pondered alone over the changes and misfortunes of the past five years. A neighboring church-clock striking the hour of seven aroused him from his meditations. He arranged the confused mass of papers before him — looked toward the door, as if expecting some one to enter — then, finding himself still alone, recurred to the one special paper which had first suggested his long train of gloomy thoughts. The few lines it contained were signed in cipher, and ran thus:

"You are aware that your superintendent, Danville, obtained leave of absence last week to attend to some affairs of his at Lyons, and that he is not expected back just yet for a day or two. While he is away, push on the affair of Trudaine. Collect all the evidence, and hold yourself in readiness to act on it at a moment's notice. Don't leave the office till you have heard from me again. If you have a copy of the Private Instructions respecting Danville, which you wrote for me, send it to my house. I wish to refresh my memory. Your original letter is burned."

Here the note abruptly terminated. As he folded it up and put it in his pocket, Lomaque sighed. This was a very rare expression of feeling with him. He leaned back in his chair, and beat his nails impatiently on the table. Suddenly there was a faint little tap at the room door, and eight or ten men — evidently familiars of the new French Inquisition — quietly entered, and ranged themselves against the wall.

Lomaque nodded to two of them. "Picard and Magloire, go and sit down at that desk. I shall want you after the rest are gone." Saying this, Lomaque handed certain sealed and docketed papers to the other men waiting in the room, who received them in silence, bowed, and went out. Innocent spectators might have thought them clerks taking bills of lading from a merchant. Who could have imagined that the giving and receiving of Denunciations, Arrest-orders, and Death-warrants — the providing of its doomed human meal for the all-devouring guillotine — could have been managed so coolly and quietly, with such unruffled calmness of official routine?

"Now," said Lomaque, turning to the two men at the desk, as the door closed, "have you got those notes about you?" (They answered in the affirmative.) "Picard, you have the first particulars of this affair of Trudaine; so you must begin reading. I have sent in the reports; but we may as well go over the evidence again from the commencement, to make sure that nothing has been left out. If any corrections are to be made, now is the time to make them. Read, Picard, and lose as little time as you possibly can."

Thus admonished, Picard drew some long slips of paper from his pocket, and began reading from them as follows:

"Minutes of evidence collected concerning Louis Trudaine, suspected, on the denunciation of Citizen Superintendent Danville, of hostility to the sacred cause of liberty, and of disaffection to the sovereignty of the people. (1.) The suspected person is placed under secret observation, and these facts are elicited: He is twice seen passing at night from his own house to a house in the Rue de Clery. On the first night he carries with him money — on the second, papers. He returns without either. These particulars have been obtained through a citizen engaged to help Trudaine in housekeeping (one of the sort called Servants in the days of the Tyrants). This man is a good patriot, who can be trusted to watch Trudaine's actions. (2.) The inmates of the house in the Rue de Clery are numerous, and in some cases not so well known to the Government as could be wished. It is found difficult to gain certain information about the person or persons visited by Trudaine without having recourse to an arrest. (3.) An arrest is thought premature at this preliminary stage of the proceedings, being likely to stop the development of conspiracy, and give warning to the guilty to fly. Order thereupon given to watch and wait for the present. (4.) Citizen Superintendent Danville quits Paris for a short time. The office of watching Trudaine is then taken out of the hands of the undersigned, and is confided to his comrade, Magloire.— Signed, PICARD. Countersigned, LOMAQUE."

Having read so far, the police agent placed his papers on the writing-table, waited a moment for orders, and, receiving none, went out. No change came over the sadness and perplexity of Lomaque's face. He still beat his nails anxiously on the writing-table, and did not even look at the second agent as he ordered the man to read his report. Magloire produced some slips of paper precisely similar to Picard's and read from them in the same rapid, business-like, unmodulated tones:

"Affair of Trudaine. Minutes continued. Citizen Agent Magloire having been appointed to continue the surveillance of Trudaine, reports the discovery of additional facts of importance. (1.) Appearances make it probable that Trudaine meditates a third secret visit to the house in the Rue de Clery. The proper measures are taken for observing him closely, and the result is the implication of another person discovered to be connected with the supposed conspiracy. This person is the sister of Trudaine, and the wife of Citizen Superintendent Danville."

"Poor, lost creature! ah, poor, lost creature!" muttered Lomaque to himself, sighing again, and shifting uneasily from side to side, in his mangy old leathern armchair. Apparently, Magloire was not accustomed to sighs, interruptions, and expressions of regret from the usually imperturbable chief agent. He looked up from his papers with a stare of wonder. "Go on, Magloire!" cried Lomaque, with a sudden outburst of irritability. "Why the devil don't you go on?"—"All ready, citizen," returned Magloire, submissively, and proceeded:

"(2.) It is at Trudaine's house that the woman Danville's connection with her brother's secret designs is ascertained, through the vigilance of the before-mentioned patriot citizen. The interview of the two suspected persons is private; their conversation is carried on in whispers. Little can be overheard; but that little suffices to prove that Trudaine's sister is perfectly aware of his intention to proceed for the third time to the house in the Rue de Clery. It is further discovered that she awaits his return, and that she then goes back privately to her own house. (3.) Meanwhile, the strictest measures are taken for watching the house in the Rue de Clery. It is discovered that Trudaine's visits are paid to a man and woman known to the landlord and lodgers by the name of Dubois. They live on the fourth floor. It is impossible, at the time of the discovery, to enter this room, or to see the citizen and citoyenne Dubois, without producing an undesirable disturbance in the house and neighborhood. A police agent is left to watch the place, while search and arrest orders are applied for. The granting of these is accidentally delayed. When they are ultimately obtained, it is discovered that the man and the woman are both missing. They have not hitherto been traced. (4.) The landlord of the house is immediately arrested, as well as the police agent appointed to watch the premises. The landlord protests that he knows nothing of his tenants. It is suspected, however, that he has been tampered with, as also that Trudaine's papers, delivered to the citizen and citoyenne Dubois, are forged passports. With these and with money, it may not be impossible that they have already succeeded in escaping from France. The proper measures have been taken for stopping them, if they have not yet passed the frontiers. No further report in relation to them has yet been received (5.) Trudaine and his sister are under perpetual surveillance, and the undersigned holds himself ready for further orders.— Signed, MAGLOIRE. Countersigned, LOMAQUE."

Having finished reading his notes, Magloire placed them on the writing-table. He was evidently a favored man in the office, and he presumed upon his position; for he ventured to make a remark, instead of leaving the room in silence, like his predecessor Picard.

"When Citizen Danville returns to Paris," he began, "he will be rather astonished to find that in denouncing his wife's brother he had also unconsciously denounced his wife."

Lomaque looked up quickly, with that old weakness in his eyes which affected them in such a strangely irregular manner on certain occasions. Magloire knew what this symptom meant, and would have become confused if he had not been a police agent. As it was, he quietly backed a step or two from the table, and held his tongue.

"Friend Magloire," said Lomaque, winking mildly, "your last remark looks to me like a question in disguise. I put questions constantly to others; I never answer questions myself. You want to know, citizen, what our superintendent's secret motive is for denouncing his wife's brother? Suppose you try and find that out for yourself. It will be famous practice for you, friend Magloire — famous practice after office hours."

"Any further orders?" inquired Magloire, sulkily.

"None in relation to the reports," returned Lomaque. "I find nothing to alter or add on a revised hearing. But I shall have a little note ready for you immediately. Sit down at the other desk, friend Magloire; I am very fond of you when you are not inquisitive; pray sit down."

While addressing this polite invitation to the agent in his softest voice, Lomaque produced his pocketbook, and drew from it a little note, which he opened and read through attentively. It was headed: "Private Instructions relative to Superintendent Danville," and proceeded thus:

"The undersigned can confidently assert, from long domestic experience in Danville's household that his motive for denouncing his wife's brother is purely a personal one, and is not in the most remote degree connected with politics. Briefly, the facts are these: Louis Trudaine, from the first, opposed his sister's marriage with Danville, distrusting the latter's temper and disposition. The marriage, however, took place, and the brother resigned himself to await results — taking the precaution of living in the same neighborhood as his sister, to interpose, if need be, between the crimes which the husband might commit and the sufferings which the wife might endure. The results soon exceeded his worst anticipations, and called for the interposition for which he had prepared himself. He is a man of inflexible firmness, patience, and integrity, and he makes the protection and consolation of his sister the business of his life. He gives his brother-inlaw no pretext for openly quarreling with him. He is neither to be deceived, irritated, nor tired out, and he is Danville's superior every way — in conduct, temper, and capacity. Under these circumstances, it is unnecessary to say that his brother-inlaw's enmity toward him is of the most implacable kind, and equally unnecessary to hint at the perfectly plain motive of the denunciation.

"As to the suspicious circumstances affecting not Trudaine only, but his sister as well, the undersigned regrets his inability, thus far, to offer either explanation or suggestion. At this preliminary stage, the affair seems involved in impenetrable mystery."

Lomaque read these lines through, down to his own signature at the end. They were the duplicate Secret Instructions demanded from him in the paper which he had been looking over before the entrance of the two police agents. Slowly, and, as it seemed, unwillingly, he folded the note up in a fresh sheet of paper, and was preparing to seal it when a tap at the door stopped him. "Come in," he cried, irritably; and a man in traveling costume, covered with dust, entered, quietly whispered a word or two in his ear, and then went out. Lomaque started at the whisper, and, opening his note again, hastily wrote under his signature: "I have just heard that Danville has hastened his return to Paris, and may be expected back to-night." Having traced these lines, he closed, sealed, and directed the letter, and gave it to Magloire. The police agent looked at the address as he left the room; it was "To Citizen Robespierre, Rue Saint-Honore."

Left alone again, Lomaque rose, and walked restlessly backward and forward, biting his nails.

"Danville comes back to-night," he said to himself, "and the crisis comes with him. Trudaine a conspirator! Bah! conspiracy can hardly be the answer to the riddle this time. What is?"

He took a turn or two in silence — then stopped at the open window, looking out on what little glimpse the street afforded him of the sunset sky. "This time five years," he said, "Trudaine was talking to me on that bench overlooking the river; and Sister Rose was keeping poor hatchet-faced old Lomaque's cup of coffee hot for him! Now I am officially bound to suspect them both; perhaps to arrest them; perhaps — I wish this job had fallen into other hands. I don't want it — I don't want it at any price!"

He returned to the writing-table and sat down to his papers, with the dogged air of a man determined to drive away vexing thoughts by dint of sheer hard work. For more than an hour he labored on resolutely, munching a bit of dry bread from time to time. Then he paused a little, and began to think again. Gradually the summer twilight faded, and the room grew dark.

"Perhaps we shall tide over to-night, after all — who knows?" said Lomaque, ringing his handbell for lights. They were brought in, and with them ominously returned the police agent Magloire with a small sealed packet. It contained an arrest-order and a tiny three-cornered note, looking more like a love-letter, or a lady's invitation to a party, than anything else. Lomaque opened the note eagerly and read these lines neatly written, and signed with Robespierre's initials — M. R.— formed elegantly in cipher:

"Arrest Trudaine and his sister to-night. On second thoughts, I am not sure, if Danville comes back in time to be present, that it may not be all the better. He is unprepared for his wife's arrest. Watch him closely when it takes place, and report privately to me. I am afraid he is a vicious man; and of all things I abhor Vice."

"Any more work for me to-night?" asked Magloire, with a yawn.

"Only an arrest," replied Lomaque. "Collect our men; and when you're ready get a coach at the door."

"We were just going to supper," grumbled Magloire to himself, as he went out. "The devil seize the Aristocrats! They're all in such a hurry to get to the guillotine that they won't even give a man time to eat his victuals in peace!"

"There's no choice now," muttered Lomaque, angrily thrusting the arrest-order and the three-cornered note into his pocket. "His father was the saving of me; he himself welcomed me like an equal; his sister treated me like a gentleman, as the phrase went in those days; and now —"

He stopped and wiped his forehead — then unlocked his desk, produced a bottle of brandy, and poured himself out a glass of the liquor, which he drank by sips, slowly.

"I wonder whether other men get softer-hearted as they grow older!" he said. "I seem to do so, at any rate. Courage! courage! what must be, must. If I risked my head to do it, I couldn't stop this arrest. Not a man in the office but would be ready to execute it, if I wasn't."

Here the rumble of carriage-wheels sounded outside.

"There's the coach!" exclaimed Lomaque, locking up the brandy-bottle, and taking his hat. "After all, as this arrest is to be made, it's as well for them that I should make it."

Consoling himself as he best could with this reflection, Chief Police Agent Lomaque blew out the candles, and quitted the room.

PART SECOND. CHAPTER II.

*I*gnorant of the change in her husband's plans, which was to bring him back to Paris a day before the time that had been fixed for his return, Sister Rose had left her solitary home to spend the evening with her brother. They had sat talking together long after sunset, and had let the darkness steal on them insensibly, as people will who are only occupied with quiet, familiar conversation. Thus it happened, by a curious coincidence, that just as Lomaque was blowing out his candles at the office Rose was lighting the reading-lamp at her brother's lodgings.

Five years of disappointment and sorrow had sadly changed her to outward view. Her face looked thinner and longer; the once delicate red and white of her complexion was gone; her figure had wasted under the influence of some weakness, which had already made her stoop a little when she walked. Her manner had lost its maiden shyness, only to become unnaturally quiet and subdued. Of all the charms which had so fatally, yet so innocently, allured her heartless husband, but one remained — the winning gentleness of her voice. It might be touched now and then with a note of sadness, but the soft attraction of its even, natural tone still remained. In the marring of all other harmonies, this one harmony had been preserved unchanged. Her brother, though his face was careworn, and his manner sadder than of old, looked less altered from his former self. It is the most fragile material which soonest shows the flaw. The world's idol, Beauty, holds its frailest tenure of existence in the one Temple where we most love to worship it.

"And so you think, Louis, that our perilous undertaking has really ended well by this time?" said Rose, anxiously, as she lighted the lamp and placed the glass shade over it. "What a relief it is only to hear you say you think we have succeeded at last!"

"I said I hope, Rose," replied her brother.

"Well, even hoped is a great word from you, Louis — a great word from any one in this fearful city, and in these days of Terror."

She stopped suddenly, seeing her brother raise his hand in warning. They looked at each other in silence and listened. The sound of footsteps going slowly past the house — ceasing for a moment just beyond it — then going on again — came through the open window. There was nothing else, out-of-doors or in, to disturb the silence of the night — the deadly silence of Terror which, for months past, had hung over Paris. It was a significant sign of the times, that even a passing footstep, sounding a little strangely at night, was subject for suspicion, both to brother and sister — so common a subject, that they suspended their conversation as a matter of course, without exchanging a word of explanation, until the tramp of the strange footsteps had died away.

"Louis," continued Rose, dropping her voice to a whisper, after nothing more was audible, "when may I trust our secret to my husband?"

"Not yet!" rejoined Trudaine, earnestly. "Not a word, not a hint of it, till I give you leave. Remember, Rose, you promised silence from the first. Everything depends on your holding that promise sacred till I release you from it."

"I will hold it sacred; I will indeed, at all hazards, under all provocations," she answered.

"That is quite enough to reassure me — and now, love, let us change the subject. Even these walls may have ears, and the closed door yonder may be no protection." He looked toward it uneasily while he spoke. "By-the-by, I have come round to your way of thinking, Rose, about that new servant of mine — there is something false in his face. I wish I had been as quick to detect it as you were."

Rose glanced at him affrightedly. "Has he done anything suspicious? Have you caught him watching you? Tell me the worst, Louis."

"Hush! hush! my dear, not so loud. Don't alarm yourself; he has done nothing suspicious."

"Turn him off — pray, pray turn him off, before it is too late!"

"And be denounced by him, in revenge, the first night he goes to his Section. You forget that servants and masters are equal now. I am not supposed to keep a servant at all. I have a citizen living with me who lays me under domestic obligations, for which I make a pecuniary acknowledgment. No! no! if I do anything, I must try if I can't entrap him into giving me warning. But we have got to another unpleasant subject already — suppose I change the topic again? You will find a little book on that table there, in the corner — tell me what you think of it."

The book was a copy of Corneille's "Cid," prettily bound in blue morocco. Rose was enthusiastic in her praises. "I found it in a bookseller's shop, yesterday," said her brother, "and bought it as a present for you. Corneille is not an author to compromise any one, even in these times. Don't you remember saying the other day that you felt ashamed of knowing but little of our greatest dramatist?" Rose remembered well, and smiled almost as happily as in the old times over her present. "There are some good engravings at the beginning of each act," continued Trudaine, directing her attention rather earnestly to the illustrations, and then suddenly leaving her side when he saw that she became interested in looking at them.

He went to the window — listened — then drew aside the curtain, and looked up and down the street. No living soul was in sight. "I must have been mistaken," he thought, returning hastily to his sister; "but I certainly fancied I was followed in my walk today by a spy."

"I wonder," asked Rose, still busy over her book, "I wonder, Louis, whether my husband would let me go with you to see 'Le Cid' the next time it is acted."

"No!" cried a voice at the door; "not if you went on your knees to ask him."

Rose turned round with a scream. There stood her husband on the threshold, scowling at her, with his hat on, and his hands thrust doggedly into his pockets. Trudaine's servant announced him, with an insolent smile, during the pause that followed the discovery. "Citizen Superintendent Danville, to visit the citoyenne, his wife," said the fellow, making a mock bow to his master.

Rose looked at her brother, then advanced a few paces toward the door. "This is a surprise," she said, faintly; "has anything happened? We — we didn't expect you." Her voice failed her as she saw her husband advancing, pale to his very lips with suppressed anger.

"How dare you come here, after what I told you?" he asked, in quick, low tones.

She shrank at his voice almost as if he had struck her. The blood flew into her brother's face as he noticed the action; but he controlled himself, and, taking her hand, led her in silence to a chair.

"I forbid you to sit down in his house," said Danville, advancing still; "I order you to come back with me! Do you hear? I order you."

He was approaching nearer to her, when he caught Trudaine's eye fixed on him, and stopped. Rose started up, and placed herself between them.

"Oh, Charles, Charles!" she said to her husband, "be friends with Louis tonight, and be kind again to me. I have a claim to ask that much of you, though you may not think it!"

He turned away from her, and laughed contemptuously. She tried to speak again, but Trudaine touched her on the arm, and gave her a warning look.

"Signals!" exclaimed Danville; "secret signals between you!"

His eye, as he glanced suspiciously at his wife, fell on Trudaine's gift-book, which she still held unconsciously.

"What book is that?" he asked.

"Only a play of Corneille's," answered Rose; "Louis has just made me a present of it."

At this avowal Danville's suppressed anger burst beyond all control.

"Give it him back!" he cried, in a voice of fury. "You shall take no presents from him; the venom of the household spy soils everything he touches. Give it him back!" She hesitated. "You won't?" He tore the book from her with an oath, threw it on the floor, and set his foot on it.

"Oh, Louis! Louis! for God's sake, remember."

Trudaine was stepping forward as the book fell to the floor. At the same moment his sister threw her arms round him. He stopped, turning from fiery red to ghastly pale.

"No, no, Louis!" she said, clasping him closer; "not after five years' patience. No — no!"

He gently detached her arms.

"You are right, love. Don't be afraid; it is all over now."

Saying that, he put her from him, and in silence took up the book from the floor.

"Won't *that* offend you even?" said Danville, with an insolent smile. "You have a wonderful temper — any other man would have called me out!"

Trudaine looked back at him steadily; and taking out his handkerchief, passed it over the soiled cover of the book.

"If I could wipe the stain of your blood off my conscience as easily as I can wipe the stain of your boot off this book," he said quietly, "you should not live another hour. Don't cry, Rose," he continued, turning again to his sister: "I will take care of your book for you until you can keep it yourself."

"You will do this! you will do that!" cried Danville, growing more and more exasperated, and letting his anger got the better even of his cunning now. "Talk less confidently of the future — you don't know what it has in store for you. Govern your tongue when you are in my presence; a day may come when you will want my help — my help; do you hear that?"

Trudaine turned his face from his sister, as if he feared to let her see it when those words were spoken.

"The man who followed me today was a spy — Danville's spy!" That thought flashed across his mind, but he gave it no utterance. There was an instant's pause of silence; and through it there came heavily on the still night air the rumbling of distant wheels. The sound advanced nearer and nearer — advanced and ceased under the window.

Danville hurried to it, and looked out eagerly. "I have not hastened my return without reason. I wouldn't have missed this arrest for anything!" thought he, peering into the night.

The stars were out, but there was no moon. He could not recognize either the coach or the persons who got out of it, and he turned again into the interior of the room. His wife had sunk into a chair, her brother was locking up in a cabinet the book which he had promised to take care of for her. The dead silence made the noise of slowly ascending footsteps on the stairs painfully audible. At last the door opened softly.

"Citizen Danville, health and fraternity!" said Lomaque, appearing in the doorway, followed by his agents. "Citizen Louis Trudaine?" he continued, beginning with the usual form.

Rose started out of her chair; but her brother's hand was on her lips before she could speak.

"My name is Louis Trudaine," he answered.

"Charles!" cried his sister, breaking from him and appealing to her husband, "who are these men? What are they here for?"

He gave her no answer.

"Louis Trudaine," said Lomaque, slowly, drawing the order from his pocket, "in the name of the Republic, I arrest you."

"Rose, come back," cried Trudaine.

It was too late; she had broken from him, and in the recklessness of terror, had seized her husband by the arm.

"Save him!" she cried. "Save him, by all you hold dearest in the world! You are that man's superior, Charles — order him from the room!"

Danville roughly shook her hand off his arm.

"Lomaque is doing his duty. Yes," he added, with a glance of malicious triumph at Trudaine, "yes, doing his duty. Look at me as you please — your looks won't move me. I denounced you! I admit it — I glory in it! I have rid myself of an enemy, and the State of a bad citizen. Remember your secret visits to the house in the Rue de Clery!"

His wife uttered a cry of horror. She seized his arm again with both hands — frail, trembling hands — that seemed suddenly nerved with all the strength of a man's.

"Come here — come here! I must and will speak to you!"

She dragged him by main force a few paces back, toward an unoccupied corner of the room. With deathly cheeks and wild eyes she raised herself on tiptoe, and put her lips to her husband's ear. At that instant Trudaine called to her:

"Rose, if you speak I am lost!"

She stopped at the sound of his voice, dropped her hold on her husband's arm, and faced her brother, shuddering.

"Rose," he continued, "you have promised, and your promise is sacred. If you prize your honor, if you love me, come here — come here, and be silent."

He held out his hand. She ran to him; and, laying her head on his bosom, burst into a passion of tears.

Danville turned uneasily toward the police agents. "Remove your prisoner," he said. "You have done your duty here."

"Only half of it," retorted Lomaque, eying him attentively. "Rose Danville —"

"My wife!" exclaimed the other. "What about my wife?"

"Rose Danville," continued Lomaque, impassibly, "you are included in the arrest of Louis Trudaine."

Rose raised her head quickly from her brother's breast. His firmness had deserted him — he was trembling. She heard him whispering to himself, "Rose, too! Oh, my God! I was not prepared for that." She heard these words, and dashed the tears from her eyes, and kissed him, saying:

"I am glad of it, Louis. We risked all together — we shall now suffer together. I am glad of it!"

Danville looked incredulously at Lomaque, after the first shock of astonishment was over.

"Impossible!" he exclaimed. "I never denounced my wife. There is some mistake; you have exceeded your orders."

"Silence!" retorted Lomaque, imperiously. "Silence, citizen, and respect to a decree of the Republic!"

"You blackguard! show me the arrest-order!" said Danville. "Who has dared to denounce my wife?"

"You have!" said Lomaque, turning on him with a grin of contempt. "You — and 'blackguard' back in your teeth! You, in denouncing her brother! Aha! we work hard in our office; we don't waste time in calling names — we make discoveries. If Trudaine is guilty, your wife is implicated in his guilt. We know it; and we arrest her."

"I resist the arrest," cried Danville. "I am the authority here. Who opposes me?"

The impassible chief agent made no answer. Some new noise in the street struck his quick ear. He ran to the window and looked out eagerly.

"Who opposes me?" reiterated Danville.

"Hark!" exclaimed Lomaque, raising his hand. "Silence, and listen!"

The heavy, dull tramp of men marching together became audible as he spoke. Voices humming low and in unison the Marseillaise hymn, joined solemnly with the heavy, regular footfalls. Soon the flare of torch-light began to glimmer redder and redder under the dim, starlight sky.

"Do you hear that? Do you see the advancing torch-light?" cried

Lomaque, pointing exultingly into the street. "Respect to the national hymn, and to the man who holds in the hollow of his hand the destinies of all France! Hat off, Citizen Danville! Robespierre is in the street. His bodyguard, the Hard-hitters, are lighting him on his way to the Jacobin Club! Who shall oppose you, did you say? Your master and mine; the man whose signature is at the bottom of this order — the man who with a scratch of his pen can send both our heads rolling together into the sack of the guillotine! Shall I call to him as he passes the house? Shall I tell him that Superintendent Danville resists me in making an arrest? Shall I? Shall I?" And in the immensity of his contempt, Lomaque seemed absolutely to rise in stature, as he thrust the arrest order under Danville's eyes and pointed to the signature with the head of his stick.

Rose looked round in terror, as Lomaque spoke his last words — looked round, and saw her husband recoil before the signature on the arrest order, as if the guillotine itself had suddenly arisen before him. Her brother felt her shrinking back in his arms, and trembled for the preservation of her self-control if the terror and suspense of the arrest lasted any longer.

"Courage, Rose, courage!" he said. "You have behaved nobly; you must not fail now. No, no! Not a word more. Not a word till I am able to think clearly again, and to decide what is best. Courage, love; our lives depend on it. Citizen," he continued, addressing himself to Lomaque, "proceed with your duty — we are ready."

The heavy marching footsteps outside were striking louder and louder on the ground; the chanting voices were every moment swelling in volume; the dark street was flaming again with the brightening torch-light, as Lomaque, under pretext of giving Trudaine his hat, came close to him, and, turning his back toward Danville, whispered: "I have not forgotten the eve of the wedding and the bench on the river bank."

Before Trudaine could answer, he had taken Rose's cloak and hood from one of his assistants, and was helping her on with it. Danville, still pale and trembling, advanced a step when he saw these preparations for departure, and addressed a word or two to his wife; but he spoke in low tones, and the fast-advancing march of feet and sullen low roar of singing outside drowned his voice. An oath burst from his lips, and he struck his fist, in impotent fury, on a table near him.

"The seals are set on everything in this room and in the bedroom," said Magloire, approaching Lomaque, who nodded and signed to him to bring up the other police agents at the door.

"Ready," cried Magloire, coming forward immediately with his men, and raising his voice to make himself heard. "Where to?"

Robespierre and his Hard-hitters were passing the house. The smoke of the torch-light was rolling in at the window; the tramping footsteps struck heavier and heavier on the ground; the low sullen roar of the Marseillaise was swelling to its loudest, as Lomaque referred for a moment to his arrest-order, and then answered:

"To the prison of St. Lazare!"

PART SECOND. CHAPTER III.

The head jailer of St. Lazare stood in the outer hall of the prison, two days after the arrest at Trudaine's lodgings, smoking his morning pipe. Looking toward the courtyard gate, he saw the wicket opened, and a privileged man let in, whom he soon recognized as the chief agent of the second section of Secret Police. "Why, friend Lomaque," cried the jailer, advancing toward the courtyard, "what brings you here this morning, business or pleasure?"

"Pleasure, this time, citizen. I have an idle hour or two to spare for a walk. I find myself passing the prison, and I can't resist calling in to see how my friend the head jailer is getting on." Lomaque spoke in a surprisingly brisk and airy manner. His eyes were suffering under a violent fit of weakness and winking; but he smiled, notwithstanding, with an air of the most inveterate cheerfulness. Those old enemies of his, who always distrusted him most when his eyes were most affected, would have certainly disbelieved every word of the friendly speech he had just made, and would have assumed it as a matter of fact that his visit to the head jailer had some specially underhand business at the bottom of it.

"How am I getting on?" said the jailer, shaking his head. "Overworked, friend — overworked. No idle hours in our department. Even the guillotine is getting too slow for us!"

"Sent off your batch of prisoners for trial this morning?" asked Lomaque, with an appearance of perfect unconcern.

"No; they're just going," answered the other. "Come and have a look at them." He spoke as if the prisoners were a collection of pictures on view, or a set of dresses just made up. Lomaque nodded his head, still with his air of happy, holiday carelessness. The jailer led the way to an inner hall; and, pointing lazily with his pipe-stem, said: "Our morning batch, citizen, just ready for the baking."

In one corner of the hall were huddled together more than thirty men and women of all ranks and ages; some staring round them with looks of blank despair; some laughing and gossiping recklessly. Near them lounged a guard of "Patriots," smoking, spitting, and swearing. Between the patriots and the prisoners sat, on a rickety stool, the second jailer — a humpbacked man, with an immense red mustache — finishing his breakfast of broad beans, which he scooped out of a basin with his knife, and washed down with copious draughts of wine from a bottle. Carelessly as Lomaque looked at the shocking scene before him, his quick eyes contrived to take note of every prisoner's face, and to descry in a few minutes Trudaine and his sister standing together at the back of the group.

"Now then, Apollo!" cried the head jailer, addressing his subordinate by a facetious prison nickname, "don't be all day starting that trumpery batch of yours. And harkye, friend, I have leave of absence, on business, at my Section this afternoon. So it will be your duty to read the list for the guillotine, and chalk the prisoners' doors before the cart comes tomorrow morning. 'Ware the bottle, Apollo, today; 'ware the bottle, for fear of accidents with the death-list tomorrow."

"Thirsty July weather, this — eh, citizen?" said Lomaque, leaving the head jailer, and patting the hunchback in the friendliest manner on the shoulder. "Why, how you have got your batch huddled up together this morning! Shall I help you to shove them into marching order? My time is quite at your disposal. This is a holiday morning with me!"

"Ha, ha, ha! what a jolly dog he is on his holiday morning!" exclaimed the head jailer, as Lomaque — apparently taking leave of his natural character altogether in the exhilaration of an hour's unexpected leisure — began pushing and pulling the prisoners into rank, with humorous mock apologies, at which not the officials only, but many of the victims themselves — reckless victims of a reckless tyranny — laughed heartily. Persevering to the last in his practical jest, Lomaque contrived to get close to Trudaine for a minute, and to give him one significant look before he seized him by the shoulders, like the rest. "Now, then, rear-guard," cried Lomaque, pushing Trudaine on, "close the line of march, and mind you keep step with your young woman there. Pluck up your spirits, citoyenne! one gets used to everything in this world, even to the guillotine!"

While he was speaking and pushing at the same time, Trudaine felt a piece of paper slip quickly between his neck and his cravat. "Courage!" he whispered, pressing his sister's hand, as he saw her shuddering under the assumed brutality of Lomaque's joke.

Surrounded by the guard of "Patriots," the procession of prisoners moved slowly into the outer courtyard, on its way to the revolutionary tribunal, the humpbacked jailer bringing up the rear. Lomaque was about to follow at some little distance, but the head jailer hospitably expostulated. "What a hurry you're in!" said he. "Now that incorrigible drinker, my second in command, has gone off with his batch, I don't mind asking you to step in and have a drop of wine."

"Thank you," answered Lomaque; "but I have rather a fancy for hearing the trial this morning. Suppose I come back afterward? What time do you go to your Section? At two o'clock, eh? Good! I shall try if I can't get here soon after one." With these words he nodded and went out. The brilliant sunlight in the courtyard made him wink faster than ever. Had any of his old enemies been with him, they would have whispered within themselves, "If you mean to come back at all, Citizen Lomaque, it will not be soon after one!"

On his way through the streets, the chief agent met one or two police office friends, who delayed his progress; so that when he arrived at the revolutionary tribunal the trials of the day were just about to begin.

The principal article of furniture in the Hall of Justice was a long, clumsy, deal table, covered with green baize. At the head of this table sat the president and his court, with their hats on, backed by a heterogeneous collection of patriots officially connected in various ways with the proceedings that were to take place. Below the front of the table, a railed-off space, with a gallery beyond, was appropriated to the general public — mostly represented, as to the gallery, on this occasion, by women, all sitting together on forms, knitting, shirt-mending, and baby-linen-making, as coolly as if they were at home. Parallel with the side of the table furthest from the great door of entrance was a low platform railed off, on which the prisoners, surrounded by their guard, were now assembled to await their trial. The sun shone in brightly from a high window, and a hum of ceaseless talking pervaded the hall cheerfully as Lomaque entered it. He was a privileged man here, as at the prison; and he made his way in by a private door, so as to pass to the prisoners' platform, and to walk round it, before he got to a place behind the president's chair. Trudaine, standing with his sister on the outermost limits of the group, nodded significantly as Lomaque looked up at him for an instant. He had contrived, on his way to the tribunal, to get an opportunity of reading the paper which the chief agent had slipped into his cravat. It contained these lines:

"I have just discovered who the citizen and citoyenne Dubois are. There is no chance for you but to confess everything. By that means you may inculpate a certain citizen holding authority, and may make it his interest, if he loves his own life, to save yours and your sister's."

Arrived at the back of the president's chair, Lomaque recognized his two trusty subordinates, Magloire and Picard, waiting among the assembled patriot officials, to give their evidence. Beyond them, leaning against the wall, addressed by no one, and speaking to no one, stood the superintendent, Danville. Doubt and suspense were written in every line of his face; the fretfulness of an uneasy mind expressed itself in his slightest gesture — even in his manner of passing a handkerchief from time to time over his face, on which the perspiration was gathering thick and fast already.

"Silence!" cried the usher of the court for the time being — a hoarse-voiced man in top-boots with a huge saber buckled to his side, and a bludgeon in his hand. "Silence for the Citizen President!" he reiterated, striking his bludgeon on the table.

The president rose and proclaimed that the sitting for the day had begun; then sat down again.

The momentary silence which followed was interrupted by a sudden confusion among the prisoners on the platform. Two of the guards sprang in among them. There was the thump of a heavy fall — a scream of terror from some of the female prisoners — then another dead silence, broken by one of the guards, who walked across the hall with a bloody knife in his hand, and laid it on the table. "Citizen President," he said, "I have to report that one of the prisoners has just stabbed himself." There was a murmuring exclamation, "Is that all?" among the women spectators, as they resumed their work. Suicide at the bar of justice was no uncommon occurrence, under the Reign of Terror.

"Name?" asked the president, quietly taking up his pen and opening a book.

"Martigne," answered the humpbacked jailer, coming forward to the table.

"Description?"

"Ex-royalist coach-maker to the tyrant Capet."

"Accusation?"

"Conspiracy in prison."

The president nodded, and entered in the book: "Martigne, coachmaker. Accused of conspiring in prison. Anticipated course of law by suicide. Action accepted as sufficient confession of guilt. Goods confiscated. 1st Thermidor, year two of the Republic."

"Silence!" cried the man with the bludgeon, as the president dropped a little sand on the entry, and signing to the jailer that he might remove the dead body, closed the book.

"Any special cases this morning?" resumed the president, looking round at the group behind him.

"There is one," said Lomaque, making his way to the back of the official chair. "Will it be convenient to you, citizen, to take the case of Louis Trudaine and Rose Danville first? Two of my men are detained here as witnesses, and their time is valuable to the Republic."

The president marked a list of names before him, and handed it to the crier or usher, placing the figures one and two against Louis Trudaine and Rose Danville.

While Lomaque was backing again to his former place behind the chair, Danville approached and whispered to him, "There is a rumor that secret information has reached you about the citizen and citoyenne Dubois. Is it true? Do you know who they are?"

"Yes," answered Lomaque; "but I have superior orders to keep the information to myself just at present."

The eagerness with which Danville put his question, and the disappointment he showed on getting no satisfactory answer to it, were of a nature to satisfy the observant chief agent that his superintendent was really as ignorant as he appeared to be on the subject of the man and woman Dubois. That one mystery, at any rate was still, for Danville, a mystery unrevealed.

"Louis Trudaine! Rose Danville!" shouted the crier, with another rap of his bludgeon.

The two came forward, at the appeal, to the front railing of the platform. The first sight of her judges, the first shock on confronting the pitiless curiosity of the audience, seemed to overwhelm Rose. She turned from deadly pale to crimson, then to pale again, and hid her face on her brother's shoulder. How fast she heard his heart throbbing! How the tears filled her eyes as she felt that his fear was all for her!

"Now," said the president, writing down their names. "Denounced by whom?"

Magloire and Picard stepped forward to the table. The first answered —"By Citizen Superintendent Danville."

The reply made a great stir and sensation among both prisoners and audience.

"Accused of what?" pursued the president.

"The male prisoner, of conspiracy against the Republic; the female prisoner, of criminal knowledge of the same."

"Produce your proofs in answer to this order."

Picard and Magloire opened their minutes of evidence, and read to the president the same particulars which they had formerly read to Lomaque in the secret police office.

"Good," said the president, when they had done, "we need trouble ourselves with nothing more than the identifying of the citizen and citoyenne Dubois, which, of course, you are prepared for. Have you heard the evidence?" he continued, turning to the prisoners; while Picard and Magloire consulted together in whispers, looking perplexedly toward the chief agent, who stood silent behind them. "Have you heard the evidence, prisoners? Do you wish to say anything? If you do, remember that the time of this tribunal is precious, and that you will not be suffered to waste it."

"I demand permission to speak for myself and for my sister," answered Trudaine. "My object is to save the time of the tribunal by making a confession."

The faint whispering, audible among the women spectators a moment before, ceased instantaneously as he pronounced the word confession. In the breathless silence, his low, quiet tones penetrated to the remotest corners of the hall; while, suppressing externally all evidences of the death-agony of hope within him, he continued his address in these words:

"I confess my secret visits to the house in the Rue de Clery. I confess that the persons whom I went to see are the persons pointed at in the evidence. And, lastly, I confess that my object in communicating with them as I did was to supply them with the means of leaving France. If I had acted from political motives to the political prejudice of the existing government, I admit that I should be guilty of that conspiracy against the Republic with which I am charged. But no political purpose animated, no political necessity urged me, in performing the action which has brought me to the bar of this tribunal. The persons whom I aided in leaving France were without political influence or political connections. I acted solely from private motives of humanity toward them and toward others — motives which a good republican may feel, and yet not turn traitor to the welfare of his country."

"Are you ready to inform the court, next, who the man and woman Dubois really are?" inquired the president, impatiently.

"I am ready," answered Trudaine. "But first I desire to say one word in reference to my sister, charged here at the bar with me." His voice grew less steady, and, for the first time, his color began to change, as Rose lifted her face from his shoulder and looked up at him eagerly. "I implore the tribunal to consider my sister as innocent of all active participation in what is charged against me as a crime —" He went on. "Having spoken with candor about myself, I have some claim to be believed when I speak of her; when I assert that she neither did help me nor could help me. If there be blame, it is mine only; if punishment, it is I alone who should suffer."

He stopped suddenly, and grew confused. It was easy to guard himself from the peril of looking at Rose, but he could not escape the hard trial to his self-possession of hearing her, if she spoke. Just as he pronounced the last sentence, she raised her face again from his shoulder, and eagerly whispered to him:

"No, no, Louis! Not that sacrifice, after all the others — not that, though you should force me into speaking to them myself!"

She abruptly quitted her hold of him, and fronted the whole court in an instant. The railing in front of her shook with the quivering of her arms and hands as she held by it to support herself! Her hair lay tangled on her shoulders; her face had assumed a strange fixedness; her gentle blue eyes, so soft and tender at all other times, were lit up wildly. A low hum of murmured curiosity and admiration broke from the women of the audience. Some rose eagerly from the benches; others cried:

"Listen, listen! she is going to speak!"

She did speak. Silvery and pure the sweet voice, sweeter than ever in sadness, stole its way through the gross sounds — through the coarse humming and the hissing whispers.

"My lord the president," began the poor girl firmly. Her next words were drowned in a volley of hisses from the women.

"Ah! aristocrat, aristocrat! None of your accursed titles here!" was their shrill cry at her. She fronted that cry, she fronted the fierce gestures which accompanied it, with the steady light still in her eyes, with the strange rigidity still fastened on her face. She would have spoken again through the uproar and execration, but her brother's voice overpowered her.

"Citizen president," he cried, "I have not concluded. I demand leave to complete my confession. I implore the tribunal to attach no importance to what my sister says. The trouble and terror of this day have shaken her intellects. She is not responsible for her words — I assert it solemnly, in the face of the whole court!"

The blood flew up into his white face as he made the asseveration. Even at that supreme moment the great heart of the man reproached him for yielding himself to a deception, though the motive of it was to save his sister's life.

"Let her speak! let her speak!" exclaimed the women, as Rose, without moving, without looking at her brother, without seeming even to have heard what he said, made a second attempt to address her judges, in spite of Trudaine's interposition.

"Silence!" shouted the man with the bludgeon. "Silence, you women! the citizen president is going to speak."

"The prisoner Trudaine has the ear of the court," said the president, "and may continue his confession. If the female prisoner wishes to speak, she may be heard afterward. I enjoin both the accused persons to make short work of it with their addresses to me, or they will make their case worse instead of better. I command silence among the audience, and if I am not obeyed, I will clear the hall. Now, prisoner Trudaine, I invite you to proceed. No more about your sister; let her speak for herself. Your business and ours is with the man and woman Dubois. Are you, or are you not, ready to tell the court who they are?"

"I repeat that I am ready," answered Trudaine. "The citizen Dubois is a

servant. The woman Dubois is the mother of the man who denounces me —
Superintendent Danville."

A low, murmuring, rushing sound of hundreds of exclaiming voices, all speaking, half-suppressedly, at the same moment, followed the delivery of the answer. No officer of the court attempted to control the outburst of astonishment. The infection of it spread to the persons on the platform, to the crier himself, to the judges of the tribunal, lounging, but the moment before, so carelessly silent in their chairs. When the noise was at length quelled, it was subdued in the most instantaneous manner by one man, who shouted from the throng behind the president's chair:

"Clear the way there! Superintendent Danville is taken ill!"

A vehement whispering and contending of many voices interrupting each other, followed; then a swaying among the assembly of official people; then a great stillness; then the sudden appearance of Danville, alone, at the table.

The look of him, as he turned his ghastly face toward the audience, silenced and steadied them in an instant, just as they were on the point of falling into fresh confusion. Every one stretched forward eagerly to hear what he would say. His lips moved; but the few words that fell from them were inaudible, except to the persons who happened to be close by him. Having spoken, he left the table supported by a police agent, who was seen to lead him toward the private door of the court, and, consequently, also toward the prisoners' platform. He stopped, however, halfway, quickly turned his face from the prisoners, and pointing toward the public door at the opposite side of the hall, caused himself to be led out into the air by that direction. When he had gone the president, addressing himself partly to Trudaine and partly to the audience, said:

"The Citizen Superintendent Danville has been overcome by the heat in the court. He has retired by my desire, under the care of a police agent, to recover in the open air; pledging himself to me to come back and throw a new light on the extraordinary and suspicious statement which the prisoner has just made. Until the return of Citizen Danville, I order the accused, Trudaine, to suspend any further acknowledgment of complicity which he may have to address to me. This matter must be cleared up before other matters are entered on. Meanwhile, in order that the time of the tribunal may not be wasted, I authorize the female prisoner to take this opportunity of making any statement concerning herself which she may wish to address to the judges."

"Silence him!" "Remove him out of court!" "Gag him!" "Guillotine him!" These cries rose from the audience the moment the president had done speaking. They were all directed at Trudaine, who had made a last desperate effort to persuade his sister to keep silence, and had been detected in the attempt by the spectators.

"If the prisoner speaks another word to his sister, remove him," said the president, addressing the guard round the platform.

"Good! we shall hear her at last. Silence! silence!" exclaimed the women, settling themselves comfortably on their benches, and preparing to resume their work.

"Rose Danville, the court is waiting to hear you," said the president, crossing his legs and leaning back luxuriously in his large armchair.

Amid all the noise and confusion of the last few minutes, Rose had stood ever in the same attitude, with that strangely fixed expression never altering on her face but once. When her husband made his way to the side of the table and stood there prominently alone, her lips trembled a little, and a faint shade of color passed swiftly over her cheeks. Even that slight change had vanished now — she was paler, stiller, more widely altered from her former self than ever, as she faced the president and said these words:

"I wish to follow my brother's example and make my confession, as he has made his. I would rather he had spoken for me; but he is too generous to say any words except such as he thinks may save me from sharing his punishment. I refuse to be saved, unless he is saved with me. Where he goes when he leaves this place, I will go; what he suffers, I will suffer; if he is to die, I believe God will grant me the strength to die resignedly with him!"

She paused for a moment, and half turned toward Trudaine — then checked herself instantly and went on: "This is what I now wish to say, as to my share in the offense charged against my brother. Some time ago, he told me one day that he had seen my husband's mother in Paris, disguised as a poor woman; that he had spoken to her, and forced her to acknowledge herself. Up to this time we had all felt certain that she had left France, because she held old-fashioned opinions which it is dangerous for people to hold now — had left France before we came to Paris. She told my brother that she had indeed gone (with an old, tried servant of the family to help and protect her) as far as Marseilles; and that, finding unforeseen difficulty there in getting further, she had taken it as a warning from Providence not to desert her son, of whom she was very passionately fond, and from whom she had been most unwilling to depart. Instead of waiting in exile for quieter times, she determined to go and hide herself in Paris, knowing her son was going there too. She assumed the name of her old and faithful servant, who declined to the last to leave her unprotected; and she proposed to live in the strictest secrecy and retirement, watching, unknown, the career of her son, and ready at a moment's notice to disclose herself to him, when the settlement of public affairs might reunite her safely to her beloved child. My brother thought this plan full of danger, both for herself, for her son, and for the honest old man who was risking his head for his mistress's sake. I thought so too; and in an evil hour I said to Louis: 'Will you try in secret to get my husband's mother away, and see that her faithful servant makes her really leave France this time?' I wrongly asked my brother to do this for a selfish reason of my own — a reason connected with my married life, which has not been a happy one. I had not succeeded in gaining my husband's affection, and was not treated kindly by him. My brother — who has always loved me far more dearly, I am afraid, than I have ever deserved — my brother increased his kindness to me, seeing me treated unkindly by my husband. This made ill-blood between them. My thought, when I asked my brother to do for me what I have said, was, that if we two in secret saved my husband's mother, without danger to him, from imperiling herself and her son, we should, when the time came for speaking of what we had done, appear to my husband in a new and better light. I should have shown how well I deserved his love, and Louis would have shown how well he deserved his brother-inlaw's gratitude; and so we should have made home happy at last, and all three have lived together affectionately. This was my thought; and when I told it to my brother, and asked him if there would be much risk, out of his kindness and indulgence toward me, he said 'No.' He had so used me to accept sacrifices for my happiness that I let him endanger himself to help me in my little household plan. I repent this bitterly now; I ask his pardon with my whole heart. If he is acquitted, I will try to show myself worthier of his love. If he is found guilty, I, too, will go to the scaffold, and die with my brother, who risked his life for my sake."

She ceased as quietly as she had begun, and turned once more to her brother.

As she looked away from the court and looked at him, a few tears came into her eyes, and something of the old softness of form and gentleness of expression seemed to return to her face. He let her take his hand, but he seemed purposely to avoid meeting the anxious gaze she fixed on him. His head sunk on his breast; he drew his breath heavily, his countenance darkened and grew distorted, as if he were suffering some sharp pang of physical pain. He bent down a little, and, leaning his elbow on the rail before him, covered his face with his hand; and so quelled the rising agony, so forced back the scalding tears to his heart. The audience had heard Rose in silence, and they preserved the same tranquillity when she had done. This was a rare tribute to a prisoner from the people of the Reign of Terror.

The president looked round at his colleagues, and shook his head suspiciously.

"This statement of the female prisoner's complicates the matter very seriously," said he. "Is there anybody in court," he added, looking at the persons behind his chair, "who knows where the mother of Superintendent Danville and the servant are now?"

Lomaque came forward at the appeal, and placed himself by the table.

"Why, citizen agent!" continued the president, looking hard at him, "are you overcome by the heat, too?"

"The fit seemed to take him, citizen president, when the female prisoner had made an end of her statement," exclaimed Magloire, pressing forward officiously.

Lomaque gave his subordinate a look which sent the man back directly to the shelter of the official group; then said, in lower tones than were customary with him:

"I have received information relative to the mother of Superintendent Danville and the servant, and am ready to answer any questions that may be put to me."

"Where are they now?" asked the president.

"She and the servant are known to have crossed the frontier, and are supposed to be on their way to Cologne. But, since they have entered Germany, their whereabouts is necessarily a matter of uncertainty to the republican authorities."

"Have you any information relative to the conduct of the old servant while he was in Paris?"

"I have information enough to prove that he was not an object for political suspicion. He seems to have been simply animated by servile zeal for the woman's interests; to have performed for her all the menial offices of a servant in private; and to have misled the neighbors by affected equality with her in public."

"Have you any reason to believe that Superintendent Danville was privy to his mother's first attempt at escaping from France?"

"I infer it from what the female prisoner has said, and for other reasons which it would be irregular to detail before the tribunal. The proofs can no doubt be obtained if I am allowed time to communicate with the authorities at Lyons and Marseilles."

At this moment Danville re-entered the court; and, advancing to the table, placed himself close by the chief agent's side. They looked each other steadily in the face for an instant.

"He has recovered from the shock of Trudaine's answer," thought Lomaque, retiring. "His hand trembles, his face is pale, but I can see regained self-possession in his eye, and I dread the consequences already."

"Citizen president," began Danville, "I demand to know if anything has transpired affecting my honor and patriotism in my absence?"

He spoke apparently with the most perfect calmness, but he looked nobody in the face. His eyes were fixed steadily on the green baize of the table beneath him.

"The female prisoner has made a statement, referring principally to herself and her brother," answered the president, "but incidentally mentioning a previous attempt on your mother's part to break existing laws by emigrating from France. This portion of the confession contains in it some elements of suspicion which seriously affect you —"

"They shall be suspicions no longer — at my own peril I will change them to certainties!" exclaimed Danville, extending his arm theatrically, and looking up for the first time. "Citizen president, I avow it with the fearless frankness of a good patriot; I was privy to my mother's first attempt at escaping from France."

Hisses and cries of execration followed this confession. He winced under them at first; but recovered his self-possession before silence was restored.

"Citizens, you have heard the confession of my fault," he resumed, turning with desperate assurance toward the audience; "now hear the atonement I have made for it at the altar of my country."

He waited at the end of that sentence, until the secretary to the tribunal had done writing it down in the report book of the court.

"Transcribe faithfully to the letter!" cried Danville, pointing solemnly to the open page of the volume. "Life and death hang on my words."

The secretary took a fresh dip of ink, and nodded to show that he was ready. Danville went on:

"In these times of glory and trial for France," he proceeded, pitching his voice to a tone of deep emotion, "what are all good citizens most sacredly bound to do? To immolate their dearest private affections and interests before their public duties! On the first attempt of my mother to violate the laws against emigration, by escaping from France, I failed in making the heroic sacrifice which inexorable patriotism demanded of me. My situation was more terrible than the situation of Brutus sitting in judgment on his own sons. I had not the Roman fortitude to rise equal to it. I erred, citizens — erred as Coriolanus did, when his august mother pleaded with him for the safety of Rome! For that error I deserved to be purged out of the republican community; but I escaped my merited punishment — nay, I even rose to the honor of holding an office under the Government. Time passed; and again my mother attempted an escape from France. Again, inevitable fate brought my civic virtue to the test. How did I meet this second supremest trial? By an atonement for past weakness, terrible as the trial itself. Citizens, you will shudder; but you will applaud while you tremble. Citizens, look! and while you look, remember well the evidence given at the opening of this case. Yonder stands the enemy of his country, who intrigued to help my mother to escape; here stands the patriot son, whose voice was the first, the only voice, to denounce him for the crime!" As he spoke, he pointed to Trudaine, then struck himself on the breast, then folded his arms, and looked sternly at the benches occupied by the spectators.

"Do you assert," exclaimed the president, "that at the time when you denounced Trudaine, you knew him to be intriguing to aid your mother's escape?"

"I assert it," answered Danville.

The pen which the president held dropped from his hand at that reply; his colleagues started, and looked at each other in blank silence.

A murmur of "Monster! monster!" began with the prisoners on the platform, and spread instantly to the audience, who echoed and echoed it again; the fiercest woman-republican on the benches joined cause at last with the haughtiest woman-aristocrat on the platform. Even in that sphere of direst discords, in that age of sharpest enmities, the one touch of Nature preserved its old eternal virtue, and roused the mother-instinct which makes the whole world kin.

Of the few persons in the court who at once foresaw the effect of Danville's answer on the proceedings of the tribunal, Lomaque was one. His sallow face whitened as he looked toward the prisoners' platform.

"They are lost," he murmured to himself, moving out of the group in which he had hitherto stood. "Lost! The lie which has saved that villain's head leaves them without the shadow of a hope. No need to stop for the sentence — Danville's infamous presence of mind has given them up to the guillotine!" Pronouncing these words, he went out hurriedly by a door near the platform, which led to the prisoners' waiting-room.

Rose's head sank again on her brother's shoulder. She shuddered, and leaned back faintly on the arm which he extended to support her. One of the female prisoners tried to help Trudaine in speaking consolingly to her; but the consummation of her husband's perfidy seemed to have paralyzed her at heart. She murmured once in her brother's ear, "Louis! I am resigned to die — nothing but death is left for me after the degradation of having loved that man." She said those words and closed her eyes wearily, and spoke no more.

"One other question, and you may retire," resumed the president, addressing Danville. "Were you cognizant of your wife's connection with her brother's conspiracy?"

Danville reflected for a moment, remembered that there were witnesses in court who could speak to his language and behavior on the evening of his wife's arrest, and resolved this time to tell the truth.

"I was not aware of it," he answered. "Testimony in my favor can be called which will prove that when my wife's complicity was discovered I was absent from Paris."

Heartlessly self-possessed as he was, the public reception of his last reply had shaken his nerve. He now spoke in low tones, turning his back on the spectators, and fixing his eyes again on the green baize of the table at which he stood.

"Prisoners, have you any objection to make, any evidence to call, invalidating the statement by which Citizen Danville has cleared himself of suspicion?" inquired the president.

"He has cleared himself by the most execrable of all falsehoods," answered Trudaine. "If his mother could be traced and brought here, her testimony would prove it."

"Can you produce any other evidence in support of your allegation?" asked the president.

"I cannot."

"Citizen Superintendent Danville, you are at liberty to retire. Your statement will be laid before the authority to whom you are officially responsible. Either you merit a civic crown for more than Roman virtue, or —" Having got thus far, the president stopped abruptly, as if unwilling to commit himself too soon to an opinion, and merely repeated, "You may retire."

Danville left the court immediately, going out again by the public door. He was followed by murmurs from the women's benches, which soon ceased, however, when the president was observed to close his note-book, and turn round toward his colleagues. "The sentence!" was the general whisper now. "Hush, hush — the sentence!"

After a consultation of a few minutes with the persons behind him, the president rose, and spoke the momentous words:

"Louis Trudaine and Rose Danville, the revolutionary tribunal, having heard the charge against you, and having weighed the value of what you have said in answer to it, decides that you are both guilty, and condemns you to the penalty of death."

Having delivered the sentence in those terms, he sat down again, and placed a mark against the two first condemned names on the list of prisoners. Immediately afterward the next case was called on, and the curiosity of the audience was stimulated by a new trial.

PART SECOND. CHAPTER IV.

The waiting-room of the revolutionary tribunal was a grim, bare place, with a dirty stone floor, and benches running round the walls. The windows were high and barred; and at the outer door, leading into the street, two sentinels kept watch. On entering this comfortless retreat from the court, Lomaque found it perfectly empty. Solitude was just then welcome to him. He remained in the waiting-room, walking slowly from end to end over the filthy pavement, talking eagerly and incessantly to himself.

After a while, the door communicating with the tribunal opened, and the humpbacked jailer made his appearance, leading in Trudaine and Rose.

"You will have to wait here," said the little man, "till the rest of them have been tried and sentenced; and then you will all go back to prison in a lump. Ha, citizen," he continued, observing Lomaque at the other end of the hall, and bustling up to him. "Here still, eh? If you were going to stop much longer, I should ask a favor of you."

"I am in no hurry," said Lomaque, with a glance at the two prisoners.

"Good!" cried the humpback, drawing his hand across his mouth; "I am parched with thirst, and dying to moisten my throat at the wine-shop over the way. Just mind that man and woman while I'm gone, will you? It's the merest form — there's a guard outside, the windows are barred, the tribunal is within hail. Do you mind obliging me?"

"On the contrary, I am glad of the opportunity."

"That's a good fellow — and, remember, if I am asked for, you must say I was obliged to quit the court for a few minutes, and left you in charge."

With these words, the humpbacked jailer ran off to the wine-shop.

He had scarcely disappeared before Trudaine crossed the room, and caught Lomaque by the arm.

"Save her," he whispered; "there is an opportunity — save her!" His face was flushed — his eyes wandered — his breath on the chief agent's cheek, while he spoke, felt scorching hot. "Save her!" he repeated, shaking Lomaque by the arm, and dragging him toward the door. "Remember all you owe to my father — remember our talk on that bench by the river — remember what you said to me yourself on the night of the arrest — don't wait to think — save her, and leave me without a word! If I die alone, I can die as a man should; if she goes to the scaffold by my side, my heart will fail me — I shall die the death of a coward! I have lived for her life — let me die for it, and I die happy!"

He tried to say more, but the violence of his agitation forbade it. He could only shake the arm he held again and again, and point to the bench on which Rose sat — her head sunk on her bosom, her hands crossed listlessly on her lap.

"There are two armed sentinels outside — the windows are barred — you are without weapons — and even if you had them, there is a guard-house within hail on one side of you, and the tribunal on the other. Escape from this room is impossible," answered Lomaque.

"Impossible!" repeated the other, furiously. "You traitor! you coward! can you look at her sitting there helpless, her very life ebbing away already with every minute that passes, and tell me coolly that escape is impossible?"

In the frenzy of his grief and despair, he lifted his disengaged hand threateningly while he spoke. Lomaque caught him by the wrist, and drew him toward a window open at the top.

"You are not in your right senses," said the chief agent, firmly; "anxiety and apprehension on your sister's account have shaken your mind. Try to compose yourself, and listen to me. I have something important to say —" (Trudaine looked at him incredulously.) "Important," continued Lomaque, "as affecting your sister's interests at this terrible crisis."

That last appeal had an instantaneous effect. Trudaine's outstretched hand dropped to his side, and a sudden change passed over his expression.

"Give me a moment," he said, faintly; and turning away, leaned against the wall and pressed his burning forehead on the chill, damp stone. He did not raise his head again till he had mastered himself, and could say quietly, "Speak; I am fit to hear you, and sufficiently in my senses to ask your forgiveness for what I said just now."

"When I left the tribunal and entered this room," Lomaque began in a whisper, "there was no thought in my mind that could be turned to good account, either for your sister or for you. I was fit for nothing but to deplore the failure of the confession which I came to St. Lazare to suggest to you as your best plan of defense. Since then, an idea has struck me, which may be useful — an idea so desperate, so uncertain — involving a proposal so absolutely dependent, as to its successful execution, on the merest chance, that I refuse to confide it to you except on one condition."

"Mention the condition! I submit to it before hand."

"Give me your word of honor that you will not mention what I am about to say to your sister until I grant you permission to speak. Promise me that when you see her shrinking before the terrors of death to-night, you will have self-restraint enough to abstain from breathing a word of hope to her. I ask this, because there are ten — twenty — fifty chances to one that there *is* no hope."

"I have no choice but to promise," answered Trudaine.

Lomaque produced his pocket-book and pencil before he spoke again.

"I will enter into particulars as soon as I have asked a strange question of you," he said. "You have been a great experimenter in chemistry in your time — is your mind calm enough, at such a trying moment as this, to answer a question which is connected with chemistry in a very humble way? You seem astonished. Let me put the question at once. Is there any liquid or powder, or combination of more than one ingredient known, which will remove writing from paper, and leave no stain behind?"

"Certainly! But is that all the question? Is there no greater difficulty?"

"None. Write the prescription, whatever it may be, on that leaf," said the other, giving him the pocket-book. "Write it down, with plain directions for use." Trudaine obeyed. "This is the first step," continued Lomaque, putting the book in his pocket, "toward the accomplishment of my purpose — my uncertain purpose, remember! Now, listen; I am going to put my own head in danger for the chance of saving yours and your sister's by tampering with the death-list. Don't interrupt me! If I can save one, I can save the other. Not a word about gratitude! Wait till you know the extent of your obligation. I tell you plainly, at the outset, there is a motive of despair, as well as a motive of pity, at the bottom of the action in which I am now about to engage. Silence! I insist on it. Our time is short; it is for me to speak, and for you to listen. The president of the tribunal has put the deathmark against your names on the prison list of today. That list, when the trials are over and it is marked to the end, will be called in this room before you are taken to St. Lazare. It will then be sent to Robespierre, who will keep it, having a copy made of it the moment it is delivered, for circulation among his colleagues — St. Just, and the rest. It is my business to make a duplicate of this copy in the first instance. The duplicate will be compared with the original, and possibly with the copy, too, either by Robespierre himself, or by some one in whom he can place implicit trust, and will then be sent to St. Lazare without passing through my hands again. It will be read in public the moment it is received, at the grating of the prison, and will afterward be kept by the jailer, who will refer to it, as he goes round in the evening with a piece of chalk, to mark the cell doors of the prisoners destined for the guillotine tomorrow. That duty happens, today, to fall to the hunchback whom you saw speaking to me. He is a confirmed drinker, and I mean to tempt him with such wine as he rarely tastes. If — after the reading of the list in public, and before the marking of the cell doors — I can get him to sit down to the bottle, I will answer for making him drunk, for getting the list out of his pocket, and for wiping your names out of it with the prescription you have just written for me. I shall write all the names, one under another, just irregularly enough in my duplicate to prevent the interval left by the erasure from being easily observed. If I succeed in this, your door will not be marked, and your names will not be called tomorrow morning when the tumbrils come for the guillotine. In the present confusion of prisoners pouring in every day for trial, and prisoners pouring out every day for execution, you will have the best possible chance of security against awkward inquiries, if you play your cards properly, for a good fortnight or ten days at least. In that time —"

"Well! well!" cried Trudaine, eagerly.

Lomaque looked toward the tribunal door, and lowered his voice to a fainter whisper before he continued, "In that time Robespierre's own head may fall into the sack! France is beginning to sicken under the Reign of Terror. Frenchmen of the Moderate faction, who have lain hidden for months in cellars and lofts, are beginning to steal out and deliberate by twos and threes together, under cover of the night. Robespierre has not ventured for weeks past to face the Convention Committee. He only speaks among his own friends at the Jacobins. There are rumors of a terrible discovery made by Carnot, of a desperate resolution taken by Tallien. Men watching behind the scenes see that the last days of the Terror are at hand. If Robespierre is beaten in the approaching struggle, you are saved — for the new reign must be a Reign of Mercy. If he conquers, I have only put off the date of your death and your sister's, and have laid my own neck under the axe. Those are your chances — this is all I can do."

He paused, and Trudaine again endeavored to speak such words as might show that he was not unworthy of the deadly risk which Lomaque was prepared to encounter. But once more the chief agent peremptorily and irritably interposed:

"I tell you, for the third time," he said, "I will listen to no expressions of gratitude from you till I know when I deserve them. It is true that I recollect your father's timely kindness to me — true that I have not forgotten what passed, five years since at your house by the river-side. I remember everything, down to what you would consider the veriest trifle — that cup of coffee, for instance, which your sister kept hot for me. I told you then that you would think better of me some day. I know that you do now. But this is not all. You want to glorify me to my face for risking my life for you. I won't hear you, because my risk is of the paltriest kind. I am weary of my life. I can't look back to it with pleasure. I am too old to look forward to what is left of it with hope. There was something in that night at your house before the wedding — something in what you said, in what your sister did — which altered me. I have had my days of gloom and self-reproach, from time to time, since then. I have sickened at my slavery, and subjection, and duplicity, and cringing, first under one master then under another. I have longed to look back at my life, and comfort myself with the sight of some good action, just as a frugal man comforts himself with the sight of his little savings laid by in an old drawer. I can't do this, and I want to do it. The want takes me like a fit, at uncertain intervals — suddenly, under the most incomprehensible influences. A glance up at the blue sky — starlight over the houses of this great city, when I look out at the night from my garret window — a child's voice coming suddenly, I don't know where from — the piping of my neighbor's linnet in his little cage — now one trifling thing, now another — wakes up that want in me in a moment. Rascal as I am, those few simple words your sister spoke to the judge went through and through me like a knife. Strange, in a man like me, isn't it? I am amazed at it myself. *My* life? Bah! I've let it out for hire to be kicked about by rascals from one dirty place to another, like a football! It's my whim to give it a last kick myself, and throw it away decently before it lodges on the dunghill forever. Your sister kept a good cup of coffee hot for me, and I give her a bad life in return for the compliment. You want to thank me for it? What folly! Thank me when I have done something useful. Don't thank me for that!"

He snapped his fingers contemptuously as he spoke, and walked away to the outer door to receive the jailer, who returned at that moment.

"Well," inquired the hunchback, "has anybody asked for me?"

"No," answered Lomaque; "not a soul has entered the room. What sort of wine did you get?"

"So-so! Good at a pinch, friend — good at a pinch."

"Ah! you should go to my shop and try a certain cask, filled with a particular vintage."

"What shop? Which vintage?"

"I can't stop to tell you now; but we shall most likely meet again today. I expect to be at the prison this afternoon. Shall I ask for you? Good! I won't forget!" With those farewell words he went out, and never so much as looked back at the prisoners before he closed the door.

Trudaine returned to his sister, fearful lest his face should betray what had passed during the extraordinary interview between Lomaque and himself. But, whatever change there might be in his expression, Rose did not seem to notice it. She was still strangely inattentive to all outward things. That spirit of resignation, which is the courage of women in all great emergencies, seemed now to be the one animating spirit that fed the flame of life within her.

When her brother sat down by her, she only took his hand gently and said: "Let us stop together like this, Louis, till the time comes. I am not afraid of it, for I have nothing but you to make me love life, and you, too, are going to die. Do you remember the time when I used to grieve that I had never had a child to be some comfort to me? I was thinking, a moment ago, how terrible it would have been now, if my wish had been granted. It is a blessing for me, in this great misery, that I am childless. Let us talk of old days, Louis, as long as we can — not of my husband; or my marriage — only of the old times, before I was a burden and a trouble to you."

Chapter V.

The day wore on. By ones and twos and threes at a time, the condemned prisoners came from the tribunal, and collected in the waiting-room. At two o'clock all was ready for the calling over of the death-list. It was read and verified by an officer of the court; and then the jailer took his prisoners back to St. Lazare.

Evening came. The prisoners' meal had been served; the duplicate of the death-list had been read in public at the grate; the cell doors were all locked. From the day of their arrest, Rose and her brother, partly through the influence of a bribe, partly through Lomaque's intercession, had been confined together in one cell; and together they now awaited the dread event of the morrow.

To Rose that event was death — death, to the thought of which, at least, she was now resigned. To Trudaine the fast-nearing future was darkening hour by hour, with the uncertainty which is worse than death; with the faint, fearful, unpartaken suspense, which keeps the mind ever on the rack, and wears away the heart slowly. Through the long unsolaced agony of that dreadful night, but one relief came to him. The tension of every nerve, the crushing weight of the one fatal oppression that clung to every thought, relaxed a little when Rose's bodily powers began to sink under her mental exhaustion — when her sad, dying talk of the happy times that were passed ceased softly, and she laid her head on his shoulder, and let the angel of slumber take her yet for a little while, even though she lay already under the shadow of the angel of death.

The morning came, and the hot summer sunrise. What life was left in the terror-struck city awoke for the day faintly; and still the suspense of the long night remained unlightened. It was drawing near the hour when the tumbrils were to come for the victims doomed on the day before. Trudaine's ear could detect even the faintest sound in the echoing prison region outside his cell. Soon, listening near the door, he heard voices disputing on the other side of it. Suddenly, the bolts were drawn back, the key turned in the lock, and he found himself standing face to face with the hunchback and one of the subordinate attendants on the prisoners.

"Look!" muttered this last man sulkily, "there they are, safe in their cell, just as I said; but I tell you again they are not down in the list. What do you mean by bullying me about not chalking their door, last night, along with the rest? Catch me doing your work for you again, when you're too drunk to do it yourself!"

"Hold your tongue, and let me have another look at the list!" returned the hunchback, turning away from the cell door, and snatching a slip of paper from the other's hand. "The devil take me if I can make head or tail of it!" he exclaimed, scratching his head, after a careful examination of the list. "I could swear that I read over their names at the grate yesterday afternoon with my own lips; and yet, look as long as I may, I certainly can't find them written down here. Give us a pinch, friend. Am I awake, or dreaming? drunk or sober this morning?"

"Sober, I hope," said a quiet voice at his elbow. "I have just looked in to see how you are after yesterday."

"How I am, Citizen Lomaque? Petrified with astonishment. You yourself took charge of that man and woman for me, in the waiting-room, yesterday morning; and as for myself, I could swear to having read their names at the grate yesterday afternoon. Yet this morning here are no such things as these said names to be found in the list! What do you think of that?"

"And what do you think," interrupted the aggrieved subordinate, "of his having the impudence to bully me for being careless in chalking the doors, when he was too drunk to do it himself? too drunk to know his right hand from his left! If I wasn't the best-natured man in the world, I should report him to the head jailer."

"Quite right of you to excuse him, and quite wrong of him to bully you," said Lomaque, persuasively. "Take my advice," he continued, confidentially, to the hunchback, "and don't trust too implicitly to that slippery memory of yours, after our little drinking bout yesterday. You could not really have read their names at the grate, you know, or of course they would be down on the list. As for the waiting-room at the tribunal, a word in your ear: chief agents of police know strange secrets. The president of the court condemns and pardons in public; but there is somebody else, with the power of ten thousand presidents, who now and then condemns and pardons in private. You can guess who. I say no more, except that I recommend you to keep your head on your shoulders, by troubling it about nothing but the list there in your hand. Stick to that literally, and nobody can blame you. Make a fuss about mysteries that don't concern you, and —"

Lomaque stopped, and holding his hand edgewise, let it drop significantly over the hunchback's head. That action and the hints which preceded it seemed to bewilder the little man more than ever. He stared perplexedly at Lomaque; uttered a word or two of rough apology to his subordinate, and rolling his misshapen head portentously, walked away with the death-list crumpled up nervously in his hand.

"I should like to have a sight of them, and see if they really are the same man and woman whom I looked after yesterday morning in the waiting-room," said Lomaque, putting his hand on the cell door, just as the deputy-jailer was about to close it again.

"Look in, by all means," said the man. "No doubt you will find that drunken booby as wrong in what he told you about them as he is about everything else."

Lomaque made use of the privilege granted to him immediately. He saw Trudaine sitting with his sister in the corner of the cell furthest from the door, evidently for the purpose of preventing her from overhearing the conversation outside. There was an unsettled look, however, in her eyes, a slowly-heightening color in her cheeks, which showed her to be at least vaguely aware that something unusual had been taking place in the corridor.

Lomaque beckoned to Trudaine to leave her, and whispered to him: "The prescription has worked well. You are safe for today. Break the news to your sister as gently as you can. Danville —" He stopped and listened till he satisfied himself, by the sound of the deputy-jailer's footsteps, that the man was lounging toward the further end of the corridor. "Danville," he resumed, "after having mixed with the people outside the grate yesterday, and having heard your names read, was arrested in the evening by secret order from Robespierre, and sent to the Temple. What charge will be laid to him, or when he will be brought to trial, it is impossible to say. I only know that he is arrested. Hush! don't talk now; my friend outside is coming back. Keep quiet — hope everything from the chances and changes of public affairs; and comfort yourself with the thought that you are both safe for today."

"And tomorrow?" whispered Trudaine.

"Don't think of tomorrow," returned Lomaque, turning away hurriedly to the door "Let tomorrow take care of itself."

PART THIRD. CHAPTER I.

*O*n a spring morning, in the year seventeen hundred and ninety-eight, the public conveyance then running between Chalons-sur-Marne and Paris sat down one of its outside passengers at the first post-station beyond Meaux. The traveler, an old man, after looking about him hesitatingly for a moment or two, betook himself to a little inn opposite the post-house, known by the sign of the Piebald Horse, and kept by the Widow Duval — a woman who enjoyed and deserved the reputation of being the fastest talker and the best maker of *gibelotte* in the whole locality.

Although the traveler was carelessly noticed by the village idlers, and received without ceremony by the Widow Duval, he was by no means so ordinary and uninteresting a stranger as the rustics of the place were pleased to consider him. The time had been when this quiet, elderly, unobtrusive applicant for refreshment at the Piebald House was trusted with the darkest secrets of the Reign of Terror, and was admitted at all times and seasons to speak face to face with Maximilian Robespierre himself. The Widow Duval and the hangers-on in front of the post-house would have been all astonished indeed if any well-informed personage from the metropolis had been present to tell them that the modest old traveler with the shabby little carpet-bag was an ex-chief agent of the secret police of Paris!

Between three and four years had elapsed since Lomaque had exercised, for the last time, his official functions under the Reign of Terror. His shoulders had contracted an extra stoop, and his hair had all fallen off, except at the sides and back of his head. In some other respects, however, advancing age seemed to have improved rather than deteriorated him in personal appearance.

His complexion looked healthier, his expression cheerfuller, his eyes brighter than they had ever been of late years. He walked, too, with a brisker step than the step of old times in the police office; and his dress, although it certainly did not look like the costume of a man in affluent circumstances, was cleaner and far more nearly worn than ever it had been in the past days of his political employment at Paris.

He sat down alone in the inn parlor, and occupied the time, while his hostess had gone to fetch the half-bottle of wine that he ordered, in examining a dirty old card which he extricated from a mass of papers in his pocket-book, and which bore, written on it, these lines:

"When the troubles are over, do not forget those who remember you with eternal gratitude. Stop at the first post-station beyond Meaux, on the high-road to Paris, and ask at the inn for Citizen Maurice, whenever you wish to see us or to hear of us again."

"Pray," inquired Lomaque, putting the card in his pocket when the Widow Duval brought in the wine, "can you inform me whether a person named Maurice lives anywhere in this neighborhood?"

"Can I inform you?" repeated the voluble widow. "Of course I can! Citizen Maurice, and the citoyenne, his amiable sister — who is not to be passed over because you don't mention her, my honest man — lives within ten minutes' walk of my house. A charming cottage, in a charming situation, inhabited by two charming people — so quiet, so retiring, such excellent pay. I supply them with everything — fowls, eggs, bread, butter, vegetables (not that they eat much of anything), wine (which they don't drink half enough of to do them good); in short, I victual the dear little hermitage, and love the two amiable recluses with all my heart. Ah! they have had their troubles, poor people, the sister especially, though they never talk about them. When they first came to live in our neighborhood —"

"I beg pardon, citoyenne, but if you would only be so kind as to direct me —"

"Which is three — no, four — no, three years and a half ago — in short, just after the time when that Satan of a man, Robespierre, had his head cut off (and serve him right!), I said to my husband (who was on his last legs then, poor man!) 'She'll die'— meaning the lady. She didn't though. My fowls, eggs, bread, butter, vegetables, and wine carried her through — always in combination with the anxious care of Citizen Maurice. Yes, yes! let us be tenderly conscientious in giving credit where credit is due; let us never forget that the citizen Maurice contributed something to the cure of the interesting invalid, as well as the victuals and drink from the Piebald Horse. There she is now, the prettiest little woman in the prettiest little cottage —"

"Where? Will you be so obliging as to tell me where?"

"And in excellent health, except that she is subject now and then to nervous attacks; having evidently, as I believe, been struck with some dreadful fright — most likely during that accursed time of the Terror; for they came from Paris — you don't drink, honest man! Why don't you drink? Very, very pretty in a pale way; figure perhaps too thin — let me pour it out for you — but an angel of gentleness, and attached in such a touching way to the citizen Maurice —"

"Citizen hostess, will you, or will you not, tell me where they live?"

"You droll little man, why did you not ask me that before, if you wanted to know? Finish your wine, and come to the door. There's your change, and thank you for your custom, though it isn't much. Come to the door, I say, and don't interrupt me! You're an old man — can you see forty yards before you? Yes, you can! Don't be peevish — that never did anybody any good yet. Now look back, along the road where I am pointing. You see a large heap of stones? Good. On the other side of the heap of stones there is a little path; you can't see that, but you can remember what I tell you? Good. You go down the path till you get to a stream; down the stream till you get to a bridge; down the other bank of the stream (after crossing the bridge) till you get to an old water-mill — a jewel of a water-mill, famous for miles round; artists from the four quarters of the globe are always coming to sketch it. Ah! what, you are getting peevish again? You won't wait? Impatient old man, what a life your wife must lead, if you have got one! Remember the bridge. Ah! your poor wife and children, I pity them; your daughters especially! Pst! pst! Remember the bridge — peevish old man, remember the bridge!"

Walking as fast as he could out of hearing of the Widow Duval's tongue, Lomaque took the path by the heap of stones which led out of the high-road, crossed the stream, and arrived at the old water-mill. Close by it stood a cottage — a rough, simple building, with a strip of garden in front. Lomaque's observant eyes marked the graceful arrangement of the flower-beds, and the delicate whiteness of the curtains that hung behind the badly-glazed narrow windows. "This must be the place," he said to himself, as he knocked at the door with his stick. "I can see the traces of her hand before I cross the threshold."

The door was opened. "Pray, does the citizen Maurice —" Lomaque began, not seeing clearly, for the first moment, in the dark little passage.

Before he could say any more his hand was grasped, his carpet-bag was taken from him, and a well-known voice cried, "Welcome! a thousand thousand times welcome, at last! Citizen Maurice is not at home; but Louis Trudaine takes his place, and is overjoyed to see once more the best and dearest of his friends!"

"I hardly know you again. How you are altered for the better!" exclaimed Lomaque, as they entered the parlor of the cottage.

"Remember that you see me after a long freedom from anxiety. Since I have lived here, I have gone to rest at night, and have not been afraid of the morning," replied Trudaine. He went out into the passage while he spoke, and called at the foot of the one flight of stairs which the cottage possessed, "Rose! Rose! come down! The friend whom you most wished to see has arrived at last."

She answered the summons immediately. The frank, friendly warmth of her greeting; her resolute determination, after the first inquiries were over, to help the guest to take off his upper coat with her own hands, so confused and delighted Lomaque, that he hardly knew which way to turn, or what to say.

"This is even more trying, in a pleasant way, to a lonely old fellow like me," he was about to add, "than the unexpected civility of the hot cup of coffee years ago"; but remembering what recollections even that trifling circumstance might recall, he checked himself.

"More trying than what?" asked Rose, leading him to a chair.

"Ah! I forget. I am in my dotage already!" he answered, confusedly. "I have not got used just yet to the pleasure of seeing your kind face again." It was indeed a pleasure to look at that face now, after Lomaque's last experience of it. Three years of repose, though they had not restored to Rose those youthful attractions which she had lost forever in the days of the Terror, had not passed without leaving kindly outward traces of their healing progress. Though the girlish roundness had not returned to her cheeks, or the girlish delicacy of color to her complexion, her eyes had recovered much of their old softness, and her expression all of its old winning charm. What was left of latent sadness in her face, and of significant quietness in her manner, remained gently and harmlessly — remained rather to show what had been once than what was now.

When they were all seated, there was, however, something like a momentary return to the suspense and anxiety of past days in their faces, as Trudaine, looking earnestly at Lomaque, asked, "Do you bring any news from Paris?"

"None," he replied; "but excellent news, instead, from Rouen. I have heard, accidentally, through the employer whom I have been serving since we parted, that your old house by the river-side is to let again."

Rose started from her chair. "Oh, Louis, if we could only live there once more! My flower-garden?" she continued to Lomaque.

"Cultivated throughout," he answered, "by the late proprietor."

"And the laboratory?" added her brother.

"Left standing," said Lomaque. "Here is a letter with all the particulars. You may depend upon them, for the writer is the person charged with the letting of the house."

Trudaine looked over the letter eagerly.

"The price is not beyond our means," he said. "After our three years' economy here, we can afford to give something for a great pleasure."

"Oh, what a day of happiness it will be when we go home again!" cried Rose. "Pray write to your friend at once," she added, addressing Lomaque, "and say we take the house, before any one else is beforehand with us!"

He nodded, and folding up the letter mechanically in the old official form, made a note on it in the old official manner. Trudaine observed the action, and felt its association with past times of trouble and terror. His face grew grave again as he said to Lomaque, "And is this good news really all the news of importance you have to tell us?"

Lomaque hesitated, and fidgeted in his chair. "What other news I have will bear keeping," he replied. "There are many questions I should like to ask first, about your sister and yourself. Do you mind allowing me to refer for a moment to the time when we last met?"

He addressed this inquiry to Rose, who answered in the negative; but her voice seemed to falter, even in saying the one word "No." She turned her head away when she spoke; and Lomaque noticed that her hands trembled as she took up some work lying on a table near, and hurriedly occupied herself with it.

"We speak as little about that time as possible," said Trudaine, looking significantly toward his sister; "but we have some questions to ask you in our turn; so the allusion, for this once, is inevitable. Your sudden disappearance at the very crisis of that time of danger has not yet been fully explained to us. The one short note which you left behind you helped us to guess at what had happened rather than to understand it."

"I can easily explain it now," answered Lomaque. "The sudden overthrow of the Reign of Terror, which was salvation to you, was destruction to me. The new republican reign was a reign of mercy, except for the tail of Robespierre, as the phrase ran then. Every man who had been so wicked or so unfortunate as to be involved, even in the meanest capacity, with the machinery of the government of Terror, was threatened, and justly, with the fate of Robespierre. I, among others, fell under this menace of death. I deserved to die, and should have resigned myself to the guillotine but for you. From the course taken by public events, I knew you would be saved; and although your safety was the work of circumstances, still I had a hand in rendering it possible at the outset; and a yearning came over me to behold you both free again with my own eyes — a selfish yearning to see in you a living, breathing, real result of the one good impulse of my heart, which I could look back on with satisfaction. This desire gave me a new interest in life. I resolved to escape death if it were possible. For ten days I lay hidden in Paris. After that — thanks to certain scraps of useful knowledge which my experience in the office of secret police had given me — I succeeded in getting clear of Paris and in making my way safely to Switzerland. The rest of my story is so short and so soon told that I may as well get it over at once. The only relation I knew of in the world to apply to was a cousin of mine (whom I had never seen before), established as a silk-mercer at Berne. I threw myself on this man's mercy. He discovered that I was likely, with my business habits, to be of some use to him, and he took me into his house. I worked for what he pleased to give me, traveled about for him in Switzerland, deserved his confidence, and won it. Till within the last few months I remained with him; and only left my employment to enter, by my master's own desire, the house of his brother, established also as a silk-mercer, at Chalons-sur-Marne. In the counting-house of this merchant I am corresponding clerk, and am only able to come and see you now by offering to undertake a special business mission for my employer at Paris. It is drudgery, at my time of life, after all I have gone through — but my hard work is innocent work. I am not obliged to cringe for every crown-piece I put in my pocket — not bound to denounce, deceive, and dog to death other men, before I can earn my bread, and scrape together money enough to bury me. I am ending a bad, base life harmlessly at last. It is a poor thing to do, but it is something done — and even that contents a man at my age. In short, I am happier than I used to be, or at least less ashamed when I look people like you in the face."

"Hush! hush!" interrupted Rose, laying her hand on his arm. "I cannot allow you to talk of yourself in that way, even in jest."

"I was speaking in earnest," answered Lomaque, quietly; "but I won't weary you with any more words about myself. My story is told."

"All?" asked Trudaine. He looked searchingly, almost suspiciously, at Lomaque, as he put the question. "All?" he repeated. "Yours is a short story, indeed, my good friend! Perhaps you have forgotten some of it?"

Again Lomaque fidgeted and hesitated.

"Is it not a little hard on an old man to be always asking questions of him, and never answering one of his inquiries in return?" he said to Rose, very gayly as to manner, but rather uneasily as to look.

"He will not speak out till we two are alone," thought Trudaine. "It is best to risk nothing, and to humor him."

"Come, come," he said aloud; "no grumbling. I admit that it is your turn to hear our story now; and I will do my best to gratify you. But before I begin," he added, turning to his sister, "let me suggest, Rose, that if you have any household matters to settle upstairs —"

"I know what you mean," she interrupted, hurriedly, taking up the work which, during the last few minutes, she had allowed to drop into her lap; "but I am stronger than you think; I can face the worst of our recollections composedly. Go on, Louis; pray go on — I am quite fit to stop and hear you."

"You know what we suffered in the first days of our suspense, after the success of your stratagem," said Trudaine, turning to Lomaque. "I think it was on the evening after we had seen you for the last time at St. Lazare that strange, confused rumors of an impending convulsion in Paris first penetrated within our prison walls. During the next few days the faces of our jailers were enough to show us that those rumors were true, and that the Reign of Terror was actually threatened with overthrow at the hands of the Moderate Party. We had hardly time to hope everything from this blessed change before the tremendous news of Robespierre's attempted suicide, then of his condemnation and execution, reached us. The confusion produced in the prison was beyond all description. The accused who had been tried and the accused who had not been tried got mingled together. From the day of Robespierre's arrest, no orders came to the authorities, no death-lists reached the prison. The jailers, terrified by rumors that the lowest accomplices of the tyrant would be held responsible, and be condemned with him, made no attempt to maintain order. Some of them — that hunchback man among the rest — deserted their duties altogether. The disorganization was so complete, that when the commissioners from the new Government came to St. Lazare, some of us were actually half starving from want of the bare necessities of life. To inquire separately into our cases was found to be impossible. Sometimes the necessary papers were lost; sometimes what documents remained were incomprehensible to the new commissioners. They were obliged, at last, to make short work of it by calling us up before them in dozens. Tried or not tried, we had all been arrested by the tyrant, had all been accused of conspiracy against him, and were all ready to hail the new Government as the salvation of France. In nine cases out of ten, our best claim to be discharged was derived from these circumstances. We were trusted by Tallien and the men of the Ninth Thermidor, because we had been suspected by Robespierre, Couthon, and St. Just. Arrested informally, we were now liberated informally. When it came to my sister's turn and mine, we were not under examination five minutes. No such thing as a searching question was asked of us; I believe we might even have given our own names with perfect impunity. But I had previously instructed Rose that we were to assume our mother's maiden name — Maurice. As the citizen and citoyenne Maurice, accordingly, we passed out of prison — under the same name we have lived ever since in hiding here. Our past repose has depended, our future happiness will depend, on our escape from death being kept the profoundest secret among us three. For one all sufficient reason, which you can easily guess at, the brother and sister Maurice must still know nothing of Louis Trudaine and Rose Danville, except that they were two among the hundreds of victims guillotined during the Reign of Terror."

He spoke the last sentence with a faint smile, and with the air of a man trying, in spite of himself, to treat a grave subject lightly. His face clouded again, however, in a moment, when he looked toward his sister, as he ceased. Her work had once more dropped on her lap, her face was turned away so that he could not see it; but he knew by the trembling of her clasped hands, as they rested on her knee, and by the slight swelling of the veins on her neck which she could not hide from him, that her boasted strength of nerve had deserted her. Three years of repose had not yet enabled her to hear her marriage name uttered, or to be present when past times of deathly suffering and terror were referred to, without betraying the shock in her face and manner. Trudaine looked saddened, but in no way surprised by what he saw. Making a sign to Lomaque to say nothing, he rose and took up his sister's hood, which lay on a window-seat near him.

"Come, Rose," he said, "the sun is shining, the sweet spring air is inviting us out. Let us have a quiet stroll along the banks of the stream. Why should we keep our good friend here cooped up in this narrow little room, when we have miles and miles of beautiful landscape to show him on the other side of the threshold? Come, it is high treason to Queen Nature to remain indoors on such a morning as this."

Without waiting for her to reply, he put on her hood, drew her arm through his, and led the way out. Lomaque's face grew grave as he followed them.

"I am glad I only showed the bright side of my budget of news in her presence," thought he. "She is not well at heart yet. I might have hurt her, poor thing! I might have hurt her again sadly, if I had not held my tongue!"

They walked for a little while down the banks of the stream, talking of indifferent matters; then returned to the cottage. By that time Rose had recovered her spirits, and could listen with interest and amusement to Lomaque's dryly-humorous description of his life as a clerk at Chalons-sur-Marne. They parted for a little while at the cottage door. Rose retired to the upstairs room from which she had been summoned by her brother. Trudaine and Lomaque returned to wander again along the banks of the stream.

With one accord, and without a word passing between them, they left the neighborhood of the cottage hurriedly; then stopped on a sudden, and attentively looked each other in the face — looked in silence for an instant. Trudaine spoke first.

"I thank you for having spared her," he began, abruptly. "She is not strong enough yet to bear hearing of a new misfortune, unless I break the tidings to her first."

"You suspect me, then, of bringing bad news?" said Lomaque.

"I know you do. When I saw your first look at her, after we were all seated in the cottage parlor, I knew it. Speak without fear, without caution, without one useless word of preface. After three years of repose, if it pleases God to afflict us again, I can bear the trial calmly; and, if need be, can strengthen her to bear it calmly, too. I say again, Lomaque, speak at once, and speak out! I know your news is bad, for I know beforehand that it is news of Danville."

"You are right; my bad news is news of him."

"He has discovered the secret of our escape from the guillotine?"

"No — he has not a suspicion of it. He believes — as his mother, as every one does — that you were both executed the day after the Revolutionary Tribunal sentenced you to death."

"Lomaque, you speak positively of that belief of his — but you cannot be certain of it."

"I can, on the most indisputable, the most startling evidence — on the authority of Danville's own act. You have asked me to speak out —"

"I ask you again — I insist on it! Your news, Lomaque — your news, without another word of preface!"

"You shall have it without another word of preface. Danville is on the point of being married."

As the answer was given they both stopped by the bank of the stream, and again looked each other in the face. There was a minute of dead silence between them. During that minute, the water bubbling by happily over its bed of pebbles seemed strangely loud, the singing of birds in a little wood by the stream-side strangely near and shrill, in both their ears. The light breeze, for all its midday warmth, touched their cheeks coldly; and the spring sunlight pouring on their faces felt as if it were glimmering on them through winter clouds.

"Let us walk on," said Trudaine, in a low voice. "I was prepared for bad news, yet not for that. Are you certain of what you have just told me?"

"As certain as that the stream here is flowing by our side. Hear how I made the discovery, and you will doubt no longer. Before last week I knew nothing of Danville, except that his arrest on suspicion by Robespierre's order was, as events turned out, the saving of his life. He was imprisoned, as I told you, on the evening after he had heard your names read from the death-list at the prison grate. He remained in confinement at the Temple, unnoticed in the political confusion out-of-doors, just as you remained unnoticed at St. Lazare, and he profited precisely in the same manner that you profited by the timely insurrection which overthrew the Reign of Terror. I knew this, and I knew that he walked out of prison in the character of a persecuted victim of Robespierre's — and, for better than three years past, I knew no more. Now listen. Last week I happened to be waiting in the shop of my employer, Citizen Clairfait, for some papers to take into the counting-house, when an old man enters with a sealed parcel, which he hands to one of the shopmen, saying:

"'Give that to Citizen Clairfait.'

"'Any name?' says the shopman.

"'The name is of no consequence,' answers the old man; 'but if you please, you can give mine. Say the parcel came from Citizen Dubois;' and then he goes out. His name, in connection with his elderly look, strikes me directly.

"'Does that old fellow live at Chalons?' I ask.

"'No,' says the shopman. 'He is here in attendance on a customer of ours — an old ex-aristocrat named Danville. She is on a visit in our town.'

"I leave you to imagine how that reply startles and amazes me. The shopman can answer none of the other questions I put to him; but the next day I am asked to dinner by my employer (who, for his brother's sake, shows me the utmost civility). On entering the room, I find his daughter just putting away a lavender-colored silk scarf, on which she has been embroidering in silver what looks to me very like a crest and coat-of-arms.

"'I don't mind your seeing what I am about, Citizen Lomaque,' says she; 'for I know my father can trust you. That scarf is sent back to us by the purchaser, an ex-emigrant lady of the old aristocratic school, to have her family coat-of-arms embroidered on it.'

"'Rather a dangerous commission even in these mercifully democratic times, is it not?' says I.

"'The old lady, you must know,' says she, 'is as proud as Lucifer; and having got back safely to France in these days of moderate republicanism, thinks she may now indulge with impunity in all her old-fashioned notions. She has been an excellent customer of ours, so my father thought it best to humor her, without, however, trusting her commission to any of the workroom women to execute. We are not living under the Reign of Terror now, certainly; still there is nothing like being on the safe side.'

"'Nothing,' I answer. 'Pray what is this ex-emigrant's name?'

"'Danville,' replies the citoyenne Clairfait. 'She is going to appear in that fine scarf at her son's marriage.'

"'Marriage!' I exclaim, perfectly thunderstruck.

"'Yes,' says she. 'What is there so amazing in that? By all accounts, the son, poor man, deserves to make a lucky marriage this time. His first wife was taken away from him in the Reign of Terror by the guillotine.'

"'Who is he going to marry?' I inquire, still breathless.

"'The daughter of General Berthelin — an ex-aristocrat by family, like the old lady; but by principle as good a republican as ever lived — a hard-drinking, loud-swearing, big-whiskered old soldier, who snaps his fingers at his ancestors and says we are all descended from Adam, the first genuine sans-culotte in the world.'

"In this way the citoyenne Clairfait gossips on all dinner-time, but says nothing more of any importance. I, with my old police-office habits, set to the next day, and try to make some discoveries for myself. The sum of what I find out is this: Danville's mother is staying with General Berthelin's sister and daughter at Chalons, and Danville himself is expected to arrive every day to escort them all three to Paris, where the marriage-contract is to be signed at the general's house. Discovering this, and seeing that prompt action is now of the most vital importance, I undertake, as I told you, my employer's commission for Paris, depart with all speed, and stop here on my way. Wait! I have not done yet. All the haste I can make is not haste enough to give me a good start of the wedding party. On my road here, the diligence by which I travel is passed by a carriage, posting along at full speed. I cannot see inside that carriage; but I look at the box-seat, and recognize on it the old man Dubois. He whirls by in a cloud of dust, but I am certain of him; and I say to myself what I now say again to you, no time is to be lost!"

"No time *shall* be lost," answers, Trudaine, firmly. "Three years have passed," he continued, in a lower voice, speaking to himself rather than to Lomaque; "three years since the day when I led my sister out of the gates of the prison — three years since I said in my heart, 'I will be patient, and will not seek to avenge myself. Our wrongs cry from earth to heaven; from man who inflicts to God who redresses. When the day of reckoning comes, let it be the day of his vengeance, not of mine.' In my heart I said those words — I have been true to them — I have waited. The day has come, and the duty it demands of me shall be fulfilled."

There was a moment's silence before Lomaque spoke again. "Your sister?" he began, hesitatingly.

"It is there only that my purpose falters," said the other, earnestly. "If it were but possible to spare her all knowledge of this last trial, and to leave the accomplishment of the terrible task to me alone?"

"I think it is possible," interposed Lomaque. "Listen to what I advise. We must depart for Paris by the diligence tomorrow morning, and we must take your sister with us — tomorrow will be time enough; people don't sign marriage-contracts on the evening after a long day's journey. We must go then, and we must take your sister. Leave the care of her in Paris, and the responsibility of keeping her in ignorance of what you are doing, to me. Go to this General Berthelin's house at a time when you know Danville is there (we can get that knowledge through the servants); confront him without a moment's previous warning; confront him as a man risen from the dead; confront him before every soul in the room though the room should be full of people — and leave the rest to the self-betrayal of a panic-stricken man. Say but three words, and your duty will be done; you may return to your sister, and may depart with her in safety to your old retreat at Rouen, or where else you please, on the very day when you have put it out of her infamous husband's power to add another to the list of his crimes."

"You forget the suddenness of the journey to Paris," said Trudaine. "How are we to account for it without the risk of awakening my sister's suspicions?"

"Trust that to me," answered Lomaque. "Let us return to the cottage at once. No, not you," he added, suddenly, as they turned to retrace their steps. "There is that in your face which would betray us. Leave me to go back alone — I will say that you have gone to give some orders at the inn. Let us separate immediately. You will recover your self-possession — you will get to look yourself again sooner — if you are left alone. I know enough of you to know that. We will not waste another minute in explanations; even minutes are precious to us on such a day as this. By the time you are fit to meet your sister again, I shall have had time to say all I wish to her, and shall be waiting at the cottage to tell you the result."

He looked at Trudaine, and his eyes seemed to brighten again with something of the old energy and sudden decision of the days when he was a man in office under the Reign of Terror. "Leave it to me," he said; and, waving his hand, turned away quickly in the direction of the cottage.

Nearly an hour passed before Trudaine ventured to follow him. When he at length entered the path which led to the garden gate, he saw his sister waiting at the cottage door. Her face looked unusually animated; and she ran forward a step or two to meet him.

"Oh, Louis!" she said, "I have a confession to make, and I must beg you to hear it patiently to the end. You must know that our good Lomaque, though he came in tired from his walk, occupied himself the first thing, at my request, in writing the letter which is to secure to us our dear old home by the banks of the Seine. When he had done, he looked at me, and said, 'I should like to be present at your happy return to the house where I first saw you.' 'Oh, come, come with us!' I said directly. 'I am not an independent man,' he answered; 'I have a margin of time allowed me at Paris, certainly, but it is not long — if I were only my own master —' and then he stopped. Louis, I remembered all we owed to him; I remembered that there was no sacrifice we ought not to be too glad to make for his sake; I felt the kindness of the wish he had expressed; and perhaps I was a little influenced by my own impatience to see once more my flower-garden and the rooms where we used to be so happy. So I said to him, 'I am sure Louis will agree with me that our time is yours, and that we shall be only too glad to advance our departure so as to make traveling leisure enough for you to come with us to Rouen. We should be worse than ungrateful —' He stopped me. 'You have always been good to me,' he said. 'I must not impose on your kindness now. No, no, you have formalities to settle before you can leave this place.' 'Not one,' I said — for we have not, as you know, Louis? 'Why, here is your furniture to begin with,' he said. 'A few chairs and tables hired from the inn,' I answered; 'we have only to give the landlady our key, to leave a letter for the owner of the cottage, and then —' He laughed. 'Why, to hear you talk, one would think you were as ready to travel as I am!' 'So we are,' I said, 'quite as ready, living in the way we do here.' He shook his head; but you will not shake yours, Louis, I am sure, now you have heard all my long story? You can't blame me can you?"

Before Trudaine could answer, Lomaque looked out of the cottage window.

"I have just been telling my brother every thing," said Rose, turning round toward him.

"And what does he say?" asked Lomaque.

"He says what I say," replied Rose, answering for her brother; "that our time is your time — the time of our best and dearest friend."

"Shall it be done, then?" asked Lomaque, with a meaning look at Trudaine.

Rose glanced anxiously at her brother; his face was much graver than she had expected to see it, but his answer relieved her from all suspense.

"You are quite right, love, to speak as you did," he said, gently. Then, turning to Lomaque, he added, in a firmer voice, "It shall be done!"

PART THIRD. CHAPTER II.

wo days after the traveling-carriage described by Lomaque had passed the diligence on the road to Paris, Madame Danville sat in the drawing-room of an apartment in the Rue de Grenelle, handsomely dressed for driving out. After consulting a large gold watch that hung at her side, and finding that it wanted a quarter of an hour only to two o'clock, she rang her hand-bell, and said to the maid-servant who answered the summons, "I have five minutes to spare. Send Dubois here with my chocolate."

The old man made his appearance with great alacrity. After handing the cup of chocolate to his mistress, he ventured to use the privilege of talking, to which his long and faithful services entitled him, and paid the old lady a compliment. "I am rejoiced to see madame looking so young and in such good spirits this morning," he said, with a low bow and a mild, deferential smile.

"I think I have some reason for being in good spirits on the day when my son's marriage-contract is to be signed," said Madame Danville, with a gracious nod of the head. "Ha, Dubois, I shall live yet to see him with a patent of nobility in his hand. The mob has done its worst; the end of this infamous revolution is not far off; our order will have its turn again soon, and then who will have such a chance at court as my son? He is noble already through his mother, he will then be noble also through his wife. Yes, yes; let that coarse-mannered, passionate, old soldier-father of hers be as unnaturally republican as he pleases, he has inherited a name which will help my son to a peerage! The Vicomte D'Anville (D with an apostrophe, Dubois, you understand?), the Vicomte D'Anville — how prettily it sounds!"

"Charmingly, madame — charmingly. Ah! this second marriage of my young master's begins under much better auspices than the first."

The remark was an unfortunate one. Madame Danville frowned portentously, and rose in a great hurry from her chair.

"Are your wits failing you, you old fool?" she exclaimed, indignantly. "What do you mean by referring to such a subject as that, on this day, of all others? You are always harping on those two wretched people who were guillotined, as if you thought I could have saved their lives. Were you not present when my son and I met, after the time of the Terror? Did you not hear my first words to him, when he told me of the catastrophe? Were they not 'Charles, I love you; but if I thought you had let those two unfortunates, who risked themselves to save me, die without risking your life in return to save them, I would break my heart rather than ever look at you or speak to you again!' Did I not say that? And did he not answer, 'Mother, my life was risked for them. I proved my devotion by exposing myself to arrest — I was imprisoned for my exertions — and then I could do no more!' Did you not stand by and hear him give that answer, overwhelmed while he spoke by generous emotion? Do you not know that he really was imprisoned in the Temple? Do you dare to think that we are to blame after that? I owe you much, Dubois, but if you are to take liberties with me —"

"Oh, madame! I beg pardon a thousand times. I was thoughtless — only thoughtless —"

"Silence! Is my coach at the door? Very well. Get ready to accompany me. Your master will not have time to return here. He will meet me, for the signing of the contract, at General Berthelin's house at two precisely. Stop! Are there many people in the street? I can't be stared at by the mob as I go to my carriage."

Dubois hobbled penitently to the window and looked out, while his mistress walked to the door.

"The street is almost empty, madame," he said. "Only a man with a woman on his arm, stopping and admiring your carriage. They seem like decent people, as well as I can tell without my spectacles. Not mob, I should say, madame; certainly not mob!"

"Very well. Attend me downstairs; and bring some loose silver with you, in case those two decent people should be fit objects for charity. No orders for the coachman, except that he is to go straight to the general's house."

The party assembled at General Berthelin's to witness the signature of the marriage-contract, comprised, besides the persons immediately interested in the ceremony of the day, some young ladies, friends of the bride, and a few officers, who had been comrades of her father's in past years. The guests were distributed, rather unequally, in two handsome apartments opening into each other — one called in the house the drawing-room, and the other the library. In the drawing-room were assembled the notary, with the contract ready, the bride, the young ladies, and the majority of General Berthelin's friends. In the library, the remainder of the military guests were amusing themselves at a billiard-table until the signing of the contract should take place, while Danville and his future father-inlaw walked up and down the room together, the first listening absently, the last talking with all his accustomed energy, and with more than his accustomed allowance of barrack-room expletives. The general had taken it into his head to explain some of the clauses in the marriage-contract to the bridegroom, who, though far better acquainted with their full scope and meaning than his father-inlaw, was obliged to listen for civility's sake. While the old soldier was still in the midst of his long and confused harangue, a clock struck on the library mantel-piece.

"Two o'clock!" exclaimed Danville, glad of any pretext for interrupting the talk about the contract. "Two o'clock; and my mother not here yet! What can be delaying her?"

"Nothing," cried the general. "When did you ever know a woman punctual, my lad? If we wait for your mother — and she's such a rabid aristocrat that she would never forgive us for not waiting — we shan't sign the contract yet this half-hour. Never mind! let's go on with what we were talking about. Where the devil was I when that cursed clock struck and interrupted us? Now then, Black Eyes, what's the matter?"

This last question was addressed to Mademoiselle Berthelin, who at that moment hastily entered the library from the drawing-room. She was a tall and rather masculine-looking girl, with superb black eyes, dark hair growing low on her forehead, and something of her father's decision and bluntness in her manner of speaking.

"A stranger in the other room, papa, who wants to see you. I suppose the servants showed him upstairs, thinking he was one of the guests. Ought I to have had him shown down again?"

"A nice question! How should I know? Wait till I have seen him, miss, and then I'll tell you!" With these words the general turned on his heel, and went into the drawing-room.

His daughter would have followed him, but Danville caught her by the hand.

"Can you be hard-hearted enough to leave me here alone?" he asked.

"What is to become of all my bosom friends in the next room, you selfish man, if I stop here with you?" retorted mademoiselle, struggling to free herself.

"Call them in here," said Danville gayly, making himself master of her other hand.

She laughed, and drew him away toward the drawing-room.

"Come," she cried, "and let all the ladies see what a tyrant I am going to marry. Come, and show them what an obstinate, unreasonable, wearisome —"

Her voice suddenly failed her; she shuddered, and turned faint. Danville's hand had in one instant grown cold as death in hers; the momentary touch of his fingers, as she felt their grasp loosen, struck some mysterious chill through her from head to foot. She glanced round at him affrightedly, and saw his eyes looking straight into the drawing-room. They were fixed in a strange, unwavering, awful stare, while, from the rest of his face, all expression, all character, all recognizable play and movement of feature, had utterly gone. It was a breathless, lifeless mask — a white blank. With a cry of terror, she looked where he seemed to be looking; and could see nothing but the stranger standing in the middle of the drawing-room. Before she could ask a question — before she could speak even a single word — her father came to her, caught Danville by the arm, and pushed her roughly back into the library.

"Go there, and take the women with you," he said, in a quick, fierce whisper. "Into the library!" he continued, turning to the ladies, and raising his voice. "Into the library, all of you, along with my daughter."

The women, terrified by his manner, obeyed him in the greatest confusion. As they hurried past him into the library, he signed to the notary to follow; and then closed the door of communication between the two rooms.

"Stop where you are!" he cried, addressing the old officers, who had risen from their chairs. "Stay, I insist on it! Whatever happens, Jacques Berthelin has done nothing to be ashamed of in the presence of his old friends and companions. You have seen the beginning, now stay and see the end."

While he spoke, he walked into the middle of the room. He had never quitted his hold of Danville's arm; step by step they advanced together to the place where Trudaine was standing.

"You have come into my house, and asked me for my daughter in marriage — and I have given her to you," said the general, addressing Danville, quietly. "You told me that your first wife and her brother were guillotined three years ago in the time of the Terror — and I believed you. Now look at that man — look him straight in the face. He has announced himself to me as the brother of your wife, and he asserts that his sister is alive at this moment. One of you two has deceived me. Which is it?"

Danville tried to speak, but no sound passed his lips; tried to wrench his arm from the grasp that was on it, but could not stir the old soldier's steady hand.

"Are you afraid? are you a coward? Can't you look him in the face?" asked the general, tightening his hold sternly.

"Stop! stop!" interposed one of the old officers, coming forward. "Give him time. This may be a case of strange accidental resemblance, which would be enough, under the circumstances, to discompose any man. You will excuse me, citizen," he continued, turning to Trudaine; "but you are a stranger. You have given us no proof of your identity."

"There is the proof," said Trudaine, pointing to Danville's face.

"Yes, yes," pursued the other; "he looks pale and startled enough, certainly. But I say again, let us not be too hasty; there are strange cases on record of accidental resemblances, and this may be one of them!"

As he repeated those words, Danville looked at him with a faint, cringing gratitude, stealing slowly over the blank terror of his face. He bowed his head, murmured something, and gesticulated confusedly with the hand that he was free to use.

"Look!" cried the old officer; "look, Berthelin; he denies the man's identity."

"Do you hear that?" said the general, appealing to Trudaine. "Have you proofs to confute him? If you have, produce them instantly."

Before the answer could be given the door leading into the drawing-room from the staircase was violently flung open, and Madame Danville — her hair in disorder, her face in its colorless terror looking like the very counterpart of her son's — appeared on the threshold, with the old man Dubois and a group of amazed and startled servants behind her.

"For God's sake, don't sign! for God's sake, come away!" she cried. "I have seen your wife — in the spirit, or in the flesh, I know not which — but I have seen her. Charles! Charles! as true as Heaven is above us, I have seen your wife!"

"You have seen her in the flesh, living and breathing as you see her brother yonder," said a firm, quiet voice, from among the servants on the landing outside.

"Let that man enter, whoever he is!" cried the general.

Lomaque passed Madame Danville on the threshold. She trembled as he brushed by her; then, supporting herself by the wall, followed him a few paces into the room. She looked first at her son — after that, at Trudaine — after that back again at her son. Something in her presence silenced every one. There fell a sudden stillness over all the assembly — a stillness so deep that the eager, frightened whispering, and sharp rustling of dresses among the women in the library, became audible from the other side of the closed door.

"Charles," she said, slowly advancing; "why do you look —" She stopped, and fixed her eyes again on her son more earnestly than before; then turned them suddenly on Trudaine. "You are looking at my son, sir," she said, "and I see contempt in your face. By what right do you insult a man whose grateful sense of his mother's obligations to you made him risk his life for the saving of yours and your sister's? By what right have you kept the escape of my son's wife from death by the guillotine — an escape which, for all I know to the contrary, his generous exertions were instrumental in effecting — a secret from my son? By what right, I demand to know, has your treacherous secrecy placed us in such a position as we now stand in before the master of this house?"

An expression of sorrow and pity passed over Trudaine's face while she spoke. He retired a few steps, and gave her no answer. The general looked at him with eager curiosity, and, dropping his hold of Danville's arm, seemed about to speak; but Lomaque stepped forward at the same time, and held up his hand to claim attention.

"I think I shall express the wishes of Citizen Trudaine," he said, addressing Madame Danville, "if I recommend this lady not to press for too public an answer to her questions."

"Pray who are you, sir, who take it on yourself to advise me?" she retorted, haughtily. "I have nothing to say to you, except that I repeat those questions, and that I insist on their being answered."

"Who is this man?" asked the general, addressing Trudaine, and pointing to Lomaque.

"A man unworthy of credit," cried Danville, speaking audibly for the first time, and darting a look of deadly hatred at Lomaque. "An agent of police under Robespierre."

"And in that capacity capable of answering questions which refer to the transactions of Robespierre's tribunals," remarked the ex-chief agent, with his old official self-possession.

"True!" exclaimed the general; "the man is right — let him be heard."

"There is no help for it," said Lomaque, looking at Trudaine; "leave it to me — it is fittest that I should speak. I was present," he continued, in a louder voice, "at the trial of Citizen Trudaine and his sister. They were brought to the bar through the denunciation of Citizen Danville. Till the confession of the male prisoner exposed the fact, I can answer for Danville's not being aware of the real nature of the offenses charged against Trudaine and his sister. When it became known that they had been secretly helping this lady to escape from France, and when Danville's own head was consequently in danger, I myself heard him save it by a false assertion that he had been aware of Trudaine's conspiracy from the first —"

"Do you mean to say," interrupted the general, "that he proclaimed himself in open court as having knowingly denounced the man who was on trial for saving his mother?"

"I do," answered Lomaque. (A murmur of horror and indignation rose from all the strangers present at that reply.) "The reports of the Tribunal are existing to prove the truth of what I say," he went on. "As to the escape of Citizen Trudaine and the wife of Danville from the guillotine, it was the work of political circumstances, which there are persons living to speak to if necessary; and of a little stratagem of mine, which need not be referred to now.

And, last, with reference to the concealment which followed the escape, I beg to inform you that it was abandoned the moment we knew of what was going on here; and that it was only persevered in up to this time, as a natural measure of precaution on the part of Citizen Trudaine. From a similar motive we now abstain from exposing his sister to the shock and the peril of being present here. What man with an atom of feeling would risk letting her even look again on such a husband as that?"

He glanced round him, and pointed to Danville, as he put the question. Before a word could be spoken by any one else in the room, a low wailing cry of "My mistress! my dear, dear mistress!" directed all eyes first on the old man Dubois, then on Madame Danville.

She had been leaning against the wall, before Lomaque began to speak; but she stood perfectly upright now. She neither spoke nor moved. Not one of the light gaudy ribbons flaunting on her disordered head-dress so much as trembled. The old servant Dubois was crouched on his knees at her side, kissing her cold right hand, chafing it in his, reiterating his faint, mournful cry, "Oh! my mistress! my dear, dear mistress!" but she did not appear to know that he was near her. It was only when her son advanced a step or two toward her that she seemed to awaken suddenly from that death-trance of mental pain. Then she slowly raised the hand that was free, and waved him back from her. He stopped in obedience to the gesture, and endeavored to speak. She waved her hand again, and the deathly stillness of her face began to grow troubled. Her lips moved a little — she spoke.

"Oblige me, sir, for the last time, by keeping silence. You and I have henceforth nothing to say to each other. I am the daughter of a race of nobles, and the widow of a man of honor. You are a traitor and a false witness — a thing from which all true men and true women turn with contempt. I renounce you! Publicly, in the presence of these gentlemen, I say it — I have no son."

She turned her back on him; and, bowing to the other persons in the room with the old formal courtesy of by-gone times, walked slowly and steadily to the door. Stopping there, she looked back; and then the artificial courage of the moment failed her. With a faint, suppressed cry she clutched at the hand of the old servant, who still kept faithfully at her side; he caught her in his arms, and her head sank on his shoulder.

"Help him!" cried the general to the servants near the door. "Help him to take her into the next room!"

The old man looked up suspiciously from his mistress to the persons who were assisting him to support her. With a strange, sudden jealousy he shook his hand at them. "Home," he cried; "she shall go home, and I will take care of her. Away! you there — nobody holds her head but Dubois. Downstairs! downstairs to her carriage! She has nobody but me now, and I say that she shall be taken home."

As the door closed, General Berthelin approached Trudaine, who had stood silent and apart, from the time when Lomaque first appeared in the drawing-room.

"I wish to ask your pardon," said the old soldier, "because I have wronged you by a moment of unjust suspicion. For my daughter's sake, I bitterly regret that we did not see each other long ago; but I thank you, nevertheless, for coming here, even at the eleventh hour."

While he was speaking, one of his friends came up, and touching him on the shoulder, said: "Berthelin, is that scoundrel to be allowed to go?"

The general turned on his heel directly, and beckoned contemptuously to Danville to follow him to the door. When they were well out of ear-shot, he spoke these words:

"You have been exposed as a villain by your brother-inlaw, and renounced as a liar by your mother. They have done their duty by you, and now it only remains for me to do mine. When a man enters the house of another under false pretenses, and compromises the reputation of his daughter, we old army men have a very expeditious way of making him answer for it. It is just three o'clock now; at five you will find me and one of my friends —"

He stopped, and looked round cautiously — then whispered the rest in Danville's ear — threw open the door, and pointed downstairs.

"Our work here is done," said Lomaque, laying his hand on Trudaine's arm. "Let us give Danville time to get clear of the house, and then leave it too."

"My sister! where is she?" asked Trudaine, eagerly.

"Make your mind easy about her. I will tell you more when we get out."

"You will excuse me, I know," said General Berthelin, speaking to all the persons present, with his hand on the library door, "if I leave you. I have bad news to break to my daughter, and private business after that to settle with a friend."

He saluted the company, with his usual bluff nod of the head, and entered the library. A few minutes afterward, Trudaine and Lomaque left the house.

"You will find your sister waiting for you in our apartment at the hotel," said the latter. "She knows nothing, absolutely nothing, of what has passed."

"But the recognition?" asked Trudaine, amazedly. "His mother saw her. Surely she —"

"I managed it so that she should be seen, and should not see. Our former experience of Danville suggested to me the propriety of making the experiment, and my old police-office practice came in useful in carrying it out. I saw the carriage standing at the door, and waited till the old lady came down. I walked your sister away as she got in, and walked her back again past the window as the carriage drove off. A moment did it, and it turned out as useful as I thought it would. Enough of that! Go back now to your sister. Keep indoors till the night mail starts for Rouen. I have had two places taken for you on speculation. Go! resume possession of your house, and leave me here to transact the business which my employer has intrusted to me, and to see how matters end with Danville and his mother. I will make time somehow to come and bid you good-by at Rouen, though it should be only for a single day. Bah! no thanks. Give us your hand. I was ashamed to take it eight years ago — I can give it a hearty shake now! There is your way; here is mine. Leave me to my business in silks and satins, and go you back to your sister, and help her to pack up for the night mail."

PART THIRD. CHAPTER III.

*T*hree more days have passed. It is evening. Rose, Trudaine and Lomaque are seated together on the bench that overlooks the windings of the Seine. The old familiar scene spreads before them, beautiful as ever — unchanged, as if it was but yesterday since they had all looked on it for the last time.

They talk together seriously and in low voices. The same recollections fill their hearts — recollections which they refrain from acknowledging, but the influence of which each knows by instinct that the other partakes. Sometimes one leads the conversation, sometimes another; but whoever speaks, the topic chosen is always, as if by common consent, a topic connected with the future.

The evening darkens in, and Rose is the first to rise from the bench. A secret look of intelligence passes between her and her brother, and then she speaks to Lomaque.

"Will you follow me into the house," she asks, "with as little delay as possible? I have something that I very much wish to show you."

Her brother waits till she is out of hearing, then inquires anxiously what has happened at Paris since the night when he and Rose left it.

"Your sister is free," Lomaque answers.

"The duel took place, then?"

"The same day. They were both to fire together. The second of his adversary asserts that he was paralyzed with terror; his own second declares that he was resolved, however he might have lived, to confront death courageously by offering his life at the first fire to the man whom he had injured. Which account is true, I know not. It is only certain that he did not discharge his pistol, that he fell by his antagonist's first bullet, and that he never spoke afterward."

"And his mother?"

"It is hard to gain information. Her doors are closed; the old servant guards her with jealous care. A medical man is in constant attendance, and there are reports in the house that the illness from which she is suffering affects her mind more than her body. I could ascertain no more."

After that answer they both remain silent for a little while, then rise from the bench and walk toward the house.

"Have you thought yet about preparing your sister to hear of all that has happened?" Lomaque asks, as he sees the lamp-light glimmering in the parlor window.

"I shall wait to prepare her till we are settled again here — till the first holiday pleasure of our return has worn off, and the quiet realities of our every-day life of old have resumed their way," answers Trudaine.

They enter the house. Rose beckons to Lomaque to sit down near her, and places pen and ink and an open letter before him.

"I have a last favor to ask of you," she says, smiling.

"I hope it will not take long to grant," he rejoins; "for I have only to-night to be with you. To-morrow morning, before you are up, I must be on my way back to Chalons."

"Will you sign that letter?" she continues, still smiling, "and then give it to me to send to the post? It was dictated by Louis, and written by me, and it will be quite complete, if you will put your name at the end of it."

"I suppose I may read it?"

She nods, and Lomaque reads these lines:

"CITIZEN— I beg respectfully to apprise you that the commission you intrusted to me at Paris has been performed.

"I have also to beg that you will accept my resignation of the place I hold in your counting-house. The kindness shown me by you and your brother before you, emboldens me to hope that you will learn with pleasure the motive of my withdrawal. Two friends of mine, who consider that they are under some obligations to me, are anxious that I should pass the rest of my days in the quiet and protection of their home. Troubles of former years have knit us together as closely as if we were all three members of one family. I need the repose of a happy fireside as much as any man, after the life I have led; and my friends assure me so earnestly that their whole hearts are set on establishing the old man's easy-chair by their hearth, that I cannot summon resolution enough to turn my back on them and their offer.

"Accept, then, I beg of you, the resignation which this letter contains, and with it the assurance of my sincere gratitude and respect.

"To Citizen Clairfait, Silk-mercer,

"Chalons-sur-Marne."

After reading these lines, Lomaque turned round to Trudaine and attempted to speak; but the words would not come at command. He looked up at Rose, and tried to smile; but his lip only trembled. She dipped the pen in the ink, and placed it in his hand. He bent his head down quickly over the paper, so that she could not see his face; but still he did not write his name. She put her hand caressingly on his shoulder, and whispered to him:

"Come, come, humor 'Sister Rose.' She must have her own way now she is back again at home."

He did not answer — his head sank lower — he hesitated for an instant — then signed his name in faint, trembling characters, at the end of the letter.

She drew it away from him gently. A few tear-drops lay on the paper. As she dried them with her handkerchief she looked at her brother.

"They are the last he shall ever shed, Louis; you and I will take care of that!"

EPILOGUE TO THE THIRD STORY.

I have now related all that is eventful in the history of Sister Rose. To the last the three friends dwelt together happily in the cottage on the river bank. Mademoiselle Clairfait was fortunate enough to know them, before Death entered the little household and took away, in the fullness of time, the eldest of its members. She describes Lomaque, in her quaint foreign English, as "a brave, big heart"; generous, affectionate, and admirably free from the small obstinacies and prejudices of old age, except on one point: he could never be induced to take his coffee, of an evening, from any other hand than the hand of Sister Rose.

I linger over these final particulars with a strange unwillingness to separate myself from them, and give my mind to other thoughts. Perhaps the persons and events that have occupied my attention for so many nights past have some peculiar interest for me that I cannot analyze. Perhaps the labor and time which this story has cost me have especially endeared it to my sympathies, now that I have succeeded in completing it. However that may be, I have need of some resolution to part at last with Sister Rose, and return, in the interests of my next and Fourth Story, to English ground.

I have experienced so much difficulty, let me add, in deciding on the choice of a new narrative out of my collection, that my wife has lost all patience, and has undertaken, on her own responsibility, to relieve me of my unreasonable perplexities. By her advice — given, as usual, without a moment's hesitation — I cannot do better than tell the story of The Lady of Glenwith Grange.

THE ANGLER'S STORY OF THE LADY OF GLENWITH GRANGE.

PROLOGUE TO THE FOURTH STORY.

*M*y practice in the art of portrait-painting, if it has done nothing else, has at least fitted me to turn my talents (such as they are) to a great variety of uses. I have not only taken the likenesses of men, women, and children, but have also extended the range of my brush, under stress of circumstances, to horses, dogs, houses, and in one case even to a bull — the terror and glory of his parish, and the most truculent sitter I ever had. The beast was appropriately named "Thunder and Lightning," and was the property of a gentleman-farmer named Garthwaite, a distant connection of my wife's family.

How it was that I escaped being gored to death before I had finished my picture is more than I can explain to this day. "Thunder and Lightning" resented the very sight of me and my color-box, as if he viewed the taking of his likeness in the light of a personal insult. It required two men to coax him, while a third held him by a ring in his nostrils, before I could venture on beginning to work. Even then he always lashed his tail, and jerked his huge head, and rolled his fiery eyes with a devouring anxiety to have me on his horns for daring to sit down quietly and look at him. Never, I can honestly say, did I feel more heartily grateful for the blessings of soundness of limb and wholeness of skin, than when I had completed the picture of the bull!

One morning, when I had but little more than half done my unwelcome task, my friend and I were met on our way to the bull's stable by the farm bailiff, who informed us gravely that "Thunder and Lightning" was just then in such an especially surly state of temper as to render it quite unsafe for me to think of painting him. I looked inquiringly at Mr. Garthwaite, who smiled with an air of comic resignation, and said, "Very well, then, we have nothing for it but to wait till tomorrow. What do you say to a morning's fishing, Mr. Kerby, now that my bull's bad temper has given us a holiday?"

I replied, with perfect truth, that I knew nothing about fishing. But Mr. Garthwaite, who was as ardent an angler in his way as Izaak Walton himself, was not to be appeased even by the best of excuses. "It is never too late to learn," cried he. "I will make a fisherman of you in no time, if you will only attend to my directions." It was impossible for me to make any more apologies, without the risk of appealing discourteous. So I thanked my host for his friendly intentions, and, with some secret misgivings, accepted the first fishing-rod that he put into my hands.

"We shall soon get there," said Mr. Garthwaite. "I am taking you to the best mill-stream in the neighborhood." It was all one to me whether we got there soon or late and whether the stream was good or bad. However, I did my best to conceal my unsportsman-like apathy; and tried to look quite happy and very impatient to begin, as we drew near to the mill, and heard louder and louder the gushing of many waters all round it.

Leading the way immediately to a place beneath the falling stream, where there was a deep, eddying pool, Mr. Garthwaite baited and threw in his line before I had fixed the joints of my fishing-rod. This first difficulty overcome, I involuntarily plunged into some excellent, but rather embarrassing, sport with my line and hook. I caught every one of my garments, from head to foot; I angled for my own clothes with the dexterity and success of Izaak Walton himself. I caught my hat, my jacket, my waistcoat, my trousers, my fingers, and my thumbs — some devil possessed my hook; some more than eel-like vitality twirled and twisted in every inch of my line. By the time my host arrived to assist me, I had attached myself to my fishing-rod, apparently for life. All difficulties yielded, however, to his patience and skill; my hook was baited for me, and thrown in; my rod was put into my hand; my friend went back to his place; and we began at last to angle in earnest.

We certainly caught a few fish (in *my* case, I mean, of course, that the fish caught themselves); but they were scanty in number and light in weight. Whether it was the presence of the miller's foreman — a gloomy personage, who stood staring disastrously upon us from a little flower-garden on the opposite bank — that cast adverse influence over our sport; or whether my want of faith and earnestness as an angler acted retributively on my companion as well as myself, I know not; but it is certain that he got almost as little reward for his skill as I got for my patience. After nearly two hours of intense expectation on my part, and intense angling on his, Mr. Garthwaite jerked his line out of the water in a rage, and bade me follow him to another place, declaring that the stream must have been netted by poachers in the night, who had taken all the large fish away with them, and had thrown in the small ones to grow until their next visit. We moved away, further down the bank, leaving the imperturbable foreman still in the flower-garden, staring at us speechlessly on our departure, exactly as he had already stared at us on our approach.

"Stop a minute," said Mr. Garthwaite suddenly, after we had walked some distance in silence by the side of the stream, "I have an idea. Now we are out for a day's angling, we won't be balked. Instead of trying the water here again, we will go where I know, by experience, that the fishing is excellent. And what is more, you shall be introduced to a lady whose appearance is sure to interest you, and whose history, I can tell you beforehand, is a very remarkable one."

"Indeed," I said. "May I ask in what way?"

"She is connected," answered Mr. Garthwaite, "with an extraordinary story, which relates to a family once settled in an old house in this neighborhood. Her name is Miss Welwyn; but she is less formally known an among the poor people about here, who love her dearly, and honor her almost superstitiously, as the Lady of Glenwith Grange. Wait till you have seen her before you ask me to say anything more. She lives in the strictest retirement; I am almost the only visitor who is admitted. Don't say you had rather not go in. Any friend of mine will be welcome at the Grange (the scene of the story, remember), for my sake — the more especially because I have never abused my privilege of introduction. The place is not above two miles from here, and the stream (which we call, in our county dialect, Glenwith Beck) runs through the ground."

As we walked on, Mr. Garthwaite's manner altered. He became unusually silent and thoughtful. The mention of Miss Welwyn's name had evidently called up some recollections which were not in harmony with his every-day mood. Feeling that to talk to him on any indifferent subject would be only to interrupt his thoughts to no purpose, I walked by his side in perfect silence, looking out already with some curiosity and impatience for a first view of Glenwith Grange. We stopped at last close by an old church, standing on the outskirts of a pretty village. The low wall of the churchyard was bounded on one side by a plantation, and was joined by a park paling, in which I noticed a small wicket-gate. Mr. Garthwaite opened it, and led me along a shrubbery path, which conducted us circuitously to the dwelling-house.

We had evidently entered by a private way, for we approached the building by the back. I looked up at it curiously, and saw standing at one of the windows on the lower floor a little girl watching us as we advanced. She seemed to be about nine or ten years old. I could not help stopping a moment to look up at her, her clear complexion and her long dark hair were so beautiful. And yet there was something in her expression — a dimness and vacancy in her large eyes — a changeless, unmeaning smile on her parted lips —

which seemed to jar with all that was naturally attractive in her face; which perplexed, disappointed, and even shocked me, though I hardy knew why. Mr. Garthwaite, who had been walking along thoughtfully, with his eyes on the ground, turned back when he found me lingering behind him; looked up where I was looking; started a little, I thought; then took my arm, whispered rather impatiently, "Don't say anything about having seen that poor child when you are introduced to Miss Welwyn; I'll tell you why afterward," and led me round hastily to the front of the building.

It was a very dreary old house, with a lawn in front thickly sprinkled with flower-beds, and creepers of all sorts climbing in profusion about the heavy stone porch and the mullions of the lower windows. In spite of these prettiest of all ornaments clustering brightly round the building — in spite of the perfect repair in which it was kept from top to bottom — there was something repellent to me in the aspect of the whole place: a deathly stillness hung over it, which fell oppressively on my spirits. When my companion rang the loud, deep-toned bell, the sound startled me as if we had been committing a crime in disturbing the silence. And when the door was opened by an old female servant (while the hollow echo of the bell was still vibrating in the air), I could hardly imagine it possible that we should be let in. We were admitted, however, without the slightest demur. I remarked that there was the same atmosphere of dreary repose inside the house which I had already observed, or rather felt, outside it. No dogs barked at our approach — no doors banged in the servants' offices — no heads peeped over the banisters — not one of the ordinary domestic consequences of an unexpected visit in the country met either eye or ear. The large shadowy apartment, half library, half breakfast-room, into which we were ushered, was as solitary as the hall of entrance; unless I except such drowsy evidences of life as were here presented to us in the shape of an Angola cat and a gray parrot — the first lying asleep in a chair, the second sitting ancient, solemn, and voiceless, in a large cage.

Mr. Garthwaite walked to the window when we entered, without saying a word. Determining to let his taciturn humor have its way, I asked him no questions, but looked around the room to see what information it would give me (and rooms often do give such information) about the character and habits of the owner of the house.

Two tables covered with books were the first objects that attracted me. On approaching them, I was surprised to find that the all-influencing periodical literature of the present day — whose sphere is already almost without limit; whose readers, even in our time, may be numbered by millions — was entirely unrepresented on Miss Welwyn's table. Nothing modern, nothing contemporary, in the world of books, presented itself. Of all the volumes beneath my hand, not one bore the badge of the circulating library, or wore the flaring modern livery of gilt cloth. Every work that I took up had been written at least fifteen or twenty years since. The prints hanging round the walls (toward which I next looked) were all engraved from devotional subjects by the old masters; the music-stand contained no music of later date than the compositions of Haydn and Mozart. Whatever I examined besides, told me, with the same consistency, the same strange tale. The owner of these possessions lived in the by-gone time; lived among old recollections and old associations — a voluntary recluse from all that was connected with the passing day. In Miss Welwyn's house, the stir, the tumult, the "idle business" of the world evidently appealed in vain to sympathies which grew no longer with the growing hour.

As these thoughts were passing through my mind, the door opened and the lady herself appeared.

She looked certainly past the prime of life; longer past it, as I afterward discovered, than she really was. But I never remember, in any other face, to have seen so much of the better part of the beauty of early womanhood still remaining, as I saw in hers. Sorrow had evidently passed over the fair, calm countenance before me, but had left resignation there as its only trace. Her expression was still youthful — youthful in its kindness and its candor especially. It was only when I looked at her hair, that was now growing gray — at her wan, thin hands — at the faint lines marked round her mouth — at the sad serenity of her eyes, that I fairly detected the mark of age; and, more than that, the token of some great grief, which had been conquered, but not banished. Even from her voice alone — from the peculiar uncertainty of its low, calm tones when she spoke — it was easy to conjecture that she must have passed through sufferings, at some time of her life, which had tried to the quick the noble nature that they could not subdue.

Mr. Garthwaite and she met each other almost like brother and sister; it was plain that the friendly intimacy between them had been of very long duration. Our visit was a short one. The conversation never advanced beyond the commonplace topics suited to the occasion. It was, therefore, from what I saw, and not from what I heard, that I was enabled to form my judgment of Miss Welwyn. Deeply as she had interested me — far more deeply than I at all know how to explain in fitting words — I cannot say that I was unwilling to depart when we rose to take leave. Though nothing could be more courteous and more kind than her manner toward me during the whole interview, I could still perceive that it cost her some effort to repress in my presence the shades of sadness and reserve which seemed often ready to steal over her. And I must confess that when I once or twice heard the half-sigh stifled, and saw the momentary relapse into thoughtfulness suddenly restrained, I felt an indefinable awkwardness in my position which made me ill at ease; which set me doubting whether, as a perfect stranger, I had done right in suffering myself to be introduced where no new faces could awaken either interest or curiosity;

where no new sympathies could ever be felt, no new friendships ever be formed.

As soon as we had taken leave of Miss Welwyn, and were on our way to the stream in her grounds, I more than satisfied Mr. Garthwaite that the impression the lady had produced on me was of no transitory kind, by overwhelming him with questions about her — not omitting one or two incidental inquiries on the subject of the little girl whom I had seen at the back window. He only rejoined that his story would answer all my questions; and that he would begin to tell it as soon as we had arrived at Glenwith Beck, and were comfortably settled to fishing.

Five minutes more of walking brought us to the bank of the stream, and showed us the water running smoothly and slowly, tinged with the softest green luster from the reflections of trees which almost entirely arched it over. Leaving me to admire the view at my ease, Mr. Garthwaite occupied himself with the necessary preparations for angling, baiting my hook as well as his own. Then, desiring me to sit near him on the bank, he at last satisfied my curiosity by beginning his story. I shall relate it in his own manner, and, as nearly as possible, in his own words.

THE ANGLER'S STORY OF THE LADY
OF GLENWITH GRANGE.

I have known Miss Welwyn long enough to be able to bear personal testimony to the truth of many of the particulars which I am now about to relate. I knew her father, and her younger sister Rosamond; and I was acquainted with the Frenchman who became Rosamond's husband. These are the persons of whom it will be principally necessary for me to speak. They are the only prominent characters in my story.

Miss Welwyn's father died some years since. I remember him very well — though he never excited in me, or in any one else that I ever heard of, the slightest feeling of interest. When I have said that he inherited a very large fortune, amassed during his father's time, by speculations of a very daring, very fortunate, but not always very honorable kind, and that he bought this old house with the notion of raising his social position, by making himself a member of our landed aristocracy in these parts, I have told you as much about him, I suspect, as you would care to hear. He was a thoroughly commonplace man, with no great virtues and no great vices in him. He had a little heart, a feeble mind, an amiable temper, a tall figure, and a handsome face. More than this need not, and cannot, be said on the subject of Mr. Welwyn's character.

I must have seen the late Mrs. Welwyn very often as a child; but I cannot say that I remember anything more of her than that she was tall and handsome, and very generous and sweet-tempered toward me when I was in her company. She was her husband's superior in birth, as in everything else; was a great reader of books in all languages; and possessed such admirable talents as a musician, that her wonderful playing on the organ is remembered and talked of to this day among the old people in our country houses about here. All her friends, as I have heard, were disappointed when she married Mr. Welwyn, rich as he was; and were afterward astonished to find her preserving the appearance, at least, of being perfectly happy with a husband who, neither in mind nor heart, was worthy of her.

It was generally supposed (and I have no doubt correctly) that she found her great happiness and her great consolation in her little girl Ida — now the lady from whom we have just parted. The child took after her mother from the first — inheriting her mother's fondness for books, her mother's love of music, her mother's quick sensibilities, and, more than all, her mother's quiet firmness, patience, and loving kindness of disposition. From Ida's earliest years, Mrs. Welwyn undertook the whole superintendence of her education. The two were hardly ever apart, within doors or without. Neighbors and friends said that the little girl was being brought up too fancifully, and was not enough among other children, was sadly neglected as to all reasonable and practical teaching, and was perilously encouraged in those dreamy and imaginative tendencies of which she had naturally more than her due share. There was, perhaps, some truth in this; and there might have been still more, if Ida had possessed an ordinary character, or had been reserved for an ordinary destiny. But she was a strange child from the first, and a strange future was in store for her.

Little Ida reached her eleventh year without either brother or sister to be her playfellow and companion at home. Immediately after that period, however, her sister Rosamond was born. Though Mr. Welwyn's own desire was to have had a son, there were, nevertheless, great rejoicings yonder in the old house on the birth of this second daughter. But they were all turned, only a few months afterward, to the bitterest grief and despair: the Grange lost its mistress. While Rosamond was still an infant in arms, her mother died.

Mrs. Welwyn had been afflicted with some disorder after the birth of her second child, the name of which I am not learned enough in medical science to be able to remember. I only know that she recovered from it, to all appearance, in an unexpectedly short time; that she suffered a fatal relapse, and that she died a lingering and a painful death. Mr. Welwyn (who, in after years, had a habit of vaingloriously describing his marriage as "a love-match on both sides") was really fond of his wife in his own frivolous, feeble way, and suffered as acutely as such a man could suffer, during the latter days of her illness, and at the terrible time when the doctors, one and all, confessed that her life was a thing to be despaired of. He burst into irrepressible passions of tears, and was always obliged to leave the sick-room whenever Mrs. Welwyn spoke of her approaching end. The last solemn words of the dying woman, the tenderest messages that she could give, the dearest parting wishes that she could express, the most earnest commands that she could leave behind her, the gentlest reasons for consolation that she could suggest to the survivors among those who loved her, were not poured into her husband's ear, but into her child's. From the first period of her illness, Ida had persisted in remaining in the sick-room, rarely speaking, never showing outwardly any signs of terror or grief, except when she was removed from it; and then bursting into hysterical passions of weeping, which no expostulations, no arguments, no commands — nothing, in short, but bringing her back to the bedside — ever availed to calm. Her mother had been her playfellow, her companion her dearest and most familiar friend; and there seemed something in the remembrance of this which, instead of overwhelming the child with despair, strengthened her to watch faithfully and bravely by her dying parent to the very last.

When the parting moment was over, and when Mr. Welwyn, unable to bear the shock of being present in the house of death at the time of his wife's funeral, left home and went to stay with one of his relations in a distant part of England, Ida, whom it had been his wish to take away with him, petitioned earnestly to be left behind. "I promised mamma before she died that I would be as good to my little sister Rosamond as she had been to me," said the child, simply; "and she told me in return that I might wait here and see her laid in her grave." There happened to be an aunt of Mrs. Welwyn, and an old servant of the family, in the house at this time, who understood Ida much better than her father did, and they persuaded him not to take her away. I have heard my mother say that the effect of the child's appearance at the funeral on her, and on all who went to see it, was something that she could never think of without the tears coming into her eyes, and could never forget to the last day of her life.

It must have been very shortly after this period that I saw Ida for the first time.

I remember accompanying my mother on a visit to the old house we have just left, in the summer, when I was at home for the holidays. It was a lovely, sunshiny morning. There was nobody indoors, and we walked out into the garden. As we approached that lawn yonder, on the other side of the shrubbery, I saw, first, a young woman in mourning (apparently a servant) sitting reading; then a little girl, dressed all in black, moving toward us slowly over the bright turf, and holding up before her a baby, whom she was trying to teach to walk. She looked, to my ideas, so very young to be engaged in such an occupation as this, and her gloomy black frock appeared to be such an unnaturally grave garment for a mere child of her age, and looked so doubly dismal by contrast with the brilliant sunny lawn on which she stood, that I quite started when I first saw her, and eagerly asked my mother who she was. The answer informed me of the sad family story, which I have been just relating to you. Mrs. Welwyn had then been buried about three months; and

Ida, in her childish way, was trying, as she had promised, to supply her mother's place to her infant sister Rosamond.

I only mention this simple incident, because it is necessary, before I proceed to the eventful part of my narrative, that you should know exactly in what relation the sisters stood toward one another from the first. Of all the last parting words that Mrs. Welwyn had spoken to her child, none had been oftener repeated, none more solemnly urged, than those which had commended the little Rosamond to Ida's love and care. To other persons, the full, the all-trusting dependence which the dying mother was known to have placed in a child hardly eleven years old, seemed merely a proof of that helpless desire to cling even to the feeblest consolations, which the approach of death so often brings with it. But the event showed that the trust so strangely placed had not been ventured vainly when it was committed to young and tender hands. The whole future existence of the child was one noble proof that she had been worthy of her mother's dying confidence, when it was first reposed in her. In that simple incident which I have just mentioned the new life of the two motherless sisters was all foreshadowed.

Time passed. I left school — went to college — traveled in Germany, and stayed there some time to learn the language. At every interval when I came home, and asked about the Welwyns, the answer was, in substance, almost always the same. Mr. Welwyn was giving his regular dinners, performing his regular duties as a county magistrate, enjoying his regular recreations as an a amateur farmer and an eager sportsman. His two daughters were never separate. Ida was the same strange, quiet, retiring girl, that she had always been; and was still (as the phrase went) "spoiling" Rosamond in every way in which it was possible for an elder sister to spoil a younger by too much kindness.

I myself went to the Grange occasionally, when I was in this neighborhood, in holiday and vacation time; and was able to test the correctness of the picture of life there which had been drawn for me. I remember the two sisters, when Rosamond was four or five years old; and when Ida seemed to me, even then, to be more like the child's mother than her sister. She bore with her little caprices as sisters do not bear with one another. She was so patient at lesson-time, so anxious to conceal any weariness that might overcome her in play hours, so proud when Rosamond's beauty was noticed, so grateful for Rosamond's kisses when the child thought of bestowing them, so quick to notice all that Rosamond did, and to attend to all that Rosamond said, even when visitors were in the room, that she seemed, to my boyish observation, altogether different from other elder sisters in other family circles into which I was then received.

I remember then, again, when Rosamond was just growing to womanhood, and was in high spirits at the prospect of spending a season in London, and being presented at court. She was very beautiful at that time — much handsomer than Ida. Her "accomplishments" were talked of far and near in our country circles. Few, if any, of the people, however, who applauded her playing and singing, who admired her water-color drawings, who were delighted at her fluency when she spoke French, and amazed at her ready comprehension when she read German, knew how little of all this elegant mental cultivation and nimble manual dexterity she owed to her governess and masters, and how much to her elder sister. It was Ida who really found out the means of stimulating her when she was idle; Ida who helped her through all her worst difficulties; Ida who gently conquered her defects of memory over her books, her inaccuracies of ear at the piano, her errors of taste when she took the brush and pencil in hand. It was Ida alone who worked these marvels, and whose all-sufficient reward for her hardest exertions was a chance word of kindness from her sister's lips. Rosamond was not unaffectionate, and not ungrateful; but she inherited much of her father's commonness and frivolity of character. She became so accustomed to owe everything to her sister — to resign all her most trifling difficulties to Ida's ever-ready care — to have all her tastes consulted by Ida's ever-watchful kindness — that she never appreciated, as it deserved, the deep, devoted love of which she was the object. When Ida refused two good offers of marriage, Rosamond was as much astonished as the veriest strangers, who wondered why the elder Miss Welwyn seemed bent on remaining single all her life.

When the journey to London, to which I have already alluded, took place, Ida accompanied her father and sister. If she had consulted her own tastes, she would have remained in the country; but Rosamond declared that she should feel quite lost and helpless twenty times a day, in town, without her sister. It was in the nature of Ida to sacrifice herself to any one whom she loved, on the smallest occasions as well as the greatest. Her affection was as intuitively ready to sanctify Rosamond's slightest caprices as to excuse Rosamond's most thoughtless faults. So she went to London cheerfully, to witness with pride all the little triumphs won by her sister's beauty; to hear, and never tire of hearing, all that admiring friends could say in her sister's praise.

At the end of the season Mr. Welwyn and his daughters returned for a short time to the country; then left home again to spend the latter part of the autumn and the beginning of the winter in Paris.

They took with them excellent letters of introduction, and saw a great deal of the best society in Paris, foreign as well as English. At one of the first of the evening parties which they attended, the general topic of conversation was the conduct of a certain French nobleman, the Baron Franval, who had returned to his native country after a long absence, and who was spoken of in terms of high eulogy by the majority of the guests present. The history of who Franval was, and of what he had done, was readily communicated to Mr. Welwyn and his daughters, and was briefly this:

The baron inherited little from his ancestors besides his high rank and his ancient pedigree. On the death of his parents, he and his two unmarried sisters (their only surviving children) found the small territorial property of the Franvals, in Normandy, barely productive enough to afford a comfortable subsistence for the three. The baron, then a young man of three-and-twenty endeavored to obtain such military or civil employment as might become his rank; but, although the Bourbons were at that time restored to the throne of France, his efforts were ineffectual. Either his interest at court was bad, or secret enemies were at work to oppose his advancement. He failed to obtain even the slightest favor; and, irritated by undeserved neglect, resolved to leave France, and seek occupation for his energies in foreign countries, where his rank would be no bar to his bettering his fortunes, if he pleased, by engaging in commercial pursuits.

An opportunity of the kind that he wanted unexpectedly offered itself. He left his sisters in care of an old male relative of the family at the chateau in Normandy, and sailed, in the first instance, to the West Indies; afterward extending his wanderings to the continent of South America, and there engaging in mining transactions on a very large scale. After fifteen years of absence (during the latter part of which time false reports of his death had reached Normandy), he had just returned to France, having realized a handsome independence, with which he proposed to widen the limits of his ancestral property, and to give his sisters (who were still, like himself, unmarried) all the luxuries and advantages that affluence could bestow. The baron's independent spirit and generous devotion to the honor of his family and the happiness of his surviving relatives were themes of general admiration in most of the social circles of Paris. He was expected to arrive in the capital every day; and it was naturally enough predicted that his reception in society there could not fail to be of the most flattering and most brilliant kind.

The Welwyns listened to this story with some little interest; Rosamond, who was very romantic, being especially attracted by it, and openly avowing to her father and sister, when they got back to their hotel, that she felt as ardent a curiosity as anybody to see the adventurous and generous baron. The desire was soon gratified. Franval came to Paris, as had been anticipated — was introduced to the Welwyns — met them constantly in society — made no favorable impression on Ida, but won the good opinion of Rosamond from the first; and was regarded with such high approval by their father, that when he mentioned his intentions of visiting England in the spring of the new year, he was cordially invited to spend the hunting season at Glenwith Grange.

I came back from Germany about the same time that the Welwyns returned from Paris, and at once set myself to improve my neighborly intimacy with the family. I was very fond of Ida; more fond, perhaps, than my vanity will now allow me to —; but that is of no consequence. It is much more to the purpose to tell you that I heard the whole of the baron's story enthusiastically related by Mr. Welwyn and Rosamond; that he came to the Grange at the appointed time; that I was introduced to him; and that he produced as unfavorable an impression upon me as he had already produced upon Ida.

It was whimsical enough; but I really could not tell why I disliked him, though I could account very easily, according to my own notions, for his winning the favor and approval of Rosamond and her father. He was certainly a handsome man as far as features went; he had a winning gentleness and graceful respect in his manner when he spoke to women; and he sang remarkably well, with one of the sweetest tenor voices I ever heard. These qualities alone were quite sufficient to attract any girl of Rosamond's disposition; and I certainly never wondered why he was a favorite of hers.

Then, as to her father, the baron was not only fitted to win his sympathy and regard in the field, by proving himself an ardent sportsman and an excellent rider; but was also, in virtue of some of his minor personal peculiarities, just the man to gain the friendship of his host. Mr. Welwyn was as ridiculously prejudiced as most weak-headed Englishmen are, on the subject of foreigners in general. In spite of his visit to Paris, the vulgar notion of a Frenchman continued to be *his* notion, both while he was in France and when he returned from it. Now, the baron was as unlike the traditional "Mounseer" of English songs, plays, and satires, as a man could well be; and it was on account of this very dissimilarity that Mr. Welwyn first took a violent fancy to him, and then invited him to his house. Franval spoke English remarkably well; wore neither beard, mustache, nor whiskers; kept his hair cut almost unbecomingly short; dressed in the extreme of plainness and modest good taste; talked little in general society; uttered his words, when he did speak, with singular calmness and deliberation; and, to crown all, had the greater part of his acquired property invested in English securities. In Mr. Welwyn's estimation, such a man as this was a perfect miracle of a Frenchman, and he admired and encouraged him accordingly.

I have said that I disliked him, yet could not assign a reason for my dislike; and I can only repeat it now. He was remarkably polite to me; we often rode together in hunting, and sat near each other at the Grange table; but I could never become familiar with him. He always gave me the idea of a man who had some mental reservation in saying the most trifling thing. There was a constant restraint, hardly perceptible to most people, but plainly visible, nevertheless, to me, which seemed to accompany his lightest words, and to hang about his most familiar manner. This, however, was no just reason for my secretly disliking and distrusting him as I did. Ida said as much to me, I remember, when I confessed to her what my feelings toward him were, and tried (but vainly) to induce her to be equally candid with me in return. She seemed to shrink from the tacit condemnation of Rosamond's opinion which such a confidence on her part would have implied. And yet she watched the growth of that opinion — or, in other words, the growth of her sister's liking for the baron — with an apprehension and sorrow which she tried fruitlessly to conceal. Even her father began to notice that her spirits were not so good as usual, and to suspect the cause of her melancholy. I remember he jested, with all the dense insensibility of a stupid man, about Ida having invariably been jealous, from a child, if Rosamond looked kindly upon anybody except her elder sister.

The spring began to get far advanced toward summer. Franval paid a visit to London; came back in the middle of the season to Glenwith Grange; wrote to put off his departure for France; and at last (not at all to the surprise of anybody who was intimate with the Welwyns) proposed to Rosamond, and was accepted. He was candor and generosity itself when the preliminaries of the marriage-settlement were under discussion. He quite overpowered Mr. Welwyn and the lawyers with references, papers, and statements of the distribution and extent of his property, which were found to be perfectly correct. His sisters were written to, and returned the most cordial answers; saying that the state of their health would not allow them to come to England for the marriage; but adding a warm invitation to Normandy for the bride and her family. Nothing, in short, could be more straightforward and satisfactory than the baron's behavior, and the testimonies to his worth and integrity which the news of the approaching marriage produced from his relatives and his friends.

The only joyless face at the Grange now was Ida's. At any time it would have been a hard trial to her to resign that first and foremost place which she had held since childhood in her sister's heart, as she knew she must resign it when Rosamond married. But, secretly disliking and distrusting Franval as she did, the thought that he was soon to become the husband of her beloved sister filled her with a vague sense of terror which she could not explain to herself; which it was imperatively necessary that she should conceal; and which, on those very accounts, became a daily and hourly torment to her that was almost more than she could bear.

One consolation alone supported her: Rosamond and she were not to be separated. She knew that the baron secretly disliked her as much as she disliked him; she knew that she must bid farewell to the brighter and happier part of her life on the day when she went to live under the same roof with her sister's husband; but, true to the promise made years and years ago by her dying mother's bed — true to the affection which was the ruling and beautiful feeling of her whole existence — she never hesitated about indulging Rosamond's wish, when the girl, in her bright, light-hearted way, said that she could never get on comfortably in the marriage state unless she had Ida to live with her and help her just the same as ever. The baron was too polite a man even to *look* dissatisfied when he heard of the proposed arrangement; and it was therefore settled from the beginning that Ida was always to live with her sister.

The marriage took place in the summer, and the bride and bridegroom went to spend their honeymoon in Cumberland. On their return to Glenwith Grange, a visit to the baron's sisters, in Normandy, was talked of; but the execution of this project was suddenly and disastrously suspended by the death of Mr. Welwyn, from an attack of pleurisy.

In consequence of this calamity, the projected journey was of course deferred; and when autumn and the shooting season came, the baron was unwilling to leave the well-stocked preserves of the Grange. He seemed, indeed, to grow less and less inclined, as time advanced, for the trip to Normandy; and wrote excuse after excuse to his sisters, when letters arrived from them urging him to pay the promised visit. In the winter-time, he said he would not allow his wife to risk a long journey. In the spring, his health was pronounced to be delicate. In the genial summer-time, the accomplishment of the proposed visit would be impossible, for at that period the baroness expected to become a mother. Such were the apologies which Franval seemed almost glad to be able to send to his sisters in France.

The marriage was, in the strictest sense of the term, a happy one. The baron, though he never altogether lost the strange restraint and reserve of his manner, was, in his quiet, peculiar way, the fondest and kindest of husbands. He went to town occasionally on business, but always seemed glad to return to the baroness; he never varied in the politeness of his bearing toward his wife's sister; he behaved with the most courteous hospitality toward all the friends of the Welwyns; in short, he thoroughly justified the good opinion which Rosamond and her father had formed of him when they first met at Paris. And yet no experience of his character thoroughly re-assured Ida. Months passed on quietly and pleasantly; and still that secret sadness, that indefinable, unreasonable apprehension on Rosamond's account, hung heavily on her sister's heart.

At the beginning of the first summer months, a little domestic inconvenience happened, which showed the baroness, for the first time, that her husband's temper could be seriously ruffled — and that by the veriest trifle. He was in the habit of taking in two French provincial newspapers — one published at Bordeaux and the other at Havre. He always opened these journals the moment they came, looked at one particular column of each with the deepest attention, for a few minutes, then carelessly threw them aside into his waste-paper basket. His wife and her sister were at first rather surprised at the manner in which he read his two papers; but they thought no more of it when he explained that he only took them in to consult them about French commercial intelligence, which might be, occasionally, of importance to him.

These papers were published weekly. On the occasion to which I have just referred, the Bordeaux paper came on the proper day, as usual; but the

Havre paper never made its appearance. This trifling circumstance seemed to make the baron seriously uneasy. He wrote off directly to the country post-office and to the newspaper agent in London. His wife, astonished to see his tranquillity so completely overthrown by so slight a cause, tried to restore his good humor by jesting with him about the missing newspaper. He replied by the first angry and unfeeling words that she had heard issue from his lips. She was then within about six weeks of her confinement, and very unfit to bear harsh answers from anybody — least of all from her husband.

On the second day no answer came. On the afternoon of the third, the baron rode off to the post town to make inquiries. About an hour after he had gone, a strange gentleman came to the Grange and asked to see the baroness. On being informed that she was not well enough to receive visitors, he sent up a message that his business was of great importance and that he would wait downstairs for a second answer.

On receiving this message, Rosamond turned, as usual, to her elder sister for advice. Ida went downstairs immediately to see the stranger. What I am now about to tell you of the extraordinary interview which took place between them, and of the shocking events that followed it, I have heard from Miss Welwyn's own lips.

She felt unaccountably nervous when she entered the room. The stranger bowed very politely, and asked, in a foreign accent, if she were the Baroness Franval. She set him right on this point, and told him she attended to all matters of business for the baroness; adding that, if his errand at all concerned her sister's husband, the baron was not then at home.

The stranger answered that he was aware of it when he called, and that the unpleasant business on which he came could not be confided to the baron — at least, in the first instance.

She asked why. He said he was there to explain; and expressed himself as feeling greatly relieved at having to open his business to her, because she would, doubtless, be best able to prepare her sister for the bad news that he was, unfortunately, obliged to bring. The sudden faintness which overcame her, as he spoke those words, prevented her from addressing him in return. He poured out some water for her from a bottle which happened to be standing on the table, and asked if he might depend on her fortitude. She tried to say "Yes"; but the violent throbbing of her heart seemed to choke her. He took a foreign newspaper from his pocket, saying that he was a secret agent of the French police — that the paper was the Havre *Journal* , for the past week, and that it had been expressly kept from reaching the baron, as usual, through his (the agent's) interference. He then opened the newspaper, and begged that she would nerve herself sufficiently (for her sister's sake) to read certain lines, which would give her some hint of the business that brought him there. He pointed to the passage as he spoke. It was among the "Shipping Entries," and was thus expressed:

"Arrived, the *Berenice* , from San Francisco, with a valuable cargo of hides. She brings one passenger, the Baron Franval, of Chateau Franval, in Normandy."

As Miss Welwyn read the entry, her heart, which had been throbbing violently but the moment before, seemed suddenly to cease from all action, and she began to shiver, though it was a warm June evening. The agent held the tumbler to her lips, and made her drink a little of the water, entreating her very earnestly to take courage and listen to him. He then sat down, and referred again to the entry, every word he uttered seeming to burn itself in forever (as she expressed it) on her memory and her heart.

He said: "It has been ascertained beyond the possibility of doubt that there is no mistake about the name in the lines you have just read. And it is as certain as that we are here, that there is only *one* Baron Franval now alive. The question, therefore, is, whether the passenger by the *Berenice* is the true baron, or — I beg you most earnestly to bear with me and to compose yourself — or the husband of your sister. The person who arrived last week at Havre was scouted as an impostor by the ladies at the chateau, the moment he presented himself there as the brother, returning to them after sixteen years of absence. The authorities were communicated with, and I and my assistants were instantly sent for from Paris.

"We wasted no time in questioning the supposed impostor. He either was, or affected to be, in a perfect frenzy of grief and indignation. We just ascertained, from competent witnesses, that he bore an extraordinary resemblance to the real baron, and that he was perfectly familiar with places and persons in and about the chateau; we just ascertained that, and then proceeded to confer with the local authorities, and to examine their private entries of suspected persons in their jurisdiction, ranging back over a past period of twenty years or more. One of the entries thus consulted contained these particulars: 'Hector Auguste Monbrun, son of a respectable proprietor in Normandy. Well educated; gentleman-like manners. On bad terms with his family. Character: bold, cunning, unscrupulous, self-possessed. Is a clever mimic. May be easily recognized by his striking likeness to the Baron Franval. Imprisoned at twenty for theft and assault.'"

Miss Welwyn saw the agent look up at her after he had read this extract from the police-book, to ascertain if she was still able to listen to him. He asked, with some appearance of alarm, as their eyes met, if she would like some more water. She was just able to make a sign in the negative. He took a second extract from his pocket-book, and went on.

He said: "The next entry under the same name was dated four years later, and ran thus, 'H. A. Monbrun, condemned to the galleys for life, for assassination, and other crimes not officially necessary to be here specified. Escaped from custody at Toulon. Is known, since the expiration of his first term of imprisonment, to have allowed his beard to grow, and to have worn his hair long, with the intention of rendering it impossible for those acquainted with him in his native province to recognize him, as heretofore, by his likeness to the Baron Franval.' There were more particulars added, not important enough for extract. We immediately examined the supposed impostor; for, if he was Monbrun, we knew that we should find on his shoulder the two letters of the convict brand, 'T. F.,' standing for *Travaux Forces* . After the minutest exami-nation with the mechanical and chemical tests used on such occasions, not the slightest trace of the brand was to be found. The moment this astounding discovery was made, I started to lay an embargo on the forthcoming numbers of the Havre *Journal* for that week, which were about to be sent to the English agent in London. I arrived at Havre on Saturday (the morning of publication), in time to execute my design. I waited there long enough to communicate by telegraph with my superiors in Paris, then hastened to this place. What my errand here is, you may —"

He might have gone on speaking for some moments longer; but Miss Welwyn heard no more.

Her first sensation of returning consciousness was the feeling that water was being sprinkled on her face. Then she saw that all the windows in the room had been set wide open, to give her air; and that she and the agent were still alone. At first she felt bewildered, and hardly knew who he was; but he soon recalled to her mind the horrible realities that had brought him there, by apologizing for not having summoned assistance when she fainted. He said it was of the last importance, in Franval's absence, that no one in the house should imagine that anything unusual was taking place in it. Then, after giving her an interval of a minute or two to collect what little strength she had left, he added that he would not increase her sufferings by saying anything more, just then, on the shocking subject of the investigation which it was his duty to make — that he would leave her to recover herself, and to consider what was the best course to be taken with the baroness in the present terrible emergency — and that he would privately return to the house between eight and nine o'clock that evening, ready to act as Miss Welwyn wished, and to afford her and her sister any aid and protection of which they might stand in need. With these words he bowed, and noiselessly quitted the room.

For the first few awful minutes after she was left alone, Miss Welwyn sat helpless and speechless; utterly numbed in heart, and mind, and body — then a sort of instinct (she was incapable of thinking) seemed to urge her to conceal the fearful news from her sister as long as possible. She ran upstairs to Rosa-mond's sitting-room, and called through the door (for she dared not trust herself in her sister's presence) that the visitor had come on some troublesome business from their late father's lawyers, and that she was going to shut herself up, and write some long letters in connection with that business. After she had got into her own room, she was never sensible of how time was passing — never conscious of any feeling within her, except a baseless, helpless hope that the French police might yet be proved to have made some terrible mistake — until she heard a violent shower of rain come on a little after sunset. The noise of the rain, and the freshness it brought with it in the air, seemed to awaken her as if from a painful and a fearful sleep. The power of reflection returned to her; her heart heaved and bounded with an overwhelming terror, as the thought of Rosamond came back vividly to it; her memory recurred despairingly to the long-past day of her mother's death, and to the farewell promise she had made by her mother's bedside. She burst into an hysterical passion of weeping that seemed to be tearing her to pieces. In the midst of it she heard the clatter of a horse's hoofs in the courtyard, and knew that Rosamond's husband had come back.

Dipping her handkerchief in cold water, and passing it over her eyes as she left the room, she instantly hastened to her sister.

Fortunately the daylight was fading in the old-fashioned chamber that Rosamond occupied. Before they could say two words to each other, Franval was in the room. He seemed violently irritated; said that he had waited for the arrival of the mail — that the missing newspaper had not come by it — that he had got wet through — that he felt a shivering fit coming on — and that he believed he had caught a violent cold. His wife anxiously suggested some simple remedies. He roughly interrupted her, saying there was but one remedy, the remedy of going to bed; and so left them without another word. She just put her handkerchief to her eyes, and said softly to her sister, "How he is changed!" then spoke no more. They sat silent for half an hour or longer. After that, Rosamond went affectionately and forgivingly to see how her husband was. She returned, saying that he was in bed, and in a deep, heavy sleep; and predicting hopefully that he would wake up quite well the next morning. In a few minutes more the clock stuck nine; and Ida heard the servant's step ascending the stairs. She suspected what his errand was, and went out to meet him. Her presentiment had not deceived her; the police agent had arrived, and was waiting for her downstairs.

He asked her if she had said anything to her sister, or had thought of any plan of action, the moment she entered the room; and, on receiving a reply in the negative, inquired, further, if "the baron" had come home yet. She answered that he had; that he was ill and tired, and vexed, and that he had gone to bed. The agent asked in an eager whisper if she knew that he was asleep, and alone in bed? and, when he received her reply, said that he must go up into the bedroom directly.

She began to feel the faintness coming over her again, and with it sensations of loathing and terror that she could neither express to others nor define to herself. He said that if she hesitated to let him avail himself of this unexpected opportunity, her scruples might lead to fatal results He reminded her that if "the baron" were really the convict Monbrun, the claims of society and of justice demanded that he should be discovered by the first available means; and that if he were not — if some inconceivable mistake had really been committed — then such a plan for getting immediately at the truth as was now proposed would insure the delivery of an innocent man from suspicion; and at the same time spare him the knowledge that he had ever been suspected. This last argument had its effect on Miss Welwyn. The baseless, helpless hope that the French authorities might yet be proved to be in error, which she had already felt in her own room, returned to her now. She suffered the agent to lead her upstairs.

He took the candle from her hand when she pointed to the door; opened it softly; and, leaving it ajar, went into the room.

She looked through the gap with a feverish, horror-struck curiosity. Franval was lying on his side in a profound sleep, with his back turned toward the door. The agent softly placed the candle upon a small reading-table between the door and the bedside, softly drew down the bed-clothes a little away from the sleeper's back, then took a pair of scissors from the toilet-table, and very gently and slowly began to cut away, first the loose folds, then the intervening strips of linen, from the part of Franval's night-gown that was over his shoulders. When the upper part of his back had been bared in this way, the agent took the candle and held it near the flesh. Miss Welwyn heard him ejaculate some word under his breath, then saw him looking round to where she was standing, and beckoning to her to come in.

Mechanically she obeyed; mechanically she looked down where his finger was pointing. It was the convict Monbrun — there, just visible under the bright light of the candle, were the fatal letters "T. F." branded on the villain's shoulder!

Though she could neither move nor speak, the horror of this discovery did not deprive her of her consciousness. She saw the agent softly draw up the bed-clothes again into their proper position, replace the scissors on the toilet-table, and take from it a bottle of smelling-salts. She felt him removing her from the bedroom, and helping her quickly downstairs, giving her the salts to smell to by the way. When they were alone again, he said, with the first appearance of agitation that he had yet exhibited, "Now, madam, for God's sake, collect all your courage, and be guided by me. You and your sister had better leave the house immediately. Have you any relatives in the neighborhood with whom you could take refuge?" They had none. "What is the name of the nearest town where you could get good accommodation for the night?" Harleybrook (he wrote the name down on his tablets). "How far off is it?"

Twelve miles. "You had better have the carriage out at once, to go there with as little delay as possible, leaving me to pass the night here. I will communicate with you tomorrow at the principal hotel. Can you compose yourself sufficiently to be able to tell the head servant, if I ring for him, that he is to obey my orders till further notice?" The servant was summoned, and received his instructions, the agent going out with him to see that the carriage was got ready quietly and quickly. Miss Welwyn went upstairs to her sister.

How the fearful news was first broken to Rosamond, I cannot relate to you. Miss Welwyn has never confided to me, has never confided to anybody, what happened at the interview between her sister and herself that night. I can tell you nothing of the shock they both suffered, except that the younger and the weaker died under it; that the elder and the stronger has never recovered from it, and never will.

They went away the same night, with one attendant, to Harleybrook, as the agent had advised. Before daybreak Rosamond was seized with the pains of premature labor. She died three days after, unconscious of the horror of her situation, wandering in her mind about past times, and singing old tunes that Ida had taught her as she lay in her sister's arms.

The child was born alive, and lives still. You saw her at the window as we came in at the back way to the Grange. I surprised you, I dare say, by asking you not to speak of her to Miss Welwyn. Perhaps you noticed something vacant in the little girl's expression. I am sorry to say that her mind is more vacant still. If "idiot" did not sound like a mocking word, however tenderly and pityingly one may wish to utter it, I should tell you that the poor thing had been an idiot from her birth.

You will, doubtless, want to hear now what happened at Glenwith Grange after Miss Welwyn and her sister had left it. I have seen the letter which the police agent sent the next morning to Harleybrook; and, speaking from my recollection of that, I shall be able to relate all you can desire to know.

First, as to the past history of the scoundrel Monbrun, I need only tell you that he was identical with an escaped convict, who, for a long term of years, had successfully eluded the vigilance of the authorities all over Europe, and in America as well. In conjunction with two accomplices, he had succeeded in possessing himself of large sums of money by the most criminal means. He also acted secretly as the "banker" of his convict brethren, whose dishonest gains were all confided to his hands for safe-keeping. He would have been certainly captured, on venturing back to France, along with his two associates, but for the daring imposture in which he took refuge; and which, if the true Baron Franval had really died abroad, as was reported, would, in all probability, never have been found out.

Besides his extraordinary likeness to the baron, he had every other requisite for carrying on his deception successfully. Though his parents were not wealthy, he had received a good education. He was so notorious for his gentle-man-like manners among the villainous associates of his crimes and excesses, that they nicknamed him "the Prince." All his early life had been passed in the neighborhood of the Chateau Franval. He knew what were the circumstances which had induced the baron to leave it. He had been in the country to which the baron had emigrated. He was able to refer familiarly to persons and locali-ties, at home and abroad, with which the baron was sure to be acquainted. And, lastly, he had an expatriation of fifteen years to plead for him as his all-sufficient excuse, if he made any slight mistakes before the baron's sisters, in his assumed character of their long-absent brother. It will be, of course, hardly necessary for me to tell you, in relation to this part of the subject, that the true Franval was immediately and honorably reinstated in the family rights of which the impostor had succeeded for a time in depriving him.

According to Monbrun's own account, he had married poor Rosamond purely for love; and the probabilities certainly are, that the pretty, innocent English girl had really struck the villain's fancy for the time; and that the easy, quiet life he was leading at the Grange pleased him, by contrast with his perilous and vagabond existence of former days. What might have happened if he had had time enough to grow wearied of his ill-fated wife and his English home, it is now useless to inquire. What really did happen on the morning when he awoke after the flight of Ida and her sister can be briefly told.

As soon as his eyes opened they rested on the police agent, sitting quietly by the bedside, with a loaded pistol in his hand. Monbrun knew immediately that he was discovered; but he never for an instant lost the self-possession for which he was famous. He said he wished to have five minutes allowed him to deliberate quietly in bed, whether he should resist the French authorities on English ground, and so gain time by obliging the one Government to apply specially to have him delivered up by the other — or whether he should accept the terms officially offered to him by the agent, if he quietly allowed himself to be captured. He chose the latter course — it was suspected, because he wished to communicate personally with some of his convict associates in France, whose fraudulent gains were in his keeping, and because he felt boast-fully confident of being able to escape again, whenever he pleased. Be his secret motives, however, what they might, he allowed the agent to conduct him peaceably from the Grange; first writing a farewell letter to poor Rosa-mond, full of heartless French sentiment and glib sophistries about Fate and Society. His own fate was not long in overtaking him. He attempted to escape again, as it had been expected he would, and was shot by the sentinel on duty at the time. I remember hearing that the bullet entered his head and killed him on the spot.

My story is done. It is ten years now since Rosamond was buried in the churchyard yonder; and it is ten years also since Miss Welwyn returned to be the lonely inhabitant of Glenwith Grange. She now lives but in the remembrances that it calls up before her of her happier existence of former days. There is hardly an object in the old house which does not tenderly and solemnly remind her of the mother, whose last wishes she lived to obey; of the sister, whose happiness was once her dearest earthly care. Those prints that you noticed on the library walls Rosamond used to copy in the past time, when her pencil was often guided by Ida's hand. Those music-books that you were looking over, she and her mother have played from together through many a long and quiet summer's evening. She has no ties now to bind her to the present but the poor child whose affliction it is her constant effort to lighten, and the little peasant population around her, whose humble cares and wants and sorrows she is always ready to relieve. Far and near her modest charities have penetrated among us; and far and near she is heartily beloved and blessed in many a laborer's household. There is no poor man's hearth, not in this village only, but for miles away from it as well, at which you would not be received with the welcome given to an old friend, if you only told the cottagers that you knew the Lady of Glenwith Grange!

THE NUN'S STORY OF GABRIEL'S MARRIAGE

PROLOGUE TO THE FIFTH STORY.

*T*he next piece of work which occupied my attention after taking leave of Mr. Garthwaite, offered the strongest possible contrast to the task which had last engaged me. Fresh from painting a bull at a farmhouse, I set forth to copy a Holy Family, by Correggio, at a convent of nuns. People who go to the Royal Academy Exhibition, and see pictures by famous artists, painted year after year in the same marked style which first made them celebrated, would be amazed indeed if they knew what a Jack-of-all-trades a poor painter must become before he can gain his daily bread.

The picture by Correggio which I was now commissioned to copy had been lent to the nuns by a Catholic gentleman of fortune, who prized it as the gem of his collection, and who had never before trusted it out of his own hands. My copy, when completed, was to be placed over the high altar of the convent chapel; and my work throughout its progress was to be pursued entirely in the parlor of the nunnery, and always in the watchful presence of one or other of the inmates of the house. It was only on such conditions that the owner of the Correggio was willing to trust his treasure out of his own hands, and to suffer it to be copied by a stranger. The restrictions he imposed, which I thought sufficiently absurd, and perhaps offensively suspicious as well, were communicated to me politely enough before I was allowed to undertake the commission. Unless I was inclined to submit to precautionary regulations which would affect any other artist exactly as they affected me, I was told not to think of offering to make the copy; and the nuns would then address themselves to some other person in my profession. After a day's consideration, I submitted to the restrictions, by my wife's advice, and saved the nuns the trouble of making application for a copier of Correggio in any other quarter.

I found the convent was charmingly situated in a quiet little valley in the West of England. The parlor in which I was to paint was a large, well-lighted apartment; and the village inn, about half a mile off, afforded me cheap and excellent quarters for the night. Thus far, therefore, there was nothing to complain of. As for the picture, which was the next object of interest to me, I was surprised to find that the copying of it would be by no means so difficult a task as I had anticipated. I am rather of a revolutionary spirit in matters of art, and am bold enough to think that the old masters have their faults as well as their beauties. I can give my opinion, therefore, on the Correggio at the convent independently at least. Looked at technically, the picture was a fine specimen of coloring and execution; but looked at for the higher merits of delicacy, elevation, and feeling for the subject, it deserved copying as little as the most commonplace work that any unlucky modern artist ever produced. The faces of the Holy Family not only failed to display the right purity and tenderness of expression, but absolutely failed to present any expression at all. It is flat heresy to say so, but the valuable Correggio was nevertheless emphatically, and, in so many words, a very uninteresting picture.

So much for the convent and the work that I was to do in it. My next anxiety was to see how the restrictions imposed on me were to be carried out. The first day, the Mother Superior herself mounted guard in the parlor — a stern, silent, fanatical-looking woman, who seemed determined to awe me and make me uncomfortable, and who succeeded thoroughly in the execution of her purpose. The second day she was relieved by the officiating priest of the convent — a mild, melancholy, gentleman-like man, with whom I got on tolerably well. The third day, I had for overlooker the portress of the house — a dirty, dismal, deaf, old woman, who did nothing but knit stockings and chew orris-root. The fourth day, a middle-aged nun, whom I heard addressed as Mother Martha, occupied the post of guardian to the precious Correggio; and with her the number of my overlookers terminated. She, and the portress, and the priest, and the Mother Superior, relieved each other with military regularity, until I had put the last touch to my copy. I found them ready for me every morning on entering the parlor, and I left them in the chair of observation every evening on quitting it. As for any young and beautiful nuns who might have been in the building, I never so much as set eyes on the ends of their veils. From the door to the parlor, and from the parlor to the door, comprised the whole of my experience of the inside of the convent.

The only one of my superintending companions with whom I established anything like a familiar acquaintance was Mother Martha. She had no outward attractions to recommend her; but she was simple, good-humored, ready to gossip, and inquisitive to a perfectly incredible degree. Her whole life had been passed in the nunnery; she was thoroughly accustomed to her seclusion, thoroughly content with the monotonous round of her occupations; not at all anxious to see the world for herself; but, on the other hand, insatiably curious to know all about it from others. There was no question connected with myself, my wife, my children, my friends, my profession, my income, my travels, my favorite amusements, and even my favorite sins, which a woman could ask a man, that Mother Martha did not, in the smallest and softest of voices, ask of me. Though an intelligent, well-informed person in all that related to her own special vocation, she was a perfect child in everything else. I constantly caught myself talking to her, just as I should have talked at home to one of my own little girls.

I hope no one will think that, in expressing myself thus, I am writing disparagingly of the poor nun. On two accounts, I shall always feel compassionately and gratefully toward Mother Martha. She was the only person in the convent who seemed sincerely anxious to make her presence in the parlor as agreeable to me as possible; and she good-humoredly told me the story which it is my object in these pages to introduce to the reader. In both ways I am deeply indebted to her; and I hope always to remember the obligation.

The circumstances under which the story came to be related to me may be told in very few words.

The interior of a convent parlor being a complete novelty to me, I looked around with some interest on first entering my painting-room at the nunnery. There was but little in it to excite the curiosity of any one. The floor was covered with common matting, and the ceiling with plain whitewash. The furniture was of the simplest kind; a low chair with a praying-desk fixed to the back, and a finely carved oak book-case, studded all over with brass crosses, being the only useful objects that I could discern which had any conventional character about them. As for the ornaments of the room, they were entirely beyond my appreciation. I could feel no interest in the colored prints of saints, with gold platters at the backs of their heads, that hung on the wall; and I could see nothing particularly impressive in the two plain little alabaster pots for holy water, fastened, one near the door, the other over the chimney-piece. The only object, indeed, in the whole room which in the slightest degree attracted my curiosity was an old worm-eaten wooden cross, made in the rudest manner, hanging by itself on a slip of wall between two windows. It was so strangely rough and misshapen a thing to exhibit prominently in a neat roam, that I suspected some history must be attached to it, and resolved to speak to my friend the nun about it at the earliest opportunity.

"Mother Martha," said I, taking advantage of the first pause in the succession of quaintly innocent questions which she was as usual addressing to me, "I have been looking at that rough old cross hanging between the windows, and fancying that it must surely be some curiosity —"

"Hush! hush!" exclaimed the nun, "you must not speak of that as a 'curiosity'; the Mother Superior calls it a Relic."

"I beg your pardon," said I; "I ought to have chosen my expressions more carefully —"

"Not," interposed Mother Martha, nodding to show me that my apology need not be finished —"not that it is exactly a relic in the strict Catholic sense of the word; but there were circumstances in the life of the person who made it —" Here she stopped, and looked at me doubtfully.

"Circumstances, perhaps, which it is not considered advisable to communicate to strangers," I suggested.

"Oh, no!" answered the nun, "I never heard that they were to be kept a secret. They were not told as a secret to me."

"Then you know all about them?" I asked.

"Certainly. I could tell you the whole history of the wooden cross; but it is all about Catholics, and you are a Protestant."

"That, Mother Martha, does not make it at all less interesting to me."

"Does it not, indeed?" exclaimed the nun, innocently. "What a strange man you are! and what a remarkable religion yours must be! What do your priests say about ours? Are they learned men, your priests?"

I felt that my chance of hearing Mother Martha's story would be a poor one indeed, if I allowed her to begin a fresh string of questions. Accordingly, I dismissed the inquiries about the clergy of the Established Church with the most irreverent briefness, and recalled her attention forthwith to the subject of the wooden cross.

"Yes, yes," said the good-natured nun; "surely you shall hear all I can tell you about it; but —" she hesitated timidly, "but I must ask the Mother Superior's leave first."

Saying these words, she summoned the portress, to my great amusement, to keep guard over the inestimable Correggio in her absence, and left the room. In less than five minutes she came back, looking quite happy and important in her innocent way.

"The Mother Superior," she said, "has given me leave to tell all I know about the wooden cross. She says it may do you good, and improve your Protestant opinion of us Catholics."

I expressed myself as being both willing and anxious to profit by what I heard; and the nun began her narrative immediately.

She related it in her own simple, earnest, minute way; dwelling as long on small particulars as on important incidents; and making moral reflections for my benefit at every place where it was possible to introduce them. In spite, however, of these drawbacks in the telling of it, the story interested and impressed me in no ordinary degree; and I now purpose putting the events of it together as skillfully and strikingly as I can, in the hope that this written version of the narrative may appeal as strongly to the reader's sympathies as the spoken version did to mine.

CHAPTER I.

One night, during the period of the first French Revolution, the family of Francois Sarzeau, a fisherman of Brittany, were all waking and watching at a late hour in their cottage on the peninsula of Quiberon. Francois had gone out in his boat that evening, as usual, to fish. Shortly after his departure, the wind had risen, the clouds had gathered; and the storm, which had been threatening at intervals throughout the whole day, burst forth furiously about nine o'clock. It was now eleven; and the raging of the wind over the barren, heathy peninsula still seemed to increase with each fresh blast that tore its way out upon the open sea; the crashing of the waves on the beach was awful to hear; the dreary blackness of the sky terrible to behold. The longer they listened to the storm, the oftener they looked out at it, the fainter grew the hopes which the fisherman's family still strove to cherish for the safety of Francois Sarzeau and of his younger son who had gone with him in the boat.

There was something impressive in the simplicity of the scene that was now passing within the cottage.

On one side of the great, rugged, black fire-place crouched two little girls; the younger half asleep, with her head in her sister's lap. These were the daughters of the fisherman; and opposite to them sat their eldest brother, Gabriel. His right arm had been badly wounded in a recent encounter at the national game of the *Soule* , a sport resembling our English foot-ball; but played on both sides in such savage earnest by the people of Brittany as to end always in bloodshed, often in mutilation, sometimes even in loss of life. On the same bench with Gabriel sat his betrothed wife — a girl of eighteen — clothed in the plain, almost monastic black-and-white costume of her native district. She was the daughter of a small farmer living at some little distance from the coast. Between the groups formed on either side of the fire-place, the vacant space was occupied by the foot of a truckle-bed. In this bed lay a very old man, the father of Francois Sarzeau. His haggard face was covered with deep wrinkles; his long white hair flowed over the coarse lump of sacking which served him for a pillow, and his light gray eyes wandered incessantly, with a strange expression of terror and suspicion, from person to person, and from object to object, in all parts of the room. Whenever the wind and sea whistled and roared at their loudest, he muttered to himself and tossed his hands fretfully on his wretched coverlet. On these occasions his eyes always fixed themselves intently on a little delf image of the Virgin placed in a niche over the fire-place. Every time they saw him look in this direction Gabriel and the young girls shuddered and crossed themselves; and even the child, who still kept awake, imitated their example. There was one bond of feeling at least between the old man and his grandchildren, which connected his age and their youth unnaturally and closely together. This feeling was reverence for the superstitions which had been handed down to them by their ancestors from centuries and centuries back, as far even as the age of the Druids. The spirit warnings of disaster and death which the old man heard in the wailing of the wind, in the crashing of the waves, in the dreary, monotonous rattling of the casement, the young man and his affianced wife and the little child who cowered by the fireside heard too. All differences in sex, in temperament, in years, superstition was strong enough to strike down to its own dread level, in the fisherman's cottage, on that stormy night.

Besides the benches by the fireside and the bed, the only piece of furniture in the room was a coarse wooden table, with a loaf of black bread, a knife, and a pitcher of cider placed on it. Old nets, coils of rope, tattered sails, hung, about the walls and over the wooden partition which separated the room into two compartments. Wisps of straw and ears of barley drooped down through the rotten rafters and gaping boards that made the floor of the granary above.

These different objects, and the persons in the cottage, who composed the only surviving members of the fisherman's family, were strangely and wildly lit up by the blaze of the fire and by the still brighter glare of a resin torch stuck into a block of wood in the chimney-corner. The red and yellow light played full on the weird face of the old man as he lay opposite to it, and glanced fitfully on the figures of the young girl, Gabriel, and the two children; the great, gloomy shadows rose and fell, and grew and lessened in bulk about the walls like visions of darkness, animated by a supernatural specter-life, while the dense obscurity outside spreading before the curtainless window seemed as a wall of solid darkness that had closed in forever around the fisherman's house. The night scene within the cottage was almost as wild and as dreary to look upon as the night scene without.

For a long time the different persons in the room sat together without speaking, even without looking at each other. At last the girl turned and whispered something into Gabriel's ear:

"Perrine, what were you saying to Gabriel?" asked the child opposite, seizing the first opportunity of breaking the desolate silence — doubly desolate at her age — which was preserved by all around her.

"I was telling him," answered Perrine, simply, "that it was time to change the bandages on his arm; and I also said to him, what I have often said before, that he must never play at that terrible game of the *Soule* again."

The old man had been looking intently at Perrine and his grandchild as they spoke. His harsh, hollow voice mingled with the last soft tones of the young girl, repeating over and over again the same terrible words, "Drowned! drowned! Son and grandson, both drowned! both drowned!"

"Hush, grandfather," said Gabriel, "we must not lose all hope for them yet. God and the Blessed Virgin protect them!" He looked at the little delf image, and crossed himself; the others imitated him, except the old man. He still tossed his hands over the coverlet, and still repeated, "Drowned! drowned!"

"Oh, that accursed *Soule!* " groaned the young man. "But for this wound I should have been with my father. The poor boy's life might at least have been saved; for we should then have left him here."

"Silence!" exclaimed the harsh voice from the bed. "The wail of dying men rises louder than the loud sea; the devil's psalm-singing roars higher than the roaring wind! Be silent, and listen! Francois drowned! Pierre drowned! Hark! Hark!"

A terrific blast of wind burst over the house as he spoke, shaking it to its center, overpowering all other sounds, even to the deafening crash of the waves. The slumbering child awoke, and uttered a scream of fear. Perrine, who had been kneeling before her lover binding the fresh bandages on his wounded arm, paused in her occupation, trembling from head to foot. Gabriel looked toward the window; his experience told him what must be the hurricane fury of that blast of wind out at sea, and he sighed bitterly as he murmured to himself, "God help them both — man's help will be as nothing to them now!"

"Gabriel!" cried the voice from the bed in altered tones — very faint and trembling.

He did not hear or did not attend to the old man. He was trying to soothe and encourage the young girl at his feet.

"Don't be frightened, love," he said, kissing her very gently and tenderly on the forehead. "You are as safe here as anywhere. Was I not right in saying that it would be madness to attempt taking you back to the farmhouse this evening? You can sleep in that room, Perrine, when you are tired — you can sleep with the two girls."

"Gabriel! brother Gabriel!" cried one of the children. "Oh, look at grandfather!"

Gabriel ran to the bedside. The old man had raised himself into a sitting position; his eyes were dilated, his whole face was rigid with terror, his hands were stretched out convulsively toward his grandson. "The White Women!" he screamed. "The White Women; the grave-diggers of the drowned are out on the sea!"

The children, with cries of terror, flung themselves into Perrine's arms; even Gabriel uttered an exclamation of horror, and started back from the bedside.

Still the old man reiterated, "The White Women! The White Women! Open the door, Gabriel! look-out westward, where the ebb-tide has left the sand dry. You'll see them bright as lightning in the darkness, mighty as the angels in stature, sweeping like the wind over the sea, in their long white garments, with their white hair trailing far behind them! Open the door, Gabriel! You'll see them stop and hover over the place where your father and your brother have been drowned; you'll see them come on till they reach the sand, you'll see them dig in it with their naked feet and beckon awfully to the raging sea to give up its dead. Open the door, Gabriel — or, though it should be the death of me, I will get up and open it myself!"

Gabriel's face whitened even to his lips, but he made a sign that he would obey. It required the exertion of his whole strength to keep the door open against the wind while he looked out.

"Do you see them, grandson Gabriel? Speak the truth, and tell me if you see them," cried the old man.

"I see nothing but darkness — pitch darkness," answered Gabriel, letting the door close again.

"Ah! woe! woe!" groaned his grandfather, sinking back exhausted on the pillow. "Darkness to *you;* but bright as lightning to the eyes that are allowed to see them. Drowned! drowned! Pray for their souls, Gabriel — *I* see the White Women even where I lie, and dare not pray for them. Son and grandson drowned! both drowned!"

The young man went back to Perrine and the children.

"Grandfather is very ill to-night," he whispered. "You had better all go into the bedroom, and leave me alone to watch by him."

They rose as he spoke, crossed themselves before the image of the Virgin, kissed him one by one, and, without uttering a word, softly entered the little room on the other side of the partition. Gabriel looked at his grandfather, and saw that he lay quiet now, with his eyes closed as if he were already dropping asleep. The young man then heaped some fresh logs on the fire, and sat down by it to watch till morning.

Very dreary was the moaning of the night storm; but it was not more dreary than the thoughts which now occupied him in his solitude — thoughts darkened and distorted by the terrible superstitions of his country and his race. Ever since the period of his mother's death he had been oppressed by the conviction that some curse hung over the family. At first they had been prosperous, they had got money, a little legacy had been left them. But this good fortune had availed only for a time; disaster on disaster strangely and suddenly succeeded. Losses, misfortunes, poverty, want itself had overwhelmed them; his father's temper had become so soured, that the oldest friends of Francois Sarzeau declared he was changed beyond recognition. And now, all this past misfortune — the steady, withering, household blight of many years — had ended in the last, worst misery of all — in death. The fate of his father and his brother admitted no longer of a doubt; he knew it, as he listened to the storm, as he reflected on his grandfather's words, as he called to mind his own experience of the perils of the sea. And this double bereavement had fallen on him just as the time was approaching for his marriage with Perrine; just when misfortune was most ominous of evil, just when it was hardest to bear! Forebodings, which he dared not realize, began now to mingle with the bitterness of his grief, whenever his thoughts wandered from the present to the future; and as he sat by the lonely fireside, murmuring from time to time the Church prayer for the repose of the dead, he almost involuntarily mingled with it another prayer, expressed only in his own simple words, for the safety of the living — for the young girl whose love was his sole earthly treasure; for the motherless children who must now look for protection to him alone.

He had sat by the hearth a long, long time, absorbed in his thoughts, not once looking round toward the bed, when he was startled by hearing the sound of his grandfather's voice once more.

"Gabriel," whispered the old man, trembling and shrinking as he spoke, "Gabriel, do you hear a dripping of water — now slow, now quick again — on the floor at the foot of my bed?"

"I hear nothing, grandfather, but the crackling of the fire, and the roaring of the storm outside."

"Drip, drip, drip! Faster and faster; plainer and plainer. Take the torch, Gabriel; look down on the floor — look with all your eyes. Is the place wet there? Is it the rain from heaven that is dropping through the roof?"

Gabriel took the torch with trembling fingers and knelt down on the floor to examine it closely. He started back from the place, as he saw that it was quite dry — the torch dropped upon the hearth — he fell on his knees before the statue of the Virgin and hid his face.

"Is the floor wet? Answer me, I command you — is the floor wet?" asked the old man, quickly and breathlessly.

Gabriel rose, went back to the bedside, and whispered to him that no drop of rain had fallen inside the cottage. As he spoke the words, he saw a change pass over his grandfather's face — the sharp features seemed to wither up on a sudden; the eager expression to grow vacant and death-like in an instant. The voice, too, altered; it was harsh and querulous no more; its tones became strangely soft, slow, and solemn, when the old man spoke again.

"I hear it still," he said, "drip! drip! faster and plainer than ever. That ghostly dropping of water is the last and the surest of the fatal signs which have told of your father's and your brother's deaths to-night, and I know from the place where I hear it — the foot of the bed I lie on — that it is a warning to me of my own approaching end. I am called where my son and my grandson have gone before me; my weary time in this world is over at last. Don't let Perrine and the children come in here, if they should awake — they are too young to look at death."

Gabriel's blood curdled when he heard these words — when he touched his grandfather's hand, and felt the chill that it struck to his own — when he listened to the raging wind, and knew that all help was miles and miles away from the cottage. Still, in spite of the storm, the darkness, and the distance, he thought not for a moment of neglecting the duty that had been taught him from his childhood — the duty of summoning the priest to the bedside of the dying. "I must call Perrine," he said, "to watch by you while I am away."

"Stop!" cried the old man. "Stop, Gabriel; I implore, I command you not to leave me!"

"The priest, grandfather — your confession —"

"It must be made to you. In this darkness and this hurricane no man can keep the path across the heath. Gabriel, I am dying — I should be dead before you got back. Gabriel, for the love of the Blessed Virgin, stop here with me till I die — my time is short — I have a terrible secret that I must tell to somebody before I draw my last breath! Your ear to my mouth — quick! quick!"

As he spoke the last words, a slight noise was audible on the other side of the partition, the door half opened, and Perrine appeared at it, looking affrightedly into the room. The vigilant eyes of the old man — suspicious even in death — caught sight of her directly.

"Go back!" he exclaimed faintly, before she could utter a word; "go back — push her back, Gabriel, and nail down the latch in the door, if she won't shut it of herself!"

"Dear Perrine! go in again," implored Gabriel. "Go in, and keep the children from disturbing us. You will only make him worse — you can be of no use here!"

She obeyed without speaking, and shut the door again.

While the old man clutched him by the arm, and repeated, "Quick! quick! your ear close to my mouth," Gabriel heard her say to the children (who were both awake), "Let us pray for grandfather." And as he knelt down by the bedside, there stole on his ear the sweet, childish tones of his little sisters, and the soft, subdued voice of the young girl who was teaching them the prayer, mingling divinely with the solemn wailing of wind and sea, rising in a still and awful purity over the hoarse, gasping whispers of the dying man.

"I took an oath not to tell it, Gabriel — lean down closer! I'm weak, and they mustn't hear a word in that room — I took an oath not to tell it; but death is a warrant to all men for breaking such an oath as that. Listen; don't lose a word I'm saying! Don't look away into the room: the stain of blood-guilt has defiled it forever! Hush! hush! hush! Let me speak. Now your father's dead, I can't carry the horrid secret with me into the grave. Just remember, Gabriel — try if you can't remember the time before I was bedridden, ten years ago and more — it was about six weeks, you know, before your mother's death; you can remember it by that. You and all the children were in that room with your mother; you were asleep, I think; it was night, not very late — only nine o'clock. Your father and I were standing at the door, looking out at the heath in the moonlight. He was so poor at that time, he had been obliged to sell his own boat, and none of the neighbors would take him out fishing with them — your father wasn't liked by any of the neighbors. Well; we saw a stranger coming toward us; a very young man, with a knapsack on his back. He looked like a gentleman, though he was but poorly dressed. He came up, and told us he was dead tired, and didn't think he could reach the town that night and asked if we would give him shelter till morning. And your father said yes, if he would make no noise, because the wife was ill, and the children were asleep. So he said all he wanted was to go to sleep himself before the fire. We had nothing to give him but black bread. He had better food with him than that, and undid his knapsack to get at it, and — and — Gabriel! I'm sinking — drink! something to drink — I'm parched with thirst."

Silent and deadly pale, Gabriel poured some of the cider from the pitcher on the table into a drinking-cup, and gave it to the old man. Slight as the stimulant was, its effect on him was almost instantaneous. His dull eyes brightened a little, and he went on in the same whispering tones as before:

"He pulled the food out of his knapsack rather in a hurry, so that some of the other small things in it fell on the floor. Among these was a pocketbook, which your father picked up and gave him back; and he put it in his coat-pocket — there was a tear in one of the sides of the book, and through the hole some bank-notes bulged out. I saw them, and so did your father (don't move away, Gabriel; keep close, there's nothing in me to shrink from). Well, he shared his food, like an honest fellow, with us; and then put his hand in his pocket, and gave me four or five livres, and then lay down before the fire to go to sleep. As he shut his eyes, your father looked at me in a way I didn't like. He'd been behaving very bitterly and desperately toward us for some time past, being soured about poverty, and your mother's illness, and the constant crying out of you children for more to eat. So when he told me to go and buy some wood, some bread, and some wine with money I had got, I didn't like, somehow, to leave him alone with the stranger; and so made excuses, saying (which was true) that it was too late to buy things in the village that night. But he told me in a rage to go and do as he bid me, and knock the people up if the shop was shut. So I went out, being dreadfully afraid of your father — as indeed we all were at that time — but I couldn't make up my mind to go far from the house; I was afraid of something happening, though I didn't dare to think what. I don't know how it was, but I stole back in about ten minutes on tiptoe to the cottage; I looked in at the window, and saw — O God! forgive him! O God! forgive me!— I saw — I— more to drink, Gabriel! I can't speak again — more to drink!"

The voices in the next room had ceased; but in the minute of silence which now ensued, Gabriel heard his sisters kissing Perrine, and wishing her good-night. They were all three trying to go asleep again.

"Gabriel, pray yourself, and teach your children after you to pray, that your father may find forgiveness where he is now gone. I saw him as plainly as I now see you, kneeling with his knife in one hand over the sleeping man. He was taking the little book with the notes in it out of the stranger's pocket. He got the book into his possession, and held it quite still in his hand for an instant, thinking. I believe — oh no! no! I'm sure — he was repenting; I'm sure he was going to put the book back; but just at that moment the stranger moved, and raised one of his arms, as if he was waking up. Then the temptation of the devil grew too strong for your father — I saw him lift the hand with the knife in it — but saw nothing more. I couldn't look in at the window — I couldn't move away — I couldn't cry out; I stood with my back turned toward the house, shivering all over, though it was a warm summer-time, and hearing no cries, no noises at all, from the room behind me. I was too frightened to know how long it was before the opening of the cottage door made me turn round; but when I did, I saw your father standing before me in the yellow moonlight, carrying in his arms the bleeding body of the poor lad who had shared his food with us and slept on our hearth. Hush! hush! Don't groan and sob in that way! Stifle it with the bedclothes. Hush! you'll wake them in the next room!"

"Gabriel — Gabriel!" exclaimed a voice from behind the partition. "What has happened? Gabriel! let me come out and be with you!"

"No! no!" cried the old man, collecting the last remains of his strength in the attempt to speak above the wind, which was just then howling at the loudest; "stay where you are — don't speak, don't come out — I command you! Gabriel" (his voice dropped to a faint whisper), "raise me up in bed — you must hear the whole of it now; raise me; I'm choking so that I can hardly speak. Keep close and listen — I can't say much more. Where was I?— Ah, your father! He threatened to kill me if I didn't swear to keep it secret; and in terror of my life I swore. He made me help him to carry the body — we took it all across the heath — oh! horrible, horrible, under the bright moon —(lift me higher, Gabriel). You know the great stones yonder, set up by the heathens; you know the hollow place under the stones they call 'The Merchant's Table'; we had plenty of room to lay him in that, and hide him so; and then we ran back to the cottage. I never dared to go near the place afterward; no, nor your father either! (Higher, Gabriel! I'm choking again.) We burned the pocket-book and the knapsack — never knew his name — we kept the money to spend. (You're not lifting me; you're not listening close enough!) Your father said it was a legacy, when you and your mother asked about the money. (You hurt me, you shake me to pieces, Gabriel, when you sob like that.) It brought a curse on us, the money; the curse has drowned your father and your brother; the curse is killing me; but I've confessed — tell the priest I confessed before I died. Stop her; stop Perrine! I hear her getting up. Take his bones away from the Merchant's Table, and bury them for the love of God! and tell the priest (lift me higher, lift me till I am on my knees)— if your father was alive, he'd murder me; but tell the priest — because of my guilty soul — to pray, and — remember the Merchant's Table — to bury, and to pray — to pray always for —"

As long as Perrine heard faintly the whispering of the old man, though no word that he said reached her ear, she shrank from opening the door in the partition. But, when the whispering sounds, which terrified her she knew not how or why, first faltered, then ceased altogether; when she heard the sobs that followed them; and when her heart told her who was weeping in the next room — then, she began to be influenced by a new feeling which was stronger than the strongest fear, and she opened the door without hesitation, almost without trembling.

The coverlet was drawn up over the old man; Gabriel was kneeling by the bedside, with his face hidden. When she spoke to him, he neither answered nor looked at her. After a while the sobs that shook him ceased; but still he never moved, except once when she touched him, and then he shuddered — shuddered under *her* hand! She called in his little sisters, and they spoke to him, and still he uttered no word in reply. They wept. One by one, often and often, they entreated him with loving words; but the stupor of grief which held him speechless and motionless was beyond the power of human tears, stronger even than the strength of human love.

It was near daybreak, and the storm was lulling, but still no change occurred at the bedside. Once or twice, as Perrine knelt near Gabriel, still vainly endeavoring to arouse him to a sense of her presence, she thought she heard the old man breathing feebly, and stretched out her hand toward the coverlet; but she could not summon courage to touch him or to look at him. This was the first time she had ever been present at a death-bed; the stillness in the room, the stupor of despair that had seized on Gabriel, so horrified her, that she was almost as helpless as the two children by her side. It was not till the dawn looked in at the cottage window — so coldly, so drearily, and yet so re-assuringly — that she began to recover her self-possession at all. Then she knew that her best resource would be to summon assistance immediately from the nearest house. While she was trying to persuade the two children to remain alone in the cottage with Gabriel during her temporary absence, she was startled by the sound of footsteps outside the door. It opened, and a man appeared on the threshold, standing still there for a moment in the dim, uncertain light.

She looked closer — looked intently at him. It was Francois Sarzeau himself.

CHAPTER II.

The fisherman was dripping with wet; but his face, always pale and inflexible, seemed to be but little altered in expression by the perils through which he must have passed during the night. Young Pierre lay almost insensible in his arms. In the astonishment and fright of the first moment, Perrine screamed as she recognized him.

"There, there, there!" he said, peevishly, advancing straight to the hearth with his burden; "don't make a noise. You never expected to see us alive again, I dare say. We gave ourselves up as lost, and only escaped after all by a miracle."

He laid the boy down where he could get the full warmth of the fire; and then, turning round, took a wicker-covered bottle from his pocket, and said, "If it hadn't been for the brandy —" He stopped suddenly — started — put down the bottle on the bench near him — and advanced quickly to the bedside.

Perrine looked after him as he went; and saw Gabriel, who had risen when the door was opened, moving back from the bed as Francois approached. The young man's face seemed to have been suddenly struck to stone — its blank, ghastly whiteness was awful to look at. He moved slowly backward and backward till he came to the cottage wall — then stood quite still, staring on his father with wild, vacant eyes, moving his hands to and fro before him, muttering, but never pronouncing one audible word.

Francois did not appear to notice his son; he had the coverlet of the bed in his hand.

"Anything the matter here?" he asked, as he drew it down.

Still Gabriel could not speak. Perrine saw it, and answered for him.

"Gabriel is afraid that his poor grandfather is dead," she whispered, nervously.

"Dead!" There was no sorrow in the tone as he echoed the word. "Was he very bad in the night before his death happened? Did he wander in his mind? He has been rather light-headed lately."

"He was very restless, and spoke of the ghostly warnings that we all know of; he said he saw and heard many things which told him from the other world that you and Pierre — Gabriel!" she screamed, suddenly interrupting herself, "look at him! Look at his face! Your grandfather is not dead!"

At this moment, Francois was raising his father's head to look closely at him. A faint spasm had indeed passed over the deathly face; the lips quivered, the jaw dropped. Francois shuddered as he looked, and moved away hastily from the bed. At the same instant Gabriel started from the wall; his expression altered, his pale cheeks flushed suddenly, as he snatched up the wicker-cased bottle, and poured all the little brandy that was left in it down his grandfather's throat.

The effect was nearly instantaneous; the sinking vital forces rallied desperately. The old man's eyes opened again, wandered round the room, then fixed themselves intently on Francois as he stood near the fire. Trying and terrible as his position was at that moment, Gabriel still retained self-possession enough to whisper a few words in Perrine's ear. "Go back again into the bedroom, and take the children with you," he said. "We may have something to speak about which you had better not hear."

"Son Gabriel, your grandfather is trembling all over," said Francois. "If he is dying at all, he is dying of cold; help me to lift him, bed and all, to the hearth."

"No, no! don't let him touch me!" gasped the old man. "Don't let him look at me in that way! Don't let him come near me, Gabriel! Is it his ghost? or is it himself?"

As Gabriel answered he heard a knocking at the door. His father opened it, and disclosed to view some people from the neighboring fishing village, who had come — more out of curiosity than sympathy — to inquire whether Francois and the boy Pierre had survived the night. Without asking any one to enter, the fisherman surlily and shortly answered the various questions addressed to him, standing in his own doorway. While he was thus engaged, Gabriel heard his grandfather muttering vacantly to himself, "Last night — how about last night, grandson? What was I talking about last night? Did I say your father was drowned? Very foolish to say he was drowned, and then see him come back alive again! But it wasn't that — I'm so weak in my head, I can't remember. What was it, Gabriel? Something too horrible to speak of? Is that what you're whispering and trembling about? I said nothing horrible. A crime! Bloodshed! I know nothing of any crime or bloodshed here — I must have been frightened out of my wits to talk in that way! The Merchant's Table? Only a big heap of old stones! What with the storm, and thinking I was going to die, and being afraid about your father, I must have been light-headed. Don't give another thought to that nonsense, Gabriel! I'm better now. We shall all live to laugh at poor grandfather for talking nonsense about crime and bloodshed in his sleep. Ah, poor old man — last night — light-headed — fancies and nonsense of an old man — why don't you laugh at it? I'm laughing — so light-headed, so light —"

He stopped suddenly. A low cry, partly of terror and partly of pain, escaped him; the look of pining anxiety and imbecile cunning which had distorted his face while he had been speaking, faded from it forever. He shivered a little, breathed heavily once or twice, then became quite still.

Had he died with a falsehood on his lips?

Gabriel looked round and saw that the cottage door was closed, and that his father was standing against it. How long he had occupied that position, how many of the old man's last words he had heard, it was impossible to conjecture, but there was a lowering suspicion in his harsh face as he now looked away from the corpse to his son, which made Gabriel shudder; and the first question that he asked, on once more approaching the bedside, was expressed in tones which, quiet as they were, had a fearful meaning in them.

"What did your grandfather talk about last night?" he asked.

Gabriel did not answer. All that he had heard, all that he had seen, all the misery and horror that might yet be to come, had stunned his mind. The unspeakable dangers of his present position were too tremendous to be realized. He could only feel them vaguely in the weary torpor that oppressed his heart; while in every other direction the use of his faculties, physical and mental, seemed to have suddenly and totally abandoned him.

"Is your tongue wounded, son Gabriel, as well as your arm?" his father went on, with a bitter laugh. "I come back to you, saved by a miracle; and you never speak to me. Would you rather I had died than the old man there? He can't hear you now — why shouldn't you tell me what nonsense he was talking last night? You won't? I say you shall!" (He crossed the room and put his back to the door.) "Before either of us leave this place, you shall confess it! You know that my duty to the Church bids me to go at once and tell the priest of your grandfather's death. If I leave that duty unfulfilled, remember it is through your fault! *You* keep me here — for here I stop till I'm obeyed. Do you hear that, idiot? Speak! Speak instantly, or you shall repeat it to the day of your death! I ask again — what did your grandfather say to you when he was wandering in his mind last night?"

"He spoke of a crime committed by another, and guiltily kept secret by him," answered Gabriel, slowly and sternly. "And this morning he denied his own words with his last living breath. But last night, if he spoke the truth —"

"The truth!" echoed Francois. "What truth?"

He stopped, his eyes fell, then turned toward the corpse. For a few minutes he stood steadily contemplating it; breathing quickly, and drawing his hand several times across his forehead. Then he faced his son once more. In that short interval he had become in outward appearance a changed man; expression, voice, and manner, all were altered.

"Heaven forgive me!" he went on, "but I could almost laugh at myself, at this solemn moment, for having spoken and acted just now so much like a fool! Denied his words, did he? Poor old man! they say sense often comes back to light-headed people just before death; and he is a proof of it. The fact is, Gabriel, my own wits must have been a little shaken — and no wonder — by what I went through last night, and what I have come home to this morning. As if you, or anybody, could ever really give serious credit to the wandering speeches of a dying old man! (Where is Perrine? Why did you send her away?) I don't wonder at your still looking a little startled, and feeling low in your mind, and all that — for you've had a trying night of it, trying in every way. He must have been a good deal shaken in his wits last night, between fears about himself and fears about me. (To think of my being angry with you, Gabriel, for being a little alarmed — very naturally — by an old man's queer fancies!) Come out, Perrine — come out of the bedroom whenever you are tired of it: you must learn sooner or later to look at death calmly. Shake hands, Gabriel; and let us make it up, and say no more about what has passed. You won't? Still angry with me for what I said to you just now? Ah! you'll think better about it by the time I return. Come out, Perrine; we've no secrets here."

"Where are you going to?" asked Gabriel, as he saw his father hastily open the door.

"To tell the priest that one of his congregation is dead, and to have the death registered," answered Francois. "These are *my* duties, and must be performed before I take any rest."

He went out hurriedly as he said these words. Gabriel almost trembled at himself when he found that he breathed more freely, that he felt less horribly oppressed both in mind and body, the moment his father's back was turned. Fearful as thought was now, it was still a change for the better to be capable of thinking at all. Was the behavior of his father compatible with innocence? Could the old man's confused denial of his own words in the morning, and in the presence of his son, be set for one instant against the circumstantial confession that he had made during the night alone with his grandson? These were the terrible questions which Gabriel now asked himself, and which he shrank involuntarily from answering. And yet that doubt, the solution of which would, one way or the other, irrevocably affect the whole future of his life, must sooner or later be solved at any hazard!

Was there any way of setting it at rest? Yes, one way — to go instantly, while his father was absent, and examine the hollow place under the Merchant's Table. If his grandfather's confession had really been made while he was in possession of his senses, this place (which Gabriel knew to be covered in from wind and weather) had never been visited since the commission of the crime by the perpetrator, or by his unwilling accomplice; though time had destroyed all besides, the hair and the bones of the victim would still be left to bear witness to the truth — if truth had indeed been spoken. As this conviction grew on him, the young man's cheek paled; and he stopped irresolute half-way between the hearth and the door. Then he looked down doubtfully at the corpse on the bed; and then there came upon him suddenly a revulsion of feeling. A wild, feverish impatience to know the worst without another instant of delay possessed him. Only telling Perrine that he should be back soon, and that she must watch by the dead in his absence, he left the cottage at once, without waiting to hear her reply, even without looking back as he closed the door behind him.

There were two tracks to the Merchant's Table. One, the longer of the two, by the coast cliffs; the other across the heath. But this latter path was also, for some little distance, the path which led to the village and the church. He was afraid of attracting his father's attention here, so he took the direction of the coast. At one spot the track trended inland, winding round some of the many Druid monuments scattered over the country. This place was on high ground, and commanded a view, at no great distance, of the path leading to the village, just where it branched off from the heathy ridge which ran in the direction of the Merchant's Table. Here Gabriel descried the figure of a man standing with his back toward the coast.

This figure was too far off to be identified with absolute certainty, but it looked like, and might well be, Francois Sarzeau. Whoever he was, the man was evidently uncertain which way he should proceed. When he moved forward, it was first to advance several paces toward the Merchant's Table; then he went back again toward the distant cottages and the church. Twice he hesitated thus; the second time pausing long before he appeared finally to take the way that led to the village.

Leaving the post of observation among the stones, at which he had instinctively halted for some minutes past, Gabriel now proceeded on his own path. Could this man really be his father? And if it were so, why did Francois Sarzeau only determine to go to the village where his business lay, after having twice vainly attempted to persevere in taking the exactly opposite direction of the Merchant's Table? Did he really desire to go there? Had he heard the name mentioned, when the old man referred to it in his dying words? And had he failed to summon courage enough to make all safe by removing — This last question was too horrible to be pursued; Gabriel stifled it affrightedly in his own heart as he went on.

He reached the great Druid monument without meeting a living soul on his way. The sun was rising, and the mighty storm-clouds of the night were parting asunder wildly over the whole eastward horizon. The waves still leaped and foamed gloriously: but the gale had sunk to a keen, fresh breeze. As Gabriel looked up, and saw how brightly the promise of a lovely day was written in the heavens, he trembled as he thought of the search which he was now about to make. The sight of the fair, fresh sunrise jarred horribly with the suspicions of committed murder that were rankling foully in his heart. But he knew that his errand must be performed, and he nerved himself to go through with it; for he dared not return to the cottage until the mystery had been cleared up at once and forever.

The Merchant's Table was formed by two huge stones resting horizontally on three others. In the troubled times of more than half a century ago, regular tourists were unknown among the Druid monuments of Brittany; and the entrance to the hollow place under the stones — since often visited by strangers — was at this time nearly choked up by brambles and weeds. Gabriel's first look at this tangled nook of briers convinced him that the place had not been entered perhaps for years, by any living being. Without allowing himself to hesitate (for he felt that the slightest delay might be fatal to his resolution), he passed as gently as possible through the brambles, and knelt down at the low, dusky, irregular entrance of the hollow place under the stones.

His heart throbbed violently, his breath almost failed him; but he forced himself to crawl a few feet into the cavity, and then groped with his hand on the ground about him.

He touched something! Something which it made his flesh creep to handle; something which he would fain have dropped, but which he grasped tight in spite of himself. He drew back into the outer air and sunshine. Was it a human bone? No! he had been the dupe of his own morbid terror — he had only taken up a fragment of dried wood!

Feeling shame at such self-deception as this, he was about to throw the wood from him before he re-entered the place, when another idea occurred to him.

Though it was dimly lighted through one or two chinks in the stones, the far part of the interior of the cavity was still too dusky to admit of perfect examination by the eye, even on a bright sunshiny morning. Observing this, he took out the tinder-box and matches, which, like the other inhabitants of the district, he always carried about with him for the purpose of lighting his pipe, determining to use the piece of wood as a torch which might illuminate the darkest corner of the place when he next entered it. Fortunately the wood had remained so long and had been preserved so dry in its sheltered position, that it caught fire almost as easily as a piece of paper. The moment it was fairly aflame Gabriel went into the cavity, penetrating at once — this time — to its furthest extremity.

He remained among the stones long enough for the wood to burn down nearly to his hand. When he came out, and flung the burning fragment from him, his face was flushed deeply, his eyes sparkled. He leaped carelessly on to the heath, over the bushes through which he had threaded his way so warily but a few minutes before, exclaiming, "I may marry Perrine with a clear conscience now; I am the son of as honest a man as there is in Brittany!"

He had closely examined the cavity in every corner, and not the slightest sign that any dead body had ever been laid there was visible in the hollow place under the Merchant's Table.

CHAPTER III.

"*I* may marry Perrine with a clear conscience now!"

There are some parts of the world where it would be drawing no natural picture of human nature to represent a son as believing conscientiously that an offense against life and the laws of hospitality, secretly committed by his father, rendered him, though innocent of all participation in it, unworthy to fulfill his engagement with his affianced wife. Among the simple inhabitants of Gabriel's province, however, such acuteness of conscientious sensibility as this was no extraordinary exception to all general rules. Ignorant and superstitious as they might be, the people of Brittany practiced the duties of hospitality as devoutly as they practiced the duties of the national religion. The presence of the stranger-guest, rich or poor, was a sacred presence at their hearths. His safety was their especial charge, his property their especial responsibility. They might be half starved, but they were ready to share the last crust with him, nevertheless, as they would share it with their own children.

Any outrage on the virtue of hospitality, thus born and bred in the people, was viewed by them with universal disgust, and punished with universal execration. This ignominy was uppermost in Gabriel's thoughts by the side of his grandfather's bed; the dread of this worst dishonor, which there was no wiping out, held him speechless before Perrine, shamed and horrified him so that he felt unworthy to look her in the face; and when the result of his search at the Merchant's Table proved the absence there of all evidence of the crime spoken of by the old man, the blessed relief, the absorbing triumph of that discovery, was expressed entirely in the one thought which had prompted his first joyful words: He could marry Perrine with a clear conscience, for he was the son of an honest man!

When he returned to the cottage, Francois had not come back. Perrine was astonished at the change in Gabriel's manner; even Pierre and the children remarked it. Rest and warmth had by this time so far recovered the younger brother, that he was able to give some account of the perilous adventures of the night at sea. They were still listening to the boy's narrative when Francois at last returned. It was now Gabriel who held out his hand, and made the first advances toward reconciliation.

To his utter amazement, his father recoiled from him. The variable temper of Francois had evidently changed completely during his absence at the village. A settled scowl of distrust darkened his face as he looked at his son.

"I never shake hands with people who have once doubted me," he exclaimed, loudly and irritably; "for I always doubt them forever after. You are a bad son! You have suspected your father of some infamy that you dare not openly charge him with, on no other testimony than the rambling nonsense of a half-witted, dying old man. Don't speak to me! I won't hear you! An innocent man and a spy are bad company. Go and denounce me, you Judas in disguise! I don't care for your secret or for you. What's that girl Perrine doing here still? Why hasn't she gone home long ago? The priest's coming; we don't want strangers in the house of death. Take her back to the farmhouse, and stop there with her, if you like; nobody wants you here!"

There was something in the manner and look of the speaker as he uttered these words, so strange, so sinister, so indescribably suggestive of his meaning much more than he said, that Gabriel felt his heart sink within him instantly; and almost at the same moment this fearful question forced itself irresistibly on his mind: might not his father have followed him to the Merchant's Table?

Even if he had been desired to speak, he could not have spoken now, while that question and the suspicion that it brought with it were utterly destroying all the re-assuring hopes and convictions of the morning. The mental suffering produced by the sudden change from pleasure to pain in all his thoughts, reacted on him physically. He felt as if he were stifling in the air of the cottage, in the presence of his father; and when Perrine hurried on her walking attire, and with a face which alternately flushed and turned pale with every moment, approached the door, he went out with her as hastily as if he had been flying from his home. Never had the fresh air and the free daylight felt like heavenly and guardian influences to him until now!

He could comfort Perrine under his father's harshness, he could assure her of his own affection, which no earthly influence could change, while they walked together toward the farmhouse; but he could do no more. He durst not confide to her the subject that was uppermost in his mind; of all human beings she was the last to whom he could reveal the terrible secret that was festering at his heart. As soon as they got within sight of the farmhouse, Gabriel stopped; and, promising to see her again soon, took leave of Perrine with assumed ease in his manner and with real despair in his heart. Whatever the poor girl might think of it, he felt, at that moment, that he had not courage to face her father, and hear him talk happily and pleasantly, as his custom was, of Perrine's approaching marriage.

Left to himself, Gabriel wandered hither and thither over the open heath, neither knowing nor caring in what direction he turned his steps. The doubts about his father's innocence which had been dissipated by his visit to the Merchant's Table, that father's own language and manner had now revived — had even confirmed, though he dared not yet acknowledge so much to himself. It was terrible enough to be obliged to admit that the result of his morning's search was, after all, not conclusive — that the mystery was, in very truth, not yet cleared up. The violence of his father's last words of distrust; the extraordinary and indescribable changes in his father's manner while uttering them — what did these things mean? Guilt or innocence? Again, was it any longer reasonable to doubt the death-bed confession made by his grandfather? Was it not, on the contrary, far more probable that the old man's denial in the morning of his own words at night had been made under the influence of a panic terror, when his moral consciousness was bewildered, and his intellectual faculties were sinking? The longer Gabriel thought of these questions, the less competent — possibly also the less willing — he felt to answer them. Should he seek advice from others wiser than he? No; not while the thousandth part of a chance remained that his father was innocent.

This thought was still in his mind, when he found himself once more in sight of his home. He was still hesitating near the door, when he saw it opened cautiously. His brother Pierre looked out, and then came running toward him. "Come in, Gabriel; oh, do come in!" said the boy, earnestly. "We are afraid to be alone with father. He's been beating us for talking of you."

Gabriel went in. His father looked up from the hearth where he was sitting, muttered the word "Spy!" and made a gesture of contempt but did not address a word directly to his son. The hours passed on in silence; afternoon waned into evening, and evening into night; and still he never spoke to any of his children. Soon after it was dark, he went out, and took his net with him, saying that it was better to be alone on the sea than in the house with a spy.

When he returned the next morning there was no change in him. Days passed — weeks, months, even elapsed, and still, though his manner insensibly became what it used to be toward his other children, it never altered toward his eldest son At the rare periods when they now met, except when absolutely obliged to speak, he preserved total silence in his intercourse with Gabriel. He would never take Gabriel out with him in the boat; he would never sit alone with Gabriel in the house; he would never eat a meal with

Gabriel; he would never let the other children talk to him about Gabriel; and he would never hear a word in expostulation, a word in reference to anything his dead father had said or done on the night of the storm, from Gabriel himself.

The young man pined and changed, so that even Perrine hardly knew him again, under this cruel system of domestic excommunication; under the wearing influence of the one unchanging doubt which never left him; and, more than all, under the incessant reproaches of his own conscience, aroused by the sense that he was evading a responsibility which it was his solemn, his immediate duty to undertake. But no sting of conscience, no ill treatment at home, and no self-reproaches for failing in his duty of confession as a good Catholic, were powerful enough in their influence over Gabriel to make him disclose the secret, under the oppression of which his very life was wasting away. He knew that if he once revealed it, whether his father was ultimately proved to be guilty or innocent, there would remain a slur and a suspicion on the family, and on Perrine besides, from her approaching connection with it, which in their time and in their generation could never be removed. The reproach of the world is terrible even in the crowded city, where many of the dwellers in our abiding-place are strangers to us — but it is far more terrible in the country, where none near us are strangers, where all talk of us and know of us, where nothing intervenes between us and the tyranny of the evil tongue. Gabriel had not courage to face this, and dare the fearful chance of life-long ignominy — no, not even to serve the sacred interests of justice, of atonement, and of truth.

CHAPTER IV.

*W*hile Gabriel still remained prostrated under the affliction that was wasting his energies of body and mind, Brittany was visited by a great public calamity, in which all private misfortunes were overwhelmed for a while.

It was now the time when the ever-gathering storm of the French Revolution had risen to its hurricane climax. Those chiefs of the new republic were in power whose last, worst madness it was to decree the extinction of religion and the overthrow of everything that outwardly symbolized it throughout the whole of the country that they governed. Already this decree had been executed to the letter in and around Paris; and now the soldiers of the Republic were on their way to Brittany, headed by commanders whose commission was to root out the Christian religion in the last and the surest of the strongholds still left to it in France.

These men began their work in a spirit worthy of the worst of their superiors who had sent them to do it. They gutted churches, they demolished chapels, they overthrew road-side crosses wherever they found them. The terrible guillotine devoured human lives in the villages of Brittany as it had devoured them in the streets of Paris; the musket and the sword, in highway and byway, wreaked havoc on the people — even on women and children kneeling in the act of prayer; the priests were tracked night and day from one hiding-place, where they still offered up worship, to another, and were killed as soon as overtaken — every atrocity was committed in every district; but the Christian religion still spread wider than the widest bloodshed; still sprang up with ever-renewed vitality from under the very feet of the men whose vain fury was powerless to trample it down. Everywhere the people remained true to their Faith; everywhere the priests stood firm by them in their sorest need. The executioners of the Republic had been sent to make Brittany a country of apostates; they did their worst, and left it a country of martyrs.

One evening, while this frightful persecution was still raging, Gabriel happened to be detained unusually late at the cottage of Perrine's father. He had lately spent much of his time at the farm house; it was his only refuge now from that place of suffering, of silence, and of secret shame, which he had once called home! Just as he had taken leave of Perrine for the night, and was about to open the farmhouse door, her father stopped him, and pointed to a chair in the chimney-corner.

"Leave us alone, my dear," said the old man to his daughter; "I want to speak to Gabriel. You can go to your mother in the next room."

The words which Pere Bonan — as he was called by the neighbors — had now to say in private were destined to lead to very unexpected events. After referring to the alteration which had appeared of late in Gabriel's manner, the old man began by asking him, sorrowfully but not suspiciously, whether he still preserved his old affection for Perrine. On receiving an eager answer in the affirmative, Pere Bonan then referred to the persecution still raging through the country, and to the consequent possibility that he, like others of his countrymen, might yet be called to suffer, and perhaps to die, for the cause of his religion. If this last act of self-sacrifice were required of him, Perrine would be left unprotected, unless her affianced husband performed his promise to her, and assumed, without delay, the position of her lawful guardian. "Let me know that you will do this," concluded the old man; "I shall be resigned to all that may be required of me, if I can only know that I shall not die leaving Perrine unprotected." Gabriel gave the promise — gave it with his whole heart. As he took leave of Pere Bonan, the old man said to him:

"Come here tomorrow; I shall know more then than I know now — I shall be able to fix with certainty the day for the fulfillment of your engagement with Perrine."

Why did Gabriel hesitate at the farmhouse door, looking back on Pere Bonan as though he would fain say something, and yet not speaking a word? Why, after he had gone out and had walked onward several paces, did he suddenly stop, return quickly to the farmhouse, stand irresolute before the gate, and then retrace his steps, sighing heavily as he went, but never pausing again on his homeward way? Because the torment of his horrible secret had grown harder to bear than ever, since he had given the promise that had been required of him. Because, while a strong impulse moved him frankly to lay bare his hidden dread and doubt to the father whose beloved daughter was soon to be his wife, there was a yet stronger passive influence which paralyzed on his lips the terrible confession that he knew not whether he was the son of an honest man, or the son of an assassin, and a robber. Made desperate by his situation, he determined, while he hastened homeward, to risk the worst, and ask that fatal question of his father in plain words. But this supreme trial for parent and child was not to be. When he entered the cottage, Francois was absent. He had told the younger children that he should not be home again before noon on the next day.

Early in the morning Gabriel repaired to the farmhouse, as he had been bidden. Influenced, by his love for Perrine, blindly confiding in the faint hope (which, in despite of heart and conscience, he still forced himself to cherish) that his father might be innocent, he now preserved the appearance at least of perfect calmness. "If I tell my secret to Perrine's father, I risk disturbing in him that confidence in the future safety of his child for which I am his present and only warrant." Something like this thought was in Gabriel's mind, as he took the hand of Pere Bonan, and waited anxiously to hear what was required of him on that day.

"We have a short respite from danger, Gabriel," said the old man. "News has come to me that the spoilers of our churches and the murderers of our congregations have been stopped on their way hitherward by tidings which have reached them from another district. This interval of peace and safety will be a short one — we must take advantage of it while it is yet ours. My name is among the names on the list of the denounced. If the soldiers of the Republic find me here — but we will say nothing more of this; it is of Perrine and of you that I must now speak. On this very evening your marriage may be solemnized with all the wonted rites of our holy religion, and the blessing may be pronounced over you by the lips of a priest. This evening, therefore, Gabriel, you must become the husband and the protector of Perrine. Listen to me attentively, and I will tell you how."

This was the substance of what Gabriel now heard from Pere Bonan:

Not very long before the persecutions broke out in Brittany, a priest, known generally by the name of Father Paul, was appointed to a curacy in one of the northern districts of the province. He fulfilled all the duties of his station in such a manner as to win the confidence and affection of every member of his congregation, and was often spoken of with respect, even in parts of the country distant from the scene of his labors. It was not, however, until the troubles broke out, and the destruction and bloodshed began, that he became renowned far and wide, from one end of Brittany to another. From the date of the very first persecutions the name of Father Paul was a rallying-cry of the hunted peasantry; he was their great encouragement under oppression, their example in danger, their last and only consoler in the hour of death. Wherever havoc and ruin raged most fiercely, wherever the pursuit was hottest and the slaughter most cruel, there the intrepid priest was sure to be seen pursuing his sacred duties in defiance of every peril. His hair-breadth escapes from death; his extraordinary re-appearances in parts of the country where no one ever expected to see him again, were regarded by the poorer classes with superstitious awe. Wherever Father Paul appeared, with his black dress, his calm face, and the ivory crucifix which he always carried in his hand, the people reverenced him as more than mortal; and grew at last to believe, that, single-handed, he would successfully defend his religion against the armies of the Republic. But their simple confidence in his powers of resistance was soon destined to be shaken. Fresh re-enforcements arrived in Brittany, and overran the whole province from one end to the other. One morning, after celebrating service in a dismantled church, and after narrowly escaping with his life from those who pursued him, the priest disappeared. Secret inquiries were made after him in all directions; but he was heard of no more.

Many weary days had passed, and the dispirited peasantry had already mourned him as dead, when some fishermen on the northern coast observed a ship of light burden in the offing, making signals to the shore. They put off to her in their boats; and on reaching the deck saw standing before them the well-remembered figure of Father Paul.

The priest had returned to his congregations, and had founded the new altar that they were to worship at on the deck of the ship! Razed from the face of the earth, their church had not been destroyed — for Father Paul and the priests who acted with him had given that church a refuge on the sea. Henceforth, their children could still be baptized, their sons and daughters could still be married, the burial of their dead could still be solemnized, under the sanction of the old religion for which, not vainly, they had suffered so patiently and so long.

Throughout the remaining time of trouble the services were uninterrupted on board the ship. A code of signals was established by which those on shore were always enabled to direct their brethren at sea toward such parts of the coast as happened to be uninfested by the enemies of their worship. On the morning of Gabriel's visit to the farmhouse these signals had shaped the course of the ship toward the extremity of the peninsula of Quiberon. The people of the district were all prepared to expect the appearance of the vessel some time in the evening, and had their boats ready at a moment's notice to put off, and attend the service. At the conclusion of this service Pere Bonan had arranged that the marriage of his daughter and Gabriel was to take place.

They waited for evening at the farmhouse. A little before sunset the ship was signaled as in sight; and then Pere Bonan and his wife, followed by Gabriel and Perrine, set forth over the heath to the beach. With the solitary exception of Francois Sarzeau, the whole population of the neighborhood was already assembled there, Gabriel's brother and sisters being among the number.

It was the calmest evening that had been known for months. There was not a cloud in the lustrous sky — not a ripple on the still surface of the sea. The smallest children were suffered by their mothers to stray down on the beach as they pleased; for the waves of the great ocean slept as tenderly and noiselessly on their sandy bed as if they had been changed into the waters of an inland lake. Slow, almost imperceptible, was the approach of the ship — there was hardly a breath of wind to carry her on — she was just drifting gently with the landward set of the tide at that hour, while her sails hung idly against the masts. Long after the sun had gone down, the congregation still waited and watched on the beach. The moon and stars were arrayed in their glory of the night before the ship dropped anchor. Then the muffled tolling of a bell came solemnly across the quiet waters; and then, from every creek along the shore, as far as the eye could reach, the black forms of the fishermen's boats shot out swift and stealthy into the shining sea.

By the time the boats had arrived alongside of the ship, the lamp had been kindled before the altar, and its flame was gleaming red and dull in the radiant moonlight. Two of the priests on board were clothed in their robes of office, and were waiting in their appointed places to begin the service. But there was a third, dressed only in the ordinary attire of his calling, who mingled with the congregation, and spoke a few words to each of the persons composing it, as, one by one, they mounted the sides of the ship. Those who had never seen him before knew by the famous ivory crucifix in his hand that the priest who received them was Father Paul. Gabriel looked at this man, whom he now beheld for the first time, with a mixture of astonishment and awe; for he saw that the renowned chief of the Christians of Brittany was, to all appearance, but little older than himself.

The expression on the pale, calm face of the priest was so gentle and kind, that children just able to walk tottered up to him, and held familiarly by the skirts of his black gown, whenever his clear blue eyes rested on theirs, while he beckoned them to his side. No one would ever have guessed from the countenance of Father Paul what deadly perils he had confronted, but for the scar of a saber-wound, as yet hardly healed, which ran across his forehead. That wound had been dealt while he was kneeling before the altar in the last church in Brittany which had escaped spoliation. He would have died where he knelt, but for the peasants who were praying with him, and who, unarmed as they were, threw themselves like tigers on the soldiery, and at awful sacrifice of their own lives saved the life of their priest. There was not a man now on board the ship who would have hesitated, had the occasion called for it again, to have rescued him in the same way.

The service began. Since the days when the primitive Christians worshiped amid the caverns of the earth, can any service be imagined nobler in itself, or sublimer in the circumstances surrounding it, than that which was now offered up? Here was no artificial pomp, no gaudy profusion of ornament, no attendant grandeur of man's creation. All around this church spread the hushed and awful majesty of the tranquil sea. The roof of this cathedral was the immeasurable heaven, the pure moon its one great light, the countless glories of the stars its only adornment. Here were no hired singers or rich priest-princes; no curious sight-seers, or careless lovers of sweet sounds. This congregation and they who had gathered it together, were all poor alike, all persecuted alike, all worshiping alike, to the overthrow of their worldly interests, and at the imminent peril of their lives. How brightly and tenderly the moonlight shone upon the altar and the people before it! how solemnly and divinely the deep harmonies, as they chanted the penitential Psalms, mingled with the hoarse singing of the freshening night breeze in the rigging of the ship! how sweetly the still rushing murmur of many voices, as they uttered the responses together, now died away, and now rose again softly into the mysterious night!

Of all the members of the congregation — young or old — there was but one over whom that impressive service exercised no influence of consolation or of peace; that one was Gabriel. Often, throughout the day, his reproaching conscience had spoken within him again and again. Often when he joined the little assembly on the beach, he turned away his face in secret shame and apprehension from Perrine and her father. Vainly, after gaining the deck of the ship, did he try to meet the eye of Father Paul as frankly, as readily, and as affectionately as others met it. The burden of concealment seemed too heavy to be borne in the presence of the priest — and yet, torment as it was, he still bore it! But when he knelt with the rest of the congregation and saw Perrine kneeling by his side — when he felt the calmness of the solemn night and the still sea filling his heart — when the sounds of the first prayers spoke with a dread spiritual language of their own to his soul — then the remembrance of the confession which he had neglected, and the terror of receiving unprepared the sacrament which he knew would be offered to him — grew too vivid to be endured; the sense that he merited no longer, though once worthy of it, the confidence in his perfect truth and candor placed in him by the woman with whom he was soon to stand before the altar, overwhelmed him with shame: the mere act of kneeling among that congregation, the passive accomplice by his silence and secrecy, for aught he knew to the contrary, of a crime which it was his bounden duty to denounce, appalled him as if he had already committed sacrilege that could never be forgiven. Tears flowed down his cheeks, though he strove to repress them: sobs burst from him, though he tried to stifle them. He knew that others besides Perrine were looking at him in astonishment and alarm; but he could neither control himself, nor move to leave his place, nor raise his eyes even — until suddenly he felt a hand laid on his shoulder. That touch, slight as it was, ran through him instantly He looked up, and saw Father Paul standing by his side.

Beckoning him to follow, and signing to the congregation not to suspend their devotions, he led Gabriel out of the assembly — then paused for a moment, reflecting — then beckoning him again, took him into the cabin of the ship, and closed the door carefully.

"You have something on your mind," he said, simply and quietly, taking the young man by the hand. "I may be able to relieve you, if you tell me what it is."

As Gabriel heard these gentle words, and saw, by the light of a lamp which burned before a cross fixed against the wall, the sad kindness of expression with which the priest was regarding him, the oppression that had lain so long on his heart seemed to leave it in an instant. The haunting fear of ever divulging his fatal suspicions and his fatal secret had vanished, as it were, at the touch of Father Paul's hand. For the first time he now repeated to another ear — the sounds of prayer and praise rising grandly the while from the congregation above — his grandfather's death-bed confession, word for word almost, as he had heard it in the cottage on the night of the storm.

Once, and once only, did Father Paul interrupt the narrative, which in whispers was addressed to him. Gabriel had hardly repeated the first two or three sentences of his grandfather's confession, when the priest, in quick, altered tones, abruptly asked him his name and place of abode.

As the question was answered, Father Paul's calm face became suddenly agitated; but the next moment, resolutely resuming his self-possession, he bowed his head as a sign that Gabriel was to continue; clasped his trembling hands, and raising them as if in silent prayer, fixed his eyes intently on the cross. He never looked away from it while the terrible narrative proceeded. But when Gabriel described his search at the Merchant's Table; and, referring to his father's behavior since that time, appealed to the priest to know whether he might even yet, in defiance of appearances, be still filially justified in doubting whether the crime had been really perpetrated — then Father Paul moved near to him once more, and spoke again.

"Compose yourself, and look at me," he said, with his former sad kindness of voice and manner. "I can end your doubts forever. Gabriel, your father was guilty in intention and in act; but the victim of his crime still lives. I can prove it."

Gabriel's heart beat wildly; a deadly coldness crept over him as he saw Father Paul loosen the fastening of his cassock round the throat.

At that instant the chanting of the congregation above ceased; and then the sudden and awful stillness was deepened rather than interrupted by the faint sound of one voice praying. Slowly and with trembling fingers the priest removed the band round his neck — paused a little — sighed heavily — and pointed to a scar which was now plainly visible on one side of his throat. He said something at the same time; but the bell above tolled while he spoke. It was the signal of the elevation of the Host. Gabriel felt an arm passed round him, guiding him to his knees, and sustaining him from sinking to the floor. For one moment longer he was conscious that the bell had stopped, that there was dead silence, that Father Paul was kneeling by him beneath the cross, with bowed head — then all objects around vanished; and he saw and knew nothing more.

When he recovered his senses, he was still in the cabin; the man whose life his father had attempted was bending over him, and sprinkling water on his face; and the clear voices of the women and children of the congregation were joining the voices of the men in singing the *Agnus Dei*.

"Look up at me without fear, Gabriel," said the priest. "I desire not to avenge injuries: I visit not the sins of the father on the child. Look up, and listen! I have strange things to speak of; and I have a sacred mission to fulfill before the morning, in which you must be my guide."

Gabriel attempted to kneel and kiss his hand but Father Paul stopped him, and said, pointing to the cross: "Kneel to that — not to me; not to your fellow-mortal, and your friend — for I will be your friend, Gabriel; believing that God's mercy has ordered it so. And now listen to me," he proceeded, with a brotherly tenderness in his manner which went to Gabriel's heart. "The service is nearly ended. What I have to tell you must be told at once; the errand on which you will guide me must be performed before tomorrow dawns. Sit here near me, and attend to what I now say!"

Gabriel obeyed; Father Paul then proceeded thus:

"I believe the confession made to you by your grandfather to have been true in every particular. On the evening to which he referred you, I approached your cottage, as he said, for the purpose of asking shelter for the night. At that period I had been studying hard to qualify myself for the holy calling which I now pursue; and, on the completion of my studies, had indulged in the recreation of a tour on foot through Brittany, by way of innocently and agreeably occupying the leisure time then at my disposal, before I entered the priesthood. When I accosted your father I had lost my way, had been walking for many hours, and was glad of any rest that I could get for the night. It is unnecessary to pain you now, by reference to the events which followed my entrance under your father's roof. I remember nothing that happened from the time when I lay down to sleep before the fire, until the time when I recovered my senses at the place which you call the Merchant's Table. My first sensation was that of being moved into the cold air; when I opened my eyes I saw the great Druid stones rising close above me, and two men on either side of me rifling my pockets. They found nothing valuable there, and were about to leave me where I lay, when I gathered strength enough to appeal to their mercy through their cupidity. Money was not scarce with me then, and I was able to offer them a rich reward (which they ultimately received as I had promised) if they would take me to any place where I could get shelter and medical help. I supposed they inferred by my language and accent — perhaps also by the linen I wore, which they examined closely — that I belonged to the higher ranks of the community, in spite of the plainness of my outer garments; and might, therefore, be in a position to make good my promise to them. I heard one say to the other, 'Let us risk it'; and then they took me in their arms, carried me down to a boat on the beach, and rowed to a vessel in the offing. The next day they disembarked me at Paimboeuf, where I got the assistance which I so much needed. I learned, through the confidence they were obliged to place in me in order to give me the means of sending them their promised reward, that these men were smugglers, and that they were in the habit of using the cavity in which I had been laid as a place of conceal-ment for goods, and for letters of advice to their accomplices. This accounted for their finding me. As to my wound, I was informed by the surgeon who attended me that it had missed being inflicted in a mortal part by less than a quarter of an inch, and that, as it was, nothing but the action of the night air in coagulating the blood over the place, had, in the first instance, saved my life. To be brief, I recovered after a long illness, returned to Paris, and was called to the priesthood. The will of my superiors obliged me to perform the first duties of my vocation in the great city; but my own wish was to be appointed to a cure of souls in your province, Gabriel. Can you imagine why?"

The answer to this question was in Gabriel's heart; but he was still too deeply awed and affected by what he had heard to give it utterance.

"I must tell you, then, what my motive was," said Father Paul. "You must know first that I uniformly abstained from disclosing to any one where and by whom my life had been attempted. I kept this a secret from the men who rescued me — from the surgeon — from my own friends even. My reason for such a proceeding was, I would fain believe, a Christian reason. I hope I had always felt a sincere and humble desire to prove myself, by the help of God, worthy of the sacred vocation to which I was destined. But my miraculous escape from death made an impression on my mind, which gave me another and an infinitely higher view of this vocation — the view which I have since striven, and shall always strive for the future, to maintain. As I lay, during the first days of my recovery, examining my own heart, and considering in what manner it would be my duty to act toward your father when I was restored to health, a thought came into my mind which calmed, comforted, and resolved all my doubts. I said within myself, 'In a few months more I shall be called to be one of the chosen ministers of God. If I am worthy of my vocation, my first desire toward this man who has attempted to take my life should be, not to know that human justice has overtaken him, but to know that he has truly and religiously repented and made atonement for his guilt. To such repentance and atonement let it be my duty to call him; if he reject that appeal, and be hard-

212 | WILKIE COLLINS

ened only the more against me because I have forgiven him my injuries, then it will be time enough to denounce him for his crimes to his fellow-men. Surely it must be well for me, here and hereafter, if I begin my career in the holy priesthood by helping to save from hell the soul of the man who, of all others, has most cruelly wronged me.' It was for this reason, Gabriel — it was because I desired to go straightway to your father's cottage, and reclaim him after he had believed me to be dead — that I kept the secret and entreated of my superiors that I might be sent to Brittany. But this, as I have said, was not to be at first, and when my desire was granted, my place was assigned me in a far district. The persecution under which we still suffer broke out; the designs of my life were changed; my own will became no longer mine to guide me. But, through sorrow and suffering, and danger and bloodshed, I am now led, after many days, to the execution of that first purpose which I formed on entering the priesthood. Gabriel, when the service is over, and the congregation are dispersed, you must guide me to the door of your father's cottage."

He held up his hand, in sign of silence, as Gabriel was about to answer. Just then the officiating priests above were pronouncing the final benediction. When it was over, Father Paul opened the cabin door. As he ascended the steps, followed by Gabriel, Pere Bonan met them. The old man looked doubtfully and searchingly on his future son-inlaw, as he respectfully whispered a few words in the ear of the priest. Father Paul listened attentively, answered in a whisper, and then turned to Gabriel, first begging the few people near them to withdraw a little.

"I have been asked whether there is any impediment to your marriage," he said, "and have answered that there is none. What you have said to me has been said in confession, and is a secret between us two. Remember that; and forget not, at the same time, the service which I shall require of you to-night, after the marriage-ceremony is over. Where is Perrine Bonan?" he added, aloud, looking round him. Perrine came forward. Father Paul took her hand and placed it in Gabriel's. "Lead her to the altar steps," he said, "and wait there for me."

It was more than an hour later; the boats had left the ship's side; the congregation had dispersed over the face of the country — but still the vessel remained at anchor. Those who were left in her watched the land more anxiously than usual; for they knew that Father Paul had risked meeting the soldiers of the Republic by trusting himself on shore. A boat was awaiting his return on the beach; half of the crew, armed, being posted as scouts in various directions on the high land of the heath. They would have followed and guarded the priest to the place of his destination; but he forbade it; and, leaving them abruptly, walked swiftly onward with one young man only for his companion.

Gabriel had committed his brother and his sisters to the charge of Perrine.

They were to go to the farmhouse that night with his newly-married wife and her father and mother. Father Paul had desired that this might be done. When Gabriel and he were left alone to follow the path which led to the fisherman's cottage, the priest never spoke while they walked on — never looked aside either to the right or the left — always held his ivory crucifix clasped to his breast. They arrived at the door.

"Knock," whispered Father Paul to Gabriel, "and then wait here with me."

The door was opened. On a lovely moonlight night Francois Sarzeau had stood on that threshold, years since, with a bleeding body in his arms. On a lovely moonlight night he now stood there again, confronting the very man whose life he had attempted, and knowing him not.

Father Paul advanced a few paces, so that the moonlight fell fuller on his features, and removed his hat.

Francois Sarzeau looked, started, moved one step back, then stood motionless and perfectly silent, while all traces of expression of any kind suddenly vanished from his face. Then the calm, clear tones of the priest stole gently on the dead silence. "I bring a message of peace and forgiveness from a guest of former years," he said; and pointed, as he spoke, to the place where he had been wounded in the neck.

For one moment, Gabriel saw his father trembling violently from head to foot — then his limbs steadied again — stiffened suddenly, as if struck by catalepsy. His lips parted, but without quivering; his eyes glared, but without moving in the orbits. The lovely moonlight itself looked ghastly and horrible, shining on the supernatural panic deformity of that face! Gabriel turned away his head in terror. He heard the voice of Father Paul saying to him: "Wait here till I come back."

Then there was an instant of silence again — then a low groaning sound that seemed to articulate the name of God; a sound unlike his father's voice, unlike any human voice he had ever heard — and then the noise of a closing door. He looked up, and saw that he was standing alone before the cottage.

Once, after an interval, he approached the window.

He just saw through it the hand of the priest holding on high the ivory crucifix; but stopped not to see more, for he heard such words, such sounds, as drove him back to his former place. There he stayed, until the noise of something falling heavily within the cottage struck on his ear. Again he advanced toward the door; heard Father Paul praying; listened for several minutes; then heard a moaning voice, now joining itself to the voice of the priest, now choked in sobs and bitter wailing. Once more he went back out of hearing, and stirred not again from his place. He waited a long and a weary time there — so long that one of the scouts on the lookout came toward him, evidently suspicious of the delay in the priest's return. He waved the man back, and then looked again toward the door. At last he saw it open — saw Father Paul approach him, leading Francois Sarzeau by the hand.

The fisherman never raised his downcast eyes to his son's face; tears trickled silently over his cheeks; he followed the hand that led him, as a little child might have followed it, listened anxiously and humbly at the priest's side to every word that he spoke.

"Gabriel," said Father Paul, in a voice which trembled a little for the first time that night —"Gabriel, it has pleased God to grant the perfect fulfillment of the purpose which brought me to this place; I tell you this, as all that you need — as all, I believe, that you would wish — to know of what has passed while you have been left waiting for me here. Such words as I have now to speak to you are spoken by your father's earnest desire. It is his own wish that I should communicate to you his confession of having secretly followed you to the Merchant's Table, and of having discovered (as you discovered) that no evidence of his guilt remained there. This admission, he thinks, will be enough to account for his conduct toward yourself from that time to this. I have next to tell you (also at your father's desire) that he has promised in my presence, and now promises again in yours, sincerity of repentance in this manner: When the persecution of our religion has ceased — as cease it will, and that speedily, be assured of it — he solemnly pledges himself henceforth to devote his life, his strength and what worldly possessions he may have, or may acquire, to the task of re-erecting and restoring the road-side crosses which have been sacrilegiously overthrown and destroyed in his native province, and to doing good, go where he may. I have now said all that is required of me, and may bid you farewell — bearing with me the happy remembrance that I have left a father and son reconciled and restored to each other. May God bless and prosper you, and those dear to you, Gabriel! May God accept your father's repentance, and bless him also throughout his future life!"

He took their hands, pressed them long and warmly, then turned and walked quickly down the path which led to the beach. Gabriel dared not trust himself yet to speak; but he raised his arm, and put it gently round his father's neck. The two stood together so, looking out dimly through the tears that filled their eyes to the sea. They saw the boat put off in the bright track of the moonlight, and reach the vessel's side; they watched the spreading of the sails, and followed the slow course of the ship till she disappeared past a distant headland from sight.

After that, they went into the cottage together. They knew it not then, but they had seen the last, in this world, of Father Paul.

CHAPTER V.

*T*he events foretold by the good priest happened sooner even than he had anticipated. A new government ruled the destinies of France, and the persecution ceased in Brittany.

Among other propositions which were then submitted to the Parliament, was one advocating the restoration of the road-side crosses throughout the province. It was found, however, on inquiry, that these crosses were to be counted by thousands, and that the mere cost of wood required to re-erect them necessitated an expenditure of money which the bankrupt nation could ill afford to spare. While this project was under discussion, and before it was finally rejected, one man had undertaken the task which the Government shrank from attempting. When Gabriel left the cottage, taking his brother and sisters to live with his wife and himself at the farmhouse, Francois Sarzeau left it also, to perform in highway and byway his promise to Father Paul. For months and months he labored without intermission at his task; still, always doing good, and rendering help and kindness and true charity to any whom he could serve. He walked many a weary mile, toiled through many a hard day's work, humbled himself even to beg of others, to get wood enough to restore a single cross. No one ever heard him complain, ever saw him impatient, ever detected him in faltering at his task. The shelter in an outhouse, the crust of bread and drink of water, which he could always get from the peasantry, seemed to suffice him. Among the people who watched his perseverance, a belief began to gain ground that his life would be miraculously prolonged until he had completed his undertaking from one end of Brittany to the other. But this was not to be.

He was seen one cold autumn evening, silently and steadily at work as usual, setting up a new cross on the site of one which had been shattered to splinters in the troubled times. In the morning he was found lying dead beneath the sacred symbol which his own hands had completed and erected in its place during the night. They buried him where he lay; and the priest who consecrated the ground allowed Gabriel to engrave his father's epitaph in the wood of the cross. It was simply the initial letters of the dead man's name, followed by this inscription: "Pray for the repose of his soul: he died penitent, and the doer of good works."

Once, and once only, did Gabriel hear anything of Father Paul. The good priest showed, by writing to the farmhouse, that he had not forgotten the family so largely indebted to him for their happiness. The letter was dated "Rome." Father Paul said that such services as he had been permitted to render to the Church in Brittany had obtained for him a new and a far more glorious trust than any he had yet held. He had been recalled from his curacy, and appointed to be at the head of a mission which was shortly to be dispatched to convert the inhabitants of a savage and far distant land to the Christian faith. He now wrote, as his brethren with him were writing, to take leave of all friends forever in this world, before setting out — for it was well known to the chosen persons intrusted with the new mission that they could only hope to advance its object by cheerfully risking their own lives for the sake of their religion. He gave his blessing to Francois Sarzeau, to Gabriel, and to his family; and bade them affectionately farewell for the last time.

There was a postscript to the letter, which was addressed to Perrine, and which she often read afterward with tearful eyes. The writer begged that, if she should have any children, she would show her friendly and Christian remembrance of him by teaching them to pray (as he hoped she herself would pray) that a blessing might attend Father Paul's labors in the distant land.

The priest's loving petition was never forgotten. When Perrine taught its first prayer to her first child, the little creature was instructed to end the few simple words pronounced at its mother's knees, with, "God bless Father Paul."

In those words the nun concluded her narrative. After it was ended, she pointed to the old wooden cross, and said to me:

"That was one of the many that he made. It was found, a few years since, to have suffered so much from exposure to the weather that it was unfit to remain any longer in its old place. A priest in Brittany gave it to one of the nuns in this convent. Do you wonder now that the Mother Superior always calls it a Relic?"

"No," I answered. "And I should have small respect indeed for the religious convictions of any one who could hear the story of that wooden cross, and not feel that the Mother Superior's name for it is the very best that could have been chosen."

THE PROFESSOR'S STORY OF THE YELLOW MASK.

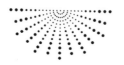

PROLOGUE TO THE SIXTH STORY.

On the last occasion when I made a lengthened stay in London, my wife and I were surprised and amused one morning by the receipt of the following note, addressed to me in a small, crabbed, foreign-looking handwriting.

"Professor Tizzi presents amiable compliments to Mr. Kerby, the artist, and is desirous of having his portrait done, to be engraved from, and placed at the beginning of the voluminous work on 'The Vital Principle; or, Invisible Essence of Life,' which the Professor is now preparing for the press — and posterity.

"The Professor will give five pounds; and will look upon his face with satisfaction, as an object perpetuated for public contemplation at a reasonable rate, if Mr. Kerby will accept the sum just mentioned.

"In regard to the Professor's ability to pay five pounds, as well as to offer them, if Mr. Kerby should, from ignorance, entertain injurious doubts, he is requested to apply to the Professor's honorable friend, Mr. Lanfray, of Rockleigh Place."

But for the reference at the end of this strange note, I should certainly have considered it as a mere trap set to make a fool of me by some mischievous friend. As it was, I rather doubted the propriety of taking any serious notice of Professor Tizzi's offer; and I might probably have ended by putting the letter in the fire without further thought about it, but for the arrival by the next post of a note from Mr. Lanfray, which solved all my doubts, and sent me away at once to make the acquaintance of the learned discoverer of the Essence of Life.

"Do not be surprised" (Mr. Lanfray wrote) "if you get a strange note from a very eccentric Italian, one Professor Tizzi, formerly of the University of Padua. I have known him for some years. Scientific inquiry is his monomania, and vanity his ruling passion. He has written a book on the principle of life, which nobody but himself will ever read; but which he is determined to publish, with his own portrait for frontispiece. If it is worth your while to accept the little he can offer you, take it by all means, for he is a character worth knowing. He was exiled, I should tell you, years ago, for some absurd political reason, and has lived in England ever since. All the money he inherits from his father, who was a mail contractor in the north of Italy, goes in books and experiments; but I think I can answer for his solvency, at any rate, for the large sum of five pounds. If you are not very much occupied just now, go and see him. He is sure to amuse you."

Professor Tizzi lived in the northern suburb of London. On approaching his house, I found it, so far as outward appearance went, excessively dirty and neglected, but in no other respect different from the "villas" in its neighborhood. The front garden door, after I had rang twice, was opened by a yellow-faced, suspicious old foreigner, dressed in worn-out clothes, and completely and consistently dirty all over, from top to toe. On mentioning my name and business, this old man led me across a weedy, neglected garden, and admitted me into the house. At the first step into the passage, I was surrounded by books. Closely packed in plain wooden shelves, they ran all along the wall on either side to the back of the house; and when I looked up at the carpetless staircase, I saw nothing but books again, running all the way up the wall, as far as my eye could reach. "Here is the Artist Painter!" cried the old servant, throwing open one of the parlor doors, before I had half done looking at the books, and signing impatiently to me to walk into the room.

Books again! all round the walls, and all over the floor — among them a plain deal table, with leaves of manuscript piled high on every part of it — among the leaves a head of long, elfish white hair covered with a black skull-cap, and bent down over a book — above the head a sallow, withered hand shaking itself at me as a sign that I must not venture to speak just at that moment — on the tops of the bookcases glass vases full of spirits of some kind, with horrible objects floating in the liquid — dirt on the window panes, cobwebs hanging from the ceiling, dust springing up in clouds under my intruding feet. These were the things I observed on first entering the study of Professor Tizzi.

After I had waited for a minute or so, the shaking hand stopped, descended with a smack on the nearest pile of manuscript, seized the book that the head had been bending over, and flung it contemptuously to the other end of the room. "I've refuted *you*, at any rate!" said Professor Tizzi, looking with extreme complacency at the cloud of dust raised by the fall of the rejected volume.

He turned next to me. What a grand face it was! What a broad, white forehead —— what fiercely brilliant black eyes — what perfect regularity and refinement in the other features; with the long, venerable hair, framing them in, as it were, on either side! Poor as I was, I felt that I could have painted his portrait for nothing. Titian, Vandyke, Valasquez — any of the three would have paid him to sit to them!

"Accept my humblest excuses, sir," said the old man, speaking English with a singularly pure accent for a foreigner. "That absurd book plunged me so deep down in the quagmires of sophistry and error, Mr. Kerby, that I really could not get to the surface at once when you came into the room. So you are willing to draw my likeness for such a small sum as five pounds?" he continued, rising, and showing me that he wore a long black velvet gown, instead of the paltry and senseless costume of modern times.

I informed him that five pounds was as much as I generally got for a drawing.

"It seems little," said the professor; "but if you want fame, I can make it up to you in that way. There is my great work" (he pointed to the piles of manuscript), "the portrait of my mind and the mirror of my learning; put a likeness of my face on the first page, and posterity will then be thoroughly acquainted with me, outside and in. Your portrait will be engraved, Mr. Kerby, and your name shall be inscribed under the print. You shall be associated, sir, in that way, with a work which will form an epoch in the history of human science. The Vital Principle — or, in other words, the essence of that mysterious Something which we call Life, and which extends down from Man to the feeblest insect and the smallest plant — has been an unguessed riddle from the beginning of the world to the present time. I alone have found the answer; and here it is!" He fixed his dazzling eyes on me in triumph, and smacked the piles of manuscript fiercely with both his sallow hands.

I saw that he was waiting for me to say something; so I asked if his great work had not cost a vast expenditure of time and pains.

"I am seventy, sir," said the Professor; "and I began preparing myself for that book at twenty. After mature consideration, I have written it in English (having three other foreign languages at my fingers' ends), as a substantial proof of my gratitude to the nation that has given me an asylum. Perhaps you think the work looks rather long in its manuscript state? It will occupy twelve volumes, sir, and it is not half long enough, even then, for the subject. I take two volumes (and no man could do it in less) to examine the theories of all the philosophers in the world, ancient and modern, on the Vital Principle. I take two more (and little enough) to scatter every one of the theories, *seriatim* , to the winds. I take two more (at the risk, for brevity's sake, of doing things by halves) to explain the exact stuff, or vital compound, of which the first man and woman in the world were made — calling them Adam and Eve, out of deference to popular prejudices. I take two more — but you are standing all this time, Mr. Kerby; and I am talking instead of sitting for my portrait. Pray take any books you want, anywhere off the floor, and make a seat of any height you please. Furniture would only be in my way here, so I don't trouble myself with anything of the kind."

I obediently followed the Professor's directions, and had just heaped up a pile of grimy quartos, when the old servant entered the room with a shabby little tray in his hand. In the middle of the tray I saw a crust of bread and a bit of garlic, encircled by a glass of water, a knife, salt, pepper, a bottle of vinegar, and a flask of oil.

"With your permission, I am going to breakfast," said Professor Tizzi, as the tray was set down before him on the part of his great work relating to the vital compound of Adam and Eve. As he spoke, he took up the piece of bread, and rubbed the crusty part of it with the bit of garlic, till it looked as polished as a new dining-table. That done, he turned the bread, crumb uppermost, and saturated it with oil, added a few drops of vinegar, sprinkled with pepper and salt, and, with a gleam of something very like greediness in his bright eyes, took up the knife to cut himself a first mouthful of the horrible mess that he had just concocted. "The best of breakfasts," said the Professor, seeing me look amazed. "Not a cannibal meal of chicken-life in embryo (vulgarly called an egg); not a dog's gorge of a dead animal's flesh, blood and bones, warmed with fire (popularly known as a chop); not a breakfast, sir, that lions, tigers, Caribbees, and costermongers could all partake of alike; but an innocent, nutritive, simple, vegetable meal; a philosopher's refection, a breakfast that a prize-fighter would turn from in disgust, and that a Plato would share with relish."

I have no doubt that he was right, and that I was prejudiced; but as I saw the first oily, vinegary, garlicky morsel slide noiselessly into his mouth, I began to feel rather sick. My hands were dirty with moving the books, and I asked if I could wash them before beginning to work at the likeness, as a good excuse for getting out of the room, while Professor Tizzi was unctuously disposing of his simple vegetable meal.

The philosopher looked a little astonished at my request, as if the washing of hands at irregular times and seasons offered a comparatively new subject of contemplation to him; but he rang a hand-bell on his table immediately, and told the old servant to take me up into his bedroom.

The interior of the parlor had astonished me; but a sight of the bedroom was a new sensation — not of the most agreeable kind. The couch on which the philosopher sought repose after his labors was a truckle-bed that would not have fetched half a crown at a sale. On one side of it dangled from the ceiling a complete male skeleton, looking like all that was left of a man who might have hung himself about a century ago, and who had never been disturbed since the moment of his suicide. On the other side of the bed stood a long press, in which I observed hideous colored preparations of the muscular system, and bottles with curious, twining, thread-like substances inside them, which might have been remarkable worms or dissections of nerves, scattered amicably side by side with the Professor's hair-brush (three parts worn out), with remnants of his beard on bits of shaving-paper, with a broken shoe-horn, and with a traveling looking-glass of the sort usually sold at sixpence apiece. Repetitions of the litter of books in the parlor lay all about over the floor; colored anatomical prints were nailed anyhow against the walls; rolled-up towels were scattered here, there, and everywhere in the wildest confusion, as if the room had been bombarded with them; and last, but by no means least remarkable among the other extraordinary objects in the bed-chamber, the stuffed figure of a large unshaven poodle-dog, stood on an old card-table, keeping perpetual watch over a pair of the philosopher's black breeches twisted round his forepaws.

I had started, on entering the room, at the skeleton, and I started once more at the dog. The old servant noticed me each time with a sardonic grin. "Don't be afraid," he said; "one is as dead as the other." With these words, he left me to wash my hands.

Finding little more than a pint of water at my disposal, and failing altogether to discover where the soap was kept, I was not long in performing my ablutions. Before leaving the room, I looked again at the stuffed poodle. On the board to which he was fixed, I saw painted in faded letters the word "Scarammuccia," evidently the comic Italian name to which he had answered in his lifetime. There was no other inscription; but I made up my mind that the dog must have been the Professor's pet, and that he kept the animal stuffed in his bedroom as a remembrance of past times. "Who would have suspected so great a philosopher of having so much heart!" thought I, leaving the bedroom to go downstairs again.

The Professor had done his breakfast, and was anxious to begin the sitting; so I took out my chalks and paper, and set to work at once — I seated on one pile of books and he on another.

"Fine anatomical preparations in my room, are there not, Mr. Kerby?" said the old gentleman. "Did you notice a very interesting and perfect arrangement of the intestinal ganglia? They form the subject of an important chapter in my great work."

"I am afraid you will think me very ignorant," I replied. "But I really do not know the intestinal ganglia when I see them. The object I noticed with most curiosity in your room was something more on a level with my own small capacity."

"And what was that?" asked the Professor.

"The figure of the stuffed poodle. I suppose he was a favorite of yours?"

"Of mine? No, no; a young woman's favorite, sir, before I was born; and a very remarkable dog, too. The vital principle in that poodle, Mr. Kerby, must have been singularly intensified. He lived to a fabulous old age, and he was clever enough to play an important part of his own in what you English call a Romance of Real Life! If I could only have dissected that poodle, I would have put him into my book; he should have headed my chapter on the Vital Principle of Beasts."

"Here is a story in prospect," thought I, "if I can only keep his attention up to the subject."

"He should have figured in my great work, sir," the Professor went on. "Scarammuccia should have taken his place among the examples that prove my new theory; but unfortunately he died before I was born. His mistress gave him, stuffed, as you see upstairs, to my father to take care of for her, and he has descended as an heirloom to me. Talking of dogs, Mr. Kerby, I have ascertained, beyond the possibility of doubt, that the brachial plexus in people who die of hydrophobia — but stop! I had better show you how it is — the preparation is upstairs under my wash-hand stand."

He left his seat as he spoke. In another minute he would have sent the servant to fetch the "preparation," and I should have lost the story. At the risk of his taking offense, I begged him not to move just then, unless he wished me to spoil his likeness. This alarmed, but fortunately did not irritate him. He returned to his seat, and I resumed the subject of the stuffed poodle, asking him boldly to tell me the story with which the dog was connected. The demand seemed to impress him with no very favorable opinion of my intellectual tastes; but he complied with it, and related, not without many a wearisome digression to the subject of his great work, the narrative which I propose calling by the name of "The Yellow Mask." After the slight specimens that I have given of his character and style of conversation, it will be almost unnecessary for me to premise that I tell this story as I have told the last, and "Sister Rose," in my own language, and according to my own plan in the disposition of the incidents — adding nothing, of course, to the facts, but keeping them within the limits which my disposable space prescribes to me.

I may perhaps be allowed to add in this place, that I have not yet seen or heard of my portrait in an engraved state. Professor Tizzi is still alive; but I look in vain through the publishers' lists for an announcement of his learned work on the Vital Principle. Possibly he may be adding a volume or two to the twelve already completed, by way of increasing the debt which a deeply obliged posterity is, sooner or later, sure of owing to him.

PART FIRST. CHAPTER I.

*A*bout a century ago, there lived in the ancient city of Pisa a famous Italian milliner, who, by way of vindicating to all customers her familiarity with Paris fashions, adopted a French title, and called herself the Demoiselle Grifoni. She was a wizen little woman with a mischievous face, a quick tongue, a nimble foot, a talent for business, and an uncertain disposition. Rumor hinted that she was immensely rich, and scandal suggested that she would do anything for money.

The one undeniable good quality which raised Demoiselle Grifoni above all her rivals in the trade was her inexhaustible fortitude. She was never known to yield an inch under any pressure of adverse circumstances Thus the memorable occasion of her life on which she was threatened with ruin was also the occasion on which she most triumphantly asserted the energy and decision of her character. At the height of the demoiselle's prosperity her skilled forewoman and cutter-out basely married and started in business as her rival. Such a calamity as this would have ruined an ordinary milliner; but the invincible Grifoni rose superior to it almost without an effort, and proved incontestably that it was impossible for hostile Fortune to catch her at the end of her resources. While the minor milliners were prophesying that she would shut up shop, she was quietly carrying on a private correspondence with an agent in Paris. Nobody knew what these letters were about until a few weeks had elapsed, and then circulars were received by all the ladies in Pisa, announcing that the best French forewoman who could be got for money was engaged to superintend the great Grifoni establishment. This master-stroke decided the victory. All the demoiselle's customers declined giving orders elsewhere until the forewoman from Paris had exhibited to the natives of Pisa the latest fashions from the metropolis of the world of dress.

The Frenchwoman arrived punctual to the appointed day — glib and curt, smiling and flippant, tight of face and supple of figure. Her name was Mademoiselle Virginie, and her family had inhumanly deserted her. She was set to work the moment she was inside the doors of the Grifoni establishment. A room was devoted to her own private use; magnificent materials in velvet, silk, and satin, with due accompaniment of muslins, laces, and ribbons were placed at her disposal; she was told to spare no expense, and to produce, in the shortest possible time, the finest and nearest specimen dresses for exhibition in the show-room. Mademoiselle Virginie undertook to do everything required of her, produced her portfolios of patterns and her book of colored designs, and asked for one assistant who could speak French enough to interpret her orders to the Italian girls in the work-room.

"I have the very person you want," cried Demoiselle Grifoni. "A workwoman we call Brigida here — the idlest slut in Pisa, but as sharp as a needle — has been in France, and speaks the language like a native. I'll send her to you directly."

Mademoiselle Virginie was not left long alone with her patterns and silks. A tall woman, with bold black eyes, a reckless manner, and a step as firm as a man's, stalked into the room with the gait of a tragedy-queen crossing the stage. The instant her eyes fell on the French forewoman, she stopped, threw up her hands in astonishment, and exclaimed, "Finette!"

"Teresa!" cried the Frenchwoman, casting her scissors on the table, and advancing a few steps.

"Hush! call me Brigida."

"Hush! call me Virginie."

These two exclamations were uttered at the same moment, and then the two women scrutinized each other in silence. The swarthy cheeks of the Italian turned to a dull yellow, and the voice of the Frenchwoman trembled a little when she spoke again.

"How, in the name of Heaven, have you dropped down in the world as low as this?" she asked. "I thought you were provided for when —"

"Silence!" interrupted Brigida. "You see I was not provided for. I have had my misfortunes; and you are the last woman alive who ought to refer to them."

"Do you think I have not had my misfortunes, too, since we met?" (Brigida's face brightened maliciously at those words.) "You have had your revenge," continued Mademoiselle Virginie, coldly, turning away to the table and taking up the scissors again.

Brigida followed her, threw one arm roughly round her neck, and kissed her on the cheek. "Let us be friends again," she said. The Frenchwoman laughed. "Tell me how I have had my revenge," pursued the other, tightening her grasp. Mademoiselle Virginie signed to Brigida to stoop, and whispered rapidly in her ear. The Italian listened eagerly, with fierce, suspicious eyes fixed on the door. When the whispering ceased, she loosened her hold, and, with a sigh of relief, pushed back her heavy black hair from her temples. "Now we are friends," she said, and sat down indolently in a chair placed by the worktable.

"Friends," repeated Mademoiselle Virginie, with another laugh. "And now for business," she continued, getting a row of pins ready for use by putting them between her teeth. "I am here, I believe, for the purpose of ruining the late forewoman, who has set up in opposition to us? Good! I *will* ruin her. Spread out the yellow brocaded silk, my dear, and pin that pattern on at your end, while I pin at mine. And what are your plans, Brigida? (Mind you don't forget that Finette is dead, and that Virginie has risen from her ashes.) You can't possibly intend to stop here all your life? (Leave an inch outside the paper, all round.) You must have projects? What are they?"

"Look at my figure," said Brigida, placing herself in an attitude in the middle of the room.

"Ah," rejoined the other, "it's not what it was. There's too much of it. You want diet, walking, and a French stay-maker," muttered Mademoiselle Virginie through her chevaus-defrise of pins.

"Did the goddess Minerva walk, and employ a French stay-maker? I thought she rode upon clouds, and lived at a period before waists were invented."

"What do you mean?"

"This — that my present project is to try if I can't make my fortune by sitting as a model for Minerva in the studio of the best sculptor in Pisa."

"And who is he! (Unwind me a yard or two of that black lace.)"

"The master-sculptor, Luca Lomi — an old family, once noble, but down in the world now. The master is obliged to make statues to get a living for his daughter and himself."

"More of the lace — double it over the bosom of the dress. And how is sitting to this needy sculptor to make your fortune?"

"Wait a minute. There are other sculptors besides him in the studio. There is, first, his brother, the priest — Father Rocco, who passes all his spare time with the master. He is a good sculptor in his way — has cast statues and made a font for his church — a holy man, who devotes all his work in the studio to the cause of piety."

"Ah, bah! we should think him a droll priest in France. (More pins.) You don't expect *him* to put money in your pocket, surely?"

"Wait, I say again. There is a third sculptor in the studio — actually a nobleman! His name is Fabio d'Ascoli. He is rich, young, handsome, an only child, and little better than a fool. Fancy his working at sculpture, as if he had his bread to get by it — and thinking that an amusement! Imagine a man belonging to one of the best families in Pisa mad enough to want to make a reputation as an artist! Wait! wait! the best is to come. His father and mother are dead — he has no near relations in the world to exercise authority over him — he is a bachelor, and his fortune is all at his own disposal; going a-begging, my friend; absolutely going a-begging for want of a clever woman to hold out her hand and take it from him."

"Yes, yes — now I understand. The goddess Minerva is a clever woman, and she will hold out her hand and take his fortune from him with the utmost docility."

"The first thing is to get him to offer it. I must tell you that I am not going to sit to him, but to his master, Luca Lomi, who is doing the statue of Minerva. The face is modeled from his daughter; and now he wants somebody to sit for the bust and arms. Maddalena Lomi and I are as nearly as possible the same height, I hear — the difference between us being that I have a good figure and she has a bad one. I have offered to sit, through a friend who is employed in the studio. If the master accepts, I am sure of an introduction to our rich young gentleman; and then leave it to my good looks, my various accomplishments, and my ready tongue, to do the rest."

"Stop! I won't have the lace doubled, on second thoughts. I'll have it single, and running all round the dress in curves — so. Well, and who is this friend of yours employed in the studio? A fourth sculptor?"

"No, no; the strangest, simplest little creature —"

Just then a faint tap was audible at the door of the room.

Brigida laid her finger on her lips, and called impatiently to the person outside to come in.

The door opened gently, and a young girl, poorly but very neatly dressed, entered the room. She was rather thin and under the average height; but her head and figure were in perfect proportion. Her hair was of that gorgeous auburn color, her eyes of that deep violet-blue, which the portraits of Giorgione and Titian have made famous as the type of Venetian beauty. Her features possessed the definiteness and regularity, the "good modeling" (to use an artist's term), which is the rarest of all womanly charms, in Italy as elsewhere. The one serious defect of her face was its paleness. Her cheeks, wanting nothing in form, wanted everything in color. That look of health, which is the essential crowning-point of beauty, was the one attraction which her face did not possess.

She came into the room with a sad and weary expression in her eyes, which changed, however, the moment she observed the magnificently-dressed French forewoman, into a look of astonishment, and almost of awe. Her manner became shy and embarrassed; and after an instant of hesitation, she turned back silently to the door.

"Stop, stop, Nanina," said Brigida, in Italian. "Don't be afraid of that lady. She is our new forewoman; and she has it in her power to do all sorts of kind things for you. Look up, and tell us what you want You were sixteen last birthday, Nanina, and you behave like a baby of two years old!"

"I only came to know if there was any work for me today," said the girl, in a very sweet voice, that trembled a little as she tried to face the fashionable French forewoman again.

"No work, child, that is easy enough for you to do," said Brigida. "Are you going to the studio today?"

Some of the color that Nanina's cheeks wanted began to steal over them as she answered "Yes."

"Don't forget my message, darling. And if Master Luca Lomi asks where I live, answer that you are ready to deliver a letter to me; but that you are forbidden to enter into any particulars at first about who I am, or where I live."

"Why am I forbidden?" inquired Nanina, innocently.

"Don't ask questions, baby! Do as you are told. Bring me back a nice note or message tomorrow from the studio, and I will intercede with this lady to get you some work. You are a foolish child to want it, when you might make more money here and at Florence, by sitting to painters and sculptors; though what they can see to paint or model in you I never could understand."

"I like working at home better than going abroad to sit," said Nanina, looking very much abashed as she faltered out the answer, and escaping from the room with a terrified farewell obeisance, which was an eccentric compound of a start, a bow, and a courtesy.

"That awkward child would be pretty," said Mademoiselle Virginie, making rapid progress with the cutting-out of her dress, "if she knew how to give herself a complexion, and had a presentable gown on her back. Who is she?"

"The friend who is to get me into Master Luca Lomi's studio," replied Brigida, laughing. "Rather a curious ally for me to take up with, isn't she?"

"Where did you meet with her?"

"Here, to be sure; she hangs about this place for any plain work she can get to do, and takes it home to the oddest little room in a street near the Campo Santo. I had the curiosity to follow her one day, and knocked at her door soon after she had gone in, as if I was a visitor. She answered my knock in a great flurry and fright, as you may imagine. I made myself agreeable, affected immense interest in her affairs, and so got into her room. Such a place! A mere corner of it curtained off to make a bedroom. One chair, one stool, one saucepan on the fire. Before the hearth the most grotesquely hideous unshaven poodle-dog you ever saw; and on the stool a fair little girl plaiting dinner-mats. Such was the household — furniture and all included. 'Where is your father?' I asked. 'He ran away and left us years ago,' answers my awkward little friend who has just left the room, speaking in that simple way of hers, with all the composure in the world. 'And your mother?'—'Dead.' She went up to the little mat-plaiting girl as she gave that answer, and began playing with her long flaxen hair. 'Your sister, I suppose,' said I. 'What is her name?'—'They call me La Biondella,' says the child, looking up from her mat (La Biondella, Virginie, means The Fair). 'And why do you let that great, shaggy, ill-looking brute lie before your fireplace?' I asked. 'Oh!' cried the little mat-plaiter, 'that is our dear old dog, Scarammuccia. He takes care of the house when Nanina is not at home. He dances on his hind legs, and jumps through a hoop, and tumbles down dead when I cry Bang! Scarammuccia followed us home one night, years ago, and he has lived with us ever since. He goes out every day by himself, we can't tell where, and generally returns licking his chops, which makes us afraid that he is a thief; but nobody finds him out, because he is the cleverest dog that ever lived!' The child ran on in this way about the great beast by the fireplace, till I was obliged to stop her; while that simpleton Nanina stood by, laughing and encouraging her. I asked them a few more questions, which produced some strange answers. They did not seem to know of any relations of theirs in the world. The neighbors in the house had helped them, after their father ran away, until they were old enough to help themselves; and they did not seem to think there was anything in the least wretched or pitiable in their way of living. The last thing I heard, when I left them that day, was La Biondella crying 'Bang!'— then a bark, a thump on the floor, and a scream of laughter. If it was not for their dog, I should go and see them oftener. But the ill-conditioned beast has taken a dislike to me, and growls and shows his teeth whenever I come near him."

"The girl looked sickly when she came in here. Is she always like that?"

"No. She has altered within the last month. I suspect our interesting young nobleman has produced an impression. The oftener the girl has sat to him lately, the paler and more out of spirits she has become."

"Oh! she has sat to him, has she?"

"She is sitting to him now. He is doing a bust of some Pagan nymph or other, and prevailed on Nanina to let him copy from her head and face. According to her own account the little fool was frightened at first, and gave him all the trouble in the world before she would consent."

"And now she has consented, don't you think it likely she may turn out rather a dangerous rival? Men are such fools, and take such fancies into their heads —"

"Ridiculous! A thread-paper of a girl like that, who has no manner, no talk, no intelligence; who has nothing to recommend her but an awkward, babyish prettiness! Dangerous to me? No, no! If there is danger at all, I have to dread it from the sculptor's daughter. I don't mind confessing that I am anxious to see Maddalena Lomi. But as for Nanina, she will simply be of use to me. All I know already about the studio and the artists in it, I know through her. She will deliver my message, and procure me my introduction; and when we have got so far, I shall give her an old gown and a shake of the hand; and then, good-by to our little innocent!"

"Well, well, for your sake I hope you are the wiser of the two in this matter. For my part, I always distrust innocence. Wait one moment, and I shall have the body and sleeves of this dress ready for the needle-women. There, ring the bell, and order them up; for I have directions to give, and you must interpret for me."

While Brigida went to the bell, the energetic Frenchwoman began planning out the skirt of the new dress. She laughed as she measured off yard after yard of the silk.

"What are you laughing about?" asked Brigida, opening the door and ringing a hand-bell in the passage.

"I can't help fancying, dear, in spite of her innocent face and her artless ways, that your young friend is a hypocrite."

"And I am quite certain, love, that she is only a simpleton."

PART FIRST. CHAPTER II.

*T*he studio of the master-sculptor, Luca Lomi, was composed of two large rooms unequally divided by a wooden partition, with an arched doorway cut in the middle of it.

While the milliners of the Grifoni establishment were industriously shaping dresses, the sculptors in Luca Lomi's workshop were, in their way, quite as hard at work shaping marble and clay. In the smaller of the two rooms the young nobleman (only addressed in the studio by his Christian name of Fabio) was busily engaged on his bust, with Nanina sitting before him as a model. His was not one of those traditional Italian faces from which subtlety and suspicion are always supposed to look out darkly on the world at large. Both countenance and expression proclaimed his character frankly and freely to all who saw him. Quick intelligence looked brightly from his eyes; and easy good humor laughed out pleasantly in the rather quaint curve of his lips. For the rest, his face expressed the defects as well as the merits of his character, showing that he wanted resolution and perseverance just as plainly as it showed also that he possessed amiability and intelligence.

At the end of the large room, nearest to the street door, Luca Lomi was standing by his life-size statue of Minerva; and was issuing directions, from time to time, to some of his workmen, who were roughly chiseling the drapery of another figure. At the opposite side of the room, nearest to the partition, his brother, Father Rocco, was taking a cast from a statuette of the Madonna; while Maddalena Lomi, the sculptor's daughter, released from sitting for Minerva's face, walked about the two rooms, and watched what was going on in them.

There was a strong family likeness of a certain kind between father, brother and daughter. All three were tall, handsome, dark-haired, and dark-eyed; nevertheless, they differed in expression, strikingly as they resembled one another in feature. Maddalena Lomi's face betrayed strong passions, but not an ungenerous nature. Her father, with the same indications of a violent temper, had some sinister lines about his mouth and forehead which suggested anything rather than an open disposition. Father Rocco's countenance, on the other hand, looked like the personification of absolute calmness and invincible moderation; and his manner, which, in a very firm way, was singularly quiet and deliberate, assisted in carrying out the impression produced by his face. The daughter seemed as if she could fly into a passion at a moment's notice, and forgive also at a moment's notice. The father, appearing to be just as irritable, had something in his face which said, as plainly as if in words, "Anger me, and I never pardon." The priest looked as if he need never be called on either to ask forgiveness or to grant it, for the double reason that he could irritate nobody else, and that nobody else could irritate him.

"Rocco," said Luca, looking at the face of his Minerva, which was now finished, "this statue of mine will make a sensation."

"I am glad to hear it," rejoined the priest, dryly

"It is a new thing in art," continued Luca, enthusiastically. "Other sculptors, with a classical subject like mine, limit themselves to the ideal classical face, and never think of aiming at individual character. Now I do precisely the reverse of that. I get my handsome daughter, Maddalena, to sit for Minerva, and I make an exact likeness of her. I may lose in ideal beauty, but I gain in individual character. People may accuse me of disregarding established rules; but my answer is, that I make my own rules. My daughter looks like a Minerva, and there she is exactly as she looks."

"It is certainly a wonderful likeness," said Father Rocco, approaching the statue.

"It the girl herself," cried the other. "Exactly her expression, and exactly her features. Measure Maddalena, and measure Minerva, and from forehead to chin, you won't find a hair-breadth of difference between them."

"But how about the bust and arms of the figure, now the face is done?" asked the priest, returning, as he spoke, to his own work.

"I may have the very model I want for them tomorrow. Little Nanina has just given me the strangest message. What do you think of a mysterious lady admirer who offers to sit for the bust and arms of my Minerva?"

"Are you going to accept the offer?" inquired the priest.

"I am going to receive her tomorrow; and if I really find that she is the same height as Maddalena, and has a bust and arms worth modeling, of course I shall accept her offer; for she will be the very sitter I have been looking after for weeks past. Who can she be? That's the mystery I want to find out. Which do you say, Rocco — an enthusiast or an adventuress?"

"I do not presume to say, for I have no means of knowing."

"Ah, there you are with your moderation again. Now, I do presume to assert that she must be either one or the other — or she would not have forbidden Nanina to say anything about her in answer to all my first natural inquiries. Where is Maddalena? I thought she was here a minute ago."

"She is in Fabio's room," answered Father Rocco, softly. "Shall I call her?"

"No, no!" returned Luca. He stopped, looked round at the workmen, who were chipping away mechanically at their bit of drapery; then advanced close to the priest, with a cunning smile, and continued in a whisper, "If Maddalena can only get from Fabio's room here to Fabio's palace over the way, on the Arno — come, come, Rocco! don't shake your head. If I brought her up to your church door one of these days, as Fabio d'Ascoli's betrothed, you would be glad enough to take the rest of the business off my hands, and make her Fabio d'Ascoli's wife. You are a very holy man, Rocco, but you know the difference between the clink of the money-bag and the clink of the chisel for all that!"

"I am sorry to find, Luca," returned the priest, coldly, "that you allow yourself to talk of the most delicate subjects in the coarsest way. This is one of the minor sins of the tongue which is growing on you. When we are alone in the studio, I will endeavor to lead you into speaking of the young man in the room there, and of your daughter, in terms more becoming to you, to me, and to them. Until that time, allow me to go on with my work."

Luca shrugged his shoulders, and went back to his statue. Father Rocco, who had been engaged during the last ten minutes in mixing wet plaster to the right consistency for taking a cast, suspended his occupation; and crossing the room to a corner next the partition, removed from it a cheval-glass which stood there. He lifted it away gently, while his brother's back was turned, carried it close to the table at which he had been at work, and then resumed his employment of mixing the plaster. Having at last prepared the composition for use, he laid it over the exposed half of the statuette with a neatness and dexterity which showed him to be a practiced hand at cast-taking. Just as he had covered the necessary extent of surface, Luca turned round from his statue.

"How are you getting on with the cast?" he asked. "Do you want any help?"

"None, brother, I thank you," answered the priest. "Pray do not disturb either yourself or your workmen on my account."

Luca turned again to the statue; and, at the same moment, Father Rocco softly moved the cheval-glass toward the open doorway between the two rooms, placing it at such an angle as to make it reflect the figures of the persons in the smaller studio. He did this with significant quickness and precision. It was evidently not the first time he had used the glass for purposes of secret observation.

Mechanically stirring the wet plaster round and round for the second casting, the priest looked into the glass, and saw, as in a picture, all that was going forward in the inner room. Maddalena Lomi was standing behind the young nobleman, watching the progress he made with his bust. Occasionally she took the modeling tool out of his hand, and showed him, with her sweetest smile, that she, too, as a sculptor's daughter, understood something of the sculptor's art; and now and then, in the pauses of the conversation, when her interest was especially intense in Fabio's work, she suffered her hand to drop absently on his shoulder, or stooped forward so close to him that her hair mingled for a moment with his. Moving the glass an inch or two, so as to bring Nanina well under his eye, Father Rocco found that he could trace each repetition of these little acts of familiarity by the immediate effect which they produced on the girl's face and manner. Whenever Maddalena so much as touched the young nobleman — no matter whether she did so by premeditation, or really by accident — Nanina's features contracted, her pale cheeks grew paler, she fidgeted on her chair, and her fingers nervously twisted and untwisted the loose ends of the ribbon fastened round her waist.

"Jealous," thought Father Rocco; "I suspected it weeks ago."

He turned away, and gave his whole attention for a few minutes to the mixing of the plaster. When he looked back again at the glass, he was just in time to witness a little accident which suddenly changed the relative positions of the three persons in the inner room.

He saw Maddalena take up a modeling tool which lay on a table near her, and begin to help Fabio in altering the arrangement of the hair in his bust. The young man watched what she was doing earnestly enough for a few moments; then his attention wandered away to Nanina. She looked at him reproachfully, and he answered by a sign which brought a smile to her face directly. Maddalena surprised her at the instant of the change; and, following the direction of her eyes, easily discovered at whom the smile was directed. She darted a glance of contempt at Nanina, threw down the modeling tool, and turned indignantly to the young sculptor, who was affecting to be hard at work again.

"Signor Fabio," she said, "the next time you forget what is due to your rank and yourself, warn me of it, if you please, beforehand, and I will take care to leave the room." While speaking the last words, she passed through the doorway. Father Rocco, bending abstractedly over his plaster mixture, heard her continue to herself in a whisper, as she went by him, "If I have any influence at all with my father, that impudent beggar-girl shall be forbidden the studio."

"Jealousy on the other side," thought the priest. "Something must be done at once, or this will end badly."

He looked again at the glass, and saw Fabio, after an instant of hesitation, beckon to Nanina to approach him. She left her seat, advanced half-way to his, then stopped. He stepped forward to meet her, and, taking her by the hand, whispered earnestly in her ear. When he had done, before dropping her hand, he touched her cheek with his lips, and then helped her on with the little white mantilla which covered her head and shoulders out-of-doors. The girl trembled violently, and drew the linen close to her face as Fabio walked into the larger studio, and, addressing Father Rocco, said:

"I am afraid I am more idle, or more stupid, than ever today. I can't get on with the bust at all to my satisfaction, so I have cut short the sitting, and given Nanina a half-holiday."

At the first sound of his voice, Maddalena, who was speaking to her father, stopped, and, with another look of scorn at Nanina standing trembling in the doorway, left the room. Luca Lomi called Fabio to him as she went away, and Father Rocco, turning to the statuette, looked to see how the plaster was hardening on it. Seeing them thus engaged, Nanina attempted to escape from the studio without being noticed; but the priest stopped her just as she was hurrying by him.

"My child," said he, in his gentle, quiet way, "are you going home?"

Nanina's heart beat too fast for her to reply in words; she could only answer by bowing her head.

"Take this for your little sister," pursued Father Rocco, putting a few silver coins in her hand; "I have got some customers for those mats she plaits so nicely. You need not bring them to my rooms; I will come and see you this evening, when I am going my rounds among my parishioners, and will take the mats away with me. You are a good girl, Nanina — you have always been a good girl — and as long as I am alive, my child, you shall never want a friend and an adviser."

Nanina's eyes filled with tears. She drew the mantilla closer than ever round her face, as she tried to thank the priest. Father Rocco nodded to her kindly, and laid his hand lightly on her head for a moment, then turned round again to his cast.

"Don't forget my message to the lady who is to sit to me tomorrow," said Luca to Nanina, as she passed him on her way out of the studio.

After she had gone, Fabio returned to the priest, who was still busy over his cast.

"I hope you will get on better with the bust tomorrow," said Father Rocco, politely; "I am sure you cannot complain of your model."

"Complain of her!" cried the young man, warmly; "she has the most beautiful head I ever saw. If I were twenty times the sculptor that I am, I should despair of being able to do her justice."

He walked into the inner room to look at his bust again — lingered before it for a little while — and then turned to retrace his steps to the larger studio. Between him and the doorway stood three chairs. As he went by them, he absently touched the backs of the first two, and passed the third; but just as he was entering the larger room, stopped, as if struck by a sudden recollection, returned hastily, and touched the third chair. Raising his eyes, as he approached the large studio again after doing this, he met the eyes of the priest fixed on him in unconcealed astonishment.

"Signor Fabio!" exclaimed Father Rocco, with a sarcastic smile, "who would ever have imagined that you were superstitious?"

"My nurse was," returned the young man, reddening, and laughing rather uneasily. "She taught me some bad habits that I have not got over yet." With those words he nodded and hastily went out.

"Superstitious," said Father Rocco softly to himself. He smiled again, reflected for a moment, and then, going to the window, looked into the street. The way to the left led to Fabio's palace, and the way to the right to the Campo Santo, in the neighborhood of which Nanina lived. The priest was just in time to see the young sculptor take the way to the right.

After another half-hour had elapsed, the two workmen quitted the studio to go to dinner, and Luca and his brother were left alone.

"We may return now," said Father Rocco, "to that conversation which was suspended between us earlier in the day."

"I have nothing more to say," rejoined Luca, sulkily.

"Then you can listen to me, brother, with the greater attention," pursued the priest. "I objected to the coarseness of your tone in talking of our young pupil and your daughter; I object still more strongly to your insinuation that my desire to see them married (provided always that they are sincerely attached to each other) springs from a mercenary motive."

"You are trying to snare me, Rocco, in a mesh of fine phrases; but I am not to be caught. I know what my own motive is for hoping that Maddalena may get an offer of marriage from this wealthy young gentleman — she will have his money, and we shall all profit by it. That is coarse and mercenary, if you please; but it is the true reason why I want to see Maddalena married to Fabio. You want to see it, too — and for what reason, I should like to know, if not for mine?"

"Of what use would wealthy relations be to me? What are people with money — what is money itself — to a man who follows my calling?"

"Money is something to everybody."

"Is it? When have you found that I have taken any account of it? Give me money enough to buy my daily bread, and to pay for my lodging and my coarse cassock, and though I may want much for the poor, for myself I want no more. Then have you found me mercenary? Do I not help you in this studio, for love of you and of the art, without exacting so much as journey-man's wages? Have I ever asked you for more than a few crowns to give away on feast-days among my parishioners? Money! money for a man who may be summoned to Rome tomorrow, who may be told to go at half an hour's notice on a foreign mission that may take him to the ends of the earth, and who would be ready to go the moment when he was called on! Money to a man who has no wife, no children, no interests outside the sacred circle of the Church! Brother, do you see the dust and dirt and shapeless marble chips lying around your statue there? Cover that floor instead with gold, and, though the litter may have changed in color and form, in my eyes it would be litter still."

"A very noble sentiment, I dare say, Rocco, but I can't echo it. Granting that you care nothing for money, will you explain to me why you are so anxious that Maddalena should marry Fabio? She has had offers from poorer men — you knew of them — but you have never taken the least interest in her accepting or rejecting a proposal before."

"I hinted the reason to you, months ago, when Fabio first entered the studio."

"It was rather a vague hint, brother; can't you be plainer today?"

"I think I can. In the first place, let me begin by assuring you that I have no objection to the young man himself. He may be a little capricious and undecided, but he has no incorrigible faults that I have discovered."

"That is rather a cool way of praising him, Rocco."

"I should speak of him warmly enough, if he were not the representative of an intolerable corruption, and a monstrous wrong. Whenever I think of him I think of an injury which his present existence perpetuates; and if I do speak of him coldly, it is only for that reason."

Luca looked away quickly from his brother, and began kicking absently at the marble chips which were scattered over the floor around him.

"I now remember," he said, "what that hint of yours pointed at. I know what you mean."

"Then you know," answered the priest, "that while part of the wealth which Fabio d'Ascoli possesses is honestly and incontestably his own; part, also, has been inherited by him from the spoilers and robbers of the Church —"

"Blame his ancestors for that; don't blame him."

"I blame him as long as the spoil is not restored."

"How do you know that it was spoil, after all?"

"I have examined more carefully than most men the records of the civil wars in Italy; and I know that the ancestors of Fabio d'Ascoli wrung from the Church, in her hour of weakness, property which they dared to claim as their right. I know of titles to lands signed away, in those stormy times, under the influence of fear, or through false representations of which the law takes no account. I call the money thus obtained spoil, and I say that it ought to be restored, and shall be restored, to the Church from which it was taken."

"And what does Fabio answer to that, brother?"

"I have not spoken to him on the subject."

"Why not?"

"Because I have, as yet, no influence over him. When he is married, his wife will have influence over him, and she shall speak."

"Maddalena, I suppose? How do you know that she will speak?"

"Have I not educated her? Does she not understand what her duties are toward the Church, in whose bosom she has been reared?"

Luca hesitated uneasily, and walked away a step or two before he spoke again.

"Does this spoil, as you call it, amount to a large sum of money?" he asked, in an anxious whisper.

"I may answer that question, Luca, at some future time," said the priest. "For the present, let it be enough that you are acquainted with all I undertook to inform you of when we began our conversation. You now know that if I am anxious for this marriage to take place, it is from motives entirely unconnected with self-interest. If all the property which Fabio's ancestors wrongfully obtained from the Church were restored to the Church tomorrow, not one paulo of it would go into my pocket. I am a poor priest now, and to the end of my days shall remain so. You soldiers of the world, brother, fight for your pay; I am a soldier of the Church, and I fight for my cause."

Saying these words, he returned abruptly to the statuette; and refused to speak, or leave his employment again, until he had taken the mold off, and had carefully put away the various fragments of which it consisted. This done, he drew a writing-desk from the drawer of his working-table, and taking out a slip of paper wrote these lines:

"Come down to the studio tomorrow. Fabio will be with us, but Nanina will return no more."

Without signing what he had written, he sealed it up, and directed it to "Donna Maddalena"; then took his hat, and handed the note to his brother.

"Oblige me by giving that to my niece," he said.

"Tell me, Rocco," said Luca, turning the note round and round perplexedly between his finger and thumb; "do you think Maddalena will be lucky enough to get married to Fabio?"

"Still coarse in your expressions, brother!"

"Never mind my expressions. Is it likely?"

"Yes, Luca, I think it is likely."

With those words he waved his hand pleasantly to his brother, and went out.

PART FIRST. CHAPTER III.

*F*rom the studio Father Rocco went straight to his own rooms, hard by the church to which he was attached. Opening a cabinet in his study, he took from one of its drawers a handful of small silver money, consulted for a minute or so a slate on which several names and addresses were written, provided himself with a portable inkhorn and some strips of paper, and again went out.

He directed his steps to the poorest part of the neighborhood; and entering some very wretched houses, was greeted by the inhabitants with great respect and affection. The women, especially, kissed his hands with more reverence than they would have shown to the highest crowned head in Europe. In return, he talked to them as easily and unconstrainedly as if they were his equals; sat down cheerfully on dirty bedsides and rickety benches; and distributed his little gifts of money with the air of a man who was paying debts rather than bestowing charity. Where he encountered cases of illness, he pulled out his inkhorn and slips of paper, and wrote simple prescriptions to be made up from the medicine-chest of a neighboring convent, which served the same merciful purpose then that is answered by dispensaries in our days. When he had exhausted his money, and had got through his visits, he was escorted out of the poor quarter by a perfect train of enthusiastic followers. The women kissed his hand again, and the men uncovered as he turned, and, with a friendly sign, bade them all farewell.

As soon as he was alone again, he walked toward the Campo Santo, and, passing the house in which Nanina lived, sauntered up and down the street thoughtfully for some minutes. When he at length ascended the steep staircase that led to the room occupied by the sisters, he found the door ajar. Pushing it open gently, he saw La Biondella sitting with her pretty, fair profile turned toward him, eating her evening meal of bread and grapes. At the opposite end of the room, Scarammuccia was perched up on his hindquarters in a corner, with his mouth wide open to catch the morsel of bread which he evidently expected the child to throw to him. What the elder sister was doing, the priest had not time to see; for the dog barked the moment he presented himself, and Nanina hastened to the door to ascertain who the intruder might be. All that he could observe was that she was too confused, on catching sight of him, to be able to utter a word. La Biondella was the first to speak.

"Thank you, Father Rocco," said the child, jumping up, with her bread in one hand and her grapes in the other —"thank you for giving me so much money for my dinner-mats. There they are, tied up together in one little parcel, in the corner. Nanina said she was ashamed to think of your carrying them; and I said I knew where you lived, and I should like to ask you to let me take them home!"

"Do you think you can carry them all the way, my dear?" asked the priest.

"Look, Father Rocco, see if I can't carry them!" cried La Biondella, cramming her bread into one of the pockets of her little apron, holding her bunch of grapes by the stalk in her mouth, and hoisting the packet of dinner-mats on her head in a moment. "See, I am strong enough to carry double," said the child, looking up proudly into the priest's face.

"Can you trust her to take them home for me?" asked Father Rocco, turning to Nanina. "I want to speak to you alone, and her absence will give me the opportunity. Can you trust her out by herself?"

"Yes, Father Rocco, she often goes out alone." Nanina gave this answer in low, trembling tones, and looked down confusedly on the ground.

"Go then, my dear," said Father Rocco, patting the child on the shoulder; "and come back here to your sister, as soon as you have left the mats."

La Biondella went out directly in great triumph, with Scarammuccia walking by her side, and keeping his muzzle suspiciously close to the pocket in which she had put her bread. Father Rocco closed the door after them, and then, taking the one chair which the room possessed, motioned to Nanina to sit by him on the stool.

"Do you believe that I am your friend, my child, and that I have always meant well toward you?" he began.

"The best and kindest of friends," answered Nanina.

"Then you will hear what I have to say patiently, and you will believe that I am speaking for your good, even if my words should distress you?" (Nanina turned away her head.) "Now, tell me; should I be wrong, to begin with, if I said that my brother's pupil, the young nobleman whom we call 'Signor Fabio,' had been here to see you today?" (Nanina started up affrightedly from her stool.) "Sit down again, my child; I am not going to blame you. I am only going to tell you what you must do for the future."

He took her hand; it was cold, and it trembled violently in his.

"I will not ask what he has been saying to you," continued the priest; "for it might distress you to answer, and I have, moreover, had means of knowing that your youth and beauty have made a strong impression on him. I will pass over, then, all reference to the words he may have been speaking to you; and I will come at once to what I have now to say, in my turn. Nanina, my child, arm yourself with all your courage, and promise me, before we part to-night, that you will see Signor Fabio no more."

Nanina turned round suddenly, and fixed her eyes on him, with an expression of terrified incredulity. "No more?"

"You are very young and very innocent," said Father Rocco; "but surely you must have thought before now of the difference between Signor Fabio and you. Surely you must have often remembered that you are low down among the ranks of the poor, and that he is high up among the rich and the nobly born?"

Nanina's hands dropped on the priest's knees. She bent her head down on them, and began to weep bitterly.

"Surely you must have thought of that?" reiterated Father Rocco.

"Oh, I have often, often thought of it!" murmured the girl "I have mourned over it, and cried about it in secret for many nights past. He said I looked pale, and ill, and out of spirits today, and I told him it was with thinking of that!"

"And what did he say in return?"

There was no answer. Father Rocco looked down. Nanina raised her head directly from his knees, and tried to turn it away again. He took her hand and stopped her.

"Come!" he said; "speak frankly to me. Say what you ought to say to your father and your friend. What was his answer, my child, when you reminded him of the difference between you?"

"He said I was born to be a lady," faltered the girl, still struggling to turn her face away, "and that I might make myself one if I would learn and be patient. He said that if he had all the noble ladies in Pisa to choose from on one side, and only little Nanina on the other, he would hold out his hand to me, and tell them, 'This shall be my wife.' He said love knew no difference of rank; and that if he was a nobleman and rich, it was all the more reason why he should please himself. He was so kind, that I thought my heart would burst while he was speaking; and my little sister liked him so, that she got upon his knee and kissed him. Even our dog, who growls at other strangers, stole to his side and licked his hand. Oh, Father Rocco! Father Rocco!" The tears burst out afresh, and the lovely head dropped once more, wearily, on the priest's knee.

Father Rocco smiled to himself, and waited to speak again till she was calmer.

"Supposing," he resumed, after some minutes of silence, "supposing Signor Fabio really meant all he said to you —"

Nanina started up, and confronted the priest boldly for the first time since he had entered the room.

"Supposing!" she exclaimed, her cheeks beginning to redden, and her dark blue eyes flashing suddenly through her tears "Supposing! Father Rocco, Fabio would never deceive me. I would die here at your feet, rather than doubt the least word he said to me!"

The priest signed to her quietly to return to the stool. "I never suspected the child had so much spirit in her," he thought to himself.

"I would die," repeated Nanina, in a voice that began to falter now. "I would die rather than doubt him."

"I will not ask you to doubt him," said Father Rocco, gently; "and I will believe in him myself as firmly as you do. Let us suppose, my child, that you have learned patiently all the many things of which you are now ignorant, and which it is necessary for a lady to know. Let us suppose that Signor Fabio has really violated all the laws that govern people in his high station and has taken you to him publicly as his wife. You would be happy then, Nanina; but would he? He has no father or mother to control him, it is true; but he has friends — many friends and intimates in his own rank — proud, heartless people, who know nothing of your worth and goodness; who, hearing of your low birth, would look on you, and on your husband too, my child, with contempt. He has not your patience and fortitude. Think how bitter it would be for him to bear that contempt — to see you shunned by proud women, and carelessly pitied or patronized by insolent men. Yet all this, and more, he would have to endure, or else to quit the world he has lived in from his boyhood — the world he was born to live in. You love him, I know —"

Nanina's tears burst out afresh. "Oh, how dearly — how dearly!" she murmured.

"Yes, you love him dearly," continued the priest; "but would all your love compensate him for everything else that he must lose? It might, at first; but there would come a time when the world would assert its influence over him again; when he would feel a want which you could not supply — a weariness which you could not solace. Think of his life then, and of yours. Think of the first day when the first secret doubt whether he had done rightly in marrying you would steal into his mind. We are not masters of all our impulses. The lightest spirits have their moments of irresistible depression; the bravest hearts are not always superior to doubt. My child, my child, the world is strong, the pride of rank is rooted deep, and the human will is frail at best! Be warned! For your own sake and for Fabio's, be warned in time."

Nanina stretched out her hands toward the priest in despair.

"Oh, Father Rocco! Father Rocco!" she cried, "why did you not tell me this before?"

"Because, my child, I only knew of the necessity for telling you today. But it is not too late; it is never too late to do a good action. You love Fabio, Nanina? Will you prove that love by making a great sacrifice for his good?"

"I would die for his good!"

"Will you nobly cure him of a passion which will be his ruin, if not yours, by leaving Pisa tomorrow?"

"Leave Pisa!" exclaimed Nanina. Her face grew deadly pale; she rose and moved back a step or two from the priest.

"Listen to me," pursued Father Rocco; "I have heard you complain that you could not get regular employment at needle-work. You shall have that employment, if you will go with me — you and your little sister too, of course — to Florence tomorrow."

"I promised Fabio to go to the studio," began Nanina, affrightedly. "I promised to go at ten o'clock. How can I—"

She stopped suddenly, as if her breath were failing her.

"I myself will take you and your sister to Florence," said Father Rocco, without noticing the interruption. "I will place you under the care of a lady who will be as kind as a mother to you both. I will answer for your getting such work to do as will enable you to keep yourself honestly and independently; and I will undertake, if you do not like your life at Florence, to bring you back to Pisa after a lapse of three months only. Three months, Nanina. It is not a long exile."

"Fabio! Fabio!" cried the girl, sinking again on the seat, and hiding her face.

"It is for his good," said Father Rocco, calmly: "for Fabio's good, remember."

"What would he think of me if I went away? Oh, if I had but learned to write! If I could only write Fabio a letter!"

"Am I not to be depended on to explain to him all that he ought to know?"

"How can I go away from him! Oh! Father Rocco, how can you ask me to go away from him?"

"I will ask you to do nothing hastily. I will leave you till tomorrow morning to decide. At nine o'clock I shall be in the street; and I will not even so much as enter this house, unless I know beforehand that you have resolved to follow my advice. Give me a sign from your window. If I see you wave your white mantilla out of it, I shall know that you have taken the noble resolution to save Fabio and to save yourself. I will say no more, my child; for, unless I am grievously mistaken in you, I have already said enough."

He went out, leaving her still weeping bitterly. Not far from the house, he met La Biondella and the dog on their way back. The little girl stopped to report to him the safe delivery of her dinner-mats; but he passed on quickly with a nod and a smile. His interview with Nanina had left some influence behind it, which unfitted him just then for the occupation of talking to a child.

Nearly half an hour before nine o'clock on the following morning, Father Rocco set forth for the street in which Nanina lived. On his way thither he overtook a dog walking lazily a few paces ahead in the roadway; and saw, at the same time, an elegantly-dressed lady advancing toward him. The dog stopped suspiciously as she approached, and growled and showed his teeth when she passed him. The lady, on her side, uttered an exclamation of disgust, but did not seem to be either astonished or frightened by the animal's threatening attitude. Father Rocco looked after her with some curiosity as she walked by him. She was a handsome woman, and he admired her courage. "I know that growling brute well enough," he said to himself, "but who can the lady be?"

The dog was Scarammuccia, returning from one of his marauding expeditions The lady was Brigida, on her way to Luca Lomi's studio.

Some minutes before nine o'clock the priest took his post in the street, opposite Nanina's window. It was open; but neither she nor her little sister appeared at it. He looked up anxiously as the church-clocks struck the hour; but there was no sign for a minute or so after they were all silent. "Is she hesitating still?" said Father Rocco to himself.

Just as the words passed his lips, the white mantilla was waved out of the window.

PART SECOND. CHAPTER I.

*E*ven the master-stroke of replacing the treacherous Italian forewoman by a French dressmaker, engaged direct from Paris, did not at first avail to elevate the great Grifoni establishment above the reach of minor calamities. Mademoiselle Virginie had not occupied her new situation at Pisa quite a week before she fell ill. All sorts of reports were circulated as to the cause of this illness; and the Demoiselle Grifoni even went so far as to suggest that the health of the new forewoman had fallen a sacrifice to some nefarious practices of the chemical sort, on the part of her rival in the trade. But, however the misfortune had been produced, it was a fact that Mademoiselle Virginie was certainly very ill, and another fact that the doctor insisted on her being sent to the baths of Lucca as soon as she could be moved from her bed.

Fortunately for the Demoiselle Grifoni, the Frenchwoman had succeeded in producing three specimens of her art before her health broke down. They comprised the evening-dress of yellow brocaded silk, to which she had devoted herself on the morning when she first assumed her duties at Pisa; a black cloak and hood of an entirely new shape; and an irresistibly fascinating dressing-gown, said to have been first brought into fashion by the princesses of the blood-royal of France. These articles of costume, on being exhibited in the showroom, electrified the ladies of Pisa; and orders from all sides flowed in immediately on the Grifoni establishment. They were, of course, easily executed by the inferior work-women, from the specimen designs of the French dressmaker. So that the illness of Mademoiselle Virginie, though it might cause her mistress some temporary inconvenience, was, after all, productive of no absolute loss.

Two months at the baths of Lucca restored the new forewoman to health. She returned to Pisa, and resumed her place in the private work-room. Once re-established there, she discovered that an important change had taken place during her absence. Her friend and assistant, Brigida, had resigned her situation. All inquiries made of the Demoiselle Grifoni only elicited one answer: the missing work-woman had abruptly left her place at five minutes' warning, and had departed without confiding to any one what she thought of doing, or whither she intended to turn her steps.

Months elapsed The new year came; but no explanatory letter arrived from Brigida. The spring season passed off, with all its accompaniments of dress-making and dress-buying, but still there was no news of her. The first anniversary of Mademoiselle Virginie's engagement with the Demoiselle Grifoni came round; and then at last a note arrived, stating that Brigida had returned to Pisa, and that if the French forewoman would send an answer, mentioning where her private lodgings were, she would visit her old friend that evening after business hours. The information was gladly enough given; and, punctually to the appointed time, Brigida arrived in Mademoiselle Virginie's little sitting-room.

Advancing with her usual indolent stateliness of gait, the Italian asked after her friend's health as coolly, and sat down in the nearest chair as carelessly, as if they had not been separated for more than a few days. Mademoiselle Virginie laughed in her liveliest manner, and raised her mobile French eyebrows in sprightly astonishment.

"Well, Brigida!" she exclaimed, "they certainly did you no injustice when they nicknamed you 'Care-for-Nothing,' in old Grifoni's workroom. Where have you been? Why have you never written to me?"

"I had nothing particular to write about; and besides, I always intended to come back to Pisa and see you," answered Brigida, leaning back luxuriously in her chair.

"But where have you been for nearly a whole year past? In Italy?"

"No; at Paris. You know I can sing — not very well; but I have a voice, and most Frenchwomen (excuse the impertinence) have none. I met with a friend, and got introduced to a manager; and I have been singing at the theater — not the great parts, only the second. Your amiable countrywomen could not screech me down on the stage, but they intrigued against me successfully behind the scenes. In short, I quarreled with our principal lady, quarreled with the manager, quarreled with my friend; and here I am back at Pisa, with a little money saved in my pocket, and no great notion what I am to do next."

"Back at Pisa? Why did you leave it?"

Brigida's eyes began to lose their indolent expression. She sat up suddenly in her chair, and set one of her hands heavily on a little table by her side.

"Why?" she repeated. "Because when I find the game going against me, I prefer giving it up at once to waiting to be beaten."

"Ah! you refer to that last year's project of yours for making your fortune among the sculptors. I should like to hear how it was you failed with the wealthy young amateur. Remember that I fell ill before you had any news to give me. Your absence when I returned from Lucca, and, almost immediately afterward, the marriage of your intended conquest to the sculptor's daughter, proved to me, of course, that you must have failed. But I never heard how. I know nothing at this moment but the bare fact that Maddalena Lomi won the prize."

"Tell me first, do she and her husband live together happily?"

"There are no stories of their disagreeing. She has dresses, horses, carriages; a negro page, the smallest lap-dog in Italy — in short, all the luxuries that a woman can want; and a child, by-the-by, into the bargain."

"A child?"

"Yes; a child, born little more than a week ago."

"Not a boy, I hope?"

"No; a girl."

"I am glad of that. Those rich people always want the first-born to be an heir. They will both be disappointed. I am glad of that."

"Mercy on us, Brigida, how fierce you look!"

"Do I? It's likely enough. I hate Fabio d'Ascoli and Maddalena Lomi — singly as man and woman, doubly as man and wife. Stop! I'll tell you what you want to know directly. Only answer me another question or two first. Have you heard anything about her health?"

"How should I hear? Dressmakers can't inquire at the doors of the nobility."

"True. Now one last question. That little simpleton, Nanina?"

"I have never seen or heard anything of her. She can't be at Pisa, or she would have called at our place for work."

"Ah! I need not have asked about her if I had thought a moment beforehand. Father Rocco would be sure to keep her out of Fabio's sight, for his niece's sake."

"What, he really loved that 'thread-paper of a girl' as you called her?"

"Better than fifty such wives as he has got now! I was in the studio the morning he was told of her departure from Pisa. A letter was privately given to him, telling him that the girl had left the place out of a feeling of honor, and had hidden herself beyond the possibility of discovery, to prevent him from compromising himself with all his friends by marrying her. Naturally enough, he would not believe that this was her own doing; and, naturally enough also, when Father Rocco was sent for, and was not to be found, he suspected the priest of being at the bottom of the business. I never saw a man in such a fury of despair and rage before. He swore that he would have all Italy searched for the girl, that he would be the death of the priest, and that he would never enter Luca Lomi's studio again —"

"And, as to this last particular, of course, being a man, he failed to keep his word?"

"Of course. At that first visit of mine to the studio I discovered two things. The first, as I said, that Fabio was really in love with the girl — the second, that Maddalena Lomi was really in love with him. You may suppose I looked at her attentively while the disturbance was going on, and while nobody's notice was directed on me. All women are vain, I know, but vanity never blinded my eyes. I saw directly that I had but one superiority over her — my figure. She was my height, but not well made. She had hair as dark and as glossy as mine; eyes as bright and as black as mine; and the rest of her face better than mine. My nose is coarse, my lips are too thick, and my upper lip overhangs my under too far. She had none of those personal faults; and, as for capacity, she managed the young fool in his passion as well as I could have managed him in her place."

"How?"

"She stood silent, with downcast eyes and a distressed look, all the time he was raving up and down the studio. She must have hated the girl, and been rejoiced at her disappearance; but she never showed it. 'You would be an awkward rival' (I thought to myself), 'even to a handsomer woman than I am.' However, I determined not to despair too soon, and made up my mind to follow my plan just as if the accident of the girl's disappearance had never occurred. I smoothed down the master-sculptor easily enough — flattering him about his reputation, assuring him that the works of Luca Lomi had been the objects of my adoration since childhood, telling him that I had heard of his difficulty in finding a model to complete his Minerva from, and offering myself (if he thought me worthy) for the honor — laying great stress on that word — for the honor of sitting to him. I don't know whether he was alto-gether deceived by what I told him; but he was sharp enough to see that I really could be of use, and he accepted my offer with a profusion of compli-ments. We parted, having arranged that I was to give him a first sitting in a week's time."

"Why put it off so long?"

"To allow our young gentleman time to cool down and return to the studio, to be sure. What was the use of my being there while he was away?"

"Yes, yes — I forgot. And how long was it before he came back?"

"I had allowed him more time than enough. When I had given my first sitting I saw him in the studio, and heard it was his second visit there since the day of the girl's disappearance. Those very violent men are always changeable and irresolute."

"Had he made no attempt, then, to discover Nanina?"

"Oh, yes! He had searched for her himself, and had set others searching for her, but to no purpose. Four days of perpetual disappointment had been enough to bring him to his senses. Luca Lomi had written him a peace-making letter, asking what harm he or his daughter had done, even supposing Father Rocco was to blame. Maddalena Lomi had met him in the street, and had looked resignedly away from him, as if she expected him to pass her. In short, they had awakened his sense of justice and his good nature (you see, I can impartially give him his due), and they had got him back. He was silent and sentimental enough at first, and shockingly sulky and savage with the priest —"

"I wonder Father Rocco ventured within his reach."

"Father Rocco is not a man to be daunted or defeated by anybody, I can tell you. The same day on which Fabio came back to the studio, he returned to it. Beyond boldly declaring that he thought Nanina had done quite right, and had acted like a good and virtuous girl, he would say nothing about her or her disappearance. It was quite useless to ask him questions — he denied that any one had a right to put them. Threatening, entreating, flattering — all modes of appeal were thrown away on him. Ah, my dear! depend upon it, the cleverest and politest man in Pisa, the most dangerous to an enemy and the most delightful to a friend, is Father Rocco. The rest of them, when I began to play my cards a little too openly, behaved with brutal rudeness to me. Father Rocco, from first to last, treated me like a lady. Sincere or not, I don't care — he treated me like a lady when the others treated me like —"

"There! there! don't get hot about it now. Tell me instead how you made your first approaches to the young gentleman whom you talk of so contemptuously as Fabio."

"As it turned out, in the worst possible way. First, of course, I made sure of interesting him in me by telling him that I had known Nanina. So far it was all well enough. My next object was to persuade him that she could never have gone away if she had truly loved him alone; and that he must have had some fortunate rival in her own rank of life, to whom she had sacrificed him, after gratifying her vanity for a time by bringing a young nobleman to her feet. I had, as you will easily imagine, difficulty enough in making him take this view of Nanina's flight. His pride and his love for the girl were both concerned in refusing to admit the truth of my suggestion. At last I succeeded. I brought him to that state of ruffled vanity and fretful self-assertion in which it is easiest to work on a man's feelings — in which a man's own wounded pride makes the best pitfall to catch him in. I brought him, I say, to that state, and then *she* stepped in and profited by what I had done. Is it wonderful now that I rejoice in her disappointments — that I should be glad to hear any ill thing of her that any one could tell me?"

"But how did she first get the advantage of you?"

"If I had found out, she would never have succeeded where I failed. All I know is, that she had more opportunities of seeing him than I, and that she used them cunningly enough even to deceive me. While I thought I was gaining ground with Fabio, I was actually losing it. My first suspicions were excited by a change in Luca Lomi's conduct toward me. He grew cold, neglectful — at last absolutely rude. I was resolved not to see this; but accident soon obliged me to open my eyes. One morning I heard Fabio and Maddalena talking of me when they imagined I had left the studio. I can't repeat their words, especially here. The blood flies into my head, and the cold catches me at the heart, when I only think of them. It will be enough if I tell you that he laughed at me, and that she —"

"Hush! not so loud. There are other people lodging in the house. Never mind about telling me what you heard; it only irritates you to no purpose. I can guess that they had discovered —"

"Through her — remember, all through her!"

"Yes, yes, I understand. They had discovered a great deal more than you ever intended them to know, and all through her."

"But for the priest, Virginie, I should have been openly insulted and driven from their doors. He had insisted on their behaving with decent civility toward me. They said that he was afraid of me, and laughed at the notion of his trying to make them afraid too. That was the last thing I heard. The fury I was in, and the necessity of keeping it down, almost suffocated me. I turned round to leave the place forever, when, who should I see, standing close behind me, but Father Rocco. He must have discovered in my face that I knew all, but he took no notice of it. He only asked, in his usual quiet, polite way, if I was looking for anything I had lost, and if he could help me. I managed to thank him, and to get to the door. He opened it for me respectfully, and bowed — he treated me like a lady to the last! It was evening when I left the studio in that way. The next morning I threw up my situation, and turned my back on Pisa. Now you know everything."

"Did you hear of the marriage? or did you only assume from what you knew that it would take place?"

"I heard of it about six months ago. A man came to sing in the chorus at our theater who had been employed some time before at the grand concert given on the occasion of the marriage. But let us drop the subject now. I am in a fever already with talking of it. You are in a bad situation here, my dear; I declare your room is almost stifling."

"Shall I open the other window?"

"No; let us go out and get a breath of air by the river-side. Come! take your hood and fan — it is getting dark — nobody will see us, and we can come back here, if you like, in half an hour."

Mademoiselle Virginie acceded to her friend's wish rather reluctantly. They walked toward the river. The sun was down, and the sudden night of Italy was gathering fast. Although Brigida did not say another word on the subject of Fabio or his wife, she led the way to the bank of the Arno, on which the young nobleman's palace stood.

Just as they got near the great door of entrance, a sedan-chair, approaching in the opposite direction, was set down before it; and a footman, after a moment's conference with a lady inside the chair, advanced to the porter's lodge in the courtyard. Leaving her friend to go on, Brigida slipped in after the servant by the open wicket, and concealed herself in the shadow cast by the great closed gates.

"The Marchesa Melani, to inquire how the Countess d'Ascoli and the infant are this evening," said the footman.

"My mistress has not changed at all for the better since the morning," answered the porter. "The child is doing quite well."

The footman went back to the sedan-chair; then returned to the porter's lodge.

"The marchesa desires me to ask if fresh medical advice has been sent for," he said.

"Another doctor has arrived from Florence today," replied the porter.

Mademoiselle Virginie, missing her friend suddenly, turned back toward the palace to look after her, and was rather surprised to see Brigida slip out of the wicket-gate. There were two oil lamps burning on pillars outside the doorway, and their light glancing on the Italian's face, as she passed under them, showed that she was smiling.

PART SECOND. CHAPTER II.

*W*hile the Marchesa Melani was making inquiries at the gate of the palace, Fabio was sitting alone in the apartment which his wife usually occupied when she was in health. It was her favorite room, and had been prettily decorated, by her own desire, with hangings in yellow satin and furniture of the same color. Fabio was now waiting in it, to hear the report of the doctors after their evening visit.

Although Maddalena Lomi had not been his first love, and although he had married her under circumstances which are generally and rightly considered to afford few chances of lasting happiness in wedded life, still they had lived together through the one year of their union tranquilly, if not fondly. She had molded herself wisely to his peculiar humors, had made the most of his easy disposition; and, when her quick temper had got the better of her, had seldom hesitated in her cooler moments to acknowledge that she had been wrong. She had been extravagant, it is true, and had irritated him by fits of unreasonable jealousy; but these were faults not to be thought of now. He could only remember that she was the mother of his child, and that she lay ill but two rooms away from him — dangerously ill, as the doctors had unwillingly confessed on that very day.

The darkness was closing in upon him, and he took up the handbell to ring for lights. When the servant entered there was genuine sorrow in his face, genuine anxiety in his voice, as he inquired for news from the sick-room. The man only answered that his mistress was still asleep, and then withdrew, after first leaving a sealed letter on the table by his master's side. Fabio summoned him back into the room, and asked when the letter had arrived. He replied that it had been delivered at the palace two days since, and that he had observed it lying unopened on a desk in his master's study.

Left alone again, Fabio remembered that the letter had arrived at a time when the first dangerous symptoms of his wife's illness had declared themselves, and that he had thrown it aside, after observing the address to be in a handwriting unknown to him. In his present state of suspense, any occupation was better than sitting idle. So he took up the letter with a sigh, broke the seal, and turned inquiringly to the name signed at the end.

It was "NANINA."

He started, and changed color. "A letter from her," he whispered to himself. "Why does it come at such a time as this?"

His face grew paler, and the letter trembled in his fingers. Those superstitious feelings which he had ascribed to the nursery influences of his childhood, when Father Rocco charged him with them in the studio, seemed to be overcoming him now. He hesitated, and listened anxiously in the direction of his wife's room, before reading the letter. Was its arrival ominous of good or evil? That was the thought in his heart as he drew the lamp near to him, and looked at the first lines.

"Am I wrong in writing to you?" (the letter began abruptly). "If I am, you have but to throw this little leaf of paper into the fire, and to think no more of it after it is burned up and gone. I can never reproach you for treating my letter in that way; for we are never likely to meet again.

"Why did I go away? Only to save you from the consequences of marrying a poor girl who was not fit to become your wife. It almost broke my heart to leave you; for I had nothing to keep up my courage but the remembrance that I was going away for your sake. I had to think of that, morning and night — to think of it always, or I am afraid I should have faltered in my resolution, and have gone back to Pisa. I longed so much at first to see you once more, only to tell you that Nanina was not heartless and ungrateful, and that you might pity her and think kindly of her, though you might love her no longer.

"Only to tell you that! If I had been a lady I might have told it to you in a letter; but I had never learned to write, and I could not prevail on myself to get others to take the pen for me. All I could do was to learn secretly how to write with my own hand. It was long, long work; but the uppermost thought in my heart was always the thought of justifying myself to you, and that made me patient and persevering. I learned, at last, to write so as not to be ashamed of myself, or to make you ashamed of me. I began a letter — my first letter to you — but I heard of your marriage before it was done, and then I had to tear the paper up, and put the pen down again.

"I had no right to come between you and your wife, even with so little a thing as a letter; I had no right to do anything but hope and pray for your

258 | WILKIE COLLINS

happiness. Are you happy? I am sure you ought to be; for how can your wife help loving you?

"It is very hard for me to explain why I have ventured on writing now, and yet I can't think that I am doing wrong. I heard a few days ago (for I have a friend at Pisa who keeps me informed, by my own desire, of all the pleasant changes in your life)— I heard of your child being born; and I thought myself, after that, justified at last in writing to you. No letter from me, at such a time as this, can rob your child's mother of so much as a thought of yours that is due to her. Thus, at least, it seems to me. I wish so well to your child, that I cannot surely be doing wrong in writing these lines.

"I have said already what I wanted to say — what I have been longing to say for a whole year past. I have told you why I left Pisa; and have, perhaps, persuaded you that I have gone through some suffering, and borne some heart-aches for your sake. Have I more to write? Only a word or two, to tell you that I am earning my bread, as I always wished to earn it, quietly at home — at least, at what I must call home now. I am living with reputable people, and I want for nothing. La Biondella has grown very much; she would hardly be obliged to get on your knee to kiss you now; and she can plait her dinner-mats faster and more neatly than ever. Our old dog is with us, and has learned two new tricks; but you can't be expected to remember him, although you were the only stranger I ever saw him take kindly to at first.

"It is time I finished. If you have read this letter through to the end, I am sure you will excuse me if I have written it badly. There is no date to it, because I feel that it is safest and best for both of us that you should know nothing of where I am living. I bless you and pray for you, and bid you affectionately farewell. If you can think of me as a sister, think of me sometimes still."

Fabio sighed bitterly while he read the letter. "Why," he whispered to himself, "why does it come at such a time as this, when I cannot dare not think of her?" As he slowly folded the letter up the tears came into his eyes, and he half raised the paper to his lips. At the same moment, some one knocked at the door of the room. He started, and felt himself changing color guiltily as one of his servants entered.

"My mistress is awake," the man said, with a very grave face, and a very constrained manner; "and the gentlemen in attendance desire me to say —"

He was interrupted, before he could give his message, by one of the medical men, who had followed him into the room.

"I wish I had better news to communicate," began the doctor, gently.

"She is worse, then?" said Fabio, sinking back into the chair from which he had risen the moment before.

"She has awakened weaker instead of stronger after her sleep," returned the doctor, evasively. "I never like to give up all hope till the very last, but —"

"It is cruel not to be candid with him," interposed another voice — the voice of the doctor from Florence, who had just entered the room. "Strengthen yourself to bear the worst," he continued, addressing himself to Fabio. "She is dying. Can you compose yourself enough to go to her bedside?"

Pale and speechless, Fabio rose from his chair, and made a sign in the affirmative. He trembled so that the doctor who had first spoken was obliged to lead him out of the room.

"Your mistress has some near relations in Pisa, has she not?" said the doctor from Florence, appealing to the servant who waited near him.

"Her father, sir, Signor Luca Lomi; and her uncle, Father Rocco," answered the man. "They were here all through the day, until my mistress fell asleep."

"Do you know where to find them now?"

"Signor Luca told me he should be at his studio, and Father Rocco said I might find him at his lodgings."

"Send for them both directly. Stay, who is your mistress's confessor? He ought to be summoned without loss of time."

"My mistress's confessor is Father Rocco, sir."

"Very well — send, or go yourself, at once. Even minutes may be of importance now." Saying this, the doctor turned away, and sat down to wait for any last demands on his services, in the chair which Fabio had just left.

PART SECOND. CHAPTER III.

*B*efore the servant could get to the priest's lodgings a visitor had applied there for admission, and had been immediately received by Father Rocco himself. This favored guest was a little man, very sprucely and neatly dressed, and oppressively polite in his manner. He bowed when he first sat down, he bowed when he answered the usual inquiries about his health, and he bowed, for the third time, when Father Rocco asked what had brought him from Florence.

"Rather an awkward business," replied the little man, recovering himself uneasily after his third bow. "The dressmaker, named Nanina, whom you placed under my wife's protection about a year ago —"

"What of her?" inquired the priest eagerly.

"I regret to say she has left us, with her child-sister, and their very disagreeable dog, that growls at everybody."

"When did they go?"

"Only yesterday. I came here at once to tell you, as you were so very particular in recommending us to take care of her. It is not our fault that she has gone. My wife was kindness itself to her, and I always treated her like a duchess. I bought dinner-mats of her sister; I even put up with the thieving and growling of the disagreeable dog —"

"Where have they gone to? Have you found out that?"

"I have found out, by application at the passport-office, that they have not left Florence — but what particular part of the city they have removed to, I have not yet had time to discover."

"And pray why did they leave you, in the first place? Nanina is not a girl to do anything without a reason. She must have had some cause for going away. What was it?"

The little man hesitated, and made a fourth bow.

"You remember your private instructions to my wife and myself, when you first brought Nanina to our house?" he said, looking away rather uneasily while he spoke.

"Yes; you were to watch her, but to take care that she did not suspect you. It was just possible, at that time, that she might try to get back to Pisa without my knowing it; and everything depended on her remaining at Florence. I think, now, that I did wrong to distrust her; but it was of the last importance to provide against all possibilities, and to abstain from putting too much faith in my own good opinion of the girl. For these reasons, I certainly did instruct you to watch her privately. So far you are quite right; and I have nothing to complain of. Go on."

"You remember," resumed the little man, "that the first consequence of our following your instructions was a discovery (which we immediately communicated to you) that she was secretly learning to write?"

"Yes; and I also remember sending you word not to show that you knew what she was doing; but to wait and see if she turned her knowledge of writing to account, and took or sent any letters to the post. You informed me, in your regular monthly report, that she nearer did anything of the kind."

"Never, until three days ago; and then she was traced from her room in my house to the post-office with a letter, which she dropped into the box."

"And the address of which you discovered before she took it from your house?"

"Unfortunately I did not," answered the little man, reddening and looking askance at the priest, as if he expected to receive a severe reprimand.

But Father Rocco said nothing. He was thinking. Who could she have written to? If to Fabio, why should she have waited for months and months, after she had learned how to use her pen, before sending him a letter? If not to Fabio, to what other person could she have written?

"I regret not discovering the address — regret it most deeply," said the little man, with a low bow of apology.

"It is too late for regret," said Father Rocco, coldly. "Tell me how she came to leave your house; I have not heard that yet. Be as brief as you can. I expect to be called every moment to the bedside of a near and dear relation, who is suffering from severe illness. You shall have all my attention; but you must ask it for as short a time as possible."

"I will be briefness itself. In the first place, you must know that I have — or rather had — an idle, unscrupulous rascal of an apprentice in my business."

The priest pursed up his mouth contemptuously.

"In the second place, this same good-for-nothing fellow had the impertinence to fall in love with Nanina."

Father Rocco started, and listened eagerly.

"But I must do the girl the justice to say that she never gave him the slightest encouragement; and that, whenever he ventured to speak to her, she always quietly but very decidedly repelled him."

"A good girl!" said Father Rocco. "I always said she was a good girl. It was a mistake on my part ever to have distrusted her."

"Among the other offenses," continued the little man, "of which I now find my scoundrel of an apprentice to have been guilty, was the enormity of picking the lock of my desk, and prying into my private papers."

"You ought not to have had any. Private papers should always be burned papers."

"They shall be for the future; I will take good care of that."

"Were any of my letters to you about Nanina among these private papers?"

"Unfortunately they were. Pray, pray excuse my want of caution this time. It shall never happen again."

"Go on. Such imprudence as yours can never be excused; it can only be provided against for the future. I suppose the apprentice showed my letters to the girl?"

"I infer as much; though why he should do so —"

"Simpleton! Did you not say that he was in love with her (as you term it), and that he got no encouragement?"

"Yes; I said that — and I know it to be true."

"Well! Was it not his interest, being unable to make any impression on the girl's fancy, to establish some claim to her gratitude; and try if he could not win her that way? By showing her my letters, he would make her indebted to him for knowing that she was watched in your house. But this is not the matter in question now. You say you infer that she had seen my letters. On what grounds?"

"On the strength of this bit of paper," answered the little man, ruefully producing a note from his pocket. "She must have had your letters shown to her soon after putting her own letter into the post. For, on the evening of the same day, when I went up into her room, I found that she and her sister and the disagreeable dog had all gone, and observed this note laid on the table."

Father Rocco took the note, and read these lines:

"I have just discovered that I have been watched and suspected ever since my stay under your roof. It is impossible that I can remain another night in the house of a spy. I go with my sister. We owe you nothing, and we are free to live honestly where we please. If you see Father Rocco, tell him that I can forgive his distrust of me, but that I can never forget it. I, who had full faith in him, had a right to expect that he should have full faith in me. It was always an encouragement to me to think of him as a father and a friend. I have lost that encouragement forever — and it was the last I had left to me!

"NANINA."

The priest rose from his seat as he handed the note back, and the visitor immediately followed his example.

"We must remedy this misfortune as we best may," he said, with a sigh. "Are you ready to go back to Florence tomorrow?"

The little man bowed again.

"Find out where she is, and ascertain if she wants for anything, and if she is living in a safe place. Say nothing about me, and make no attempt to induce her to return to your house. Simply let me know what you discover. The poor child has a spirit that no ordinary people would suspect in her. She must be soothed and treated tenderly, and we shall manage her yet. No mistakes, mind, this time! Do just what I tell you, and do no more. Have you anything else to say to me?"

The little man shook his head and shrugged his shoulders.

"Good-night, then," said the priest.

"Good-night," said the little man, slipping through the door that was held open for him with the politest alacrity.

"This is vexatious," said Father Rocco, taking a turn or two in the study after his visitor had gone. "It was bad to have done the child an injustice — it is worse to have been found out. There is nothing for it now but to wait till I know where she is. I like her, and I like that note she left behind her. It is bravely, delicately, and honestly written — a good girl — a very good girl, indeed!"

He walked to the window, breathed the fresh air for a few moments, and quietly dismissed the subject from his mind. When he returned to his table he had no thoughts for any one but his sick niece.

"It seems strange," he said, "that I have had no message about her yet. Perhaps Luca has heard something. It may be well if I go to the studio at once to find out."

He took up his hat and went to the door. Just as he opened it, Fabio's servant confronted him on the thresh old.

"I am sent to summon you to the palace," said the man. "The doctors have given up all hope."

Father Rocco turned deadly pale, and drew back a step. "Have you told my brother of this?" he asked.

"I was just on my way to the studio," answered the servant.

"I will go there instead of you, and break the bad news to him," said the priest.

They descended the stairs in silence. Just as they were about to separate at the street door, Father Rocco stopped the servant.

"How is the child?" he asked, with such sudden eagerness and impatience, that the man looked quite startled as he answered that the child was perfectly well.

"There is some consolation in that," said Father Rocco, walking away, and speaking partly to the servant, partly to himself. "My caution has misled me," he continued, pausing thoughtfully when he was left alone in the roadway. "I should have risked using the mother's influence sooner to procure the righteous restitution. All hope of compassing it now rests on the life of the child. Infant as she is, her father's ill-gotten wealth may yet be gathered back to the Church by her hands."

He proceeded rapidly on his way to the studio, until he reached the river-side and drew close to the bridge which it was necessary to cross in order to get to his brother's house. Here he stopped abruptly, as if struck by a sudden idea. The moon had just risen, and her light, streaming across the river, fell full upon his face as he stood by the parapet wall that led up to the bridge. He was so lost in thought that he did not hear the conversation of two ladies who were advancing along the pathway close behind him. As they brushed by him, the taller of the two turned round and looked back at his face.

"Father Rocco!" exclaimed the lady, stopping.

"Donna Brigida!" cried the priest, looking surprised at first, but recovering himself directly and bowing with his usual quiet politeness. "Pardon me if I thank you for honoring me by renewing our acquaintance, and then pass on to my brother's studio. A heavy affliction is likely to befall us, and I go to prepare him for it."

"You refer to the dangerous illness of your niece?" said Brigida. "I heard of it this evening. Let us hope that your fears are exaggerated, and that we may yet meet under less distressing circumstances. I have no present intention of leaving Pisa for some time, and I shall always be glad to thank Father Rocco for the politeness and consideration which he showed to me, under delicate circumstances, a year ago."

With these words she courtesied deferentially, and moved away to rejoin her friend. The priest observed that Mademoiselle Virginie lingered rather near, as if anxious to catch a few words of the conversation between Brigida and himself. Seeing this, he, in his turn, listened as the two women slowly walked away together, and heard the Italian say to her companion: "Virginie, I will lay you the price of a new dress that Fabio d'Ascoli marries again."

Father Rocco started when she said those words, as if he had trodden on fire.

"My thought!" he whispered nervously to himself. "My thought at the moment when she spoke to me! Marry again? Another wife, over whom I should have no influence! Other children, whose education would not be confided to me! What would become, then, of the restitution that I have hoped for, wrought for, prayed for?"

He stopped, and looked fixedly at the sky above him. The bridge was deserted. His black figure rose up erect, motionless, and spectral, with the white still light falling solemnly all around it. Standing so for some minutes, his first movement was to drop his hand angrily on the parapet of the bridge. He then turned round slowly in the direction by which the two women had walked away.

"Donna Brigida," he said, "I will lay you the price of fifty new dresses that Fabio d'Ascoli never marries again!"

He set his face once more toward the studio, and walked on without stopping until he arrived at the master-sculptor's door.

"Marry again?" he thought to himself, as he rang the bell. "Donna Brigida, was your first failure not enough for you? Are you going to try a second time?"

Luca Lomi himself opened the door. He drew Father Rocco hurriedly into the studio toward a single lamp burning on a stand near the partition between the two rooms.

"Have you heard anything of our poor child?" he asked. "Tell me the truth! tell me the truth at once!"

"Hush! compose yourself. I have heard," said Father Rocco, in low, mournful tones.

Luca tightened his hold on the priest's arm, and looked into his face with breathless, speechless eagerness.

"Compose yourself," repeated Father Rocco. "Compose yourself to hear the worst. My poor Luca, the doctors have given up all hope."

Luca dropped his brother's arm with a groan of despair. "Oh, Maddalena! my child — my only child!"

Reiterating these words again and again, he leaned his head against the partition and burst into tears. Sordid and coarse as his nature was, he really loved his daughter. All the heart he had was in his statues and in her.

After the first burst of his grief was exhausted, he was recalled to himself by a sensation as if some change had taken place in the lighting of the studio. He looked up directly, and dimly discerned the priest standing far down at the end of the room nearest the door, with the lamp in his hand, eagerly looking at something.

"Rocco!" he exclaimed, "Rocco, why have you taken the lamp away? What are you doing there?"

There was no movement and no answer. Luca advanced a step or two, and called again. "Rocco, what are you doing there?"

The priest heard this time, and came suddenly toward his brother, with the lamp in his hand — so suddenly that Luca started.

"What is it?" he asked, in astonishment. "Gracious God, Rocco, how pale you are!"

Still the priest never said a word. He put the lamp down on the nearest table. Luca observed that his hand shook. He had never seen his brother violently agitated before. When Rocco had announced, but a few minutes ago, that Maddalena's life was despaired of, it was in a voice which, though sorrowful, was perfectly calm. What was the meaning of this sudden panic — this strange, silent terror?

The priest observed that his brother was looking at him earnestly. "Come!" he said in a faint whisper, "come to her bedside: we have no time to lose. Get your hat, and leave it to me to put out the lamp."

He hurriedly extinguished the light while he spoke. They went down the studio side by side toward the door. The moonlight streamed through the window full on the place where the priest had been standing alone with the lamp in his hand. As they passed it, Luca felt his brother tremble, and saw him turn away his head.

. . . .

Two hours later, Fabio d'Ascoli and his wife were separated in this world forever; and the servants of the palace were anticipating in whispers the order of their mistress's funeral procession to the burial-ground of the Campo Santo.

PART THIRD. CHAPTER I.

*A*bout eight months after the Countess d'Ascoli had been laid in her grave in the Campo Santo, two reports were circulated through the gay world of Pisa, which excited curiosity and awakened expectation everywhere.

The first report announced that a grand masked ball was to be given at the Melani Palace, to celebrate the day on which the heir of the house attained his majority. All the friends of the family were delighted at the prospect of this festival; for the old Marquis Melani had the reputation of being one of the most hospitable, and, at the same time, one of the most eccentric men in Pisa. Every one expected, therefore, that he would secure for the entertainment of his guests, if he really gave the ball, the most whimsical novelties in the way of masks, dances, and amusements generally, that had ever been seen.

The second report was, that the rich widower, Fabio d'Ascoli, was on the point of returning to Pisa, after having improved his health and spirits by traveling in foreign countries; and that he might be expected to appear again in society, for the first time since the death of his wife, at the masked ball which was to be given in the Melani Palace. This announcement excited special interest among the young ladies of Pisa. Fabio had only reached his thirtieth year; and it was universally agreed that his return to society in his native city could indicate nothing more certainly than his desire to find a second mother for his infant child. All the single ladies would now have been ready to bet, as confidently as Brigida had offered to bet eight months before, that Fabio d'Ascoli would marry again.

For once in a way, report turned out to be true, in both the cases just mentioned. Invitations were actually issued from the Melani Palace, and Fabio returned from abroad to his home on the Arno.

In settling all the arrangements connected with his masked ball, the Marquis Melani showed that he was determined not only to deserve, but to increase, his reputation for oddity. He invented the most extravagant disguises, to be worn by some of his more intimate friends; he arranged grotesque dances, to be performed at stated periods of the evening by professional buffoons, hired from Florence. He composed a toy symphony, which included solos on every noisy plaything at that time manufactured for children's use. And not content with thus avoiding the beaten track in preparing the entertainments at the ball, he determined also to show decided originality, even in selecting the attendants who were to wait on the company. Other people in his rank of life were accustomed to employ their own and hired footmen for this purpose; the marquis resolved that his attendants should be composed of young women only; that two of his rooms should be fitted up as Arcadian bowers; and that all the prettiest girls in Pisa should be placed in them to preside over the refreshments, dressed, in accordance with the mock classical taste of the period, as shepherdesses of the time of Virgil.

The only defect of this brilliantly new idea was the difficulty of executing it. The marquis had expressly ordered that not fewer than thirty shepherdesses were to be engaged — fifteen for each bower. It would have been easy to find double this number in Pisa, if beauty had been the only quality required in the attendant damsels. But it was also absolutely necessary, for the security of the marquis's gold and silver plate, that the shepherdesses should possess, besides good looks, the very homely recommendation of a fair character. This last qualification proved, it is sad to say, to be the one small merit which the majority of the ladies willing to accept engagements at the palace did not possess. Day after day passed on; and the marquis's steward only found more and more difficulty in obtaining the appointed number of trustworthy beauties. At last his resources failed him altogether; and he appeared in his master's presence about a week before the night of the ball, to make the humiliating acknowledgment that he was entirely at his wits' end. The total number of fair shepherdesses with fair characters whom he had been able to engage amounted only to twenty-three.

"Nonsense!" cried the marquis, irritably, as soon as the steward had made his confession. "I told you to get thirty girls, and thirty I mean to have. What's the use of shaking your head when all their dresses are ordered? Thirty tunics, thirty wreaths, thirty pairs of sandals and silk stockings, thirty crooks, you scoundrel — and you have the impudence to offer me only twenty-three hands to hold them. Not a word! I won't hear a word! Get me my thirty girls, or lose your place." The marquis roared out this last terrible sentence at the top of his voice, and pointed peremptorily to the door.

The steward knew his master too well to remonstrate. He took his hat and cane, and went out. It was useless to look through the ranks of rejected volunteers again; there was not the slightest hope in that quarter. The only chance left was to call on all his friends in Pisa who had daughters out at service, and to try what he could accomplish, by bribery and persuasion, that way.

After a whole day occupied in solicitations, promises, and patient smoothing down of innumerable difficulties, the result of his efforts in the new direction was an accession of six more shepherdesses. This brought him on bravely from twenty-three to twenty-nine, and left him, at last, with only one anxiety — where was he now to find shepherdess number thirty?

He mentally asked himself that important question, as he entered a shady by-street in the neighborhood of the Campo Santo, on his way back to the Melani Palace. Sauntering slowly along in the middle of the road, and fanning himself with his handkerchief after the oppressive exertions of the day, he passed a young girl who was standing at the street door of one of the houses, apparently waiting for somebody to join her before she entered the building.

"Body of Bacchus!" exclaimed the steward (using one of those old Pagan ejaculations which survive in Italy even to the present day), "there stands the prettiest girl I have seen yet. If she would only be shepherdess number thirty, I should go home to supper with my mind at ease. I'll ask her, at any rate. Nothing can be lost by asking, and everything may be gained. Stop, my dear," he continued, seeing the girl turn to go into the house as he approached her. "Don't be afraid of me. I am steward to the Marquis Melani, and well known in Pisa as an eminently respectable man. I have something to say to you which may be greatly for your benefit. Don't look surprised; I am coming to the point at once. Do you want to earn a little money? honestly, of course. You don't look as if you were very rich, child."

"I am very poor, and very much in want of some honest work to do," answered the girl, sadly.

"Then we shall suit each other to a nicety; for I have work of the pleasantest kind to give you, and plenty of money to pay for it. But before we say anything more about that, suppose you tell me first something about yourself — who you are, and so forth. You know who I am already."

"I am only a poor work-girl, and my name is Nanina. I have nothing more, sir, to say about myself than that."

"Do you belong to Pisa?"

"Yes, sir — at least, I did. But I have been away for some time. I was a year at Florence, employed in needlework."

"All by yourself?"

"No, sir, with my little sister. I was waiting for her when you came up."

"Have you never done anything else but needlework? never been out at service?"

"Yes, sir. For the last eight months I have had a situation to wait on a lady at Florence, and my sister (who is turned eleven, sir, and can make herself very useful) was allowed to help in the nursery."

"How came you to leave this situation?"

"The lady and her family were going to Rome, sir. They would have taken me with them, but they could not take my sister. We are alone in the world, and we never have been parted from each other, and never shall be — so I was obliged to leave the situation."

"And here you are, back at Pisa — with nothing to do, I suppose?"

"Nothing yet, sir. We only came back yesterday."

"Only yesterday! You are a lucky girl, let me tell you, to have met with me. I suppose you have somebody in the town who can speak to your character?"

"The landlady of this house can, sir."

"And who is she, pray?"

"Marta Angrisani, sir."

"What! the well-known sick-nurse? You could not possibly have a better recommendation, child. I remember her being employed at the Melani Palace at the time of the marquis's last attack of gout; but I never knew that she kept a lodging-house."

"She and her daughter, sir, have owned this house longer than I can recollect. My sister and I have lived in it since I was quite a little child, and I had hoped we might be able to live here again. But the top room we used to have is taken, and the room to let lower down is far more, I am afraid, than we can afford."

"How much is it?"

Nanina mentioned the weekly rent of the room in fear and trembling. The steward burst out laughing.

"Suppose I offered you money enough to be able to take that room for a whole year at once?" he said.

Nanina looked at him in speechless amazement.

"Suppose I offered you that?" continued the steward. "And suppose I only ask you in return to put on a fine dress and serve refreshments in a beautiful room to the company at the Marquis Melani's grand ball? What should you say to that?"

Nanina said nothing. She drew back a step or two, and looked more bewildered than before.

"You must have heard of the ball," said the steward, pompously; "the poorest people in Pisa have heard of it. It is the talk of the whole city."

Still Nanina made no answer. To have replied truthfully, she must have confessed that "the talk of the whole city" had now no interest for her. The last news from Pisa that had appealed to her sympathies was the news of the

Countess d'Ascoli's death, and of Fabio's departure to travel in foreign countries. Since then she had heard nothing more of him. She was as ignorant of his return to his native city as of all the reports connected with the marquis's ball. Something in her own heart — some feeling which she had neither the desire nor the capacity to analyze — had brought her back to Pisa and to the old home which now connected itself with her tenderest recollections. Believing that Fabio was still absent, she felt that no ill motive could now be attributed to her return; and she had not been able to resist the temptation of revisiting the scene that had been associated with the first great happiness as well as with the first great sorrow of her life. Among all the poor people of Pisa, she was perhaps the very last whose curiosity could be awakened, or whose attention could be attracted by the rumor of gayeties at the Melani Palace.

But she could not confess all this; she could only listen with great humility and no small surprise, while the steward, in compassion for her ignorance, and with the hope of tempting her into accepting his offered engagement, described the arrangements of the approaching festival, and dwelt fondly on the magnificence of the Arcadian bowers, and the beauty of the shepherdesses' tunics. As soon as he had done, Nanina ventured on the confession that she should feel rather nervous in a grand dress that did not belong to her, and that she doubted very much her own capability of waiting properly on the great people at the ball. The steward, however, would hear of no objections, and called peremptorily for Marta Angrisani to make the necessary statement as to Nanina's character. While this formality was being complied with to the steward's perfect satisfaction, La Biondella came in, unaccompanied on this occasion by the usual companion of all her walks, the learned poodle Scarammuccia.

"This is Nanina's sister," said the good-natured sick-nurse, taking the first opportunity of introducing La Biondella to the great marquis's great man. "A very good, industrious little girl; and very clever at plaiting dinner-mats, in case his excellency should ever want any. What have you done with the dog, my dear?"

"I couldn't get him past the pork butcher's, three streets off," replied La Biondella. "He would sit down and look at the sausages. I am more than half afraid he means to steal some of them."

"A very pretty child," said the steward, patting La Biondella on the cheek. "We ought to have her at the hall. If his excellency should want a Cupid, or a youthful nymph, or anything small and light in that way, I shall come back and let you know. In the meantime, Nanina, consider yourself Shepherdess Number Thirty, and come to the housekeeper's room at the palace to try on your dress tomorrow. Nonsense! don't talk to me about being afraid and awkward. All you're wanted to do is to look pretty; and your glass must have told you you could do that long ago. Remember the rent of the room, my dear, and don't stand in your light and your sister's. Does the little girl like sweet-meats? Of course she does! Well, I promise you a whole box of sugar-plums to take home for her, if you will come and wait at the ball."

"Oh, go to the ball, Nanina; go to the ball!" cried La Biondella, clapping her hands.

"Of course she will go to the ball," said the nurse. "She would be mad to throw away such an excellent chance."

Nanina looked perplexed. She hesitated a little, then drew Marta Angrisani away into a corner, and whispered this question to her:

"Do you think there will be any priests at the palace where the marquis lives?"

"Heavens, child, what a thing to ask!" returned the nurse. "Priests at a masked ball! You might as well expect to find Turks performing high mass in the cathedral. But supposing you did meet with priests at the palace, what then?"

"Nothing," said Nanina, constrainedly. She turned pale, and walked away as she spoke. Her great dread, in returning to Pisa, was the dread of meeting with Father Rocco again. She had never forgotten her first discovery at Florence of his distrust of her. The bare thought of seeing him any more, after her faith in him had been shaken forever, made her feel faint and sick at heart.

"To-morrow, in the housekeeper's room," said the steward, putting on his hat, "you will find your new dress all ready for you."

Nanina courtesied, and ventured on no more objections. The prospect of securing a home for a whole year to come among people whom she knew, reconciled her — influenced as she was also by Marta Angrisani's advice, and by her sister's anxiety for the promised present — to brave the trial of appearing at the ball.

"What a comfort to have it all settled at last," said the steward, as soon as he was out again in the street. "We shall see what the marquis says now. If he doesn't apologize for calling me a scoundrel the moment he sets eyes on Number Thirty, he is the most ungrateful nobleman that ever existed."

Arriving in front of the palace, the steward found workmen engaged in planning the external decorations and illuminations for the night of the ball. A little crowd had already assembled to see the ladders raised and the scaffold-ings put up. He observed among them, standing near the outskirts of the throng, a lady who attracted his attention (he was an ardent admirer of the fair sex) by the beauty and symmetry of her figure. While he lingered for a moment to look at her, a shaggy poodle-dog (licking his chops, as if he had just had something to eat) trotted by, stopped suddenly close to the lady, sniffed suspiciously for an instant, and then began to growl at her without the slightest apparent provocation. The steward advancing politely with his stick

THE PROFESSOR'S STORY OF THE YELLOW MASK. | 273

to drive the dog away, saw the lady start, and heard her exclaim to herself amazedly:

"You here, you beast! Can Nanina have come back to Pisa?"

This last exclamation gave the steward, as a gallant man, an excuse for speaking to the elegant stranger.

"Excuse me, madam," he said, "but I heard you mention the name of Nanina. May I ask whether you mean a pretty little work-girl who lives near the Campo Santo?"

"The same," said the lady, looking very much surprised and interested immediately.

"It may be a gratification to you, madam, to know that she has just returned to Pisa," continued the steward, politely; "and, moreover, that she is in a fair way to rise in the world. I have just engaged her to wait at the marquis's grand ball, and I need hardly say, under those circumstances, that if she plays her cards properly her fortune is made."

The lady bowed, looked at her informant very intently and thoughtfully for a moment, then suddenly walked away without uttering a word.

"A curious woman," thought the steward, entering the palace. "I must ask Number Thirty about her tomorrow."

PART THIRD. CHAPTER II.

The death of Maddalena d'Ascoli produced a complete change in the lives of her father and her uncle. After the first shock of the bereavement was over, Luca Lomi declared that it would be impossible for him to work in his studio again — for some time to come at least — after the death of the beloved daughter, with whom every corner of it was now so sadly and closely associated. He accordingly accepted an engagement to assist in restoring several newly discovered works of ancient sculpture at Naples, and set forth for that city, leaving the care of his work-rooms at Pisa entirely to his brother.

On the master-sculptor's departure, Father Rocco caused the statues and busts to be carefully enveloped in linen cloths, locked the studio doors, and, to the astonishment of all who knew of his former industry and dexterity as a sculptor, never approached the place again. His clerical duties he performed with the same assiduity as ever; but he went out less than had been his custom hitherto to the houses of his friends. His most regular visits were to the Ascoli Palace, to inquire at the porter's lodge after the health of Maddalena's child, who was always reported to be thriving admirably under the care of the best nurses that could be found in Pisa. As for any communications with his polite little friend from Florence, they had ceased months ago. The information — speedily conveyed to him — that Nanina was in the service of one of the most respectable ladies in the city seemed to relieve any anxieties which he might otherwise have felt on her account. He made no attempt to justify himself to her; and only required that his over-courteous little visitor of former days should let him know whenever the girl might happen to leave her new situation.

The admirers of Father Rocco, seeing the alteration in his life, and the increased quietness of his manner, said that, as he was growing older, he was getting more and more above the things of this world. His enemies (for even Father Rocco had them) did not scruple to assert that the change in him was decidedly for the worse, and that he belonged to the order of men who are most to be distrusted when they become most subdued. The priest himself paid no attention either to his eulogists or his depreciators. Nothing disturbed the regularity and discipline of his daily habits; and vigilant Scandal, though she sought often to surprise him, sought always in vain.

Such was Father Rocco's life from the period of his niece's death to Fabio's return to Pisa.

As a matter of course, the priest was one of the first to call at the palace and welcome the young nobleman back. What passed between them at this interview never was precisely known; but it was surmised readily enough that some misunderstanding had taken place, for Father Rocco did not repeat his visit. He made no complaints of Fabio, but simply stated that he had said something, intended for the young man's good, which had not been received in a right spirit; and that he thought it desirable to avoid the painful chance of any further collision by not presenting himself at the palace again for some little time. People were rather amazed at this. They would have been still more surprised if the subject of the masked ball had not just then occupied all their attention, and prevented their noticing it, by another strange event in connection with the priest. Father Rocco, some weeks after the cessation of his intercourse with Fabio, returned one morning to his old way of life as a sculptor, and opened the long-closed doors of his brother's studio.

Luca Lomi's former workmen, discovering this, applied to him immediately for employment; but were informed that their services would not be needed. Visitors called at the studio, but were always sent away again by the disappointing announcement that there was nothing new to show them. So the days passed on until Nanina left her situation and returned to Pisa. This circumstance was duly reported to Father Rocco by his correspondent at Florence; but, whether he was too much occupied among the statues, or whether it was one result of his cautious resolution never to expose himself unnecessarily to so much as the breath of detraction, he made no attempt to see Nanina, or even to justify himself toward her by writing her a letter. All his mornings continued to be spent alone in the studio, and all his afternoons to be occupied by his clerical duties, until the day before the masked ball at the Melani Palace.

Early on that day he covered over the statues, and locked the doors of the work-rooms once more; then returned to his own lodgings, and did not go out again. One or two of his friends who wanted to see him were informed that he was not well enough to be able to receive them. If they had penetrated into his little study, and had seen him, they would have been easily satisfied that this was no mere excuse. They would have noticed that his face was startlingly pale, and that the ordinary composure of his manner was singularly disturbed.

Toward evening this restlessness increased, and his old housekeeper, on pressing him to take some nourishment, was astonished to hear him answer her sharply and irritably, for the first time since she had been in his service. A little later her surprise was increased by his sending her with a note to the Ascoli Palace, and by the quick return of an answer, brought ceremoniously by one of Fabio's servants. "It is long since he has had any communication with that quarter. Are they going to be friends again?" thought the house-keeper as she took the answer upstairs to her master.

"I feel better to-night," he said as he read it; "well enough indeed to venture out. If any one inquires for me, tell them that I am gone to the Ascoli Palace." Saying this, he walked to the door; then returned, and trying the lock of his cabinet, satisfied himself that it was properly secured; then went out.

He found Fabio in one of the large drawing-rooms of the palace, walking irritably backward and forward, with several little notes crumpled together in his hands, and a plain black domino dress for the masquerade of the ensuing night spread out on one of the tables.

"I was just going to write to you," said the young man, abruptly, "when I received your letter. You offer me a renewal of our friendship, and I accept the offer. I have no doubt those references of yours, when we last met, to the subject of second marriages were well meant, but they irritated me; and, speaking under that irritation, I said words that I had better not have spoken. If I pained you, I am sorry for it. Wait! pardon me for one moment. I have not quite done yet. It seems that you are by no means the only person in Pisa to whom the question of my possibly marrying again appears to have presented itself. Ever since it was known that I intended to renew my intercourse with society at the ball tomorrow night, I have been persecuted by anonymous letters — infamous letters, written from some motive which it is impossible for me to understand. I want your advice on the best means of discovering the writers; and I have also a very important question to ask you. But read one of the letters first yourself; any one will do as a sample of the rest."

Fixing his eyes searchingly on the priest, he handed him one of the notes. Still a little paler than usual, Father Rocco sat down by the nearest lamp, and shading his eyes, read these lines:

"COUNT FABIO—— It is the common talk of Pisa that you are likely, as a young man left with a motherless child, to marry again. Your having accepted an invitation to the Melani Palace gives a color of truth to this report. Widowers who are true to the departed do not go among all the handsomest single women in a city at a masked ball. Reconsider your determination, and remain at home. I know you, and I knew your wife, and I say to you solemnly, avoid temptation, for you must never marry again. Neglect my advice and you will repent it to the end of your life. I have reasons for what I say — serious, fatal reasons, which I cannot divulge. If you would let your wife lie easy in her grave, if you would avoid a terrible warning, go not to the masked ball!"

"I ask you, and I ask any man, if that is not infamous?" exclaimed Fabio, passionately, as the priest handed him back the letter. "An attempt to work on my fears through the memory of my poor dead wife! An insolent assumption that I want to marry again, when I myself have not even so much as thought of the subject at all! What is the secret object of this letter, and of the rest here that resemble it? Whose interest is it to keep me away from the ball? What is the meaning of such a phrase as, 'If you would let your wife lie easy in her grave'? Have you no advice to give me — no plan to propose for discovering the vile hand that traced these lines? Speak to me! Why, in Heaven's name, don't you speak?"

The priest leaned his head on his hand, and, turning his face from the light as if it dazzled his eyes, replied in his lowest and quietest tones:

"I cannot speak till I have had time to think. The mystery of that letter is not to be solved in a moment. There are things in it that are enough to perplex and amaze any man!"

"What things?"

"It is impossible for me to go into details — at least at the present moment."

"You speak with a strange air of secrecy. Have you nothing definite to say — no advice to give me?"

"I should advise you not to go to the ball."

"You would! Why?"

"If I gave you my reasons, I am afraid I should only be irritating you to no purpose."

"Father Rocco, neither your words nor your manner satisfy me. You speak in riddles; and you sit there in the dark with your face hidden from me —"

The priest instantly started up and turned his face to the light.

"I recommend you to control your temper, and to treat me with common courtesy," he said, in his quietest, firmest tones, looking at Fabio steadily while he spoke.

"We will not prolong this interview," said the young man, calming himself by an evident effort. "I have one question to ask you, and then no more to say."

The priest bowed his head, in token that he was ready to listen. He still stood up, calm, pale, and firm, in the full light of the lamp.

"It is just possible," continued Fabio, "that these letters may refer to some incautious words which my late wife might have spoken. I ask you as her spiritual director, and as a near relation who enjoyed her confidence, if you ever heard her express a wish, in the event of my surviving her, that I should abstain from marrying again?"

"Did she never express such a wish to you?"

"Never. But why do you evade my question by asking me another?"

"It is impossible for me to reply to your question."

"For what reason?"

"Because it is impossible for me to give answers which must refer, whether they are affirmative or negative, to what I have heard in confession."

"We have spoken enough," said Fabio, turning angrily from the priest. "I expected you to help me in clearing up these mysteries, and you do your best to thicken them. What your motives are, what your conduct means, it is impossible for me to know, but I say to you, what I would say in far other terms, if they were here, to the villains who have written these letters — no menaces, no mysteries, no conspiracies, will prevent me from being at the ball tomorrow. I can listen to persuasion, but I scorn threats. There lies my dress for the masquerade; no power on earth shall prevent me from wearing it tomorrow night!" He pointed, as he spoke, to the black domino and half-mask lying on the table.

"No power on *earth!*" repeated Father Rocco, with a smile, and an emphasis on the last word. "Superstitious still, Count Fabio! Do you suspect the powers of the other world of interfering with mortals at masquerades?"

Fabio started, and, turning from the table, fixed his eyes intently on the priest's face.

"You suggested just now that we had better not prolong this interview," said Father Rocco, still smiling. "I think you were right; if we part at once, we may still part friends. You have had my advice not to go to the ball, and you decline following it. I have nothing more to say. Good-night."

Before Fabio could utter the angry rejoinder that rose to his lips, the door of the room had opened and closed again, and the priest was gone.

PART THIRD. CHAPTER III.

The next night, at the time of assembling specified in the invitations to the masked ball, Fabio was still lingering in his palace, and still allowing the black domino to lie untouched and unheeded on his dressing-table. This delay was not produced by any change in his resolution to go to the Melani Palace. His determination to be present at the ball remained unshaken; and yet, at the last moment, he lingered and lingered on, without knowing why. Some strange influence seemed to be keeping him within the walls of his lonely home. It was as if the great, empty, silent palace had almost recovered on that night the charm which it had lost when its mistress died.

He left his own apartment and went to the bedroom where his infant child lay asleep in her little crib. He sat watching her, and thinking quietly and tenderly of many past events in his life for a long time, then returned to his room. A sudden sense of loneliness came upon him after his visit to the child's bedside; but he did not attempt to raise his spirits even then by going to the ball. He descended instead to his study, lighted his reading-lamp, and then, opening a bureau, took from one of the drawers in it the letter which Nanina had written to him. This was not the first time that a sudden sense of his solitude had connected itself inexplicably with the remembrance of the work-girl's letter.

He read it through slowly, and when he had done, kept it open in his hand. "I have youth, titles, wealth," he thought to himself, sadly; "everything that is sought after in this world. And yet if I try to think of any human being who really and truly loves me, I can remember but one — the poor, faithful girl who wrote these lines!"

Old recollections of the first day when he met with Nanina, of the first sitting she had given him in Luca Lomi's studio, of the first visit to the neat little room in the by-street, began to rise more and more vividly in his mind. Entirely absorbed by them, he sat absently drawing with pen and ink, on some sheets of letter-paper lying under his hand, lines and circles, and fragments of decorations, and vague remembrances of old ideas for statues, until the sudden sinking of the flame of his lamp awoke his attention abruptly to present things.

He looked at his watch. It was close on midnight.

This discovery at last aroused him to the necessity of immediate departure. In a few minutes he had put on his domino and mask, and was on his way to the ball.

Before he reached the Melani Palace the first part of the entertainment had come to an end. The "Toy Symphony" had been played, the grotesque dance performed, amid universal laughter; and now the guests were, for the most part, fortifying themselves in the Arcadian bowers for new dances, in which all persons present were expected to take part. The Marquis Melani had, with characteristic oddity, divided his two classical refreshment-rooms into what he termed the Light and Heavy Departments. Fruit, pastry, sweetmeats, salads, and harmless drinks were included under the first head, and all the stimulating liquors and solid eatables under the last. The thirty shepherdesses had been, according to the marquis's order, equally divided at the outset of the evening between the two rooms. But as the company began to crowd more and more resolutely in the direction of the Heavy Department, ten of the shepherdesses attached to the Light Department were told off to assist in attending on the hungry and thirsty majority of guests who were not to be appeased by pastry and lemonade. Among the five girls who were left behind in the room for the light refreshments was Nanina. The steward soon discovered that the novelty of her situation made her really nervous, and he wisely concluded that if he trusted her where the crowd was greatest and the noise loudest, she would not only be utterly useless, but also very much in the way of her more confident and experienced companions.

When Fabio arrived at the palace, the jovial uproar in the Heavy Department was at its height, and several gentlemen, fired by the classical costumes of the shepherdesses, were beginning to speak Latin to them with a thick utterance, and a valorous contempt for all restrictions of gender, number, and case. As soon as he could escape from the congratulations on his return to his friends, which poured on him from all sides, Fabio withdrew to seek some quieter room. The heat, noise, and confusion had so bewildered him, after the tranquil life he had been leading for many months past, that it was quite a relief to stroll through the half deserted dancing-rooms, to the opposite extremity of the great suite of apartments, and there to find himself in a second Arcadian bower, which seemed peaceful enough to deserve its name.

A few guests were in this room when he first entered it, but the distant sound of some first notes of dance music drew them all away. After a careless look at the quaint decorations about him, he sat down alone on a divan near the door, and beginning already to feel the heat and discomfort of his mask, took it off. He had not removed it more than a moment before he heard a faint cry in the direction of a long refreshment-table, behind which the five waiting-girls were standing. He started up directly, and could hardly believe his senses, when he found himself standing face to face with Nanina.

Her cheeks had turned perfectly colorless. Her astonishment at seeing the young nobleman appeared to have some sensation of terror mingled with it. The waiting-woman who happened to stand by her side instinctively stretched out an arm to support her, observing that she caught at the edge of the table as Fabio hurried round to get behind it and speak to her. When he drew near, her head drooped on her breast, and she said, faintly: "I never knew you were at Pisa; I never thought you would be here. Oh, I am true to what I said in my letter, though I seem so false to it!"

"I want to speak to you about the letter — to tell you how carefully I have kept it, how often I have read it," said Fabio.

She turned away her head, and tried hard to repress the tears that would force their way into her eyes "We should never have met," she said; "never, never have met again!"

Before Fabio could reply, the waiting-woman by Nanina's side interposed.

"For Heaven's sake, don't stop speaking to her here!" she exclaimed, impatiently. "If the steward or one of the upper servants was to come in, you would get her into dreadful trouble. Wait till tomorrow, and find some fitter place than this."

Fabio felt the justice of the reproof immediately. He tore a leaf out of his pocketbook, and wrote on it, "I must tell you how I honor and thank you for that letter. To-morrow — ten o'clock — the wicket-gate at the back of the Ascoli gardens. Believe in my truth and honor, Nanina, for I believe implicitly in yours." Having written these lines, he took from among his bunch of watch-seals a little key, wrapped it up in the note, and pressed it into her hand. In spite of himself his fingers lingered round hers, and he was on the point of speaking to her again, when he saw the waiting-woman's hand, which was just raised to motion him away, suddenly drop. Her color changed at the same moment, and she looked fixedly across the table.

He turned round immediately, and saw a masked woman standing alone in the room, dressed entirely in yellow from head to foot. She had a yellow hood, a yellow half-mask with deep fringe hanging down over her mouth, and a yellow domino, cut at the sleeves and edges into long flame-shaped points, which waved backward and forward tremulously in the light air wafted through the doorway. The woman's black eyes seemed to gleam with an evil brightness through the sight-holes of the mask, and the tawny fringe hanging before her mouth fluttered slowly with every breath she drew. Without a word or a gesture she stood before the table, and her gleaming black eyes fixed steadily on Fabio the instant he confronted her. A sudden chill struck through him, as he observed that the yellow of the stranger's domino and mask was of precisely the same shade as the yellow of the hangings and furniture which his wife had chosen after their marriage for the decoration of her favorite sitting-room.

"The Yellow Mask!" whispered the waiting-girls nervously, crowding together behind the table. "The Yellow Mask again!"

"Make her speak!"

"Ask her to have something!"

"This gentleman will ask her. Speak to her, sir. Do speak to her! She glides about in that fearful yellow dress like a ghost."

Fabio looked around mechanically at the girl who was whispering to him. He saw at the same time that Nanina still kept her head turned away, and that she had her handkerchief at her eyes. She was evidently struggling yet with the agitation produced by their unexpected meeting, and was, most probably for that reason, the only person in the room not conscious of the presence of the Yellow Mask.

"Speak to her, sir. Do speak to her!" whispered two of the waiting-girls together.

Fabio turned again toward the table. The black eyes were still gleaming at him from behind the tawny yellow of the mask. He nodded to the girls who had just spoken, cast one farewell look at Nanina, and moved down the room to get round to the side of the table at which the Yellow Mask was standing. Step by step as he moved the bright eyes followed him. Steadily and more steadily their evil light seemed to shine through and through him, as he turned the corner of the table and approached the still, spectral figure.

He came close up to the woman, but she never moved; her eyes never wavered for an instant. He stopped and tried to speak; but the chill struck through him again. An overpowering dread, an unutterable loathing seized on him; all sense of outer things — the whispering of the waiting-girls behind the table, the gentle cadence of the dance music, the distant hum of joyous talk — suddenly left him. He turned away shuddering, and quitted the room.

Following the sound of the music, and desiring before all things now to join the crowd wherever it was largest, he was stopped in one of the smaller apartments by a gentleman who had just risen from the card table, and who held out his hand with the cordiality of an old friend.

"Welcome back to the world, Count Fabio!" he began, gayly, then suddenly checked himself. "Why, you look pale, and your hand feels cold. Not ill, I hope?"

"No, no. I have been rather startled — I can't say why — by a very strangely dressed woman, who fairly stared me out of countenance."

"You don't mean the Yellow Mask?"

"Yes I do. Have you seen her?"

"Everybody has seen her; but nobody can make her unmask, or get her to speak. Our host has not the slightest notion who she is; and our hostess is horribly frightened at her. For my part, I think she has given us quite enough of her mystery and her grim dress; and if my name, instead of being nothing but plain Andrea D'Arbino, was Marquis Melani, I would say to her: 'Madam, we are here to laugh and amuse ourselves; suppose you open your lips, and charm us by appearing in a prettier dress!'"

During this conversation they had sat down together, with their backs toward the door, by the side of one of the card-tables. While D'Arbino was speaking, Fabio suddenly felt himself shuddering again, and became conscious of a sound of low breathing behind him.

He turned round instantly, and there, standing between them, and peering down at them, was the Yellow Mask!

Fabio started up, and his friend followed his example. Again the gleaming black eyes rested steadily on the young nobleman's face, and again their look chilled him to the heart.

"Yellow Lady, do you know my friend?" exclaimed D'Arbino, with mock solemnity.

There was no answer. The fatal eyes never moved from Fabio's face.

"Yellow Lady," continued the other, "listen to the music. Will you dance with me?"

The eyes looked away, and the figure glided slowly from the room.

"My dear count," said D'Arbino, "that woman seems to have quite an effect on you. I declare she has left you paler than ever. Come into the supper-room with me, and have some wine; you really look as if you wanted it."

They went at once to the large refreshment-room. Nearly all the guests had by this time begun to dance again. They had the whole apartment, therefore, almost entirely to themselves.

Among the decorations of the room, which were not strictly in accordance with genuine Arcadian simplicity, was a large looking-glass, placed over a well-furnished sideboard. D'Arbino led Fabio in this direction, exchanging greetings as he advanced with a gentleman who stood near the glass looking into it, and carelessly fanning himself with his mask.

"My dear friend!" cried D'Arbino, "you are the very man to lead us straight to the best bottle of wine in the palace. Count Fabio, let me present to you my intimate and good friend, the Cavaliere Finello, with whose family I know you are well acquainted. Finello, the count is a little out of spirits, and I have prescribed a good dose of wine. I see a whole row of bottles at your side, and I leave it to you to apply the remedy. Glasses there! three glasses, my lovely shepherdess with the black eyes — the three largest you have got."

The glasses were brought; the Cavaliere Finello chose a particular bottle, and filled them. All three gentlemen turned round to the sideboard to use it as a table, and thus necessarily faced the looking-glass.

"Now let us drink the toast of toasts," said D'Arbino. "Finello, Count Fabio — the ladies of Pisa!"

Fabio raised the wine to his lips, and was on the point of drinking it, when he saw reflected in the glass the figure of the Yellow Mask. The glittering eyes were again fixed on him, and the yellow-hooded head bowed slowly, as if in acknowledgment of the toast he was about to drink. For the third time the strange chill seized him, and he set down his glass of wine untasted.

"What is the matter?" asked D'Arbino.

"Have you any dislike, count, to that particular wine?" inquired the cavaliere.

"The Yellow Mask!" whispered Fabio. "The Yellow Mask again!"

They all three turned round directly toward the door. But it was too late — the figure had disappeared.

"Does any one know who this Yellow Mask is?" asked Finello. "One may guess by the walk that the figure is a woman's. Perhaps it may be the strange color she has chosen for her dress, or perhaps her stealthy way of moving from room to room; but there is certainly something mysterious and startling about her."

"Startling enough, as the count would tell you," said D'Arbino. "The Yellow Mask has been responsible for his loss of spirits and change of complexion, and now she has prevented him even from drinking his wine."

"I can't account for it," said Fabio, looking round him uneasily; "but this is the third room into which she has followed me — the third time she has seemed to fix her eyes on me alone. I suppose my nerves are hardly in a fit state yet for masked balls and adventures; the sight of her seems to chill me. Who can she be?"

"If she followed me a fourth time," said Finello, "I should insist on her unmasking."

"And suppose she refused?" asked his friend

"Then I should take her mask off for her."

"It is impossible to do that with a woman," said Fabio. "I prefer trying to lose her in the crowd. Excuse me, gentlemen, if I leave you to finish the wine, and then to meet me, if you like, in the great ballroom."

He retired as he spoke, put on his mask, and joined the dancers immediately, taking care to keep always in the most crowded corner of the apartment. For some time this plan of action proved successful, and he saw no more of the mysterious yellow domino. Ere long, however, some new dances were arranged, in which the great majority of the persons in the ballroom took part; the figures resembling the old English country dances in this respect, that the ladies and gentlemen were placed in long rows opposite to each other. The sets consisted of about twenty couples each, placed sometimes across, and sometimes along the apartment; and the spectators were all required to move away on either side, and range themselves close to the walls. As Fabio among others complied with this necessity, he looked down a row of dancers waiting during the performance of the orchestral prelude; and there, watching him again, from the opposite end of the lane formed by the gentlemen on one side and the ladies on the other, he saw the Yellow Mask.

He moved abruptly back, toward another row of dancers, placed at right angles to the first row; and there again; at the opposite end of the gay lane of brightly-dressed figures, was the Yellow Mask. He slipped into the middle of the room, but it was only to find her occupying his former position near the wall, and still, in spite of his disguise, watching him through row after row of dancers. The persecution began to grow intolerable; he felt a kind of angry curiosity mingling now with the vague dread that had hitherto oppressed him. Finello's advice recurred to his memory; and he determined to make the woman unmask at all hazards. With this intention he returned to the supper-room in which he had left his friends.

They were gone, probably to the ballroom, to look for him. Plenty of wine was still left on the sideboard, and he poured himself out a glass. Finding that his hand trembled as he did so, he drank several more glasses in quick succession, to nerve himself for the approaching encounter with the Yellow Mask. While he was drinking he expected every moment to see her in the looking-glass again; but she never appeared — and yet he felt almost certain that he had detected her gliding out after him when he left the ballroom.

He thought it possible that she might be waiting for him in one of the smaller apartments, and, taking off his mask, walked through several of them without meeting her, until he came to the door of the refreshment-room in which Nanina and he had recognized each other. The waiting-woman behind the table, who had first spoken to him, caught sight of him now, and ran round to the door.

"Don't come in and speak to Nanina again," she said, mistaking the purpose which had brought him to the door. "What with frightening her first, and making her cry afterward, you have rendered her quite unfit for her work. The steward is in there at this moment, very good-natured, but not very sober. He says she is pale and red-eyed, and not fit to be a shepherdess any longer, and that, as she will not be missed now, she may go home if she likes. We have got her an old cloak, and she is going to try and slip through the rooms unobserved, to get downstairs and change her dress. Don't speak to her, pray, or you will only make her cry again; and what is worse, make the steward fancy —"

She stopped at that last word, and pointed suddenly over Fabio's shoulder.

"The Yellow Mask!" she exclaimed. "Oh, sir, draw her away into the ball-room, and give Nanina a chance of getting out!"

Fabio turned directly, and approached the Mask, who, as they looked at each other, slowly retreated before him. The waiting-woman, seeing the yellow figure retire, hastened back to Nanina in the refreshment-room.

Slowly the masked woman retreated from one apartment to another till she entered a corridor brilliantly lighted up and beautifully ornamented with flow-ers. On the right hand this corridor led to the ballroom; on the left to an ante-chamber at the head of the palace staircase. The Yellow Mask went on a few paces toward the left, then stopped. The bright eyes fixed themselves as before on Fabio's face, but only for a moment. He heard a light step behind him, and then he saw the eyes move. Following the direction they took, he turned round, and discovered Nanina, wrapped up in the old cloak which was to enable her to get downstairs unobserved.

"Oh, how can I get out? how can I get out?" cried the girl, shrinking back affrightedly as she saw the Yellow Mask.

"That way," said Fabio, pointing in the direction of the ballroom. "Nobody will notice you in the cloak; it will only be thought some new disguise." He took her arm as he spoke, to reassure her, and continued in a whisper, "Don't forget tomorrow."

At the same moment he felt a hand laid on him. It was the hand of the masked woman, and it put him back from Nanina.

In spite of himself, he trembled at her touch, but still retained presence of mind enough to sign to the girl to make her escape. With a look of eager inquiry in the direction of the mask, and a half suppressed exclamation of terror, she obeyed him, and hastened away toward the ballroom.

"We are alone," said Fabio, confronting the gleaming black eyes, and reaching out his hand resolutely toward the Yellow Mask. "Tell me who you are, and why you follow me, or I will uncover your face, and solve the mystery for myself."

The woman pushed his hand aside, and drew back a few paces, but never spoke a word. He followed her. There was not an instant to be lost, for just then the sound of footsteps hastily approaching the corridor became audible.

"Now or never," he whispered to himself, and snatched at the mask.

His arm was again thrust aside; but this time the woman raised her disen-gaged hand at the same moment, and removed the yellow mask.

The lamps shed their soft light full on her face.

It was the face of his dead wife.

PART THIRD. CHAPTER IV.

*S*ignor Andrea D'Arbino, searching vainly through the various rooms in the palace for Count Fabio d'Ascoli, and trying as a last resource, the corridor leading to the ballroom and grand staircase, discovered his friend lying on the floor in a swoon, without any living creature near him. Determining to avoid alarming the guests, if possible, D'Arbino first sought help in the antechamber. He found there the marquis's valet, assisting the Cavaliere Finello (who was just taking his departure) to put on his cloak.

While Finello and his friend carried Fabio to an open window in the antechamber, the valet procured some iced water. This simple remedy, and the change of atmosphere, proved enough to restore the fainting man to his senses, but hardly — as it seemed to his friends — to his former self. They noticed a change to blankness and stillness in his face, and when he spoke, an indescribable alteration in the tone of his voice.

"I found you in a room in the corridor," said D'Arbino. "What made you faint? Don't you remember? Was it the heat?"

Fabio waited for a moment, painfully collecting his ideas. He looked at the valet, and Finello signed to the man to withdraw.

"Was it the heat?" repeated D'Arbino.

"No," answered Fabio, in strangely hushed, steady tones. "I have seen the face that was behind the yellow mask."

"Well?"

"It was the face of my dead wife."

"Your dead wife!"

"When the mask was removed I saw her face. Not as I remember it in the pride of her youth and beauty — not even as I remember her on her sick-bed — but as I remember her in her coffin."

"Count! for God's sake, rouse yourself! Collect your thoughts — remember where you are — and free your mind of its horrible delusion."

"Spare me all remonstrances; I am not fit to bear them. My life has only one object now — the pursuing of this mystery to the end. Will you help me? I am scarcely fit to act for myself."

He still spoke in the same unnaturally hushed, deliberate tones. D'Arbino and Finello exchanged glances behind him as he rose from the sofa on which he had hitherto been lying.

"We will help you in everything," said D'Arbino, soothingly. "Trust in us to the end. What do you wish to do first?"

"The figure must have gone through this room. Let us descend the staircase and ask the servants if they have seen it pass."

(Both D'Arbino and Finello remarked that he did not say *her*.)

They inquired down to the very courtyard. Not one of the servants had seen the Yellow Mask.

The last resource was the porter at the outer gate. They applied to him; and in answer to their questions he asserted that he had most certainly seen a lady in a yellow domino and mask drive away, about half an hour before, in a hired coach.

"Should you remember the coachman again?" asked D'Arbino.

"Perfectly; he is an old friend of mine."

"And you know where he lives?"

"Yes; as well as I know where I do."

"Any reward you like, if you can get somebody to mind your lodge, and can take us to that house."

In a few minutes they were following the porter through the dark, silent streets. "We had better try the stables first," said the man. "My friend, the coachman, will hardly have had time to do more than set the lady down. We shall most likely catch him just putting up his horses."

The porter turned out to be right. On entering the stable-yard, they found that the empty coach had just driven into it.

"You have been taking home a lady in a yellow domino from the masquerade?" said D'Arbino, putting some money into the coachman's hand.

"Yes, sir; I was engaged by that lady for the evening — engaged to drive her to the ball as well as to drive her home."

"Where did you take her from?"

"From a very extraordinary place — from the gate of the Campo Santo burial-ground."

During this colloquy, Finello and D'Arbino had been standing with Fabio between them, each giving him an arm. The instant the last answer was given, he reeled back with a cry of horror.

"Where have you taken her to now?" asked D'Arbino. He looked about him nervously as he put the question, and spoke for the first time in a whisper.

"To the Campo Santo again," said the coachman.

Fabio suddenly drew his arms out of the arms of his friends, and sank to his knees on the ground, hiding his face. From some broken ejaculations which escaped him, it seemed as if he dreaded that his senses were leaving him, and that he was praying to be preserved in his right mind.

"Why is he so violently agitated?" said Finello, eagerly, to his friend.

"Hush!" returned the other. "You heard him say that when he saw the face behind the yellow mask, it was the face of his dead wife?"

"Yes. But what then?"

"His wife was buried in the Campo Santo."

PART THIRD. CHAPTER V.

Of all the persons who had been present, in any capacity, at the Marquis Melani's ball, the earliest riser on the morning after it was Nanina. The agitation produced by the strange events in which she had been concerned destroyed the very idea of sleep. Through the hours of darkness she could not even close her eyes; and, as soon as the new day broke, she rose to breathe the early morning air at her window, and to think in perfect tranquillity over all that had passed since she entered the Melani Palace to wait on the guests at the masquerade.

On reaching home the previous night, all her other sensations had been absorbed in a vague feeling of mingled dread and curiosity, produced by the sight of the weird figure in the yellow mask, which she had left standing alone with Fabio in the palace corridor. The morning light, however, suggested new thoughts. She now opened the note which the young nobleman had pressed into her hand, and read over and over again the hurried pencil lines scrawled on the paper. Could there be any harm, any forgetfulness of her own duty, in using the key inclosed in the note, and keeping her appointment in the Ascoli gardens at ten o'clock? Surely not — surely the last sentence he had written, "Believe in my truth and honor, Nanina, for I believe implicitly in yours," was enough to satisfy her this time that she could not be doing wrong in listening for once to the pleading of her own heart. And besides, there in her lap lay the key of the wicket-gate. It was absolutely necessary to use that, if only for the purpose of giving it back safely into the hand of its owner.

As this last thought was passing through her mind, and plausibly overcoming any faint doubts and difficulties which she might still have left, she was startled by a sudden knocking at the street door; and, looking out of the window immediately, saw a man in livery standing in the street, anxiously peering up at the house to see if his knocking had aroused anybody.

"Does Marta Angrisani, the sick-nurse, live here?" inquired the man, as soon as Nanina showed herself at the window.

"Yes," she answered. "Must I call her up? Is there some person ill?"

"Call her up directly," said the servant; "she is wanted at the Ascoli Palace. My master, Count Fabio —"

Nanina waited to hear no more. She flew to the room in which the sick-nurse slept, and awoke her, almost roughly, in an instant.

"He is ill!" she cried, breathlessly. "Oh, make haste, make haste! He is ill, and he has sent for you!"

Marta inquired who had sent for her, and on being informed, promised to lose no time. Nanina ran downstairs to tell the servant that the sick-nurse was getting on her clothes. The man's serious expression, when she came close to him, terrified her. All her usual self-distrust vanished; and she entreated him, without attempting to conceal her anxiety, to tell her particularly what his master's illness was, and how it had affected him so suddenly after the ball.

"I know nothing about it," answered the man, noticing Nanina's manner as she put her question, with some surprise, "except that my master was brought home by two gentlemen, friends of his, about a couple of hours ago, in a very sad state; half out of his mind, as it seemed to me. I gathered from what was said that he had got a dreadful shock from seeing some woman take off her mask, and show her face to him at the ball. How that could be I don't in the least understand; but I know that when the doctor was sent for, he looked very serious, and talked about fearing brain-fever."

Here the servant stopped; for, to his astonishment, he saw Nanina suddenly turn away from him, and then heard her crying bitterly as she went back into the house.

Marta Angrisani had huddled on her clothes and was looking at herself in the glass to see that she was sufficiently presentable to appear at the palace, when she felt two arms flung round her neck; and, before she could say a word, found Nanina sobbing on her bosom.

"He is ill — he is in danger!" cried the girl. "I must go with you to help him. You have always been kind to me, Marta — be kinder than ever now. Take me with you — take me with you to the palace!"

"You, child!" exclaimed the nurse, gently unclasping her arms.

"Yes — yes! if it is only for an hour," pleaded Nanina; "if it is only for one little hour every day. You have only to say that I am your helper, and they would let me in. Marta! I shall break my heart if I can't see him, and help him to get well again."

The nurse still hesitated. Nanina clasped her round the neck once more, and laid her cheek — burning hot now, though the tears had been streaming down it but an instant before — close to the good woman's face.

"I love him, Marta; great as he is, I love him with all my heart and soul and strength," she went on, in quick, eager, whispering tones; "and he loves me. He would have married me if I had not gone away to save him from it. I could keep my love for him a secret while he was well; I could stifle it, and crush it down, and wither it up by absence. But now he is ill, it gets beyond me; I can't master it. Oh, Marta! don't break my heart by denying me! I have suffered so much for his sake, that I have earned the right to nurse him!"

Marta was not proof against this last appeal. She had one great and rare merit for a middle-aged woman — she had not forgotten her own youth.

"Come, child," said she, soothingly; "I won't attempt to deny you. Dry your eyes, put on your mantilla; and, when we get face to face with the doctor, try to look as old and ugly as you can, if you want to be let into the sick-room along with me."

The ordeal of medical scrutiny was passed more easily than Marta Angrisani had anticipated. It was of great importance, in the doctor's opinion, that the sick man should see familiar faces at his bedside. Nanina had only, therefore, to state that he knew her well, and that she had sat to him as a model in the days when he was learning the art of sculpture, to be immediately accepted as Marta's privileged assistant in the sick-room.

The worst apprehensions felt by the doctor for the patient were soon realized. The fever flew to his brain. For nearly six weeks he lay prostrate, at the mercy of death; now raging with the wild strength of delirium, and now sunk in the speechless, motionless, sleepless exhaustion which was his only repose. At last; the blessed day came when he enjoyed his first sleep, and when the doctor began, for the first time, to talk of the future with hope. Even then, however, the same terrible peculiarity marked his light dreams which had previously shown itself in his fierce delirium. From the faintly uttered, broken phrases which dropped from him when he slept, as from the wild words which burst from him when his senses were deranged, the one sad discovery inevitably resulted — that his mind was still haunted, day and night, hour after hour, by the figure in the yellow mask.

As his bodily health improved, the doctor in attendance on him grew more and more anxious as to the state of his mind. There was no appearance of any positive derangement of intellect, but there was a mental depression — an unaltering, invincible prostration, produced by his absolute belief in the reality of the dreadful vision that he had seen at the masked ball — which suggested to the physician the gravest doubts about the case. He saw with dismay that the patient showed no anxiety, as he got stronger, except on one subject. He was eagerly desirous of seeing Nanina every day by his bedside; but, as soon as he was assured that his wish should be faithfully complied with, he seemed to care for nothing more. Even when they proposed, in the hope of rousing him to an exhibition of something like pleasure, that the girl should read to him for an hour every day out of one of his favorite books, he only showed a languid satisfaction. Weeks passed away, and still, do what they would, they could not make him so much as smile.

One day Nanina had begun to read to him as usual, but had not proceeded far before Marta Angrisani informed her that he had fallen into a doze. She ceased with a sigh, and sat looking at him sadly, as he lay near her, faint and pale and mournful in his sleep — miserably altered from what he was when she first knew him. It had been a hard trial to watch by his bedside in the terrible time of his delirium; but it was a harder trial still to look at him now, and to feel less and less hopeful with each succeeding day.

While her eyes and thoughts were still compassionately fixed on him, the door of the bedroom opened, and the doctor came in, followed by Andrea D'Arbino, whose share in the strange adventure with the Yellow Mask caused him to feel a special interest in Fabio's progress toward recovery.

"Asleep, I see; and sighing in his sleep," said the doctor, going to the bedside. "The grand difficulty with him," he continued, turning to D'Arbino, "remains precisely what it was. I have hardly left a single means untried of rousing him from that fatal depression; yet, for the last fortnight, he has not advanced a single step. It is impossible to shake his conviction of the reality of that face which he saw (or rather which he thinks he saw) when the yellow mask was removed; and, as long as he persists in his own shocking view of the case, so long he will lie there, getting better, no doubt, as to his body, but worse as to his mind."

"I suppose, poor fellow, he is not in a fit state to be reasoned with?"

"On the contrary, like all men with a fixed delusion, he has plenty of intelligence to appeal to on every point, except the one point on which he is wrong. I have argued with him vainly by the hour together. He possesses, unfortunately, an acute nervous sensibility and a vivid imagination; and besides, he has, as I suspect, been superstitiously brought up as a child. It would be probably useless to argue rationally with him on certain spiritual subjects, even if his mind was in perfect health. He has a good deal of the mystic and the dreamer in his composition; and science and logic are but broken reeds to depend upon with men of that kind."

"Does he merely listen to you when you reason with him, or does he attempt to answer?"

"He has only one form of answer, and that is, unfortunately, the most difficult of all to dispose of. Whenever I try to convince him of his delusion, he invariably retorts by asking me for a rational explanation of what happened to him at the masked ball. Now, neither you nor I, though we believe firmly that he has been the dupe of some infamous conspiracy, have been able as yet to penetrate thoroughly into this mystery of the Yellow Mask. Our common sense tells us that he must be wrong in taking his view of it, and that we must be right in taking ours; but if we cannot give him actual, tangible proof of that — if we can only theorize, when he asks us for an explanation — it is but too plain, in his present condition, that every time we remonstrate with him on the subject we only fix him in his delusion more and more firmly."

"It is not for want of perseverance on my part," said D'Arbino, after a moment of silence, "that we are still left in the dark. Ever since the extraordinary statement of the coachman who drove the woman home, I have been inquiring and investigating. I have offered the reward of two hundred scudi for the discovery of her; I have myself examined the servants at the palace, the night-watchman at the Campo Santo, the police-books, the lists of keepers of hotels and lodging-houses, to hit on some trace of this woman; and I have failed in all directions. If my poor friend's perfect recovery does indeed depend on his delusion being combated by actual proof, I fear we have but little chance of restoring him. So far as I am concerned, I confess myself at the end of my resources."

"I hope we are not quite conquered yet," returned the doctor. "The proofs we want may turn up when we least expect them. It is certainly a miserable case," he continued, mechanically laying his fingers on the sleeping man's pulse. "There he lies, wanting nothing now but to recover the natural elasticity of his mind; and here we stand at his bedside, unable to relieve him of the weight that is pressing his faculties down. I repeat it, Signor Andrea, nothing will rouse him from his delusion that he is the victim of a supernatural inter-position but the production of some startling, practical proof of his error. At present he is in the position of a man who has been imprisoned from his birth in a dark room, and who denies the existence of daylight. If we cannot open the shutters and show him the sky outside, we shall never convert him to a knowledge of the truth."

Saying these words, the doctor turned to lead the way out of the room, and observed Nanina, who had moved from the bedside on his entrance, standing near the door. He stopped to look at her, shook his head good-humoredly, and called to Marta, who happened to be occupied in an adjoining room.

"Signora Marta," said the doctor, "I think you told me some time ago that your pretty and careful little assistant lives in your house. Pray, does she take much walking exercise?"

"Very little, Signor Dottore. She goes home to her sister when she leaves the palace. Very little walking exercise, indeed."

"I thought so! Her pale cheeks and heavy eyes told me as much. Now, my dear," said the doctor, addressing Nanina, "you are a very good girl, and I am sure you will attend to what I tell you. Go out every morning before you come here, and take a walk in the fresh air. You are too young not to suffer by being shut up in close rooms every day, unless you get some regular exercise. Take a good long walk in the morning, or you will fall into my hands as a patient, and be quite unfit to continue your attendance here. Now, Signor Andrea, I am ready for you. Mind, my child, a walk every day in the open air outside the town, or you will fall ill, take my word for it!"

Nanina promised compliance; but she spoke rather absently, and seemed scarcely conscious of the kind familiarity which marked the doctor's manner. The truth was, that all her thoughts were occupied with what he had been saying by Fabio's bedside. She had not lost one word of the conversation while the doctor was talking of his patient, and of the conditions on which his recovery depended. "Oh, if that proof which would cure him could only be found!" she thought to herself, as she stole back anxiously to the bedside when the room was empty.

On getting home that day she found a letter waiting for her, and was greatly surprised to see that it was written by no less a person than the master-sculptor, Luca Lomi. It was very short; simply informing her that he had just returned to Pisa, and that he was anxious to know when she could sit to him for a new bust — a commission from a rich foreigner at Naples.

Nanina debated with herself for a moment whether she should answer the letter in the hardest way, to her, by writing, or, in the easiest way, in person; and decided on going to the studio and telling the master-sculptor that it would be impossible for her to serve him as a model, at least for some time to come. It would have taken her a long hour to say this with due propriety on paper; it would only take her a few minutes to say it with her own lips. So she put on her mantilla again and departed for the studio.

On, arriving at the gate and ringing the bell, a thought suddenly occurred to her, which she wondered had not struck her before. Was it not possible that she might meet Father Rocco in his brother's work-room? It was too late to retreat now, but not too late to ask, before she entered, if the priest was in the studio. Accordingly, when one of the workmen opened the door to her, she inquired first, very confusedly and anxiously, for Father Rocco. Hearing that he was not with his brother then, she went tranquilly enough to make her apologies to the master-sculptor.

She did not think it necessary to tell him more than that she was now occupied every day by nursing duties in a sick-room, and that it was consequently out of her power to attend at the studio. Luca Lomi expressed, and evidently felt, great disappointment at her failing him as a model, and tried hard to persuade her that she might find time enough, if she chose, to sit to him, as well as to nurse the sick person. The more she resisted his arguments and entreaties, the more obstinately he reiterated them. He was dusting his favorite busts and statues, after his long absence, with a feather-brush when she came in; and he continued this occupation all the while he was talking —

urging a fresh plea to induce Nanina to reconsider her refusal to sit at every fresh piece of sculpture he came to, and always receiving the same resolute apology from her as she slowly followed him down the studio toward the door.

Arriving thus at the lower end of the room, Luca stopped with a fresh argument on his lips before his statue of Minerva. He had dusted it already, but he lovingly returned to dust it again. It was his favorite work — the only good likeness (although it did assume to represent a classical subject) of his dead daughter that he possessed. He had refused to part with it for Maddalena's sake; and, as he now approached it with his brush for the second time, he absently ceased speaking, and mounted on a stool to look at the face near and blow some specks of dust off the forehead. Nanina thought this a good opportunity of escaping from further importunities. She was on the point of slipping away to the door with a word of farewell, when a sudden exclamation from Luca Lomi arrested her.

"Plaster!" cried the master-sculptor, looking intently at that part of the hair of the statue which lay lowest on the forehead. "Plaster here!" He took out his penknife as he spoke, and removed a tiny morsel of some white substance from an interstice between two folds of the hair where it touched the face. "It *is* plaster!" he exclaimed, excitedly. "Somebody has been taking a cast from the face of my statue!"

He jumped off the stool, and looked all round the studio with an expression of suspicious inquiry. "I must have this cleared up," he said. "My statues were left under Rocco's care, and he is answerable if there has been any stealing of casts from any one of them. I must question him directly."

Nanina, seeing that he took no notice of her, felt that she might now easily effect her retreat. She opened the studio door, and repeated, for the twentieth time at least, that she was sorry she could not sit to him.

"I am sorry too, child," he said, irritably looking about for his hat. He found it apparently just as Nanina was going out; for she heard him call to one of the workmen in the inner studio, and order the man to say, if anybody wanted him, that he had gone to Father Rocco's lodgings.

PART THIRD. CHAPTER VI.

The next morning, when Nanina rose, a bad attack of headache, and a sense of languor and depression, reminded her of the necessity of following the doctor's advice, and preserving her health by getting a little fresh air and exercise. She had more than two hours to spare before the usual time when her daily attendance began at the Ascoli Palace; and she determined to employ the interval of leisure in taking a morning walk outside the town. La Biondella would have been glad enough to go too, but she had a large order for dinner-mats on hand, and was obliged, for that day, to stop in the house and work. Thus it happened that when Nanina set forth from home, the learned poodle, Scarammuccia, was her only companion.

She took the nearest way out of the town; the dog trotting along in his usual steady, observant way close at her side, pushing his great rough muzzle, from time to time, affectionately into her hand, and trying hard to attract her attention at intervals by barking and capering in front of her. He got but little notice, however, for his pains. Nanina was thinking again of all that the physician had said the day before by Fabio's bedside, and these thoughts brought with them others, equally absorbing, that were connected with the mysterious story of the young nobleman's adventure with the Yellow Mask. Thus preoccupied, she had little attention left for the gambols of the dog. Even the beauty of the morning appealed to her in vain. She felt the refreshment of the cool, fragrant air, but she hardly noticed the lovely blue of the sky, or the bright sunshine that gave a gayety and an interest to the commonest objects around her.

After walking nearly an hour, she began to feel tired, and looked about for a shady place to rest in.

Beyond and behind her there was only the high-road and the flat country; but by her side stood a little wooden building, half inn, half coffee-house, backed by a large, shady pleasure-garden, the gates of which stood invitingly open. Some workmen in the garden were putting up a stage for fireworks, but the place was otherwise quiet and lonely enough. It was only used at night as a sort of rustic Ranelagh, to which the citizens of Pisa resorted for pure air and amusement after the fatigues of the day. Observing that there were no visitors in the grounds, Nanina ventured in, intending to take a quarter of an hour's rest in the coolest place she could find before returning to Pisa.

She had passed the back of a wooden summer-house in a secluded part of the gardens, when she suddenly missed the dog from her side; and, looking round after him, saw that he was standing behind the summer-house with his ears erect and his nose to the ground, having evidently that instant scented something that excited his suspicion.

Thinking it possible that he might be meditating an attack on some unfortunate cat, she turned to see what he was watching. The carpenters engaged on the firework stage were just then hammering at it violently. The noise prevented her from hearing that Scarammuccia was growling, but she could feel that he was the moment she laid her hand on his back. Her curiosity was excited, and she stooped down close to him to look through a crack in the boards before which he stood into the summer-house.

She was startled at seeing a lady and gentleman sitting inside. The place she was looking through was not high enough up to enable her to see their faces, but she recognized, or thought she recognized, the pattern of the lady's dress as one which she had noticed in former days in the Demoiselle Grifoni's show-room. Rising quickly, her eye detected a hole in the boards about the level of her own height, caused by a knot having been forced out of the wood. She looked through it to ascertain, without being discovered, if the wearer of the familiar dress was the person she had taken her to be; and saw, not Brigida only, as she had expected, but Father Rocco as well. At the same moment the carpenters left off hammering and began to saw. The new sound from the firework stage was regular and not loud. The voices of the occupants of the summer-house reached her through it, and she heard Brigida pronounce the name of Count Fabio.

Instantly stooping down once more by the dog's side, she caught his muzzle firmly in both her hands. It was the only way to keep Scarammuccia from growling again, at a time when there was no din of hammering to prevent him from being heard. Those two words, "Count Fabio," in the mouth of another woman, excited a jealous anxiety in her. What could Brigida have to say in connection with that name? She never came near the Ascoli Palace — what right or reason could she have to talk of Fabio?

"Did you hear what I said?" she heard Brigida ask, in her coolest, hardest tone.

"No," the priest answered. "At least, not all of it."

"I will repeat it, then. I asked what had so suddenly determined you to give up all idea of making any future experiments on the superstitious fears of Count Fabio?"

"In the first place, the result of the experiment already tried has been so much more serious than I had anticipated, that I believe the end I had in view in making it has been answered already."

"Well; that is not your only reason?"

"Another shock to his mind might be fatal to him. I can use what I believe to be a justifiable fraud to prevent his marrying again; but I cannot burden myself with a crime."

"That is your second reason; but I believe you have another yet. The suddenness with which you sent to me last night to appoint a meeting in this lonely place; the emphatic manner in which you requested — I may almost say ordered — me to bring the wax mask here, suggest to my mind that something must have happened. What is it? I am a woman, and my curiosity must be satisfied. After the secrets you have trusted to me already, you need not hesitate, I think, to trust me with one more."

"Perhaps not. The secret this time is, moreover, of no great importance. You know that the wax mask you wore at the ball was made in a plaster mold taken off the face of my brother's statue?"

"Yes, I know that."

"My brother has just returned to his studio; has found a morsel of the plaster I used for the mold sticking in the hair of the statue; and has asked me, as the person left in charge of his work-rooms, for an explanation. Such an explanation as I could offer has not satisfied him, and he talks of making further inquiries. Considering that it will be used no more, I think it safest to destroy the wax mask, and I asked you to bring it here, that I might see it burned or broken up with my own eyes. Now you know all you wanted to know; and now, therefore, it is my turn to remind you that I have not yet had a direct answer to the first question I addressed to you when we met here. Have you brought the wax mask with you, or have you not?"

"I have not."

"And why?"

Just as that question was put, Nanina felt the dog dragging himself free of her grasp on his mouth. She had been listening hitherto with such painful intensity, with such all-absorbing emotions of suspense, terror, and astonishment, that she had not noticed his efforts to get away, and had continued mechanically to hold his mouth shut. But now she was aroused by the violence of his struggles to the knowledge that, unless she hit upon some new means of quieting him, he would have his mouth free, and would betray her by a growl.

In an agony of apprehension lest she should lose a word of the momentous conversation, she made a desperate attempt to appeal to the dog's fondness for her, by suddenly flinging both her arms round his neck, and kissing his rough, hairy cheek. The stratagem succeeded. Scarammuccia had, for many years past, never received any greater marks of his mistress's kindness for him than such as a pat on the head or a present of a lump of sugar might convey. His dog's nature was utterly confounded by the unexpected warmth of Nanina's caress, and he struggled up vigorously in her arms to try and return it by licking her face. She could easily prevent him from doing this, and could so gain a few minutes more to listen behind the summer-house without danger of discovery.

She had lost Brigida's answer to Father Rocco's question; but she was in time to hear her next words.

"We are alone here," said Brigida. "I am a woman, and I don't know that you may not have come armed. It is only the commonest precaution on my part not to give you a chance of getting at the wax mask till I have made my conditions."

"You never said a word about conditions before."

"True. I remember telling you that I wanted nothing but the novelty of going to the masquerade in the character of my dead enemy, and the luxury of being able to terrify the man who had brutally ridiculed me in old days in the studio. That was the truth. But it is not the less the truth that our experiment on Count Fabio has detained me in this city much longer than I ever intended, that I am all but penniless, and that I deserve to be paid. In plain words, will you buy the mask of me for two hundred scudi?"

"I have not twenty scudi in the world, at my own free disposal."

"You must find two hundred if you want the wax mask. I don't wish to threaten — but money I must have. I mention the sum of two hundred scudi, because that is the exact amount offered in the public handbills by Count Fabio's friends for the discovery of the woman who wore the yellow mask at the Marquis Melani's ball. What have I to do but to earn that money if I please, by going to the palace, taking the wax mask with me, and telling them that I am the woman. Suppose I confess in that way; they can do nothing to hurt me, and I should be two hundred scudi the richer. You might be injured, to be sure, if they insisted on knowing who made the wax model, and who suggested the ghastly disguise —"

"Wretch! do you believe that my character could be injured on the unsupported evidence of any words from your lips?"

"Father Rocco, for the first time since I have enjoyed the pleasure of your acquaintance, I find you committing a breach of good manners. I shall leave you until you become more like yourself. If you wish to apologize for calling me a wretch, and if you want to secure the wax mask, honor me with a visit before four o'clock this afternoon, and bring two hundred scudi with you. Delay till after four, and it will be too late."

An instant of silence followed; and then Nanina judged that Brigida must be departing, for she heard the rustling of a dress on the lawn in front of the summer-house. Unfortunately, Scarammuccia heard it too. He twisted himself round in her arms and growled.

The noise disturbed Father Rocco. She heard him rise and leave the summer-house. There would have been time enough, perhaps, for her to conceal herself among some trees if she could have recovered her self-possession at once; but she was incapable of making an effort to regain it. She could neither think nor move — her breath seemed to die away on her lips — as she saw the shadow of the priest stealing over the grass slowly from the front to the back of the summer-house. In another moment they were face to face.

He stopped a few paces from her, and eyed her steadily in dead silence. She still crouched against the summer-house, and still with one hand mechanically kept her hold of the dog. It was well for the priest that she did so. Scarammuccia's formidable teeth were in full view, his shaggy coat was bristling, his eyes were starting, his growl had changed from the surly to the savage note; he was ready to tear down, not Father Rocco only, but all the clergy in Pisa, at a moment's notice.

"You have been listening," said the priest, calmly. "I see it in your face. You have heard all."

She could not answer a word; she could not take her eyes from him. There was an unnatural stillness in his face, a steady, unrepentant, unfathomable despair in his eyes that struck her with horror. She would have given worlds to be able to rise to her feet and fly from his presence.

"I once distrusted you and watched you in secret," he said, speaking after a short silence, thoughtfully, and with a strange, tranquil sadness in his voice. "And now, what I did by you, you do by me. You put the hope of your life once in my hands. Is it because they were not worthy of the trust that discovery and ruin overtake me, and that you are the instrument of the retribution? Can this be the decree of Heaven — or is it nothing but the blind justice of chance?"

He looked upward, doubtingly, to the lustrous sky above him, and sighed. Nanina's eyes still followed his mechanically. He seemed to feel their influence, for he suddenly looked down at her again.

"What keeps you silent? Why are you afraid?" he said. "I can do you no harm, with your dog at your side, and the workmen yonder within call. I can do you no harm, and I wish to do you none. Go back to Pisa; tell what you have heard, restore the man you love to himself, and ruin me. That is your work; do it! I was never your enemy, even when I distrusted you. I am not your enemy now. It is no fault of yours that a fatality has been accomplished through you — no fault of yours that I am rejected as the instrument of securing a righteous restitution to the Church. Rise, child, and go your way, while I go mine, and prepare for what is to come. If we never meet again, remember that I parted from you without one hard saying or one harsh look — parted from you so, knowing that the first words you speak in Pisa will be death to my character, and destruction to the great purpose of my life."

Speaking these words, always with the same calmness which had marked his manner from the first, he looked fixedly at her for a little while, sighed again, and turned away. Just before he disappeared among the trees, he said "Farewell," but so softly that she could barely hear it. Some strange confusion clouded her mind as she lost sight of him. Had she injured him, or had he injured her? His words bewildered and oppressed her simple heart. Vague doubts and fears, and a sudden antipathy to remaining any longer near the summer-house, overcame her. She started to her feet, and, keeping the dog still at her side, hurried from the garden to the highroad. There, the wide glow of sunshine, the sight of the city lying before her, changed the current of her thoughts, and directed them all to Fabio and to the future.

A burning impatience to be back in Pisa now possessed her. She hastened toward the city at her utmost speed. The doctor was reported to be in the palace when she passed the servants lounging in the courtyard. He saw the moment, she came into his presence, that something had happened, and led her away from the sick-room into Fabio's empty study. There she told him all.

"You have saved him," said the doctor, joyfully. "I will answer for his recovery. Only let that woman come here for the reward; and leave me to deal with her as she deserves. In the meantime, my dear, don't go away from the palace on any account until I give you permission. I am going to send a message immediately to Signor Andrea D'Arbino to come and hear the extraordinary disclosure that you have made to me. Go back to read to the count, as usual, until I want you again; but, remember, you must not drop a word to him yet of what you have said to me. He must be carefully prepared for all that we have to tell him; and must be kept quite in the dark until those preparations are made."

D'Arbino answered the doctor's summons in person; and Nanina repeated her story to him. He and the doctor remained closeted together for some time after she had concluded her narrative and had retired. A little before four o'clock they sent for her again into the study. The doctor was sitting by the table with a bag of money before him, and D'Arbino was telling one of the servants that if a lady called at the palace on the subject of the handbill which he had circulated, she was to be admitted into the study immediately.

As the clock struck four Nanina was requested to take possession of a window-seat, and to wait there until she was summoned. When she had obeyed, the doctor loosened one of the window-curtains, to hide her from the view of any one entering the room.

About a quarter of an hour elapsed, and then the door was thrown open, and Brigida herself was shown into the study. The doctor bowed, and D'Arbino placed a chair for her. She was perfectly collected, and thanked them for their politeness with her best grace.

"I believe I am addressing confidential friends of Count Fabio d'Ascoli?" Brigida began. "May I ask if you are authorized to act for the count, in relation to the reward which this handbill offers?"

The doctor, having examined the handbill, said that the lady was quite right, and pointed significantly to the bag of money.

"You are prepared, then," pursued Brigida, smiling, "to give a reward of two hundred scudi to any one able to tell you who the woman is who wore the yellow mask at the Marquis Melani's ball, and how she contrived to personate the face and figure of the late Countess d'Ascoli?"

"Of course we are prepared," answered D'Arbino, a little irritably. "As men of honor, we are not in the habit of promising anything that we are not perfectly willing, under proper conditions, to perform."

"Pardon me, my dear friend," said the doctor; "I think you speak a little too warmly to the lady. She is quite right to take every precaution. We have the two hundred scudi here, madam," he continued, patting the money-bag; "and we are prepared to pay that sum for the information we want. But" (here the doctor suspiciously moved the bag of scudi from the table to his lap) "we must have proofs that the person claiming the reward is really entitled to it."

Brigida's eyes followed the money-bag greedily.

"Proofs!" she exclaimed, taking a small flat box from under her cloak, and pushing it across to the doctor. "Proofs! there you will find one proof that establishes my claim beyond the possibility of doubt."

The doctor opened the box, and looked at the wax mask inside it; then handed it to D'Arbino, and replaced the bag of scudi on the table.

"The contents of that box seem certainly to explain a great deal," he said, pushing the bag gently toward Brigida, but always keeping his, hand over it. "The woman who wore the yellow domino was, I presume, of the same height as the late countess?"

"Exactly," said Brigida. "Her eyes were also of the same color as the late countess's; she wore yellow of the same shade as the hangings in the late countess's room, and she had on, under her yellow mask, the colorless wax model of the late countess's face, now in your friend's hand. So much for that part of the secret. Nothing remains now to be cleared up but the mystery of who the lady was. Have the goodness, sir, to push that bag an inch or two nearer my way, and I shall be delighted to tell you."

"Thank you, madam," said the doctor, with a very perceptible change in his manner. "We know who the lady was already."

He moved the bag of scudi while he spoke back to his own side of the table. Brigida's cheeks reddened, and she rose from her seat.

"Am I to understand, sir," she said, haughtily, "that you take advantage of my position here, as a defenseless woman, to cheat me out of the reward?"

"By no means, madam," rejoined the doctor. "We have covenanted to pay the reward to the person who could give us the information we required."

"Well, sir! have I not given you part of it? And am I not prepared to give you the whole?"

"Certainly; but the misfortune is, that another person has been beforehand with you. We ascertained who the lady in the yellow domino was, and how she contrived to personate the face of the late Countess d'Ascoli, several hours ago from another informant. That person has consequently the prior claim; and, on every principle of justice, that person must also have the reward. Nanina, this bag belongs to you — come and take it."

Nanina appeared from the window-seat. Brigida, thunderstruck, looked at her in silence for a moment; gasped out, "That girl!"— then stopped again, breathless.

"That girl was at the back of the summer-house this morning, while you and your accomplice were talking together," said the doctor.

D'Arbino had been watching Brigida's face intently from the moment of Nanina's appearance, and had quietly stolen close to her side. This was a fortunate movement; for the doctor's last words were hardly out of his mouth before Brigida seized a heavy ruler lying, with some writing materials, on the table. In another instant, if D'Arbino had not caught her arm, she would have hurled it at Nanina's head.

"You may let go your hold, sir," she said, dropping the ruler, and turning toward D'Arbino with a smile on her white lips and a wicked calmness in her steady eyes. "I can wait for a better opportunity."

With those words she walked to the door; and, turning round there, regarded Nanina fixedly.

"I wish I had been a moment quicker with the ruler," she said, and went out.

"There!" exclaimed the doctor; "I told you I knew how to deal with her as she deserved. One thing I am certainly obliged to her for — she has saved us the trouble of going to her house and forcing her to give up the mask. And now, my child," he continued, addressing Nanina, "you can go home, and one of the men-servants shall see you safe to your own door, in case that woman should still be lurking about the palace. Stop! you are leaving the bag of scudi behind you."

"I can't take it, sir."

"And why not?"

"*She* would have taken money!" Saying those words, Nanina reddened, and looked toward the door.

The doctor glanced approvingly at D'Arbino. "Well, well, we won't argue about that now," he said. "I will lock up the money with the mask for today. Come here tomorrow morning as usual, my dear. By that time I shall have made up my mind on the right means for breaking your discovery to Count Fabio. Only let us proceed slowly and cautiously, and I answer for success."

PART THIRD. CHAPTER VII.

The next morning, among the first visitors at the Ascoli Palace was the master-sculptor, Luca Lomi. He seemed, as the servants thought, agitated, and said he was especially desirous of seeing Count Fabio. On being informed that this was impossible, he reflected a little, and then inquired if the medical attendant of the count was at the palace, and could be spoken with. Both questions were answered in the affirmative, and he was ushered into the doctor's presence.

"I know not how to preface what I want to say," Luca began, looking about him confusedly. "May I ask you, in the first place, if the work-girl named Nanina was here yesterday?"

"She was," said the doctor.

"Did she speak in private with any one?"

"Yes; with me."

"Then you know everything?"

"Absolutely everything."

"I am glad at least to find that my object in wishing to see the count can be equally well answered by seeing you. My brother, I regret to say —" He stopped perplexedly, and drew from his pocket a roll of papers.

"You may speak of your brother in the plainest terms," said the doctor. "I know what share he has had in promoting the infamous conspiracy of the Yellow Mask."

"My petition to you, and through you to the count, is, that your knowledge of what my brother has done may go no further. If this scandal becomes public it will ruin me in my profession. And I make little enough by it already," said Luca, with his old sordid smile breaking out again faintly on his face.

"Pray do you come from your brother with this petition?" inquired the doctor.

"No; I come solely on my own account. My brother seems careless what happens. He has made a full statement of his share in the matter from the first; has forwarded it to his ecclesiastical superior (who will send it to the archbishop), and is now awaiting whatever sentence they choose to pass on him. I have a copy of the document, to prove that he has at least been candid, and that he does not shrink from consequences which he might have avoided by flight. The law cannot touch him, but the Church can — and to the Church he has confessed. All I ask is, that he may be spared a public exposure. Such an exposure would do no good to the count, and it would do dreadful injury to me. Look over the papers yourself, and show them, whenever you think proper, to the master of this house. I have every confidence in his honor and kindness, and in yours."

He laid the roll of papers open on the table, and then retired with great humility to the window. The doctor looked over them with some curiosity.

The statement or confession began by boldly avowing the writer's conviction that part of the property which the Count Fabio d'Ascoli had inherited from his ancestors had been obtained by fraud and misrepresentation from the Church. The various authorities on which this assertion was based were then produced in due order; along with some curious particles of evidence culled from old manuscripts, which it must have cost much trouble to collect and decipher.

The second section was devoted, at great length, to the reasons which induced the writer to think it his absolute duty, as an affectionate son and faithful servant of the Church, not to rest until he had restored to the successors of the apostles in his day the property which had been fraudulently taken from them in days gone by. The writer held himself justified, in the last resort, and in that only, in using any means for effecting this restoration, except such as might involve him in mortal sin.

The third section described the priest's share in promoting the marriage of Maddalena Lomi with Fabio; and the hopes he entertained of securing the restitution of the Church property through his influence over his niece, in the first place, and, when she had died, through his influence over her child, in the second. The necessary failure of all his projects, if Fabio married again, was next glanced at; and the time at which the first suspicion of the possible occurrence of this catastrophe occurred to his mind was noted with scrupulous accuracy.

The fourth section narrated the manner in which the conspiracy of the Yellow Mask had originated. The writer described himself as being in his brother's studio on the night of his niece's death, harassed by forebodings of the likelihood of Fabio's marrying again, and filled with the resolution to prevent any such disastrous second union at all hazards. He asserted that the idea of taking the wax mask from his brother's statue flashed upon him on a sudden, and that he knew of nothing to lead to it, except, perhaps, that he had been thinking just before of the superstitious nature of the young man's character, as he had himself observed it in the studio. He further declared that the idea of the wax mask terrified him at first; that he strove against it as against a temptation of the devil; that, from fear of yielding to this temptation, he abstained even from entering the studio during his brother's absence at Naples, and that he first faltered in his good resolution when Fabio returned to Pisa, and when it was rumored, not only that the young nobleman was going to the ball, but that he would certainly marry for the second time.

The fifth section related that the writer, upon this, yielded to temptation rather than forego the cherished purpose of his life by allowing Fabio a chance of marrying again — that he made the wax mask in a plaster mold taken from the face of his brother's statue — and that he then had two separate interviews with a woman named Brigida (of whom he had some previous knowledge), who was ready and anxious, from motives of private malice, to personate the deceased countess at the masquerade. This woman had suggested that some anonymous letters to Fabio would pave the way in his mind for the approaching impersonation, and had written the letters herself. However, even when all the preparations were made, the writer declared that he shrank from proceeding to extremities; and that he would have abandoned the whole project but for the woman Brigida informing him one day that a work-girl named Nanina was to be one of the attendants at the ball. He knew the count to have been in love with this girl, even to the point of wishing to marry her; he suspected that her engagement to wait at the ball was preconcerted; and, in consequence, he authorized his female accomplice to perform her part in the conspiracy.

The sixth section detailed the proceedings at the masquerade, and contained the writer's confession that, on the night before it, he had written to the count proposing the reconciliation of a difference that had taken place between them, solely for the purpose of guarding himself against suspicion. He next acknowledged that he had borrowed the key of the Campo Santo gate, keeping the authority to whom it was intrusted in perfect ignorance of the purpose for which he wanted it. That purpose was to carry out the ghastly delusion of the wax mask (in the very probable event of the wearer being followed and inquired after) by having the woman Brigida taken up and set down at the gate of the cemetery in which Fabio's wife had been buried.

The seventh section solemnly averred that the sole object of the conspiracy was to prevent the young nobleman from marrying again, by working on his superstitious fears; the writer repeating, after this avowal, that any such second marriage would necessarily destroy his project for promoting the ultimate restoration of the Church possessions, by diverting Count Fabio's property, in great part, from his first wife's child, over whom the priest would always have influence, to another wife and probably other children, over whom he could hope to have none.

The eighth and last section expressed the writer's contrition for having allowed his zeal for the Church to mislead him into actions liable to bring scandal on his cloth; reiterated in the strongest language his conviction that, whatever might be thought of the means employed, the end he had proposed to himself was a most righteous one; and concluded by asserting his resolution to suffer with humility any penalties, however severe, which his ecclesiastical superiors might think fit to inflict on him.

Having looked over this extraordinary statement, the doctor addressed himself again to Luca Lomi.

"I agree with you," he said, "that no useful end is to be gained now by mentioning your brother's conduct in public — always provided, however, that his ecclesiastical superiors do their duty. I shall show these papers to the count as soon as he is fit to peruse them, and I have no doubt that he will be ready to take my view of the matter."

This assurance relieved Luca Lomi of a great weight of anxiety. He bowed and withdrew.

The doctor placed the papers in the same cabinet in which he had secured the wax mask. Before he locked the doors again he took out the flat box, opened it, and looked thoughtfully for a few minutes at the mask inside, then sent for Nanina.

"Now, my child," he said, when she appeared, "I am going to try our first experiment with Count Fabio; and I think it of great importance that you should be present while I speak to him."

He took up the box with the mask in it, and beckoning to Nanina to follow him, led the way to Fabio's chamber.

PART THIRD. CHAPTER VIII.

*A*bout six months after the events already related, Signor Andrea D'Arbino and the Cavaliere Finello happened to be staying with a friend, in a seaside villa on the Castellamare shore of the bay of Naples. Most of their time was pleasantly occupied on the sea, in fishing and sailing. A boat was placed entirely at their disposal. Sometimes they loitered whole days along the shore; sometimes made trips to the lovely islands in the bay.

One evening they were sailing near Sorrento, with a light wind. The beauty of the coast tempted them to keep the boat close inshore. A short time before sunset, they rounded the most picturesque headland they had yet passed; and a little bay, with a white-sand beach, opened on their view. They noticed first a villa surrounded by orange and olive trees on the rocky heights inland; then a path in the cliff-side leading down to the sands; then a little family party on the beach, enjoying the fragrant evening air.

The elders of the group were a lady and gentleman, sitting together on the sand. The lady had a guitar in her lap and was playing a simple dance melody. Close at her side a young child was rolling on the beach in high glee; in front of her a little girl was dancing to the music, with a very extraordinary partner in the shape of a dog, who was capering on his hind legs in the most grotesque manner. The merry laughter of the girl, and the lively notes of the guitar were heard distinctly across the still water.

"Edge a little nearer in shore," said D'Arbino to his friend, who was steering; "and keep as I do in the shadow of the sail. I want to see the faces of those persons on the beach without being seen by them."

Finello obeyed. After approaching just near enough to see the countenances of the party on shore, and to be barked at lustily by the dog, they turned the boat's head again toward the offing.

"A pleasant voyage, gentlemen," cried the clear voice of the little girl. They waved their hats in return; and then saw her run to the dog and take him by the forelegs. "Play, Nanina," they heard her say. "I have not half done with my partner yet." The guitar sounded once more, and the grotesque dog was on his hind legs in a moment.

"I had heard that he was well again, that he had married her lately, and that he was away with her and her sister, and his child by the first wife," said D'Arbino; "but I had no suspicion that their place of retirement was so near us. It is too soon to break in upon their happiness, or I should have felt inclined to run the boat on shore."

"I never heard the end of that strange adventure of the Yellow Mask," said Finello. "There was a priest mixed up in it, was there not?"

"Yes; but nobody seems to know exactly what has become of him. He was sent for to Rome, and has never been heard of since. One report is, that he has been condemned to some mysterious penal seclusion by his ecclesiastical superiors — another, that he has volunteered, as a sort of Forlorn Hope, to accept a colonial curacy among rough people, and in a pestilential climate. I asked his brother, the sculptor, about him a little while ago, but he only shook his head, and said nothing."

"And the woman who wore the yellow mask?"

"She, too, has ended mysteriously. At Pisa she was obliged to sell off everything she possessed to pay her debts. Some friends of hers at a milliner's shop, to whom she applied for help, would have nothing to do with her. She left the city, alone and penniless."

The boat had approached the next headland on the coast while they were talking They looked back for a last glance at the beach. Still the notes of the guitar came gently across the quiet water; but there mingled with them now the sound of the lady's voice. She was singing. The little girl and the dog were at her feet, and the gentleman was still in his old place close at her side.

In a few minutes more the boat rounded the next headland, the beach vanished from view, and the music died away softly in the distance.

LAST LEAVES FROM LEAH'S DIARY.

3d of June.— Our stories are ended; our pleasant work is done. It is a lovely summer afternoon. The great hall at the farmhouse, after having been filled with people, is now quite deserted. I sit alone at my little work-table, with rather a crying sensation at my heart, and with the pen trembling in my fingers, as if I was an old woman already. Our manuscript has been sealed up and taken away; the one precious object of all our most anxious thoughts for months past — our third child, as we have got to call it — has gone out from us on this summer's day, to seek its fortune in the world.

A little before twelve o'clock last night, my husband dictated to me the last words of "The Yellow Mask." I laid down the pen, and closed the paper thoughtfully. With that simple action the work that we had wrought at together so carefully and so long came to a close. We were both so silent and still, that the murmuring of the trees in the night air sounded audibly and solemnly in our room.

William's collection of stories has not, thus far, been half exhausted yet; but those who understand the public taste and the interests of bookselling better than we, think it advisable not to risk offering too much to the reader at first. If individual opinions can be accepted as a fair test, our prospects of success seem hopeful. The doctor (but we must not forget that he is a friend) was so pleased with the two specimen stories we sent to him, that he took them at once to his friend, the editor of the newspaper, who showed his appreciation of what he read in a very gratifying manner. He proposed that William should publish in the newspaper, on very fair terms, any short anecdotes and curious experiences of his life as a portrait-painter, which might not be important enough to put into a book. The money which my husband has gained from time to time in this way has just sufficed to pay our expenses at the farmhouse up to within the last month; and now our excellent friends here say they will not hear anything more from us on the subject of the rent until the book is sold and we have plenty of money. This is one great relief and happiness. Another, for which I feel even more grateful, is that William's eyes have gained so much by their long rest, that even the doctor is surprised at the progress he has made. He only puts on his green shade now when he goes out into the sun, or when the candles are lit. His spirits are infinitely raised, and he is beginning to talk already of the time when he will unpack his palette and brushes, and take to his old portrait-painting occupations again.

With all these reasons for being happy, it seems unreasonable and ungracious in me to be feeling sad, as I do just at this moment. I can only say, in my own justification, that it is a mournful ceremony to take leave of an old friend; and I have taken leave twice over of the book that has been like an old friend to me — once when I had written the last word in it, and once again when I saw it carried away to London.

I packed the manuscript up with my own hands this morning, in thick brown paper, wasting a great deal of sealing-wax, I am afraid, in my anxiety to keep the parcel from bursting open in case it should be knocked about on its journey to town. Oh me, how cheap and common it looked, in its new form, as I carried it downstairs! A dozen pairs of worsted stockings would have made a larger parcel; and half a crown's worth of groceries would have weighed a great deal heavier.

Just as we had done dinner the doctor and the editor came in. The first had called to fetch the parcel — I mean the manuscript; the second had come out with him to Appletreewick for a walk. As soon as the farmer heard that the book was to be sent to London, he insisted that we should drink success to it all round. The children, in high glee, were mounted up on the table, with a glass of currant-wine apiece; the rest of us had ale; the farmer proposed the toast, and his sailor son led the cheers. We all joined in (the children included), except the editor — who, being the only important person of the party, could not, I suppose, afford to compromise his dignity by making a noise. He was extremely polite, however, in a lofty way, to me, waving his hand and bowing magnificently every time he spoke. This discomposed me a little; and I was still more flurried when he said that he had written to the London publishers that very day, to prepare them for the arrival of our book.

"Do you think they will print it, sir?" I ventured to ask.

"My dear madam, you may consider it settled," said the editor, confidently. "The letter is written — the thing is done. Look upon the book as published already; pray oblige me by looking upon the book as published already."

"Then the only uncertainty now is about how the public will receive it!" said my husband, fidgeting in his chair, and looking nervously at me.

"Just so, my dear sir, just so," answered the editor. "Everything depends upon the public — everything, I pledge you my word of honor."

"Don't look doubtful, Mrs. Kerby; there isn't a doubt about it," whispered the kind doctor, giving the manuscript a confident smack as he passed by me with it on his way to the door.

In another minute he and the editor, and the poor cheap-looking brown paper parcel, were gone. The others followed them out, and I was left in the hall alone.

Oh, Public! Public! it all depends now upon you! The children are to have new clothes from top to toe; I am to have a black silk gown; William is to buy a beautiful traveling color-box; the rent is to be paid; all our kind friends at the farmhouse are to have little presents, and our future way in this hard world is to be smoothed for us at the outset, if you will only accept a poor painter's stories which his wife has written down for him After Dark!

9 782357 284845